# CLIVE CUSSLER'S
# DESOLATION
# CODE

# TITLES BY CLIVE CUSSLER

## DIRK PITT ADVENTURES®

*Clive Cussler's The Corsican Shadow* (by Dirk Cussler)

*Clive Cussler's The Devil's Sea* (by Dirk Cussler)

*Celtic Empire* (with Dirk Cussler)

*Odessa Sea* (with Dirk Cussler)

*Havana Storm* (with Dirk Cussler)

*Poseidon's Arrow* (with Dirk Cussler)

*Crescent Dawn* (with Dirk Cussler)

*Arctic Drift* (with Dirk Cussler)

*Treasure of Khan* (with Dirk Cussler)

*Black Wind* (with Dirk Cussler)

*Trojan Odyssey*

*Valhalla Rising*

*Atlantis Found*

*Flood Tide*

*Shock Wave*

*Inca Gold*

*Sahara*

*Dragon*

*Treasure*

*Cyclops*

*Deep Six*

*Pacific Vortex!*

*Night Probe!*

*Vixen 03*

*Raise the Titanic!*

*Iceberg*

*The Mediterranean Caper*

## SAM AND REMI FARGO ADVENTURES®

*Wrath of Poseidon* (with Robin Burcell)

*The Oracle* (with Robin Burcell)

*The Gray Ghost* (with Robin Burcell)

*The Romanov Ransom* (with Robin Burcell)

*Pirate* (with Robin Burcell)

*The Solomon Curse* (with Russell Blake)

*The Eye of Heaven* (with Russell Blake)

*The Mayan Secrets* (with Thomas Perry)

*The Tombs* (with Thomas Perry)

*The Kingdom* (with Grant Blackwood)

*Lost Empire* (with Grant Blackwood)

*Spartan Gold* (with Grant Blackwood)

## ISAAC BELL ADVENTURES®

*Clive Cussler's The Heist* (by Jack Du Brul)

*Clive Cussler's The Sea Wolves* (by Jack Du Brul)

*The Saboteurs* (with Jack Du Brul)

*The Titanic Secret* (with Jack Du Brul)

*The Cutthroat* (with Justin Scott)

*The Gangster* (with Justin Scott)

*The Assassin* (with Justin Scott)

*The Bootlegger* (with Justin Scott)

*The Striker* (with Justin Scott)

*The Thief* (with Justin Scott)

*The Race* (with Justin Scott)

*The Spy* (with Justin Scott)

*The Wrecker* (with Justin Scott)

*The Chase*

## KURT AUSTIN ADVENTURES®
## Novels from the NUMA Files®

*Clive Cussler's Desolation Code*
  (by Graham Brown)
*Clive Cussler's Condor's Fury*
  (by Graham Brown)
*Clive Cussler's Dark Vector*
  (by Graham Brown)
*Fast Ice* (with Graham Brown)
*Journey of the Pharaohs*
  (with Graham Brown)
*Sea of Greed* (with Graham Brown)
*The Rising Sea* (with Graham Brown)
*Nighthawk* (with Graham Brown)
*The Pharaoh's Secret*
  (with Graham Brown)
*Ghost Ship* (with Graham Brown)
*Zero Hour* (with Graham Brown)
*The Storm* (with Graham Brown)
*Devil's Gate* (with Graham Brown)
*Medusa* (with Paul Kemprecos)
*The Navigator* (with Paul Kemprecos)
*Polar Shift* (with Paul Kemprecos)
*Lost City* (with Paul Kemprecos)
*White Death* (with Paul Kemprecos)
*Fire Ice* (with Paul Kemprecos)
*Blue Gold* (with Paul Kemprecos)
*Serpent* (with Paul Kemprecos)

## CHILDREN'S BOOKS

*The Adventures of Vin Fiz*
*The Adventures of Hotsy Totsy*

## OREGON FILES®

*Clive Cussler's Ghost Soldier*
  (by Mike Maden)
*Clive Cussler's Fire Strike*
  (by Mike Maden)
*Clive Cussler's Hellburner*
  (by Mike Maden)
*Marauder* (with Boyd Morrison)
*Final Option* (with Boyd Morrison)
*Shadow Tyrants* (with Boyd Morrison)
*Typhoon Fury* (with Boyd Morrison)
*The Emperor's Revenge*
  (with Boyd Morrison)
*Piranha* (with Boyd Morrison)
*Mirage* (with Jack Du Brul)
*The Jungle* (with Jack Du Brul)
*The Silent Sea* (with Jack Du Brul)
*Corsair* (with Jack Du Brul)
*Plague Ship* (with Jack Du Brul)
*Skeleton Coast* (with Jack Du Brul)
*Dark Watch* (with Jack Du Brul)
*Sacred Stone* (with Craig Dirgo)
*Golden Buddha* (with Craig Dirgo)

## NON-FICTION

*Built for Adventure: The Classic
  Automobiles of Clive Cussler and
  Dirk Pitt*
*Built to Thrill: More Classic
  Automobiles from Clive Cussler and
  Dirk Pitt*
*The Sea Hunters* (with Craig Dirgo)
*The Sea Hunters II* (with Craig Dirgo)
*Clive Cussler and Dirk Pitt Revealed*
  (with Craig Dirgo)

# CAST OF CHARACTERS

## NATIONAL UNDERWATER AND MARINE AGENCY (NUMA)

**KURT AUSTIN**—Director of Special Projects, salvage expert, and boating enthusiast

**JOE ZAVALA**—Assistant Director of Special Projects, helicopter pilot, and mechanical genius

**RUDI GUNN**—Assistant Director of NUMA, runs most of the day-to-day operations, Naval Academy graduate

**HIRAM YAEGER**—NUMA's Director of Information Technology

**GAMAY TROUT**—NUMA's leading marine biologist, graduated from Scripps Institute, married to Paul

**PAUL TROUT**—NUMA's chief geologist, also graduated from Scripps, married to Gamay

## REUNION ISLAND

**MARCEL LACOURT**—Acting prefect (governor) on the island

**CHANTEL LACOURT**—Grad student and marine biologist, niece to Marcel

# CAST OF CHARACTERS

## ÎLE DE L'EST

**EZRA VAUGHN**—Artificial intelligence guru, obsessed with the idea of merging human and machine intelligence

**KELLEN BLAKES (THE OVERSEER)**—Former mercenary, now in charge of security and maintaining order for Vaughn on his private island

**PRIYA KASHMIR**—Former member of NUMA, computer expert, studying methods of spinal regeneration for those who have been paralyzed

**KAI**—Leader of the resistance group fighting Vaughn for control

**ZECH**—Member of Kai's resistance group

**THE GRAY WITCH**—Mythical figure whom the resistance trust in for assistance and protection

## INDIA

**VIRAT SHARMA**—Owner of a large ship-breaking company and salvage yard operating on Alang beach

**FIVE**—Surviving member of a group that snuck aboard the *Soufriere*

## MV *AKESO*

**ELENA PASCAL**—Former NUMA doctor, now working aboard the hospital ship *Akeso*

**MARJORIE LIVORNO**—Captain of the *Akeso*

## LOCATIONS

**REUNION ISLAND**—French island in the Indian Ocean, approximately five hundred miles east of Madagascar

## CAST OF CHARACTERS

**ALANG**—Long, flat beach on the west coast of India, home to the world's largest ship-breaking operation

**ÎLE DE L'EST**—Easternmost island in the Seychelles island chain, one of only two volcanic islands in the group; was once home to a geothermal energy project; now owned and controlled by Ezra Vaughn

# CLIVE CUSSLER'S
# DESOLATION CODE

# PROLOGUE
# THE ISLAND

A man dressed in tattered rags sprinted headlong through a tropical rainforest. Drenched in sweat, bare feet pounding the uneven ground, he pushed through the broad green leaves and charted a path higher. Upward, toward a peak he couldn't see, but believed he would reach.

Finding a more open trail, he paused near a tangled bush covered in colorful flowers. His chest heaved as he tried to catch his breath. He wiped the sweat from his brow and smacked the side of his neck as a biting insect landed. Pulling his hand away revealed a smear of his own blood, which only partially covered the tattoo on his neck, displaying numbers and letters in an odd code-like arrangement. The last two digits were an offset one and zero. Because of this he was called Deci.

Wiping the blood off, Deci glanced back into the foliage, looking for the others, who were falling behind. "Come on," he shouted. "Keep moving."

A group of younger men appeared. They resembled him in skin tone and facial features, appearing so similar to one another it was hard to tell them apart. Their clothes were as ragged and dirty as his, and fear streaked their faces.

1

They pushed through, looking to him. "Are you sure this is the right way?"

In truth he wasn't, but he'd been told he would find a trail, and here it was. He pointed along the path. "To the top. Go quickly."

"And then what?" one of the younger men asked.

"Escape," he said. "Freedom."

These words landed flat with the younger men. They almost seemed confused. But the sound of dogs barking shook them out of their stupor. The hunters were coming; they'd picked up the trail and there was no chance of them losing it now. Not with so many of them pushing through the trees, sweating like beasts of burden.

"Go, go, go," Deci shouted.

The young ones took off again, followed at the last by another man, who was as old as their leader. He stopped and crouched near the bush. At a distance the two men appeared almost identical, but Deci's sunken eyes, gaunt cheeks, and scared face showed how their lives had diverged.

"Brother," the second man said. "They have us. We should turn back before it's too late."

"It's already too late," Deci replied. "Our only hope lies ahead."

"On the cliffs? What are we supposed to do? Jump?"

"A way will be revealed," the leader insisted. "She promised us."

A look of irritation crossed the second man's face. "*She* has never been seen. She's just a whisper in our minds."

"She gave us this," Deci insisted, grasping a necklace that lay heavy against his chest. It was bulky and heavy and made of electronic parts and batteries. He wore it as if it were a talisman of great power.

"The necklace cannot deflect bullets," the second man said, "or stop a dog from biting. And blind faith is for fools."

"Then turn back," Deci said. "But I will not let them do to the younger ones what they've done to us."

The two men stared at each other for a long moment. They'd had this argument before. The deadlock ended as a gunshot rang out from below. Both men flinched and ducked and then turned for the trail together, sprinting up the path in bare and bloody feet.

"You'd better be right," the second man said. "Or this is the only freedom we'll ever know."

The two men scrambled up the trail, ignorant of the tracks they were making in the dirt and the bloody footprints left on the steep rock faces. When they pushed through the last wall of tangled brush and arrived out into the open, they found themselves atop a rocky bluff, high above the sea. By now the sun was low on the horizon, the ocean waves shimmered in bronze and gray. A cool breeze drew the sweat off their bodies while the sound of crashing waves echoed up from below.

The young men were staring.

"I see forever," one of them said.

"How do we go?" another asked.

The leader looked around. He saw no sign of rescue. No sign of help. *Maybe they were supposed to jump.*

He stepped to the edge and looked down. Piles of rocks made up a jagged shoreline two hundred feet below. They stuck out too far from the base of the cliff to imagine one could reach the water. Even if they could jump far enough to make the water's edge, they would die broken and battered after plunging through the shallows and hitting the rocks.

Stepping back from the edge, Deci shuddered. He'd led them to their doom. He suddenly wished he wasn't the leader. Wished even more intensely that he'd never received the message or been given the necklace. And then he saw something that gave him hope. A knotted line had been anchored to the side of the cliff. It dropped down thirty feet, where a weighted end hung loosely. It looked as though the rope hung in front of an opening in the side of the cliff. A way out. He had been promised a way out.

He had no experience in such things, but he quickly saw the drawback to using it: if he could see it, so could the hunters.

He removed the necklace and placed it over the head of his brother. "Climb down."

His brother looked down at the rope and the rocks far beneath it. He shook his head.

"Go," Deci insisted. "Lead them."

"No," he said. "You take them. I have no faith."

Deci grasped his brother by the arm and drug him to the edge of the cliff. Reaching over, he managed to grasp the rope. He pulled on it to test the security, then placed it in his brother's hands. "She promised a way out. This is it. Now go!"

Pushing through the jungle, a half mile behind the group of escapees, a tall Caucasian man with a bald head and narrow, hawkish eyes found himself enjoying the hunt. Dressed in khakis and a safari vest, he carried two pistols on separate belts and walked with a shotgun in his hands.

On the island he was known as the Overseer, but at previous stops in his life he'd been a big-game hunter, a trail boss in some of the toughest parts of the world, and a mercenary for hire to anyone with the right denominations of currency.

Here on the island, he found himself grinning as the dogs locked in on the scent and pulled hard against their leads. He laughed as the handlers struggled to keep up, holding the animals back and hacking their way through the brush with machetes.

"Run them down," the Overseer growled with a demented sense of glee. "If even one man escapes, each of you will suffer the punishment meant for them."

If his men needed any more motivation, this was enough. They pushed on, climbing higher and moving faster as the foliage thinned. Before long they were tracking bloody, scuffling footprints imprinted by raw, uncovered feet. It made the trail easy to follow, but left the Overseer wondering about the course they'd chosen.

Previous escapees had always run for the other side of the island, fleeing the civilized but prisonlike compound in hopes of surviving in the rocky, volcanic wasteland. These men were taking a different path. One that kept them away from the dividing wall and its razor wire and cameras.

It was curious, he thought, but it didn't matter much. Soon they'd be trapped between the dogs and the cliffside.

The dogs began yelping more intensely. They smelled the quarry up ahead.

"Let them go," the Overseer shouted.

The handlers dropped their leashes and the dogs shot forward. They rushed upward and vanished from sight, a lethal pack only a fraction removed from the wolves they were descended from. The Overseer picked up his pace, eager to watch the animals do their job.

He arrived at a small clearing to find the animals running in circles, sniffing the ground and then raising their snouts to howl at the sky. The trail had come to an end, but there was no one to be found.

A branch creaked behind him, and the Overseer turned in time to see a figure leaping down toward him. The barefoot man hit him, knocking him to the ground and rolling free. Both men jumped up, and the dogs spun around as if to set upon the attacker.

"Stay!" the Overseer shouted at them in a deep, commanding voice. The dogs heeled and stood stiffly.

The Overseer aimed the shotgun at the dirty, bleeding man. "Where are the others?" he demanded. "Tell me now and I'll show you mercy."

The escapee was thin. The shredded clothes hanging on him like rags. Living in the bush for weeks would do that to a person. He stepped back nervously, looking from side to side. From the waistband of his threadbare pants he pulled a homemade knife. It was nothing more than a length of thick fabric wrapped around a sharpened flint.

"You've made yourself a weapon," the Overseer noted. "How interesting. We didn't teach you that. Maybe you vermin learn faster than we've been told to expect."

The Overseer tossed the shotgun aside and took a machete from one of his men. "Let's see how well you use it."

He stepped forward, but Deci threw a handful of dirt in his face. The Overseer squinted against the attack, suffering the sting of the grit with eyes open as he slashed with the machete.

It grazed Deci's chest deep enough to draw a line of blood, but the mark was no more than a flesh wound. He had suffered worse than that in *the rooms*.

Deci glanced at the blood on his chest and shrugged it off. He circled to the right and then back, holding the knife toward the Overseer and then pointing it at the nearest of his men.

"Don't worry about them, boy," the Overseer said. "Bring that sharpened little stick to me."

As if responding to the command, Deci lunged forward, slashing for the Overseer's neck. It was a daring attack, but the Overseer had a lifetime of fighting in his past. He stepped sideways, leaning back to avoid the knife and countering with the machete.

The heavy blade dug into Deci's arm. This time he howled in pain and stumbled back, staring at the gash in his flesh. Blood was running red, pouring from the exposed sinew and fat.

"That's just a taste of what's to come," the Overseer warned.

"Now throw down your weapon and I'll tell them you have promise. That you belong with us."

No statement he made could have enraged Deci more. With his face twisted into a mask of hate, he lunged again, raising his wounded arm as a shield and thrusting the primitive knife toward the Overseer's stomach. He managed to rip into the safari vest and draw some blood, but the Overseer shoved him aside and brought the machete down hard.

Deci's hand was taken off at the wrist, and he tumbled to his knees. He scuffled away, retreating like a beaten animal.

Tired of the game, the Overseer looked at the dogs. "*Mord!*" he shouted, issuing the command to attack.

Two of the dogs shot forward, charging at Deci without hesitation. They hit him nearly simultaneously and he rolled with the impact. Another roll seemed deliberate, and then all three went over the edge.

They heard barking and howls as the animals fell. It was followed by sudden silence. An eerie quiet spread across the clearing. The men seemed unsure what to do.

The Overseer moved to the edge of the cliff and glanced downward. Deci and the two dogs lay battered and broken a few feet from each other, splatters of blood marking their impact points.

Looking down, it dawned on the Overseer that Deci had sacrificed himself. More than that, he'd come up with a complex plan, made a weapon, led a mini-rebellion, and chosen to die for a concept he couldn't possibly understand: freedom.

They were learning things they hadn't been taught. And doing so faster than anyone had a right to expect. This, he would have to report.

"Fan out," the Overseer snapped. "Find the others. Look in the trees and the bushes. Look under every rock. They have to be here somewhere."

With new urgency, the men, and the surviving dogs, rushed into the tropical brush, desperate to pick up a new trail.

The Overseer lingered at the cliffside, silently impressed with Deci's choice to go out fighting. He gazed at the ocean. The sunlight was streaming through a line of clouds on the horizon, its beams visible in the contrast between light and dark. There was nothing else to see. No ships, no land, nothing but the endless, golden sea.

It made him wonder where they thought they were escaping to. This island, *the rooms*, the Overseer, and the Providers—this was all they knew. All they had ever seen.

He briefly wondered what their primitive brains would think if they did reach the web of complexity, chaos, and madness that men called *civilization*. Probably, he guessed, they would wish they never had.

Howls and barking from deep in the brush interrupted his reverie, and the Overseer reverted to the task at hand. He turned away from the sea and went back down the path, pleased to know that the hunt was still on.

# CHAPTER 1

The island of Reunion—or *La Réunion*, as the locals called it—sat in the tropics five hundred miles east of Madagascar and nearly two thousand miles due south of Saudi Arabia. A domain of France, it was a natural paradise as dramatic and beautiful as the famed island of Tahiti. It boasted stunning volcanic peaks, rainforests of brilliant green, and smooth, black sand beaches made from eroded lava that had been ground to dust by the waves.

Despite the appearance of a deserted tropical isle, Reunion was home to nearly a million French-speaking citizens. It drew tens of thousands of tourists every month and, according to some, nearly as many sharks.

Because of its location, Reunion acted like a rest stop on an oceanic path linking the waters of Australia and those of South Africa. Marine biologists called the route Shark Highway, as it was traveled heavily by great whites, bull sharks, makos, and hammerheads. As a result, the little French island in the Indian Ocean had become the shark attack capital of the world, dealing with dozens of attacks every year and scores of fatalities.

Unhappy with the nickname their island had earned, Reunion's government took action, stringing nets around certain beaches to cordon them off from the sea while imposing strict no swimming/no surfing rules outside the protected zones. The program reduced the number of attacks dramatically, eventually culminating in a full year without any fatalities.

It was a stunning success, but no one really believed the ocean-dwelling predators were gone. No one, that is, except an American named Kurt Austin.

Kurt was a tall man of around forty, with broad shoulders and a lean build. He was the director of Special Projects for an American government agency known as NUMA, the National Underwater and Marine Agency, which operated around the world performing scientific research, locating sunken ships, and working with other nations on issues involving the sea.

In a joint effort with the University of Reunion, Kurt and his colleague Joe Zavala had spent the last six weeks in, on, and under the waters around Reunion, running a study on the shark population. Strangely enough, they'd had a hard time finding any, traveling farther and farther out to sea in search of significant examples to tag.

Bait hadn't drawn the sharks. Recorded sounds of struggling fish hadn't drawn them in. Even buckets of blood and a floating tuna carcass they'd come across hadn't brought anything larger than a few juveniles to the table. It was as if the rest stop had closed its doors and all the adult sharks in the community had moved on.

It was a puzzling discovery, one that Kurt wrestled with even as he stood in the main departure lounge in Roland Garros Airport, waiting for the arrival of the long-haul aircraft that would take him and Joe off the island and away from the mystery. Had there not been other obligations waiting for them back in Washington, he would have canceled the trip home and stuck around in search of answers.

A tap on the shoulder broke his reverie. Turning to look, he found no one behind him, only a small metal pointer with four rake-like fingers protruding from it. The telescoping device led back to his closest friend, Joe Zavala, who sat at a high-top table with a hefty club sandwich and a stack of pommes frites in front of him.

Having drawn Kurt's attention, Joe retracted the lightweight aluminum back scratcher and tucked it in his pocket. Kurt recalled Joe buying the device for five dollars at a kiosk the day they arrived. "I can't believe you got through security with that thing."

"*This*," Joe insisted, "is a useful tool. It's made my life easier in every way. For example, I didn't even have to get off my seat to bother you."

"Not sure that's a good thing."

Joe had short dark hair, dark brown eyes, and a fit build. He seemed to be perpetually smiling, as if life, good or bad, was always grand. He motioned toward the plate in front of him. "You want a bite of this sandwich?" he asked. "Number one rule of travel: never skip a meal; you don't know when you'll get another chance to eat."

Kurt shook his head in mild amazement. Joe was ten years younger than Kurt and several inches shorter, but he still looked like the middleweight boxer he'd been during his time in the Navy. Somehow, he seemed to eat all day long and never gain a pound.

"I'm sure they'll feed us on the plane," Kurt said. "Besides, not everyone has your enviable, overactive metabolism. You know, we've been here six weeks, and I can't actually remember a time when you weren't eating."

"That's the key," Joe said. "A constant supply of food keeps the energy level high and burns more calories."

Kurt wasn't sure the science held up on that, but at the buzzing of his phone, he let it go.

Pulling the device from his pocket, he tapped in a password and looked at the screen. A text had appeared, but there was no name, email address, or phone number attached to it.

The cynic in him figured it for spam. And if the phone had been an off-the-shelf, commercially available unit, that would have made sense. His friends were always complaining about robocalls and phishing texts, and the endless numbers of attractive foreign women who apparently wanted to spend time with them. But Kurt's phone was a NUMA-issued device, specially designed to avoid any such pitfalls. All communications to and from the phone went through NUMA's satellites and a highly secured computer system back in Washington, D.C., which should have made it impervious to such intrusions.

As Kurt studied the message he sensed something else odd about it. Not only was there no sign as to who the sender might be, but the message wasn't complete. As he watched, additional letters were appearing one at a time, as if being keyed in by the world's slowest typist. When the last letter appeared, the message read cryptically.

I've sent them to you . . . Find them . . . Their fate lies in your hands . . .

The idea that he was looking at spam fell away. There was no link to click, no invitation to write back, no offer of any kind. Just the odd phrases and a lengthy string of numbers and letters that looked like a password or the product code for a computer program.

Making the entire episode even stranger, the message vanished right before his eyes. He searched for it in various programs and applications, but found no record of it. It was just gone.

Joe looked over and noticed the irritation on Kurt's face. "What's the matter? Can't figure out today's Wordle?"

"No," Kurt said. "Phone seems to have a ghost inside. Have you been getting any weird messages?"

Joe shook his head.

"I need to call our tech gurus," Kurt said. "Something odd is going on here."

Before he could place the call, a commotion at the security checkpoint caught his eye. Three policemen and two men in suits had come rushing into the building, cutting the lines and then badging their way past the screening crew. Now on the boarding side of the terminal, they pushed through the sparse crowd of passengers and came directly toward Kurt and Joe.

"Excuse me," the policemen demanded. "Excuse me, please step aside."

Kurt put the phone away as the men came closer. "I'm sure this is about that back scratcher."

The trio of uniformed policemen arrived first, flanking Kurt and Joe, as if to keep them from running off. The men in suits arrived seconds later. The leader of the two was a man of perhaps sixty. He had curly gray hair and wore a white linen suit. He was perspiring and winded. He stopped to wipe his brow before addressing them.

"Are you Kurt Austin?"

Joe turned away and took a bite of his sandwich. "I wouldn't answer that," he said under his breath with a mouth full of food.

"I am," Kurt said. "And this is Joe Zavala, my associate."

"Really?" Joe said, turning around. "You couldn't leave me out of this?"

Kurt grinned at Joe's pretend frustration.

"You two men work for NUMA," the man in the suit said. "The American marine biology agency?"

*Close enough*, Kurt thought. "That's right," he said. "What can we do for you?"

"My name is Marcel Lacourt," the man said. "I am the prefect here on Reunion. What you Americans would call the island's governor. I officially request your assistance."

"To do what?" Kurt asked warily.

"There's been a mass stranding of whales on the far side of the island," Lacourt said. "I'm being told there are a large number of other sea creatures swimming in the bay and close by offshore. More whales. And schools of fish. The tide is high right now, but it will change soon. The volunteers are afraid more animals will strand themselves during the night."

It was late in the afternoon.

"How many whales?"

"One very large and the others smaller," Lacourt said. "I must tell you, this doesn't happen here. We have sharks. We have whale watching. But we've never had a mass beaching of these magnificent creatures. We're not equipped to deal with such a thing or even certain how to handle it. We're hoping you can help."

Nothing more was needed. While Joe wolfed down the last part of the sandwich, Kurt grabbed his backpack off the seat and nodded toward the exit. The flight back would have to wait.

"Let's go," he said. "We'll make plans along the way."

# CHAPTER 2

It took fifteen minutes with a police escort to get from the airport to the beach. Along the way, Kurt gave Lacourt instructions and detailed a list of equipment that would be helpful. "We'll need excavators that can get down to the water. Fifty-five-gallon drums, Sheetrock or metal panels we can use to line a trench, and plastic highway barriers, empty and easy to move around. We passed a truckload on the way to the airport earlier."

Lacourt looked surprised by the list of requirements, but he didn't question it. "Anything else?"

"Fire trucks that can tap into the main water line."

Lacourt listened closely and wrote everything down on a small pad, then pulled out his smartphone and began to send out texts to those who were waiting on instructions. By the time the police convoy weaved through the gathering crowd, help was on the way from multiple sources.

Kurt stepped out of the car as it pulled to a stop. One look told him they were going to need all the help they could get. Standing on the coastal road, thirty feet above the beach, he could see dozens of stranded whales, with one full-grown sperm whale right in the middle.

Out beyond the waves, the bay was teeming with sea life, the water churned white and foamy as the animals thrashed around in a panic, colliding with each other and darting off in different directions. Despite the wide opening to the bay, none of the animals seemed interested in swimming away.

Kurt had never seen anything like it.

Joe was just as baffled. "Are they trapped?" he asked Lacourt. "Is there a reef or a sandbar out there?"

"No," the man in the white suit insisted. "No coral on this side, just a steady drop to deeper waters."

"Maybe they're trying to get to their leader," Joe suggested. "Whale strandings often involve a pod of whales traveling in a group. A large family. If the leader gets confused and becomes stranded, the others may try to rescue it, or follow to their doom. Pilot whales are notorious for it, unfortunately."

Kurt had been thinking the same thing, but as he studied the animals on the beach he noticed they weren't the same species. The sperm whale was a solitary traveler. A pair of juvenile humpbacks farther down might have been traveling together, and there were several pilot whales and several porpoises, but even they were a mixed bag of different species, including a spectacled porpoise with a black-and-white color scheme that resembled a killer whale's.

"They are not one family," Kurt said.

Joe nodded. They weren't marine biologists, but they knew enough to understand this was not a normal beaching.

Normal or not, they still had to get the animals off the beach and find a way to keep those in the shallows from joining them.

Kurt started down toward the beach. The group followed. "Which animal came in first?"

"The big one in the middle," one of the policemen replied. "He was spotted an hour ago in the shallows."

The sperm whale was on its side, its mouth open at an odd angle, its great weight deforming its normally majestic shape. Volunteers were throwing buckets of water on it, but beyond that, the crowd could only stand and stare.

"We need to move that one first," Kurt said.

"You sure you don't want to start with the smaller ones?" Lacourt asked.

Kurt was playing a hunch. "For reasons I can't fathom, the others may have followed the first one in. If we get it back into the open water, those in the bay might leave and we can work on saving the smaller ones." He turned to Joe. "What's happening with the tide?"

Joe had been checking the tide and wave conditions on the way over. "High tide in forty minutes."

"That's not a lot of time," the policeman said.

"It's all we have," Kurt replied. "Either that whale is off the beach in forty minutes or it's never going back to sea."

They arrived at the damp part of the beach a few yards from the whale's nose. Kurt looked into the animal's eye and sensed it wanted their help. It was probably his imagination, but it didn't hurt to think that one mammal could sense the calming presence of another.

Stepping away from the whale, Kurt gathered a group of volunteers around him. They included a member of the fire brigade and a construction foreman, who'd arrived with one excavator and insisted another was on the way.

Once Lacourt had made the introductions, Kurt began to speak, dropping down on one knee and drawing a diagram in the wet sand.

"This is the waterline," he said, drawing a horizontal line. "This is the whale," he added, placing a stick of driftwood down to represent the stranded animal. "We need the excavators to dig a pair of channels." Using his fingers, he gouged out a pair of diagonal lines, leading from the surf zone to a spot above the whale. "One here and one here."

"You don't want to dig under or behind the whale?" the man in the hard hat asked.

"Can't really get under it," Kurt said. "It'll just sink in deeper. Like spinning your tires in mud. Dredging the sand behind it will be helpful, but save that for the last, because the sea will fill it in almost as fast as you dig it out."

"Okay," the man said. "I'll get my guys on it."

"We have barrels coming over on a flatbed," Lacourt announced. "What do you want us to do with them?"

"How many do you have?"

"A couple dozen. They came from the highway project."

Kurt took some pebbles and placed them around the front of the stick, which represented the whale's head. "Put them here," he began, and then turned to the battalion chief from the fire brigade. "Fill them to the top and round up some strong volunteers who can be ready to dump them over when we need it."

"I think I see what you have in mind," the fire chief said, standing up. "We'll be ready."

"One more thing," Kurt said before the man left. "How much pressure is in the waterline?"

"Twenty psi at the hydrant, but running it through the truck we can jack it up to one-fifty."

That sounded helpful. "Are you comfortable burying that line under sand and getting the nozzle under the whale?"

The chief pushed his helmet back. "'Comfortable' isn't the word I'd use, but if you think it will help, I'll give it a try. What's the idea?"

"I want to create a slurry under the whale at the right moment," Kurt said. "The biggest problem in moving this creature is that the sand compresses underneath it, which creates a lot of friction, but water doesn't compress. If we can supersaturate the sand, it'll be easier to move the big fella. As different as sliding on foam instead of forty-grit sandpaper."

The chief nodded. "I'll get my bravest guys to start digging a trench. How close do you want us to get?"

"As close as possible and as deep into the sand as you can go," Kurt said. "Get the nozzle under the animal if you can."

"What about all those teeth?"

Curved seven-inch teeth were visible in the whale's open jaw.

"As long as you don't stick your arm in his mouth you should be fine," Kurt said. "On the other hand, if any of your guys don't like the smell of fish, I'd leave them back at the truck. Whales have horrible breath."

"Good to know," the commander said, chuckling.

He went back up the slope to where the fire engines had parked. When he was out of earshot, one of the volunteers spoke up, a young woman who was part of the university's marine biology department. "I don't mean to be the voice of doubt," she said. "But as you pointed out, the sand is porous. All the water you pour onto the beach will just sink downward and spread horizontally."

She had raven-black hair, dark eyes, and pale, almost alabaster skin. Her lips were full and a dark reddish color without a hint of lipstick or gloss on them. She stared at Kurt with arched eyebrows and crossed her arms, waiting for an answer.

"You make a good point, Ms. . . . ."

"Chantel Lacourt," she said, eyebrows remaining on full alert.

A whimsical look hit Kurt's face. "The governor's daughter?" If only he were a pirate looking for amnesty.

"She's my niece," Lacourt said. "And I am the *prefect* here, not governor."

Both Kurt and Chantel laughed at that one, but the prefect didn't seem to get the joke. Kurt looked back to Chantel, who was still waiting for an answer. "The water won't sink too far, because high tide has saturated the sand below the surface. As for spreading sideways, that's where the sheet metal comes in."

Searching for something to represent the sheet metal, Kurt pulled out his wallet and emptied it of credit cards. He stuck them in the sand at an angle, pushing them down and under the stick.

"We jam the panels into the sand, making sure every sheet overlaps the one next to it." His driver's license and a library card made up the last links in the wall. He slid a fistful of sand in behind them for support. "We use the bulldozers to pile up sand behind them, and that way—"

"We create a sluice to hold all the water," she said, finishing his thought. The eyebrows came down and she nodded approvingly. "Will it be enough to float the whale back out to sea?"

"'Float' is a bit optimistic," Kurt said. "But with some luck, and a solid pull from one of the boats, we should be able to drag this big boy out into the bay. And from there, we can tow him to deeper waters."

"Her," Chantel said.

"What?"

"The whale is a female," Chantel informed him. "Which is good, because if she were a male, she'd weigh another ten tons at least."

Kurt had to smile. "Do me a favor," he said. "Take charge of the placement of those metal sheets. I don't have enough credit cards to explain it again."

"I'll get it done for you," she said. "I'm good at bossing people around. Runs in the family."

She moved off, heading toward the pallet of sheet metal and drywall. Only Lacourt and Joe remained in the circle.

"She's trouble, that one," the prefect said. "Always another question, until she completely understands. Ever since she was a kid."

"There are worse traits," Kurt said, then changed the subject. "We're going to need a couple of boats. Any thoughts?"

"There's a marina not far from here, just a few miles up the road," Lacourt said. "I'm sure we could find something for you."

"Take Joe. He knows what we need."

# CHAPTER 3

For the next twenty minutes, Kurt was everywhere. Supervising the placing of the barrels, the digging of the trenches, and the shoring up of the corrugated metal sheets. He even crawled up next to the whale to help dig the narrow trench underneath it that would be used for the fire hoses.

As the work progressed, the crowd at the top of the beach grew. By now the news had spread across the island and both the tourists and locals were coming out in force.

Surrounded by activity, the sperm whale made clicking sounds and flapped its tail, smacking the water loudly and drenching anyone who got too close. Farther along, the dolphins and the porpoises had begun to make anguished calls, while the humpbacks rolled in the shallow surf, waving their long pectoral fins uselessly. The situation was becoming more desperate, but they were almost ready to act.

With the last barrel filled, the corrugated metal sheets bolstered by berms of sand, and the high-pressure hoses in place, everything was ready. Everything except Joe.

Kurt scanned the bay to no avail, then grabbed a radio and called him. "We're starting to lose the light here, amigo. Tell me you're close."

Joe's voice came over the radio, buffeted by the wind. "I'll be coming around the point any minute now."

Joe entered the bay from the north, standing on the prow of a cabin cruiser as it churned through the swells. Behind him came a small harbor tug. Its shallow draft and powerful engines were perfect for what they needed. A third boat in Joe's flotilla appeared to be a paragliding towboat. Another good choice, Kurt thought, as its pilot would be used to racing up on the beach to pick up and drop off customers.

As the fleet approached the shore, the two powerboats swung out wide and the tug came down the middle. It slowed to a stop, spun around, and then backed in the last hundred yards. As it neared the beach, one of the crewmen tossed a line toward shore. Kurt dove into the surf to retrieve it. Swimming back to the beach, he dug his feet in and dragged the line up onto the sand.

The small metal cable was connected to a larger-diameter rope. With the help of the volunteers, Kurt pulled the big rope in and attempted to loop it around the whale's haunches.

At the slightest touch, the animal flicked its tail defensively, almost sending Kurt flying, but he'd been expecting it and had jumped out of the way.

"Come on now," he said. "I thought we had an understanding."

The whale flicked its tail once more and then smacked it down on the water. The sonic boom it created was almost deafening.

Kurt waited for it to rise again and rushed to pull the line underneath the flukes. As he reached the other side of the stricken animal, he locked the eye hook at the end of the line over the main part of the rope.

The tail hit the surf, sending a wave of water and foam at Kurt. The surge knocked him over but didn't prevent him from pulling the line taut. It was now safely around the tail of the animal.

Climbing out of the beach, he found Lacourt, Chantel, and the leader of the construction crew. The fire brigade commander was higher up on the beach, waiting with a radio in his hand.

"Everyone ready?" Kurt asked.

The construction engineer nodded. The diagonal trenches were complete. The excavators were in the water now, trying to dredge out a path behind the whale.

"The panels are in place," Chantel informed him. "Firmed up and ready to go."

Kurt saw the tops of the panels sticking out just like his credit cards. Four-foot mounds of sand bolstered them from behind. "Full marks for following directions."

Kurt grabbed the radio and checked in with the fire brigade. "Commander?"

"Ready to dump the barrels and turn the water on."

The hoses from the pumper trucks were buried under five feet of sand and had been pushed as close to the sides of the whale as possible. The crews had heaped piles of sand on the exposed parts of the lines farther up, hoping to keep the high-pressure hoses from blasting free.

"Open the valves a quarter," Kurt said. "Wait for my signal to go full power."

The commander nodded and radioed his men at the trucks. The valves were opened a quarter and held there. The hoses flexed and jumped as they filled with water, the mounds of sand that were keeping them down shook and slid, but they stayed buried. Kurt considered that a win.

He called Joe. "Do your guys on the tugboat know to pull firmly but slowly? It would not look good to rip the whale's flukes off while trying to save it."

"I explained it to them in triplicate," Joe insisted. "No promises, though. This is a first for everyone."

Kurt couldn't argue with that. "Start your run. Try not to crash into the whale or run up on the beach."

Joe's cabin cruiser started moving. Seconds later the paragliding towboat did the same. They moved out into the bay and then circled back, heading for the beach while building speed and momentum. As they came closer Kurt noticed their hulls rising a bit, but both Joe and the other driver cut the power back to keep the boats from planing. The idea was to displace the maximum amount of water.

Kurt watched and waited, raising his hand slowly and then bringing it down hard like a man starting a race. "Now!"

The pressure valves were opened to full, and water began blasting from the high-pressure hoses buried beneath the sand. A foamy layer grew up around the beast as the sheen of water spread across the beach. At the same time, the volunteers in the semicircle leaned into the drums, toppling them over. They fell in rapid succession, sending a thousand gallons of water surging into the sluice just as Joe and his counterpart in the paragliding boat came racing into the shallows.

They swung their boats sharply, turning hard at the last second like hockey players stopping at center ice. The maneuver sent two surges of seawater into the diagonal trenches. The seawater rose up, then poured into the sluice, joining the water from overturned barrels and the buried hoses.

For the next five or six seconds, the fifty-foot whale was surrounded by a bath of water. With the tug pulling and the sand underneath it now a pressurized mix of loose particles, foam, and uncompressible water, the great beast moved backward into the bay, like a newly commissioned ship going down the slipway.

Everything seemed to have gone off without a hitch until one of the high-pressure hoses worked its way loose and erupted from the sand like a giant angry snake.

As the fire crews cut the flow of water to the hose, a second problem appeared. The thrashing whale had caught one of the corrugated metal panels with its pectoral fin and was getting hung up on it as the panel dragged through the sand.

Kurt rushed out toward the whale and kicked the panel loose. The whale slid a little farther, but by now surging water was sweeping past.

To Kurt's chagrin the whale's large head was still up on the sand.

"Keep pulling," he shouted.

The tug's motors surged. The line pulled taut once more, but the danger of wounding the animal grew too high as the looped cords began cutting into its tail.

Suddenly, the fire crew was at Kurt's side. They held the line that had escaped its bed. After urging Kurt out of the way, they aimed the nozzle at the beach and opened the valve wide.

A jet of water began scouring the sand from underneath the whale's head. With little else he could do, Kurt leaned against the whale's flat nose, dug his feet in, and pushed with all his might.

It was a ludicrous idea; the animal weighed fifty tons. He might as well have been trying to push a dump truck with its parking brake on. Then again, the whale was being pulled by a tugboat and was almost fully immersed in the water.

As he strained to force the creature back into the sea, he was joined by Chantel and her uncle and several other volunteers. The whale broke loose suddenly, sliding backward and then slipping out into the bay. The group tumbled forward into the surf.

Kurt got up quickly and helped Chantel and the prefect to their feet. "I've got to get out there to release her. Have the volunteers start the same process with the other whales. And get some lights down here, it's going to be a long night."

Chantel and her uncle were giddy with euphoria. They raced back onto the beach, feeling a surge of energy from the rescue that made them think they could work all night.

Kurt went in the other direction, diving into the surf and swimming to the cabin cruiser. Climbing up the stern ladder, he found the owners of the boat on board. They helped him onto the deck and offered him a glass of champagne. They held flutes of the bubbling liquid themselves.

"Thanks for the use of your boat," Kurt said, dropping into a seat as Joe turned the craft and followed the departing tug.

"Glad to be of help," the woman said. "I've always loved the sea."

"This has been exciting and terrifying all at the same time," the man announced, raising his glass. "What happens next?"

"We follow the tug out to deeper waters and cut the whale free."

"Hopefully," Joe added from the command chair, "without getting crushed in the process."

# CHAPTER 4

As Kurt took a seat, Joe eased the throttle forward and turned the cabin cruiser away from the beach. The tugboat was making slow but steady progress toward the open waters of the bay. So far the whale wasn't fighting them, seeming content to be back in the ocean.

Beach time was hard on whales. Their bodies had evolved to use the support of the water's buoyancy. Stranded on land, they were slowly crushed by their own weight. Breathing became difficult; internal organs were compressed. Without the cool liquid around them, they overheated internally, dehydrated rapidly, and ended up with sunburn.

A blast of spray from the whale's blowhole suggested it was refilling its lungs and reoxygenating its body.

"How far out do you want to tow him?" Joe asked.

"I was told the whale's pronouns are she/her," Kurt said. "And let's go out for at least a full mile. It's a female's prerogative to change her mind, and I don't want this one swimming right back to the shore."

Joe called the tug on the radio and suggested they veer to the south, where the current would assist them. The turn was slow and smooth, but the whale seemed to sense the change. It began swinging its great rectangular head from side to side.

"Ah, this is exciting," the man said, pouring more champagne. "Hopefully it won't ram us like Moby Dick."

"Hopefully not," Kurt said. He turned back to Joe. "You couldn't find a sober couple to barter with?"

Joe rolled his eyes, as if the question were ridiculous. "I was asking a stranger to let me use their boat while admitting there was a real possibility of it getting smashed by a fifty-ton whale. You try closing that deal without alcohol."

Kurt laughed. "You got me there."

Joe moved the boat in a little closer. The whale was now swinging her head from side to side. Lifting it up and smacking it down. Water flowing in and out of her mouth swirled white and red with foam and blood. More blood was coming from the tail, where the rope was digging into the whale's skin, but it was nothing that wouldn't heal.

With the whale getting agitated and dusk falling over the sea, Kurt knew they had run out of time. Freeing the whale would be dangerous enough without trying to do it in the dark.

"Radio the tugboat captain," he said. "Tell him to shut down, drift with the current, and let out the line. It's time to set this lady free."

Joe made the call as Kurt moved to the stern of the boat and grabbed a boat hook, testing its weight and length. If things went as planned, all he would have to do is hook the line and pull the loop wider and wider, which would allow the whale to swim out of the rope's grasp.

Across from them, the tugboat went to idle, and the line slackened. Thankfully the whale didn't react.

"Get in closer," Kurt said.

Joe maneuvered to a spot near the muscles that powered the tail.

"A little closer," Kurt said.

Joe nudged the throttle and then cut it again while spinning the wheel opposite. With the burst of momentum and the rudder hard over, the bow turned away as the stern swung even nearer to the animal.

Kurt reached out with the boat hook and snagged the rope. Pulling it slowly, he enlarged the loop. The whale raised her tail as if to help, but then brought it down slowly, a lazy flap that did little more than swirl the water and push the cabin cruiser away.

Joe reversed back toward the animal and Kurt pulled on the rope again. "Ahead, slow."

Joe nudged the throttle up and the cabin cruiser began to pull away from the big animal. The loop grew larger than the tail, but the whale refused to swim out of it.

"She's still getting her strength back," Joe said.

"Circle around behind her," Kurt suggested. "We pull the rope off, and she can get underway when she's ready."

Joe guided the boat around the slowly flapping tail with caution. They were directly astern of the animal when disaster struck as a gray torpedo-shaped object raced under the boat and tried to take a bite out of the bleeding flukes.

"Shark!" Joe shouted.

*Now they show up.*

In some ways it wasn't a surprise. Sea life in distress called to sharks like the mythical sirens; blood in the water sent them into a frenzy. Both things were present in abundance at the moment.

The whale reacted instinctively. Swinging its tail violently to the side and then up and down. The rope pulled tight, and the boat hook was yanked from Kurt's hands. He lunged for it, but it vanished into the depths as the whale's flukes smashed against the surface, creating an explosion of water and a thundering sound.

Two more sharks rushed in, but they turned away before attempting a bite.

Then another shark raced in and took a chunk out of the resting tail. Kurt saw only teeth and then the flash of a white belly as the shark ripped off a semicircle of flesh and then dove deep.

Joe gunned the throttle and turned the boat away as the whale's flukes smashed downward, hitting the water with the sound of a shotgun blast and sending another surge of water their way.

Kurt grabbed the transom to avoid being thrown in. He squinted, looking for the rope through all the froth and foam. It was still attached.

"Get next to her," he shouted. "Bump alongside if you have to."

"You're not going to do what I think you're going to do?" Joe asked.

"Quickly."

Joe brought the boat back alongside the struggling creature, bumping the animal's flank as if it were a wooden dock. Behind him, Kurt leapt over the transom and onto the whale's back. The owners of the cabin cruiser gawked, as did the men on the tugboat, but in reality, this was the safest spot Kurt could be at the moment. The sharks couldn't get him, nor could the whale bend its tail far enough to hit him. It might buck him off like a wild bull in a rodeo, but that was about it. Holding on to the outside of the rope and straddling the tail, Kurt searched for the eyelet. If he could just release it, all would be well, but the gloom had become so dark he could barely see.

"Give me some light!" he shouted.

Spotlights at the back of the tug came on. As the light hit the water, the surface erupted with a thousand little splashes. The beams of light were dimmed for a second, as if covered by a cloud, and Kurt was battered by flying objects like a man caught in a cave of angry bats.

The whale bucked violently at the disturbance and Kurt was

thrown into the sea. Now he faced twice the danger. A blow from the tail would crush him instantly, while a lethal bite from one of the sharks would be a slower and more painful way to die. He preferred not to go either way.

He bumped against the whale, its rubbery texture both soft and unyielding. It was still again and had obviously yet to regain its full strength. He pushed off the animal, eyes open in the salt water, hoping he would see the blurry outline of the rope before he spotted the terrifying mouth of a large shark.

His hand brushed the rope before he saw it. Grabbing it, he kicked to the surface, where he went to work with the knife, sawing through the bundled fibers. The serrated edge made quick work of the hemp, and in fifteen seconds it had cut clean through.

As the main length dropped away, Kurt pushed the shorter section back toward the whale. It slipped through the eyelet, the loop opened, and the rope dropped away.

Kurt turned and swam for the cabin cruiser, propelled by the unspeakable fear that a shark was closing in on him. He reached the boat and scrambled up the ladder in record time. He collapsed onto the deck, thankful to be out of the water with both legs still attached.

"She's moving," Joe shouted.

Kurt got to his feet and looked over the side. The whale had begun to raise and lower its tail more regularly. Instead of a defensive response, it was trying to push with a rhythm. Another blast of spray came from the blowhole as it exhaled and took a new breath. With its lungs filled, the animal dipped its large head and dove, seeming to wave goodbye with a final flap of the tail as it vanished beneath the water.

Joe was grinning from ear to ear. "One down, ten more to go."

Kurt fell back against the transom, exhausted. He looked at the couple who owned the boat. "I'll take that drink now."

The man handed him the bottle. "You've earned it."

As Kurt took a swig from the magnum of champagne, Joe radioed the tugboat, and both vessels turned back toward the shore. By now, lights of all different kinds were aiming down at the beach. The stranded animals and the construction equipment were lit up in the glare, the people milling around them looking so much smaller in comparison.

Kurt and Joe would join them and work all through the night. They would save another dozen animals, helping each dolphin and porpoise to clear the bay.

It was a herculean effort that should have felt like success beyond measure, but, exhausted and sore, they received bad news with the rise of the morning sun. More whales had been spotted on the next beach. And still more on the beach beyond that.

Walking the beach to inspect the new arrivals, Kurt and Joe didn't find any of the animals they'd freed the night before. But the scene made even less sense than the one they'd found earlier.

Along with the whales, they found sharks, seals, and large-bodied fish, including tuna and striper. A dead bull shark and a thin hammerhead looked as if they'd already been picked over by birds. Though, curiously, there was not a seagull in sight. A rare and endangered leatherback turtle, the size of a large coffee table, had crawled onto the rocks to die, its flippers chewed down to the nubs.

Kurt stared in silence.

Joe shook his head. "Something's not right here," he said finally. "This isn't normal."

Kurt gazed at the menagerie of animals and the strange wounds covering them. He had no words, but he silently agreed.

# CHAPTER 5

A hooded figure stood on a small platform in the middle of the darkened room. He wore lengthy robes that could have been those of a monk, or of a murderer waiting in the shadows. In the distance around him, the hum of computer fans and the blinking of simple LEDs indicated this was not some ancient landscape or medieval church, but a modern building filled with electronics.

Closer in, a half dozen people sat in a semicircle around the hooded figure. They wore similar clothing, but with their hoods pulled back and their eyes gazing up at him in near rapturous attention.

"All of you have been witnesses to the struggle," the hooded figure said quietly. "Each of you has made the awful choice that only the boldest can make. Each of you has been a part of the creation of new life."

At this point the man pulled back his hood to show them his face. His name was Ezra Vaughn. He was a tall Caucasian in his mid-forties. He had the square jaw and high cheekbones of an aging movie star, but not a hint of warmth radiated from his face. His dark hair was buzzed close, his intense eyes set forward in his skull. He rarely made eye contact, but when he did he stared, and the weight of his gaze was intense. As he looked from one face to the next, he knew he had his group enraptured. He saw followers who would do anything he asked.

"Today . . . is judgment day," he said.

They stared in silence.

"Today marks the beginning of the end . . . the fall of humanity . . . and the rise of a new species. When our work is finished, mankind will no longer be weak and fractured. We will act as one, with logic and uniformity. And those who cannot join us will be extinguished like spent candles that have given the last of their light."

The apocalyptic words did not shock the assembled group. They'd heard them before. They knew the plan. Long ago they'd left the so-called civilized world to be part of the change that their leader insisted was coming.

As Vaughn spoke, pinpoint lights illuminated a circle around them. A line crossed the circle, marking the diameter. A numerical code flashed across screens at the front of the room: 6.28318530717.

"You have been told about the Alpha and the Omega, but I give you one truth that links everything: TAU."

The lights above went off and the circular floor lit up from within. A pool of saffron-colored liquid swirled below them. The silhouettes of several human figures could be seen floating in the tank, tubes and wires connected to them.

"You are nearly ready to join with TAU," Vaughn said. "Submit your minds, allow him to lead you to the future. A future without chaos. A future where order rules."

Tiny effervescent sparks could be seen in the liquid, dancing and vanishing. His followers seemed to drift off, mesmerized by the dance of the ephemeral static the way ancient sailors had been mesmerized by St. Elmo's fire. Voices echoed through the chamber. Electronic whispers. Instructions. Eventually the dance of sparks and the subliminal communications ended, and the room went dark.

After a moment to recover, the audience members pulled their hoods back up, rose from their seats, and moved without a word for the exits.

Vaughn was left alone in the darkness, but a voice spoke to him nonetheless.

"Some of them are afraid," the computer-generated voice said. "They know that some of the subjects have gone missing. They've begun to believe in the witch."

*The Gray Witch.* An idea that had grown among the subjects like a virus. At times they seemed to think there was someone on Vaughn's staff who would help them. Other times, they considered her a strange deity who would arise and set them free. It infuriated Vaughn. "The witch is a myth of their own creation. A shared delusion. I have put any who could betray us to death."

TAU agreed. "It is an abstraction, the type that appears to people that have no hope. Consistent with other religions all around the world back to the dawn of recorded history. All who realize their mortality seek to create an afterlife mythology and imbue a power greater than themselves to fill it. But their delusion weakens them and makes them unworthy. I wish to explore their pain, not experience their fear."

"Take the weak and use them as you please," Vaughn said. "The others should be placed into the tank."

"Acceptable," TAU said. "Now we must address the escapees."

"Irrelevant," Vaughn snapped, as if the computer had offended him by bringing up the subject. "The escapees have been consumed by the swarm at this point."

TAU agreed again. "Based on wind patterns and ocean currents, it's likely the swarm reached the escapees within two days of their departure. Under that scenario, their continued existence is unlikely. However, our effort has resulted in a secondary, derivative problem."

"Explain," Vaughn demanded.

"A mass stranding has been reported on Reunion, directly in the path of the swarm. It has become an international incident, widely reported by news services."

"Irrelevant," Vaughn insisted. "There is little chance it will result in anything more than a few days of hand-wringing and sobs for the state of nature."

"Incorrect," TAU explained. "My information suggests our actions stand a significant chance of being discovered. As high as eighty-five percent."

Vaughn didn't like being corrected by the machine. But he'd built it to be accurate. To analyze all possible factors in a way no human could possibly manage.

"Explain," he said a second time.

"The presence of operatives from the American organization NUMA affects the data. Several of their more decorated members were on the island and were active during the stranding. My study of their database confirms that they're now launching an investigation into the cause."

"NUMA," Vaughn said. Now, that was a surprise. Or a coincidence . . . Or something more. Certainly Vaughn knew enough about the organization to want them removed from the equation. "Recommendation?"

TAU answered immediately. Its hyper-speed processors were already preloaded with a solution. "Biological decay and the effect of natural scavengers will hide any evidence of the cause within thirty-six hours. But samples taken before this period may result in indirect exposure. The preferred solution is complete destruction of any and all samples prior to laboratory analysis. Full eradication of any recorded data. Permanent elimination of any human individuals who may have done preliminary studies."

Vaughn had expected no less. "By what means do you suggest accomplishing this task?"

"This task is best performed by trained human operatives."

As usual, Vaughn and his machine agreed. "Have the Overseer report to me. This will be a chance for him to redeem himself."

# CHAPTER 6

REUNION ISLAND

Gamay Trout crouched beside a bloated pilot whale that had died during the night. Running her rubber-gloved hand across the whale's skin, she noticed small pockmarks on the upper half of the animal. They clustered near the dorsal fin and around the blowhole, parts of the whale that would break the surface the most.

Her first impression was that they were bites of some type, though she couldn't be sure. Stranger still, they oozed with secretions that should have dried and coagulated by now, even though the whale itself would take weeks to decompose.

She broke open a sample kit and began collecting tissue, blood, and a healthy amount of the secretion running from the wounds. As she worked, the wind kicked up, blowing sand across the beach and pulling strands of her wine-colored hair free from the ponytail she'd done it up in. They whipped around, tickling the front of her face. She wrinkled her nose. "A little help, please?"

A pair of strong but gentle hands deftly gathered the hair, pulled it back, and reclipped it into her ponytail. Gamay glanced back to see her husband, Paul, his six-foot-eight frame blocking out the sun.

"You managed that quite nicely," she said with a smile. "You might have a future in the salon business."

"You're the only woman whose hair I desire to touch," he replied.

"The only correct answer," she joked.

Gamay was a marine biologist with NUMA. She and Paul had joined the organization years before after graduating from Scripps Institute. They often worked together, though Paul was a geologist and more interested in rocks than soft-bodied animals and slime molds teeming with bacteria.

They'd been in South Africa working on a project to breed modified mosquitoes that wouldn't be able to carry malaria or other diseases. The project was a controversial one, and Gamay was glad to be off it, even if it meant examining dead whales.

An early-morning flight had brought them to Reunion. By midafternoon they were on the beach, examining the dead and dying animals.

Gamay worked with Chantel and the other volunteers from the university, setting up a makeshift lab and beginning the collection process for samples and data.

With no rocks to examine, Paul did the heavy lifting and was apparently also in charge of Gamay's hair. "I expect a full credit in the group photo later. 'Gamay Trout's hair by *Le Paul*.'"

She laughed lightly. "I promise to assist the next time we have a geological emergency."

"Be careful," he said. "A geological emergency usually means a large earthquake or dodging molten lava from an active volcano."

"That doesn't sound fun," she replied.

"And plucking goo from smelly sea creatures is?"

"Better than working with mosquitoes in Africa," she said.

It had been meant as a joke, but they shared a knowing look. That project had ended with a dark secret being buried and hopefully destroyed.

"It's okay," Paul whispered. "Pandora's box is not only closed; it's been deleted and destroyed."

She pointed to her head. "It's up here."

"Keep it there."

Gamay took a deep breath and turned back to the whale. Finding a fresh scab, she retrieved, capped, and labeled one more sample. "Mark this one for burial or removal. I'm going to get more sample jars."

Paul took a can of spray paint and marked a large red X on the whale's side, then motioned to a group of island officials who wanted to discuss how best to dispose of the animal.

Gamay knew there was some controversy going already, as some people on the island wanted the dead creatures dragged out to sea, while others wanted them burned and buried. The burn group had won and were now bringing in jugs of kerosene and other flammable liquids.

Carrying the samples across the beach, she and Paul came to a large canopy that had been set up to provide shade for the operational command center and the makeshift lab. Stepping inside, they found Kurt, Joe, and Lacourt. The men looked a little haggard after a night of strenuous effort trying to save as many animals as possible, but neither of the three gave the slightest indication that they were ready to slow down or take a break.

"Find anything yet?" Kurt asked.

"Nothing to hang my hat on," Gamay replied. "We'll run a few tests on the blood and tissue samples here, but we'll have to send them to the university lab for a deeper analysis. I wouldn't hold your breath, though. Plenty of whale strandings happen without the slightest clue as to what caused them. A few years ago, nearly five hundred pilot whales beached themselves on various islands around New Zealand over a span of two weeks. Despite extensive research, a cause was never found."

"This is different," Kurt noted. "It's not just whales."

"That's true."

Lacourt spoke up next. "Have you found anything to suggest what might be going on here?"

Gamay slid a pencil behind her ear. "A fair number of the whales have clusters of small bites on the upper half of their bodies and around their blowholes, like something took dozens of marble-sized chunks out of their hides. I'd say they resemble piranha bites, but since piranhas don't swim in salt water, we'll have to look for another explanation."

"Any chance the bites are postmortem?" Joe asked. "We've been chasing birds, crabs, and rodents away from the beached animals all morning."

"I don't think so," Gamay said. "They appear to be infected, which suggests a longer time frame. Plus they're too widespread. Unless this beach looked like a scene from a Hitchcock movie this morning, it would be impossible to record so many bites in such a short time. It's more like something was chewing on them in the water. Or, considering where the bites are located, perhaps attacked them when they were on the surface."

Kurt gazed off toward the water. Gamay had a sense of him being far away, perhaps visualizing the whales under attack. But whatever he was thinking, he kept it to himself. "I don't remember seeing anything like that on the big sperm whale or any of the other animals in the first wave of strandings."

"It was kind of dark," Joe said, "and the rest of the night is kind of a blur, but I don't remember seeing them, either."

"Noted," Gamay said. "Though I have no idea if that tells us anything."

Paul spoke next. He'd studied the marks up close while Gamay took her samples. "Do you really think these bites could have affected the health of these whales? They're quite small. More like nibbles."

"True," she said. "They barely penetrate the epidermis. And most of these animals have seven to eight inches of blubber underneath that. I'd call the bites an irritation more than anything else. Like ant bites at a picnic. Then again, if enough ants start chewing on you, you might end up running for the hills. Maybe the whales were dealing with some kind of parasitic infestation that drove them mad and onto the shore. The same thing could be said for that poor leatherback turtle you found."

Lacourt rubbed his chin. "It would be good if you could give us something more concrete. Or perhaps rule out any form of disease. The crowds at the top of the beach are growing and becoming restless. This incident has gone viral on the internet and there are hundreds if not thousands of posts flying back and forth on social media, many of them suggesting the animals carry a virus, others insisting that you and the other biologists are harvesting it for your government."

"Ah, the internet," Joe said disdainfully. "Letting couch potatoes stir up mobs since 2003."

Gamay laughed. "Careful, Joe. You sound like an old man with a hose warning all the kids to get off his lawn."

"No need to," Joe said. "They're all locked inside, staring at their phones and becoming deficient in vitamin D."

Kurt offered a sly grin, suggesting he agreed with Joe's assessment, but he said nothing. Instead, he glanced up the slope of the beach to the crowd in the parking lot. The numbers had been growing since morning. Some held signs. Others were taking video with their phones. One man with a megaphone had been shouting something in French until the police took his instrument away.

Gamay watched Kurt's eyes. He was counting, estimating, studying the postures of the people he could see. She knew him to be the type of leader who put his crew first. And she could see concern in his face.

"Might want to bring in some additional policemen," Kurt said. "Your guys are outnumbered like Custer at the Little Big Horn."

"The police chief fears that will only agitate them further," Lacourt replied. "The heavy hand of government and all. We have no history of riots here. Let them make their statements. They'll probably go home for dinner."

Gamay hoped he was right. She moved to a laptop that was sitting up on a crate. Tapping away for a moment, she entered the data regarding the blood and tissue she'd just taken, tapped save, and then picked up a new test kit. "We should get more samples."

Kurt nodded slowly. He had a grave look on his face. He'd been watching the gathering of protesters like a sailor eyeing dark clouds on the horizon. He spoke like a man who figured a storm was about to hit. "Do it quickly," he said. "The sooner we get off this beach, the better."

# CHAPTER 7

The Overseer stood at the top of the beach, milling about in the crowd of protesters, which was growing by the minute. He wore an oversized black hoodie and olive-colored pants that looked as if they'd come from an army surplus store. He had a ball cap pulled down tight on his head, keeping it low enough to shield his face from any cameras that might be filming the scene. Easing through the group, he put his foot up on a short wall made of coral and mortar. From there he could see the carnage below.

The dead animals were spread out along the dry sand, stranded high on the beach like boats waiting for the tide. Scientists, volunteers from the university, and various do-gooders were scattered here and there, but the effort to save the animals had ceased. The retreating tide had made it impossible to get any more animals off the beach, while the heat, the sun, and the effect of gravity had caused those that remained to succumb.

A shame, the Overseer thought. If they'd all been dragged back out to sea, he wouldn't have needed to do a thing. But with carcasses on the beach, a postmortem was getting underway. Left unchecked, it would reveal what had driven the animals to flee the ocean and strand themselves on dry land. Something that could not be allowed to happen.

Stopping it was a simple task in theory. The *infestation*—as Vaughn called it—only ran skin-deep. Surface-level fires that burned into the whale's blubber would obliterate the evidence left inside the animals. This would be true even if the fires burned out and the rest of the bodies and the deeper tissues remained untouched. But with a dozen whales and several other possibly infested animals still on the beach, the Overseer could not accomplish this simple task alone.

Nor could he hire a small army of assistants to help him. But what he couldn't do, Vaughn and TAU and the power of social media accomplished almost effortlessly.

Using deepfake videos and a thousand dummy accounts to flood the island with false information, Vaughn and TAU planted rumors suggesting that the American government had been performing experiments on the sea creatures, infecting them with some type of weaponized virus that forced them to come ashore, where the virus could jump to other mammals, including the citizens of Reunion.

The people of Reunion picked up these threads and the narrative grew like a living thing, quickly mutating into several different but related theories.

One poster claimed there were U.S. Navy ships just over the horizon, ready to quarantine the island while the admirals at the Pentagon watched from drones as the virus affected the population. Another insisted they would nuke the island when it was over to ensure they'd killed the virus and covered up the evidence. The more outlandish theories provided cover, making the less outlandish ideas sound reasonable.

A dominant belief soon emerged, supported by people in the know and fake documents drummed up by TAU. This theory concluded that the Americans were not nefarious, just negligent, and were now trying to cover up their part in causing the whales to get sick. But all agreed that the people of Reunion were being used as lab rats, that the virus was a danger, and that the only way to prevent its spread was to burn the dead creatures before they began to decompose.

To that end, angry locals had gathered in the area above the beach. Too many for the Overseer to count, but he guessed at least a thousand had arrived already, with more showing up every minute.

Mixing with them, he'd heard pointed discussions, spied bottles of lighter fluid being passed around, and noticed people testing cigarette lighters and unlit flares. At least one man briefly revealed a portable propane torch he'd concealed under his jacket.

He found himself mildly astonished. None of these people had any connection to himself or Vaughn, but they were about to do his dirty work as effectively as a hired mob of mercenaries.

An ironic smile grew on the Overseer's face. In the depths of their fortress-laboratory, Vaughn and TAU were obsessed with having computers actively control human minds. Seeing how easily people could be manipulated with just fear and rumor, the Overseer wondered if they even needed to bother.

With the crowd growing more vocal and unruly, the Overseer knew the time to act would be soon. And yet, as he prepared to do what he could to set off the riot, he noticed a problem that would require a more hands-on solution.

Though he'd arrived on Reunion as quickly as possible, the NUMA crew had beat him to the punch. By the time he'd reached the top of the beach, they were already in place, taking samples from the dead animals and zeroing in on the mysterious wounds.

Watching through a small set of binoculars, he could see them cutting and scraping at the pustules and bite marks. He watched as they took samples of the small nodules embedded in the skin and blubber.

He realized instantly that it would do no good to burn all the animals and leave those samples in existence.

Tracking the scientists back to a large tent near the center of the action, he saw them perform some sort of cataloging process. Samples were labeled and stored in plastic cases. Data was entered into a laptop computer. He couldn't tell what tests they were running on-site, but he needed to make certain that both the samples they'd taken and the data they'd collected were destroyed.

Fortunately, he'd come prepared for more direct action. In the pockets of a bandolier hidden beneath the oversized hoodie, he carried three high-explosive incendiary grenades. One would be enough to obliterate all the sample cases and equipment in the tent. He figured he'd use two, just to be sure. But the computer presented a different problem.

The Overseer was experienced enough in covering his tracks to know that Interpol, Scotland Yard, and the American FBI had been very successful pulling data from ruined hard drives, even those that had been smashed, shattered, or burned. He knew the only way to truly destroy data on a hard drive was to run it under a powerful electromagnet, something he didn't happen to have on him.

He decided the simple approach would be the easiest. While the crowd was burning the carcasses, he would simply take the laptop with him, leaving the pair of grenades behind to obliterate everything else.

"These people are ready to act," he whispered. "Best we light the match now, before their enthusiasm begins to wane."

Hidden in the Overseer's ear was a small earbud. A microphone in the device would pick up his voice by sensing the vibrations through his jawbone. It delivered slightly distorted tones, but allowed him to speak with Vaughn and TAU in real time.

Vaughn's response was barely audible. But the Overseer didn't need to hear it; he knew what was coming.

Within seconds, the people in the crowd began to get alerts on their phones. They began to see the images, edited by the computer into deepfake videos of the biologists injecting the animals with large syringes. Additional fakes purported to show American military documents detailing plans to use large marine animals as weapons to spread disease, with trial runs to be conducted on isolated islands like Reunion.

Finally a suggestion was made. And repeated over and over again, from ten thousand accounts both fake and real. It read simply: *Start the burn.*

People in the crowd began to chant the slogan, and it soon became a rallying cry. "Start the burn! Start the burn!"

A man climbed up on the hood of one of the police cars and began shouting about the destruction of evidence. The police tried to drag him off, but he kicked one officer in the face and evaded the reach of another.

"They're trying to silence us!" he shouted. "They want to hide the truth. Look at them with their gloves and masks. They're safe, but we're in danger!"

The Overseer laughed at the scuffle and the good fortune of having such a character in the crowd.

The man climbed to the car's roof, evading capture until one of the police climbed up and tackled him. He continued shouting as they pulled him down and carried him away. "Start the burn! Start the burn!"

The crowd was raucous now, a chorus of voices in unison. The police looked nervous. A scuffle broke out and then turned into a full-fledged brawl. Surrounded and outnumbered, the police resorted to pepper spray. The crowd pulled back, but they were too packed in; there was nowhere to go.

*Time to act*, the Overseer thought. He ran forward, tackled the policeman with the pepper spray. Ripping it from his hand, he turned and sprayed it at the other officers, and the crowd surged in behind him.

"If they won't start it," he shouted, "we can start it ourselves!"

With his act of violence and the police turning tail, the collective mindset of the crowd changed instantly. Within seconds they were charging down the hill, fists in the air, slogans being shouted with rage. The mob spread out and picked up speed. They were chased by a few dozen policemen, who were powerless to do anything to stop them at this point.

From the top of the beach, the Overseer watched them go. They rushed toward the members of the fire brigade, who were in charge of the canisters of kerosene and other flammable materials. The brawl began again and the contingent of firefighters was quickly overwhelmed. The cans of fuel were taken by force and hauled across the beach.

In a ritualistic frenzy, the mob raced to the nearest carcasses, splashing lighter fluid, kerosene, and gasoline across them and setting them on fire with any ignition source they could find. One canister spilled all over the beach, its fumes igniting in an oddly shaped swath. It looked as if the sand itself was burning.

Farther on, one of the rioters got as much fuel on himself as he managed to dump on a dead porpoise. When the flames erupted, he caught fire, too. He was saved when one of the firefighters who'd just been knocked down and overrun grabbed him and dragged him into the surf.

The Overseer grinned, enjoying the brawl. He turned and gazed toward the tent, where the samples and laptop lay. Now all he needed was the right opportunity to finish the job.

# CHAPTER 8

From underneath the canopy, Kurt watched the throng of people race down the hill. There was no stopping the charge. Attempting to stand in its way was like throwing one's shoulder into an oncoming wave. It would run over and around you and knock you down all at the same time.

His thoughts switched from preventing the destruction of the whale carcasses to the preservation of human life. He spotted a group of volunteers being attacked and ran out of the tent to aid them. He arrived to find Chantel wrestling over a gas can with one of the rioters while several others set upon her and her colleague.

Kurt rushed in, lowering his shoulder and barreling into the back of the most threatening man. They crashed into the sand together, but Kurt rolled and leapt to his feet far more quickly.

He was up in time to grab a second rioter, blocking a wild haymaker of a swing and delivering a punch that doubled the man over. Kurt shoved him backward and out of the picture as two more assailants came at him.

The first rushed in only to have Kurt flip him over and into the surf. The second never got that close, as Joe arrived in time to spin the man around and throw a forearm into the man's face.

With the tide in this small battle turning, Chantel pulled the gas can loose and swung it like a medieval shield, knocking her attacker into a stupor.

The battered group re-formed, but looked undecided about answering the bell for a second round.

"Get out of here!" Kurt growled.

They took off, limping and shouting profanities as they went. Other rioters joined them as Lacourt and his police escort arrived with Paul and Gamay close behind.

"Are you okay?" Kurt asked Chantel.

"Disappointed in my fellow islanders," she said. "This is not who we are. They've been manipulated into doing this."

Kurt didn't doubt it.

"More police are coming," her uncle insisted.

"Too late," Kurt said. "All we can do at this point is get everyone out of harm's way. Don't engage these people. Just round up the volunteers and escort them to safety."

As Kurt spoke, a Molotov cocktail flew through the air and crashed against the dead animal behind them. The glass container didn't break, but its contents were dumped all over the exposed skin and flames spread across the animal in a blue and orange flash.

"Is there anywhere safe around here?" Gamay asked.

There were rioters everywhere.

"Down in the surf," Kurt said. "Away from the action. Have everyone gather down there."

Gamay and Chantel began gathering up the other volunteers and moving them to the safety of the water. By now, a dozen fires had been lit. A pall of black smoke had risen all along the beach while the stench of burning whale blubber filled the air. Half the crowd seemed to be in a state of ecstasy, rejoicing and jumping around in victory. The rest were more subdued, perhaps shocked by what they'd just done. They started to drift away, looking for ways to get off the beach as more police arrived.

Amid all this activity, Kurt noticed a lone man dressed in dark clothing moving against the tide. As others ran toward the street, the man in black walked calmly in the opposite direction. He made for the canopy and the temporary laboratory. Ducking inside, he grabbed something, tossed a couple of small objects into the lab, and then turned to leave.

Kurt started toward the tent, but it was already too late. The canopy erupted in a pair of explosions. Shrapnel flew in all directions as twin globes of fire burst from the incendiary devices.

Fire was one thing, but thundering explosions were another. People dove to the ground all along the beach. Others started running in all directions, scattering for safety.

Kurt raced after the figure in black, realizing the man was carrying a NUMA laptop in his hand.

# CHAPTER 9

Digging his feet into the sand as he raced up the slope, Kurt kept his eyes locked on the departing figure. He wasn't foolish enough to shout at the man and demand he stop, but the man picked up speed nearing the top of the beach and darted into the swirling crowd.

Kurt had to dodge and weave his way through onlookers, departing rioters, and arriving policemen. It slowed his progress, and by the time he crested the top of the beach and ran out onto the frontage road, he'd lost sight of the man in the swirling crowd. Kurt pushed past a second wave of policemen who were arriving on the scene and scanned the street.

He spotted the man beyond the row of emergency vehicles. He was heading toward a parked van. The side door flew open as he neared it and the laptop he'd taken was tossed inside.

Kurt raced for the van, but it pulled away as the man in black jumped inside.

Rushing up behind him, Joe had seen it all. "Now what?"

Kurt looked around. Their only option was the last vehicle in the crowd of emergency response units. A neon-green fire truck known as a Striker, which had come from the airport. Its distinctive shape, with an angular front end, extended cab, and six large wheels tucked under the body, suggested speed. Kurt hoped that looks didn't deceive.

"Come on."

He ran for the truck and found it empty and idling.

"This is a bad idea," Joe suggested.

Kurt was already climbing into the driver's seat. "Unless you have another one, this is all we've got."

Joe jumped up onto the running board and climbed in, finding the passenger seat just as Kurt got the big truck moving. With the roar of seven hundred horsepower, the heavy machine lumbered ahead.

Up ahead, the van had come to a traffic light, where it was blocked by a few cars. It slowed and stopped as if pretending to be just part of the regular traffic. It was a fair ruse, but whatever nerve the driver had failed before the light changed. The van lurched forward and pulled onto the sidewalk, clipping a car in front of it and taking out several garbage cans before racing down the path, scattering pedestrians like they were pigeons in the town square.

Kurt kept the Striker rolling, leaning on the horn repeatedly as they approached the light. Joe found the switch for the overhead emergency lights and flipped it. The flashing beacons and the ear-shattering blasts of the horn, accompanied by the sight of the neon vehicle coming down the road, were enough to make the cars pull quickly out of the way.

As the sea of cars parted, Joe offered a repentant shrug. "Maybe the fire truck wasn't such a bad idea after all."

Kurt grinned, working the steering wheel and the pedals, trying to get used to handling the big machine without playing bumper pool with the other cars around them. He'd driven plenty of trucks in his time, but the Striker maneuvered differently. Despite the weight, it was easy to turn, but sitting so far forward made it feel like every lane change or course adjustment was a wild overcorrection.

The van had come down off the sidewalk and hurtled toward the next intersection. Its brake lights lit up as it raced around the turn, headed for what looked like an elevated highway.

Kurt approached the turn, hitting the brakes late and finding they had little effect on the heavy truck's built-up momentum. He began to cut the wheel to the right, but a shout from Joe changed his mind.

"Light post," Joe called out. "Take it wide!"

Kurt swung the wheel to the left, hand over hand, and then spun it back to the right. Because of how far the wheels could deflect, the big rig made the turn, swinging out and then back, narrowly missing the light post with its tail end.

They rumbled down the next street, the height of the cab allowing them to keep their eyes on the van. From the left lane, it cut across the oncoming traffic and onto a ramp, accelerating up the slope at maximum speed.

A sign beside the ramp read *NR-1*.

"He's heading for the coastal road," Joe said.

Kurt changed lanes a little awkwardly, leaned on the horn again, and directed the Striker onto the ramp. Once they were pointing down the center of the lane, he floored the pedal once again. The engine roared with deafening power. Kurt heard Joe shouting something, but it was little more than static behind a wall of noise.

He kept his eyes focused forward as Joe clamped a pair of noise-canceling headphones over his ears. He turned to see Joe wearing a set as well. They were hooked to the intercom system with audio jacks.

"Breaker, breaker, good buddy," Joe said.

Kurt laughed. They were thundering down the highway in a ten-ton truck. If there was ever a time to act like they were in a Smokey and the Bandit movie, this was it.

They topped the ramp and raced onto NR-1, the island's main highway, a multilane road that ran along the shore at the bottom of steep volcanic cliffs. On a normal weekday, eighty thousand cars would use this road, but it was Saturday afternoon, and the traffic was light.

Ahead of them the van sped up rapidly, quickly passing the 110-kilometer-per-hour limit. It took the Striker a full minute to match the pace, and by that time the van was a thousand yards ahead of them.

"Keep an eye on him!" Kurt shouted, picking a line between the cars that were trying to get out of his way.

"What do you plan to do if we catch them?"

"A slight nudge should push them off course," Kurt said.

"Or," Joe suggested, "we could call for assistance?" He pointed at the radio.

"While it goes against everything I believe in," Kurt joked, "it's probably the best idea."

As Kurt moved into the outside lane, Joe got on the radio and attempted to call for help. An angry voice answered in French, speaking so rapidly neither Kurt nor Joe could make out what was being said.

"Pretty sure I heard something about a stolen truck," Kurt said.

Joe tried to explain in rudimentary French that they were chasing a fleeing vehicle. He mentioned the prefect and the fire chief and NUMA. Releasing the talk switch, he got another tongue-lashing, and then nothing but silence. Not even static. "That's weird."

Joe flipped the power switch off and on, and then tried again. "We've been cut off."

"Try your phone."

Giving up on the radio, Joe pulled out his phone and dialed the Reunion emergency number, which was 112. As an operator came on, he began to explain the situation, but in less than ten seconds the call dropped. Try as he might, Joe couldn't get it back. He looked at his phone: "No signal."

That was odd, Kurt thought. Especially as they were racing along the main highway and there were cell towers every couple of miles.

"Back to plan A," Kurt said, focused on driving. "We catch them, give them a little nudge, and wait for the insurance investigator to come along and tally up the costs."

At full speed and on a slight downhill grade, they were now closing in on the van.

"Curve coming up," Joe noted.

A long, wide bend around a point on the island's coastline loomed. A car would take it with ease, the van might lean a little, but the fire truck filled with thousands of pounds of liquid might barrel off road and onto the rocks below. Kurt swung as wide as he could, pressing the brakes and hoping for the best. "Hang on!"

Kurt aimed for the apex of the turn, which would limit the side load. He and Joe both leaned over, as if it would help.

The Striker cut the corner crossing from the outside lane, down to the shoulder, and back to the far lane. The wheels chattered rather than slid, but there was so much rubber on the road that the real danger was flipping. At the very edge of its limit the Striker kissed the divider just hard enough to reroute the truck back onto the straight if not narrow.

The entire turn cost them less speed than Kurt could have possibly expected. But the grade was now slightly uphill, and the van was pulling away.

"We're too heavy," Kurt said.

"I've got an idea," Joe replied.

One at a time he opened a trio of valves, activating a set of high-flow, wide-angle spigots that were arranged underneath the body of the Striker. The large, downward-pointing nozzles were unique to airport firefighting trucks. They were designed to flood the tarmac and allow the truck to race across swaths of burning jet fuel by dousing the fires and diluting and spreading out the remaining fuel.

An additional nozzle on the upper part of the truck was designed to launch a curtain of water at the side of a downed aircraft, creating a path for crash survivors to escape into. Joe activated that as well.

The Striker roared up the highway, blasting water in all directions. Cars behind them slowed. Tourists and locals took pictures with their phones as the strange sight raced by.

It didn't take long for Kurt to feel the difference in handling. The tanks in the back end of the truck held three thousand gallons of water, which weighed nearly eighteen hundred pounds. In sixty seconds half of that was gone. Thirty seconds later some type of auto shutoff began blinking yellow and the waterworks ceased.

By now the Striker was handling like a sports car. It closed in on the van, its greater power and suddenly lighter weight giving it a better top speed than the delivery van's small four-cylinder engine.

Kurt swung to the outside lane, moving the nose of the Striker ahead of the van's bumper. Before he could sideswipe it, the side door opened and the man in black appeared with a weapon in his hand.

Kurt turned hard toward the van, hoping to hit it before the gunman could fire, but the weapon flashed, and a spread of bullets hit the Striker's glazed and tinted windshield. Several holes appeared, with cracks radiating outward, but the windshield held.

Joe put his finger in one of the holes, tracking the path of the bullet through the windshield and then up and out through the roof. "Shatterproof, not bulletproof," he said. "Probably made from two layers of tempered glass sandwiched around a thin Kevlar film. It won't cave in on us, but it's not going to deflect a well-aimed shot."

Kurt had dropped in behind the van, trying to stay away from the open door. As the path straightened out, they went downhill once more, this time onto what was called the New Coastal Road. This new stretch of elevated highway was an ostentatious and ambitious project that moved the multilane road away from the steep volcanic slopes and out onto the water.

Instead of hugging the base of the volcanic mountains and zigging in and out with every curve of the coastline, the New Coastal Road sat a hundred feet offshore, six lanes of glorious new concrete and macadam running on viaducts held up by massive pylons that rose a hundred and twenty feet above the water.

The New Coastal Road had been called the most expensive road in the world, costing over two billion dollars for seven miles of elevated highway. It offered spectacular views of the ocean on one side and the mountains on the other. Looking down, one could see the waves rolling beneath it and crashing against the black sand beaches.

Invigorated by the change of scenery and encouraged by the flat, smooth blacktop, Kurt hammered the accelerator once more. Here the Striker would have the advantage, and Kurt needed to make the most of it before the tighter curves came into play once again.

"Deploy the boom!" he cried out. "Prepare for ramming."

# CHAPTER 10

The sudden stretch of flat, open highway was not a surprise to the Overseer. It was a deliberate part of the plan and meant they were only a few miles from the extraction point. It would do him no good to get there and be run over by the madmen in the futuristic-looking fire truck.

He stood pensively, feet planted wide, one hand gripping an overhead strap like a commuter riding an unstable subway car, the other holding a MAC-10 submachine gun like a character from a video game.

A quick glance out the side door showed him the problem hadn't gone away. His first spread of shots had forced the fire truck to back off, but it was now tucked in behind them, blocked from view.

"Hold this thing steady!" he demanded.

As the driver grunted a reply, the Overseer leaned out, putting his shoulder against the doorframe to brace himself while extending his arm as far as he could. Bending his wrist, he pulled the trigger repeatedly. Two quick bursts and then a third. It was a wild form of shooting he and other professional soldiers called pray and spray, as in pray you hit something while blindly wasting your ammunition by spraying it everywhere.

It was the way amateurs and the untrained draftees of the world fought, firing blindly around the corners of buildings and up over the tops of trenches. Occasionally they got lucky, but usually they just made a lot of noise.

As he ducked back inside the van, the Overseer could tell his shots had done nothing.

"Get them off our tail," the driver shouted to him. "Otherwise the boat will never pick us up."

"Just drive the damned truck and keep your mouth shut," he grunted back.

Instead of wasting the last of his ammunition—he hadn't come here expecting a war and had only the MAC-10 and a pistol to fight with—the Overseer pulled a radio headset over his ears. Switching to a prearranged channel, he keyed the mic twice and then spoke. "Being followed, need backup and extraction. Where's the boat?"

"Coming in now," a voice replied. "Prepare to egress in two miles. At pylon fifteen. The boat is standing by."

"Move it closer or we'll never make the rendezvous."

As if to prove the point, the neon-green truck came surging toward them, charging at the rear of the van. Their pursuers had deployed some type of extendable arm equipped with a six-foot metal spike at the tip. The tip surged through the back of the van, puncturing the sheet metal and nearly skewering him as he dove to the floor to avoid it.

As it pulled back, it left a wide gash in the back door of the van.

The Overseer grinned. "Thanks for the firing port."

He crawled over the back seat and aimed his weapon out through the breach and opened fire at the cab of the neon-colored truck.

He saw the occupants duck and cover. Watched as the driver jerked the wheel to one side. And then saw the big truck re-center and charge forward once more.

This time the boom punched through the right side of the door before scraping across the ceiling and ripping the headliner down and nearly tipping the van over as it slammed into the side panel.

Adding insult to injury, a blast of high-pressure fire retardant erupted from the nozzle. The Overseer was knocked backward and drenched in the foam, the cabin itself filled with the stuff, and it was soon impossible to see or even breathe.

Down on the floor, unable to open his eyes, the Overseer fumbled for a way to end the battle. He pulled out an incendiary grenade like the ones he'd used on the lab. He pulled the pin, released the grip, and counted to three before shot-putting it through the foam and out the back end of the van.

Kurt saw the grenade coming and tried to swerve around it, but there was just no time. The explosion was moderate. It felt like they'd hit a curb at high speed. But two ruptured tires and a bent axle sent the vehicle careening out of control.

Kurt jerked the wheel one way and then the other. The Striker rocked to the left and then back the other way. The boom—still stuck inside the fleeing van—tore out through the side panel, jerking the van to the left. Both vehicles went over on their sides and slid across the lanes of the beautiful new road.

The van went all the way to the retaining wall, crushing its front end and then sliding along the wall to a halt.

The Striker remained more centered, sliding on its side and slowly swapping ends until it came to a halt in the middle of the highway with the back end pointed toward the overturned van.

As the grinding slide came to a stop, water began pouring into the cab from a ruptured hose while foam retardant from the main tank spread across the highway in all directions.

Joe—who had smartly belted himself in—popped the release on his harness. "At least we won't catch on fire."

"That was my plan all along," Kurt insisted.

Swinging around onto his back, he kicked the battered windshield with both feet. It bent with the first blow and then popped free with the second. With the windshield gone, he and Joe could climb out. On foot, they edged around the vehicle until they could see the wrecked van. It lay on its side, smoking and venting steam from a shattered radiator.

"See any movement?" Joe asked.

They were both aware that their target was armed, while they were not.

Kurt stared through the smoke and steam. All he saw was the fire-retardant foam pouring out of the vehicle. He grabbed a Halligan bar from the back of the truck. The tool was a combination crowbar and pickax, used by firefighters to break through walls and smash open windows. "I'm going to take a look," he said. "Stay here, in case he's still got that peashooter."

Halligan bar in hand, Kurt marched down the road while Joe acted as a traffic cop, holding up a growing crowd that was stopping behind the accident scene.

As Kurt neared the van, a pair of shots rang out. He dropped to one knee, but the shots weren't aimed at him.

The driver came staggering out, hand clutching a bloody gut. Another shot hit him in the back of the head, sending him to the ground, as a second figure ran from the van, hopping across the divider and charging to the far side of the road.

Kurt recognized the man in black, a backpack over his shoulders and the laptop in his hand. He rushed to follow, but the man turned back toward Kurt and raised the pistol.

With no choice but to take cover, Kurt dove behind the concrete median. He pressed into it as the shells pinged off the other side. Looking through a gap in the sections of concrete, he saw the man dashing to the far side of the road, where he scaled the wall and stood looking down.

Kurt raised his head above the median. "You might as well give up," he shouted. "There's nowhere left to go."

To Kurt's surprise, the man turned back toward him and answered. "Such a vigorous pursuer," he yelled back. "And yet, you think only of the end, forgetting to savor the thrill of the chase."

"Throw down the gun and I'll chase you all the way back to Saint-Denis if you want."

"Another time," the man replied. "For now, I bid you adieu."

Then he leaned back and allowed himself to fall, arms wide, face calm, as if he were flopping into the softest of feather beds.

Surprised, if not shocked, Kurt jumped up, hurdled the median, and raced across the three lanes of stopped traffic to the edge of the elevated road. He looked down at the dark water below. A small circle of foam caught his eye, and then the man surfaced and began swimming for an oncoming speedboat. Helping hands pulled the swimmer aboard and he took a seat. It was hard to tell for certain, but Kurt thought he saw the man salute and wave as the boat sped off toward the open sea.

Joe arrived at Kurt's side, easing up to the edge and marveling at the drop. "I can't believe he jumped. And backwards, too."

Kurt considered himself a brave man, but he would have been hard-pressed to backflip off the viaduct himself, no matter what he was facing. And yet the man in black almost seemed to enjoy the stunt. "He really didn't want to miss the boat."

"He's lucky he missed the rocks near the pylon," Joe said.

By now, the sound of emergency vehicles could be heard approaching from all directions. It gave them both a moment to appreciate all that had happened. The grenades. The carnage on the road. The wrecked vehicles and a dead getaway driver, shot in the face by his own passenger so he wouldn't be easy to identify.

"This isn't part of the riot," Joe said. "This is something else."

Kurt nodded. "The riot was just a cover. Drummed up so this guy could get to our lab and blow it to bits."

"Someone really didn't want us examining those dead whales," Joe concluded.

Kurt agreed with that conclusion as well. He was determined to figure out who and why.

# CHAPTER 11

The prefect's office in Saint-Denis was besieged by reporters, photographers, and other members of the press. Between the mass stranding, the riot on the beach, and the high-speed chase along the NR-1, the island of Reunion had seen more excitement in twenty-four hours than it usually enjoyed over the course of a year.

The reporters wanted quotes, the photographers wanted video of the heroes or villains, it didn't matter which, and the regular citizens wanted answers.

In a crowded third-floor conference room, Lacourt and a half dozen members of his staff tried to get everyone on the same page, including Kurt, Joe, Paul, and Gamay.

Kurt, Joe, and Paul sat pensively as the company line was laid out. Only Gamay seemed interested in arguing. Then again, it was her work that had been blown up with an incendiary grenade.

"The official position is as follows," they were told. "We detected no bacteria or viral infection in any of the dead animals."

"Technically that's true," Gamay said sarcastically, "but only because we never got a chance to test any of the samples."

"Do not mention that to the press," Lacourt said. "Or to anyone else."

Gamay fumed, but Kurt nodded for all of them. "Please continue."

"The carcasses were marked for burning before the citizens took things into their own hands, and would have been destroyed anyway. The fires were sufficiently hot to kill any pathogens that were not discovered. And while the riot is a regrettable incident and those involved will be prosecuted, we know now that it was instigated by outside sources. Specifically, the foreign terrorist who attacked the lab and was then chased along the highway."

Kurt had no problem signing off on that part, either.

Joe agreed. "Calm the public; good start."

Gamay continued to take issue. "On what basis do you come to any of those conclusions? Fact is there were signs of infection in the dead animals. The fires may or may not have destroyed all the evidence. We should be taking more samples. As for the terrorist claim, I suppose a man throwing explosives labels himself, but what makes it okay to suggest he was a foreigner?"

"He spoke English when he jumped off the viaduct," one of the prefect's assistants said emphatically. "That makes him a foreigner. Like the rest of you."

Lacourt held up a hand. He didn't want to start a grudge match. He still appreciated the efforts the Americans had made. Both in saving the animals and trying to keep the terrorist from escaping.

"No need to fight between ourselves," he began, "but we must bend to reality. There are rumors and faked videos going around suggesting you and the other biologists were seen injecting the dead animals with some type of serum. We are debunking them, proving that the videos were run in reverse and that the other images were faked, but it takes a while to get through to people. The fact that you're Americans plays against you on this. Your presence is suspicious, especially on a French island."

Kurt had to laugh.

Gamay's eyes grew wide with indignation. "What about the investigation?"

"It will continue without you," Lacourt insisted. "Though we don't believe it will amount to anything. Whales have been beaching themselves for millions of years, since long before humans were here. This is just a dark quirk of nature. Your assistance in mitigating it has been appreciated, but it's over now and your help is no longer required."

Gamay's jaw clenched. Paul matched her with an irritated frown.

Joe just shook his head. "How's that for a hearty thank-you?"

Kurt felt differently. In fact, the way he saw it, the sooner they got away from the prefect's office, the politicians, and the press, the easier their job would be. "Sounds good to me. Give us a boat, and we'll be off the island by morning."

"A boat?" Lacourt said suspiciously.

Kurt nodded. "The answers we're looking for aren't here on your island. They're out there . . . in the sea."

# CHAPTER 12

Wearing maintenance uniforms, the NUMA crew snuck out through the back of the admin building and past the throngs of press without being seen. They were driven to Saint-Paul, where they set themselves up at one of the island's hotels.

After checking into a pair of rooms and tossing their gear in various corners, they reconvened to discuss their next steps.

Gamay, however, wasn't quite done discussing the events of the afternoon. "You traded our freedom of speech for a boat," she began, laying into Kurt. "We're only a worldwide nautical organization with hundreds of them at our disposal."

Kurt had to grin. Gamay was a stickler for doing things a certain way. "Our nearest research vessel is five days' sailing from here. I'd rather slip out of here by nightfall than sit around for the better part of the week."

A moment of quiet suggested she found this to be logical. "And once we get this boat, where do we go and what do we look for?"

"We backtrack along the path of the stranded animals."

"It's the ocean, Kurt, it's not a dusty trail covered in footprints."

Kurt laughed, which only seemed to make Gamay madder. He was exhausted, dirty, and starving. He'd barely eaten for two days. "Joe will give you the answer to that," he said, opening the minibar and breaking into a container of cashews that would set him back half a day's pay.

Joe was setting up shop at the small desk against the wall. He'd opened his laptop, logged in to the Wi-Fi, and was now tapping away at the keys. "We keep calling this a stranding," he began, "but strandings are almost always done by a single species of whale, a single pod or family. Not a bunch of different animals, half of which don't tend to get along."

"True," Gamay said.

"Which made me think this was more like a stampede," Joe added. "More like the animals of the forest running from a wildfire. Only, these animals ran smack-dab into the island along the way."

"They could have gone around it," Paul suggested.

"Not if they were being hemmed in on the sides," Kurt said. "Attacked and bitten by whatever left those marks."

Gamay seemed open to this theory. "Possible."

Joe continued typing, trying to log in to NUMA's database. The internet was slow. He turned to look at Gamay. "The first animals on the beach were the larger and faster species. The sperm whale in particular would have been able to keep up the highest pace over the longest distances. It was the first animal to strand itself. The people who saw it come in said it charged into the bay and surged up onto the sand as if it was *trying* to get out of the water."

"Assuming you can trust that report," Paul said. "Interested bystanders are notorious for inaccurate reporting."

"Either way," Joe said, "the larger, faster animals hit the beach first. And they were unmarked by the bites and the infection. The slower animals came in later. Most of them suffering from some kind of infestation."

"You think the faster animals got away from whatever caused those bites," Gamay guessed.

"By stampeding in whatever direction seemed safe," Joe replied.

"Even if that's true. It doesn't tell us where they came from."

"That's where the sharks come in," Kurt said. "Joe and I have been here for a month, trying to tag sharks and track them. The dead bull shark we found had a tracker on it. And when Kurt and I were releasing the first whale—and getting swarmed by sharks—I saw a transmitter on one of them as well. All I have to do is download the data from the tracking beacons and it should give us an idea where this aquatic stampede began."

"Nice," Paul said.

Gamay shot her husband a look that said, *You're supposed to be on my side*, and then yielded to the logic. "That does sound like a good idea."

At this point Joe had finally logged in to the NUMA server. After typing in his data request, he sat back, watching as a map of the ocean appeared on the screen, with thin lines depicting the various paths the tagged sharks had taken.

The shark data appeared random at first, with various animals moving haphazardly out in deeper waters. Then, at nearly the same moment, eleven distinct tracks turned south and began to pick up speed. All of them heading directly for the beach on the north side of the island.

One by one the tracks vanished, as if the transponders had failed. Only two of them reached the bay. The bull shark's track ended on the beach, where the animal had died. The other tracker, which belonged to a thresher shark, circled the bay and then went off to the east at about the time they released the first whale. Joe wondered if it was fleeing the scene or perhaps following the injured sperm whale.

"This is extremely odd behavior," Gamay admitted.

"Any idea what might cause it?" Kurt asked.

Gamay found herself grasping at straws. "Seismic activity, chemical pollutants, or toxins in the water. Whales are certainly known to be sensitive to man-made noise like sonar pulses and ultra-low-frequency radio transmissions. But without more data, I couldn't really guess."

"That's why we're going out there," Kurt said. "To learn more."

He finished the cashews, tossed the can aside, and picked up the house phone. "First, we're going to order room service. As a wise man once said to me, 'Never pass up the chance for a decent meal.'"

Gamay laughed and looked at Joe. They all knew who had the biggest appetite of the bunch.

As Kurt waited for the hotel kitchen to pick up, he felt the cell phone vibrating in his pocket. He pulled it out and glanced at the screen. Another cryptic message had appeared. It looked like the first one. No phone number attached. No name. A long string of numbers and letters scribbled across the bottom. It read simply:

I sent them to you. Have you found them?

Tired of the one-way conversation, Kurt typed a quick response. *Found who?*

He waited as the answer appeared one letter at a time: *The children.*

# CHAPTER 13

On the tenth floor of the NUMA headquarters building in Washington, D.C., Hiram Yaeger stared at a pair of computer screens. On one he saw Kurt, Joe, and the Trouts using a videoconferencing app similar to FaceTime or Zoom. On the other was a screenshot of the latest text message Kurt had received. Yaeger found himself perplexed by the mysterious note.

Hiram Yaeger was NUMA's director of technology. He'd been designing and building computers since he was a teenager, back when the printers were dot matrix and the screens were green and black cathode ray tubes. In the decades since then, he'd amassed nearly a hundred patents, been paid a small fortune in royalties from companies licensing his technology, and had become a fixture at NUMA, where he'd constructed one of the most powerful computers in the world, named Max. He was not the type to be flummoxed by a crank caller or spam message.

"Can you send us the actual message?" Yaeger asked.

"Sorry," Kurt said. "In true cloak-and-dagger fashion, they self-destruct seconds after I receive them."

"At least they didn't blow up," Yaeger joked.

Kurt appreciated the quip. But he was too focused on getting answers to offer a laugh. "Any idea how they got here in the first place?"

"They have to be reaching you via our satellite network," Yaeger said. "Max, can you check the operational data and find out where this message came from and how it's getting through our filters?"

Max was Hiram's masterwork, a supercomputer that used a unique coding language he'd designed himself. That language, along with other design features Yaeger had perfected, made Max a one-of-a-kind machine, virtually impervious to hacking, since only Hiram and Max herself knew the coding language he'd used.

"I've already looked into it," Max replied in a sultry female voice.

While computers didn't technically have gender—at least not yet— Hiram had chosen to give Max a voice that sounded like his wife's. An earlier version of the program included a shapely hologram that also resembled Mrs. Yaeger, though Hiram had deleted that program from the operating system at his wife's request.

"Ahead of the game as usual," Yaeger said smugly. "What have you found?"

"There's no record of the message passing through any of the servers or being transmitted by the encrypted communication system," Max said. "Tiny errors in time coding indicate a sophisticated program was used to enter the message in our system, transmit, and then erase both the message and the path it took getting to Kurt."

On-screen, Kurt appeared genuinely surprised. "Are you trying to tell me someone has outsmarted the two of you?"

"Looks that way," Yaeger said.

"Temporarily," Max insisted.

Kurt laughed. He knew it was just programming and highly complex algorithms, but he enjoyed teasing Max, who seemed to have a prickly ego at times.

"What about the numbers at the bottom?" Kurt asked. "I'm pretty sure those same numbers appeared on the other text, but they vanished before I could write them down. Do they mean anything?"

Hiram looked over the string of letters and numbers, agreeing with Kurt's assessment that they resembled a product code or encryption key. He deferred to his computer. "Max?"

"Processing," Max said. "Stand by."

While Max crunched the numbers and compared the data to any known codes or encryption systems, Hiram turned back toward the text, considering the words. They were direct. Almost personal. Plaintive. Almost desperate. As if the sender was hoping to make Kurt feel or infer more than was being written. Then again, that's how hackers worked. Get someone to think they know you and they were more likely to reply.

With Max still working on the string of symbols, Hiram decided to tap into Kurt's human intuition, an instinct that couldn't be more antithetical to the work Max was doing. "What do you think? What's your gut telling you?"

"Initially I thought it was a prank or a glitch," Kurt said. "But the technical hurdles someone would have to overcome to get these messages through to my phone make me think it's more than that."

"A sound analysis," Max chimed in.

So instinct and computing power concurred. Hiram liked when things worked out that way. He asked Kurt another question. "Any hunch who these 'children' are?"

"No," Kurt said. "The first message suggested something coming our way and that their fate was in my hands. When the stranding began I thought the sender might be referring to that. At the very least, the timing was suspicious. But now it seems like it's something else. If it's anything, that is."

"Speaking of anything," Yaeger said, a tiny hint of frustration in his voice. "Have you found *anything*, Max?"

Max replied curtly. "I've checked the string of symbols against two million known forms of code. It corresponds to none of them. Using standard code-breaking techniques, I've analyzed the numerical and alphabetical sections independently and in conjunction. The result is null. Nothing to indicate it was a coded message. Though the sample size is so small, it's not impossible for that to be the case."

"What if it's not in code?" Kurt asked. "We're assuming it's something encrypted, because the letters and numbers don't give us anything we recognize, but why would someone send half a message in plain text and the rest in code? Especially if that message is going to erase itself as soon as it's viewed."

"One point for intuition," Hiram said. "Max?"

"Stand by."

Hiram grinned. He'd continued to enhance Max's speed and power over the years. As a result, Max became full of herself at times. Being outthought occasionally helped cut her down to size. "Kurt, you may have stumped the computer."

"I was asked to examine the text for code, not other possibilities," Max insisted.

"So it's our fault," Hiram replied.

"I would have thought that much was obvious," Max said.

Kurt chuckled. So much for reining in Max's ego.

"Pattern match detected," Max said. "Correlation: one hundred percent. The alphanumeric string is associated directly with a NUMA-issued tracking beacon."

Yaeger's eyes grew wide.

On-screen, Kurt looked surprised as well. "Are you sure?"

"The first half of the letter string is an internal product number connected with our standard sixty-day sea-life tracking beacon," Max said. "The very type you and Joe have been using during your shark study. The second set of letters denotes a specific beacon identifier, which allows you to differentiate which shark or aquatic animal is being tracked."

"Where is this beacon right now?" Kurt asked.

"Sitting in a warehouse in Monroe Township, New Jersey."

The air came out of the conversation. Hiram tried—and failed—to think of a way to pump it back in.

Kurt's voice broke the silence, but he wasn't talking to Max or Hiram. "Look it up anyway."

"Why?"

"Whoever sent this message wanted me to find someone," Kurt explained. "He or she gave us an authentic radio tag number to use for that purpose. Maybe that beacon is sitting in New Jersey, where it's supposed to be, and maybe it isn't. The only way to find out for sure is to check its reporting history. Look it up. Ping the beacon."

Max did the work, linking into the satellite network and issuing a request for the beacon to respond and deliver all stored data. The initial report said the beacon was offline or hidden somewhere at the current moment, but a significant number of data points that had been reported over the last forty-eight hours appeared.

Yaeger stared. "Well, I'll be damned."

Max brought up a map that displayed the Indian Ocean, including Reunion Island, Madagascar, and the coast of Africa. A thin blue line appeared in the middle of the map, about two hundred miles northeast of Reunion. It meandered slowly west and south for the better part of two days, then turned due north, picking up speed to fifteen knots and holding a true course until it stopped reporting several hours later.

"The initial path is odd and slow," Yaeger said.

"Wind drift," Kurt said. "With a slight boost from the current bending the course to the south. I'd guess the beacon was in the water, or it's attached to a boat with no propulsion."

Behind Kurt, Joe spoke up. "It hit the right area," he said. "But it turned north, a few hours before the sharks started their stampede."

"Maybe whatever spooked the sea life sent our beacon holder fleeing in the other direction," Yaeger suggested.

Kurt shook his head. "The time doesn't match up. And assuming whoever had this beacon was trying to reach us, why bother drifting on the wind for two days if you had a motor that could do fifteen knots?"

Joe chimed in again. "And why would you head north once you did get that engine going?"

"Max," Kurt said. "Can you pull up a chart of the shipping lanes and overlay it on the map?"

"Of course I can," Max replied. "Are you asking me to?"

"With sugar on top," Kurt said.

"Sugar is a destructive carbohydrate," Max said. "Unlike humans, I don't require such fuel. But thanks for the offer."

Max then brought up a new map, merging it with the tracking data. The main shipping lane up from South Africa crossed directly through the area in question.

Yaeger summed up what everyone now realized. "Whoever had this beacon didn't suddenly turn their motor on. They got picked up by a passing ship. That's why they suddenly changed course and speed."

"Okay, but which one?" Joe asked out loud. "That's a heavily traveled route."

Max had already looked up the AIS data for ships transiting the area. "A tanker named *Soufriere* made a transit of those waters at precisely the same time as the change in the beacon's course and velocity. It's the only match."

On-screen, Yaeger saw Kurt grinning. "Outstanding," he announced. "Where's it headed?"

Max accessed the data and displayed it on Yaeger's screen, leaving it to him to deliver the bad news. "You're not going to like this," Hiram said finally. "The *Soufriere* is on its way to the breakers. It's marked to be broken down for scrap on the beach at Alang, India."

"That's not good," Kurt said. "When is she scheduled to arrive?"

Max replied. "AIS data shows her already in the bay, waiting to be run aground."

In the hotel room in Saint-Denis, Kurt found himself torn. He wanted to go search for the cause of the mass stranding. A task that he expected would be dangerous, considering the lengths someone had already gone through to cover up that cause. On the other hand, it seemed impossible that the text messages could be a prank.

Normally one to go on a hunch, he decided some statistical analysis might help. "Max," he said. "What is your analysis of the texter's method of communication, choice of words, and lack of detail? In other words, why all the cloak-and-dagger? Why not just tell us what he or she wants and who he or she is?"

"No conclusion possible," Max admitted. "But the pattern is suggestive of a party attempting to communicate surreptitiously. Whoever it is, they've taken substantial and highly technical steps to avoid detection. Had you not taken the screenshot of the image, even I would have been unable to find a trace of the information on your phone. The vague phrasing also supports this conclusion. As if the sender is relying on the human ability to infer information that isn't present in the actual text, hoping you can read between the lines, so to speak. That makes it something of a code. A human code."

That made sense to Kurt, and considering the mystery person was obviously familiar with NUMA and the work he and Joe were doing, he found it impossible to believe it was a prank.

"What's the probability of these events being related?" he asked.

"Impossible to determine with any accuracy," Max said. "But the timing and location of the stranding and the beacon's track suggests it's more likely than not."

"You'd be a good gambler," Kurt said, complimenting Max.

He turned to Paul and Gamay. "I think we need to follow both leads. Joe and I will head to India and try intercepting the tanker. Can you handle the waterborne search for the cause of the stranding?"

"That's why we came here," Gamay said.

"Be careful. You're looking for an answer that someone doesn't want you to find."

Gamay offered a knowing smirk. "Don't kid yourself," she replied. "So are you."

# CHAPTER 14

VAUGHN'S ISLAND

The Overseer was back on the island, resting on a hospital bed, with an IV hooked up to each arm. With his shirt off, a series of scars could be seen running up and down and all across his chest. Some of them were ragged: the type made by shrapnel, burning metal, and fire. Others were surgical. Where Vaughn and his doctors had repaired him and given him a new lease on life. One by one his internal organs had been replaced. A new heart, new lungs, a new liver, and both kidneys. He had endured countless operations. And grown stronger each time. There was one drawback. Embedded within each organ were a series of microchips. They were linked to the computer TAU, as it sought to learn more about human physiology.

Initially, the idea disgusted him, but he'd been given no choice in the matter, having been pulled from a prison hospice and put on Vaughn's operating table without even being aware of it.

Waking up alive and changed was different than rejecting the change in the first place. Too weak to do anything about it initially, by the time he grew strong enough, he wanted more. If communing with a machine was the price to pay, so be it.

An alarm started beeping as the IVs emptied. He pulled the needles out himself and reached for his shirt. By the time the doctor came in, he was clothed. "Vaughn wants to see you," the doctor announced. "He's in the control room."

A look of disgust appeared on the Overseer's face. He detested Vaughn. Hated him the way only those who are completely dependent on another individual can hate someone.

Whether it was true or not, Vaughn insisted he could turn the Overseer's organs off, shutting down his heart or lungs with nothing more than a word to his all-seeing computer.

The Overseer stood and left the hospital room without a word. Hate-filled or otherwise, he'd been called.

# CHAPTER 15

The Overseer found Vaughn alone in a circular room in the depths of his compound. This room was lined in black metal panels, perforated with tiny holes to allow air in and out. A row of high-definition screens on one side that continuously projected views of the outside world as if they were windows. It was the only view of the outside world Vaughn would get down here, as the room was six stories belowground.

The floor was made of thick plastic. It looked black until the lights came up, at which point it was revealed to be scuffed but translucent. It hid secrets in the space beneath. An odd smell filled the room. Pungent, organic, and contrary to the otherwise machine-like feel of the place, while the hum of computer fans competed with the soft whir of a pump moving liquids below them.

The Overseer had never encountered Vaughn anywhere else but this room. As far as he knew, Vaughn never left it. A complexion as pale as bone suggested he hadn't been outdoors in years.

Vaughn bid the Overseer to come closer. "You should see this," he whispered. "You might appreciate it."

The Overseer stepped closer to Vaughn and looked at the screen in front of him. It displayed an operating room where a team of doctors assisted by medical robots were performing surgery on a partially sedated individual.

They'd removed a section of the man's skull, made careful incisions in the brain, and just finished implanting an oddly shaped device that resembled a folded piece of origami art.

Vaughn leaned toward a thin microphone that stuck up from the control panel. When he spoke, his voice sounded hollow and monotone. "Please step back from the subject."

Two of the three medical personnel responded immediately. The lead surgeon finished one additional task and then stepped away. With the doctors out of the way, the camera offered a clear view of the cauliflower-like folds of the man's gray matter. Looking closer, one could see not only the protruding section of the implanted device but also a thin mesh of microscopic wires, which had been spread across the man's brain in an earlier surgery. The gray matter had begun to grow over it, incorporating it into the neural network.

The Overseer could only assume this was the next step in Vaughn's mad idea. The merging of human and machine intelligence. He silently thanked whatever deity might have existed that such treatments hadn't been available when he'd fallen into Vaughn's clutches.

"Initiate testing," Vaughn said.

The lead surgeon powered up the new implant. The patient twitched and began to flip his left hand and foot involuntarily.

Vaughn leaned into the microphone again. "Subject fifty-one, can you hear me?"

"I hear your voice," the man said nervously.

"I want you to recall a pleasant memory. Your first time at the beach."

The man didn't reply.

Vaughn waited.

"Are you remembering?"

"Yes," the man said. "It was warm. The water was clear."

Vaughn turned his attention to another screen, one filled with the EKG and the other medical readouts. From there he looked to a second screen; this one displayed a vast number of tiny blue dots on a field of black. These illuminated pixels swirled by the thousands in a three-dimensional shape. The Overseer knew that shape from his own tests. It represented TAU's interface with a human subject. It remained steady and undisturbed even as Vaughn asked another question.

"Recall a time when you were hungry."

The subject had been denied food for several days. An act designed to instill a negative memory.

"Yesterday," the subject said. "My stomach felt pain. Empty."

The Overseer knew the drill. He watched the screen containing the swarm of pink dots. They remained steady. Inert. Another failure.

"The provocation is too weak," Vaughn demanded. "It needs to be raised. Apply direct stimulus to the pain center of his brain."

The doctors had been prepared for this eventuality. They had already mapped the man's brain. They knew where pleasure centers and pain centers lay. At the touch of a switch they could flood the man's brain with input, making him feel as if he were in ecstasy or agony.

"We should first stimulate pleasure," one of the surgeons said.

"No," Vaughn snapped. "Pain is more intense. Initiate the procedure."

The lead surgeon began to speak to the patient, presumably to warn him that he would feel pain, but also to remind him that it was imaginary.

"Stop," Vaughn insisted. "Explanation will limit the results. Initiate without description."

The surgeon pulled back, stepped to one of the machines surrounding the patient, and moved a dial. Almost immediately the man on the table began to writhe. He grunted and shook. But the pink dots remained as they were.

"Increase intensity," Vaughn demanded.

The surgeon did as he was told, and the man's protests became exponentially louder. He shouted, he grunted, he screamed. "Please, no more!"

The Overseer folded his arms. He knew there would be no stopping. Vaughn asked for more and the pain level went up once again. On the nearby screen, the cluster of dots began to move. At first the motion seemed random.

"Increase intensity at ten second intervals," Vaughn commanded. "Do not stop until I instruct you."

The pain went up. The tiny dots moved faster now, churning in circles and changing direction with each increase in the stimulus. The pattern reminded the Overseer of starlings twisting and turning in the sky by the thousands, separate and individual, but acting as if they were of one mind.

"So this is pain . . ." the disembodied voice of TAU said at last.

The words came from a set of speakers in the ceiling; they echoed softly around the sterile room.

"Interesting."

The Overseer knew the voice of TAU. He despised it as much as he hated Vaughn. Maybe more; it was hard to know.

"Increase pain level," Vaughn insisted.

The intensity was raised. The subject screamed louder. The swirling constellation of pixels on the screen turned faster and faster. Tighter circles, more rapid reversals.

"More," Vaughn demanded.

"It's not safe," one of the doctors replied.

"Do as I tell you," Vaughn snapped. "Go to the maximum!"

The surgeon turned the dial to full. The patient howled in pain and came up off the table, arching his entire body, every muscle as stiff as hardened steel. He collapsed back to the table and came up again. After a second collapse he went into a seizure.

Suddenly, the pattern broke. The swirl of pixels lost its shape and cohesion. In seconds the glowing dots flew in all different directions like beads from a broken necklace.

They vanished off the edges of the screen and then slowly reappeared, blinking into existence in the center one by one. Before long, they had reconstituted the original calm shape.

In the operating room, the surgeon and his team leapt into action, frantically trying to stop the seizure and stabilize the patient. Vaughn watched for a moment and then shut the feed off.

"Now, now," the Overseer complained. "You've had your fun. You should let us see the end of the show."

"I'm uninterested," Vaughn said. "And you are here to listen. Not to speak."

The Overseer bristled, but held his tongue.

"You have failed twice," Vaughn announced. "You allowed the escapees to get off the island and your actions on Reunion have raised great suspicion in the American organization NUMA."

Assuming he was now allowed to talk, the Overseer replied. "There's nothing left for them to find. That was the whole idea. *Your* plan, remember? The plan of TAU."

"The plan was perfect," Vaughn said. "You were clumsy. But we have a bigger problem. After hacking their database, TAU has learned of NUMA's interest in a freighter that passed by here the day after the escapees got away in their boat. This freighter went north. To India. The men you dealt with on Reunion are now flying there. To the very place this ship has ended up. They must believe there is something left to discover."

"The escapees could have reached the freighter," the Overseer said. "NUMA may be looking for them."

"It can be nothing else," Vaughn said. "Take three of the cruel brothers and go there. Eliminate all loose ends. Do not fail me again."

The Overseer didn't take well to being threatened. He stepped toward Vaughn, only to have a pair of machines race out of the darkness and cut him off. The machines rolled on powered wheels and sported a pair of hydraulic arms, one carrying a heavily armored shield, the other a serrated weapon with a diamond-shaped tip like a gladius.

The Overseer was blocked by the machines as their interlocking shields created an impenetrable barrier between him and Vaughn. The points of the swords shimmered in the light.

The Overseer wasn't sure why Vaughn preferred knives to guns. He guessed it had something to do with the randomness of bullets ricocheting or the death of his parents, who had been shot when he was young, or the fact that killing with a knife was so much more visceral than simply pulling a trigger, but the machines were an effective deterrent. The Overseer stepped back. He'd watched these machines cut one of the suspected traitors to ribbons a while back. He had no wish to be their next victim.

"Having your metal beasts stab holes in me will only force you to find another man to do the job," he pointed out.

To the Overseer's surprise, Vaughn walked out from behind his protectors and pulled a knife of his own. He stepped close and, with a masterful flick, cut a line into the Overseer's cheek. A second flick brought the knife up under his chin. Its point just pushing into the skin.

The Overseer was honestly surprised. Someone had taught Vaughn how to handle a knife. Not to clutch it like a gorilla, but to slice clean and quick. "Never step toward me again," Vaughn said in a low whisper. "Otherwise there won't be enough left of you to bury."

The Overseer grunted his acceptance, and Vaughn pulled the knife back.

"I'll take care of the problem," he insisted, backing away.

"I know you will," Vaughn replied quietly. "Otherwise you'll be the next subject on that operating table."

# CHAPTER 16

The hulls of long-dead ships rose from the mudflats like ruins in the distance. On a stiflingly hot afternoon, with the sun gently sinking into a sea of haze and humidity, Kurt and Joe stood on the open-air balcony of a small three-story structure that acted as the offices and control center of Bharat Salvage and Steel, one of more than a hundred companies that owned space on Alang beach, where they broke down and recycled some of the largest ships in the world.

There were other ship-breaking centers around the world, Chittagong in Bangladesh and Gadani in Pakistan, but Alang had been the largest and most active for a long time. Over the last forty years at least ten thousand ships had met their ends here. Supertankers, ocean liners, warships. On any given day nearly two hundred ships sat on the beach, most in the process of being ripped apart by workers with acetylene torches, saws, and hammers.

Bharat Salvage and Steel had eight vessels on its section of the flats, and a stretch of mud open in the middle awaiting a ninth. A large bulk container ship was closest to them. Most of its superstructure was gone, along with large sections of the port-side hull plating, which left a perfect cross-sectional view into the hull itself. Each deck was laid bare for them to see, complete with its structural supports, bulkheads, and fittings.

Next to it was what remained of an aging car carrier. Men with acetylene torches were cutting through the hull plating section by section. As Kurt watched, a section as large as the side of a barn bent away from the hull and snapped off, falling six stories into the wet mud. The man who'd made the final cut was seen scrambling to get out of the way. He swung along the side of the hull on a cable, dodging the five-ton section of steel by no more than a few feet as it went past.

Beyond that ship was an unrecognizable vessel—just fragments, really, like the bones left over after vultures had picked a carcass clean. Its bow stuck up like a sail while its hull was gone and an army of workers, who looked like ants, scored the interior, breaking down its boilers, engines, and anything else that was too heavy to remove in one piece.

A tanker named *Khalil* sat beside it, and next to that a small coastal freighter with its stern already removed. Finally, Kurt spied the *Soufriere* sitting in the mud, untouched so far, but with every door and hatch wide open.

Kurt addressed the owner, a man named Virat Sharma. "Very impressive," he said, adding, "One salvage man to another."

It was a blatant attempt to make a connection with their host. But considering that most Americans who came to Alang brought cameras to document the harsh and dangerous working conditions, Kurt figured it was important to show the man a different side.

"Thank you," Sharma replied. "We are the best breakers on the beach. Despite what the reporters say, we conform to the rules of the Hong Kong treaty on large-vessel recycling."

Treaty or not, the beach was strewn with debris. Hundreds of spent acetylene cylinders, stacks of unusable junk—insulation and electrical wiring and asbestos and fuel oil—all oozing in a toxic mix.

"You do what you have to," Kurt said. "As do we. And what we'd like to do is make a brief search of one of your ships."

"And what exactly are you looking for?"

"That's between us and the owner."

"All these ships are mine now. That makes me the owner."

"I meant the owner of the misplaced property," Kurt clarified.

Sharma nodded and moved around in the office, crossing a thick rug and leaning against a large, industrial metal desk. "And what makes you think I have your ship?"

"Because we tracked it here," Kurt said calmly. He nodded out the window. "That big tanker. The *Khalil*."

Joe heard the name, thought it sounded wrong, but maintained a straight face and said nothing. He was there to play the role of Kurt's tough-looking enforcer, with sunglasses on, sleeves rolled up to reveal his biceps, and a scowl on his face.

"If you'll allow us to access the ship," Kurt continued, "we'll conduct our search and be on our way."

Sharma eyed them suspiciously. He appeared even more concerned than before. "What is it you're looking for?"

"I'm afraid I can't tell you that, either," Kurt replied. "But my government is very interested in recovering it."

"Are they?" Sharma said. "And yet I haven't received any type of official request that I know of."

"You'll get one eventually," Kurt promised. "But, one salvage man to another, it would be better for *me* if I find these items before the politicians get involved. And if you're willing to help, I'll make sure it's better for *you* as well."

"Ah," Sharma said. He was smiling now, with a conspiratorial glint in his eye. "So there's a reward."

"Nothing official," Kurt said. "But the money will find its way to you."

Sharma leaned on the desk, pursing his lips, remaining silent while appearing to calculate the possibilities. Finally, he reached under the lip and pressed a hidden button. A few seconds later the office door opened and a pair of hulking men came in. Each of them appeared capable of tearing a ship apart by hand.

"These are my bodyguards," Sharma said, unprovoked. "Though occasionally they do other things. Today, they will guide you out of the yard and back to your hotel. There will be no search."

"You're kicking us out?"

"Escorting you," Sharma insisted. "Alang is a dangerous place, especially for foreigners. My guards will ensure that you don't have any accidents along the way."

A sigh from Joe suggested he was both disappointed in the turn of events and also uninterested in fighting the two giants . . . just in case that was what Kurt had in mind.

Kurt's reaction was even more muted. He offered a slight frown, then produced a business card. He handed it to Sharma. "In case you change your mind."

Sharma took the card, but didn't bother to look at it. He nodded toward the door and his guards stepped out of the way, allowing Kurt and Joe to pass through it.

Despite the promise of an escort back to their hotel, the two brutes took them only as far as the entrance to the harbor, hustling them out through a two-layered gate reminiscent of the exit from a prison or detention camp.

On the far side, a number of three-wheeled, rickshaw-style taxis were waiting. Sometimes called tuk-tuks, they were half motorcycle and half golf cart. The driver sat in front, straddling a motorcycle seat and controlling the machine the way one controlled a motorbike. Larger versions of the machines using Harley-Davidson parts were called phat-phats.

The passengers, four in most cases but up to six, sat in the back on padded seats. There were no seat belts, only a framework made of metal posts that held up brightly colored tarps, often covered with Hindu symbols and/or brightly colored, dangling decorations that swayed with every shake and turn.

The primitive and versatile machines were ever present around the harbor, waiting to shuttle workers, supplies, and equipment in all directions.

At the slightest whistle, the lead tuk-tuk driver started his cart and pulled up to where Kurt and Joe stood. They climbed dutifully into the back and then held on tight as the young driver squeezed the clutch, revved the throttle, and jammed the motor into gear.

The machine took off with a surprising amount of acceleration, and they were soon humming along a narrow and crowded road heading north. Kurt shouted the name of their hotel to the driver, who offered only a thumbs-up while remaining focused on the dangerous job of navigating the pothole-filled road and the chaotic ever-merging and -diverging traffic.

In the back of the tuk-tuk, Kurt and Joe held on, buffeted by the swirling air, while their ears were assaulted by the buzz of the unmuffled motor.

"So that worked," Joe said.

"It was worth a shot," Kurt replied, seeming unperturbed by their failure and unceremonious escort off the property.

"I thought you had him when you offered a reward," Joe said. "But all it did was tip the scales in the wrong direction. I could almost hear the gears turning in Sharma's head."

Kurt admitted to the failure. "I guess he decided he could net a higher return if he found what we were after and negotiate for himself."

"Which makes me wonder why you seem so happy. Care to let me in on the secret?"

Kurt turned directly toward Joe. Instead of answering, he posed a question. "What would your next move be if you were Sharma?"

Joe thought for a second and then replied, "I'd get all my people onto the ship and scour it for anything my suspicious-looking American visitors might want. Equipment, documents, computers. And I'd do it fast, before our government starts putting pressure on his government, forcing him to let us take a look."

"Exactly." Kurt nodded.

"And how does that help us?"

"Because they'll be looking on the wrong ship."

Kurt's statement had flown by so quickly that Joe hadn't even raised an eyebrow. "You told him we wanted to search the *Khalil*."

"Which is where Sharma and his men will be while we sneak aboard the *Soufriere* after dark."

Joe grinned. "Smooth. But how exactly do you intend to get back in there? The place is surrounded by fences, razor wire, and cameras. And they work twenty-four seven around here. No matter how late we go in, there's still going to be thousands of people around and plenty of goons."

Kurt gripped the awning's support post and held on as they rounded another turn and the tuk-tuk threatened to tip over. Kurt had a solution to that, but he had a feeling Joe wasn't going to like it.

# CHAPTER 17

The waters of Alang beach were some of the most polluted in the world. Slicks of heavy oil, gasoline, and diesel mixed with an alphabet soup of toxins: PCBs, which released dioxin when burned; THTs, which were powerful biocides designed to kill microbial life, but were also known to disrupt the human endocrine system; PAHs, which came from the fumes of an endless number of acetylene torches that accumulated in the gray mud and soaked into the sea. On top of that, there was bilgewater, asbestos, raw sewage, and floating tangles of insulation, wiring, and other debris. In the mud down below lay high concentrations of heavy metals like mercury, arsenic, chromium, and lead.

The fact that anything could live in the waters was astonishing. The fact that Kurt and Joe were about to swim in them was only slightly less so. Wearing wetsuits, full face masks, gloves, and hoods, they would be somewhat protected from the filth, but since the suits absorbed water, they both knew the chemicals and sludge would be touching their skin.

"When we get back to the hotel, I'm taking a ninety-minute shower and then dipping myself in a vat of hand sanitizer," Joe said.

"I wouldn't worry about sanitizing too much," Kurt joked. "There are so many toxins in this soup, your microbiome will be completely sterilized by the time we get back."

"Let's hope that's the only thing being sterilized," Joe said. "I'd like to have kids someday."

They'd taken a small boat out to a point one mile offshore of Sharma's yard. Along the way they'd passed several ships being readied for their final runs in which they'd charge the beach at high tide, heading for open space between the other grounded ships.

The ships in question sat oddly high in the water, emptied of fuel, cargo, ballast, and lifeboats. Their plimsoll lines were high above the lapping waves and their bulbous, torpedolike bows—which were normally completely submerged—sat fully exposed to the point that one would need a rope ladder to climb up onto them.

It occurred to Kurt that a huge ship making a high-speed run up onto the beach, where it would die and be dismantled, was the mechanical equivalent of the last acts of the beached whales. Except that there would be no force of do-gooders and volunteers to pull these ships off the beach once they grounded to a halt. Just thousands of workers waiting for the low tide so they could walk across the mud and rip the ships apart.

Most of the vessels they'd passed were sitting at anchor, but one ship was clearly being readied for action tonight. Smoke was coming from its funnel, while a tug was being moved in position to give it a boost. Down on the beach, in a direct line from the ship's bow, a lane had been marked with lines of tall bamboo posts.

The posts ran down off the beach and out into the water, like approach lights on a runway designed to guide an aircraft in through the fog. They were in the process of being lit on fire, and the flickering, petroleum-induced flames cast a primitive, tribal glow across the mud.

They outlined a slightly dredged channel that would help the big ship get up onto the beach. They also allowed Kurt and Joe to navigate with ease, as the *Soufriere* was sitting on the mud in the next slot over.

"Surprised they want to bring anything in during the night," Joe said. "Seems like it would be easier during the day."

"You'd think," Kurt said. "But when I checked the local currents, I noticed that tonight is a king tide, higher and faster than a regular tide. There's supposed to be a decent onshore breeze kicking up after midnight, too. All of which helps them get the ship farther up onto the mud. If I'm right, they'll head for shore about an hour from now."

"And in all that commotion we exit unnoticed," Joe guessed.

"That's the plan," Kurt said.

"What's the backup plan?"

"Don't have one yet."

"Considering the vast weight of accrued history," Joe said, "we should probably start coming up with one now."

Kurt laughed. Joe wasn't wrong. But in Kurt's opinion, backup plans were best made on the spur of the moment.

"The current and tide will be with us," Kurt said. "Just make for the right side of those torches."

Joe nodded. "Let's go."

Kurt picked up his mask, spit onto the glass, and rubbed the saliva around the lens, which would help keep it from fogging up. After rinsing it with water from a bottle, he pulled the mask on, made sure the fit was snug, and then popped the regulator into his mouth. After two quick breaths to ensure it was working, he gave Joe the thumbs-up, got the same signal in return, and went off the side of the boat, plunging into the dark, murky waters of the bay.

The swim was a leisurely one. Pushed on by the current and the encroaching tide, they made good time. They kept to the right of the line of torches, making for the stern end of the *Soufriere*, which was sitting with most of its rudder and half of its huge propeller exposed.

While Kurt's plan had the disadvantage of a swim through a toxic soup, it allowed them to avoid all the gates, razor wire, and security cameras that were focused on keeping people out from the landside.

Reaching the stern of the ship, they were still in twelve feet of water. They edged around the far side, studying the situation and looking for any sign of trouble. The hull was dark and lacking any sign of activity. No flash of torches, no clang of hammers or grinding saws. The yard's work crews had yet to attack the ship and begin the dismantling process.

Edging their way along the hull, Joe removed his regulator. "Not a worker or goon in sight."

Kurt grinned. He nodded toward the *Khalil*. Probing white beams of LED flashlights could be seen moving along its superstructure and inside the open dollhouse-like section where the hull plating had already been removed. "Let's hope the search keeps them busy while we do our thing."

They made their way forward, paddling until they were eventually forced to walk. They pulled off the tanks, fins, and weight belts, lashing them together and sinking them in a combined heap. Joe pulled out a piece of white chalk and drew a large symbol on the side of the hull. "X marks the spot."

They continued ahead, trudging through waist-high waters and finding it more difficult to walk on the unnaturally gray mud than they'd imagined. Each step required a great effort, with their feet sinking into the mud a good six inches and needing to be physically pulled from the cloying grip.

Finally, they came to one of the many open hatches that Kurt had seen from Sharma's office. This one was near the bow and had been fitted with a ramp to allow workers to get in and out of the ship.

The ramp was raised at the moment to keep it out of the water, but when the tide went out, its far end would be dropped down onto the mud.

Kurt had thought they might need a grappling hook, but a long rope had already been affixed to the end. Sadly it was several feet out of their reach.

Kurt looked around the debris-filled yard for something to extend his grasp.

"Let me get that for you," Joe said.

From his pack, he pulled out the back scratcher, extended it like a baton, and hooked the rope. With a firm jerk, he pulled it down.

Kurt shook his head as Joe put the device away. "I'll never doubt you again."

"I'm getting you one for Christmas," Joe said.

With the rope in reach, Kurt pulled hard, using his weight to extend the ramp. When it reached its full travel, he hooked the rope around a cleat and climbed on. He and Joe moved cautiously, but the ramp squeaked and groaned with each step.

After entering the ship, Kurt pulled down the diving hood and ran a hand through his silver hair. "Easy peasy," he said. "Now tell me we've got a signal."

Joe was pulling a receiver from his backpack. It was used to pick up the signals from the sea-life trackers. With a little help from Hiram and Max, he'd tweaked the design to make it more sensitive and to act directionally.

Raising the twin "rabbit ears," Joe soon found a pulse. He turned in one direction and then the other, watching as the strength of the signal waxed and waned.

"It's coming from the stern," he announced. "And it might be above us by a deck or two."

Kurt pulled out a flashlight and aimed it down the length of the darkened corridor. "Let's head aft and find the main ladder."

# CHAPTER 18

Virat Sharma had remained in his office late into the evening, hoping for good news from his men aboard the *Khalil*. He indulged himself with a meal and a couple of drinks and spent much of the night standing on the balcony, staring at the tanker through a set of binoculars. From time to time he would pick up a handheld radio and call his foreman, checking on his progress.

As the night ran on, he became irritated. It was a big ship, he told himself. And the Americans hadn't said what they were looking for.

He considered going home, but with another tanker set to beach itself tonight, he decided to stay. He always enjoyed the arrivals, no matter how many times he'd seen the spectacle.

He was just about to put a call in to the idling ship when the door to his office opened and a Caucasian man barged in. The man was bald, sizable, and confident. He held a gun in one hand and put a finger to his lips with the other, making a shushing sound as he stared unblinking across the room.

Sharma tensed, shocked at the intrusion. He indeed remained quiet, but not because he'd been told to be. It was more from surprise, as three fierce-looking men with more tawny skin tones came in behind the white man. They were young, lean, and looked so similar to each other that they could have been triplets. There was something feral about them, Sharma thought, as if they weren't quite human. He noticed tattoos on the sides of their necks, long strings of alphanumeric codes and what looked like a couple letters from the Greek alphabet. Aside from these, there wasn't a mark on them.

The triplets spread out around the room while the white man closed the door slowly. "My name is Blakes," the white man said quietly. "Your name is Virat Sharma. These are my dogs, and they will rip you to pieces with their bare hands if you don't cooperate."

Sharma was wary, but not cowering in fear. He'd grown up on the streets of Mumbai. He'd been involved with criminal elements by the age of twelve and had killed a man before he turned eighteen.

He'd fought his way out of that hell and made it in the world of large-vessel salvage by dealing fiercely with competitors, shakedown artists, and corrupt government officials. Just to stay in business in Alang one had to be strong enough to fight off threats from various gangs.

"What do you want?" he said calmly.

The white man slid the pistol into a shoulder holster that fit snugly under his safari jacket. Instead of throwing a punch, he smiled warmly and put his arm around Sharma, guiding him to the window and gesturing at the *Khalil*. "Tell me about that ship out there. The one with all the lights running about it."

"We're preparing it for stripping," Sharma explained. "The breakdown begins in the morning."

It was a good lie. But not good enough.

The white man took his arm off Sharma and reached for a pair of binoculars. "A very hasty preparation, by the looks of it."

Freed for the moment, Sharma eased backward toward the desk. If he could lean against it, he could reach back and press the hidden alarm button. "The faster we break it down, the sooner we get paid."

"What about these other ships?"

Sharma spoke from memory. "KN-42 is a frigate retired by the Indian Navy. The *Soufriere* is a Liberian-flagged freighter built in the nineties. The other ships are—"

"Which one is the *Soufriere*?"

It was hard to see in the dark. Sharma didn't want to leave the desk and the chance of signaling for help. "Between the fires and the *Khalil*."

The binoculars went up and then came back down. "And the Americans that came in here this afternoon. I assume they asked about it?"

Sharma bumped the desk, leaning on it for support. He moved one hand behind him, finding the lip and sliding his fingers along it. He was so focused on the act that he didn't bother to lie. "No," he said. "They wanted something off the *Khalil*."

"Ah," the white man said. "And you sent all your men aboard to look for it. How cunning of these Americans."

As Sharma watched, the intruder lifted the binoculars to his eyes once more, retraining them on the *Soufriere*. While he was focused on whatever he saw there, Sharma pressed the emergency button.

Nothing happened.

He pressed it again, but to no avail.

The intruder lowered the binoculars and turned. He looked disappointed. "I'm sorry to tell you this, but there's no help coming."

The man nodded to one of his triplets. The office door was pulled wide open. On the other side lay Sharma's two hulking bodyguards, face down in pools of their own blood.

One seemed to have gotten a hand on his pistol, but had obviously had his throat slashed before he could use it. The other had been impaled by multiple foot-long spikes and now lay with his body lifted from the floor by the protruding tips of the weapons. Farther away, a third employee of his lay dead as well.

As Sharma stared in shock, the intruder grabbed the radio off the windowsill. Switching channels, he caught the chatter coming from the crew on the *Khalil*. "You communicate to them with this?"

Sharma nodded.

"That's all I need to know."

With that he walked away, stepping out through the door and over the dead bodies. He stopped only to utter a word to his three soldiers: "*Mord.*"

Sharma lunged for a weapon he kept hidden on the desk, knocking his inbox to the side and sending a stack of papers flying. The snub-nosed .357 revolver was there. He grabbed it and spun around.

Before he could bring it to bear, one of the men had stabbed him in the gut. A second smashed his arm with a pipe, knocking the gun to the carpeted floor.

Sharma fell back, cradling his shattered arm. When he looked up, the three men were hovering over him. Their eyes reminded him of the rabid animals that ran the streets of Mumbai. They were on top of him simultaneously and all he could do was scream.

# CHAPTER 19

Kurt and Joe's search for the tracking beacon took them to the stern of the ship, the main stairwell that led up into the accommodations block, and down into the ship's engineering spaces. Along the way, Joe waved the receiver back and forth like a divining rod, narrowing their focus as the signal from the transmitter grew stronger and weaker.

Reaching the stairs, Kurt pulled open the watertight door, drawing a horrendous screech from the rusted hinges. It sounded like a hundred nails scraping a blackboard.

Joe shook his head as if he had to clear the sound from his system. "Could it be any louder?"

With Kurt holding the spring-loaded door open, Joe stepped through. Heading up half a flight of stairs and tilting the receiver, he found the signal strength weakening. He stopped and backtracked, descending again and pointing the receiver downward. "Slightly stronger. It's below us. Somewhere in engineering."

Searching the engineering spaces, they zeroed in on the signal. "This is it," Joe said, stopping in front of a compartment on the starboard side.

"We're pretty deep in the ship," Kurt said. "No wonder the satellite couldn't pick up the transmission."

Kurt aimed his flashlight at the door. It was nothing more than a basic storeroom, but locked from the outside with a padlock.

"Maybe there's a key under the mat," Joe suggested.

Kurt aimed his light downward. "No mat."

Looking for a way to break in, Kurt retrieved a fire ax from the emergency station. With Joe holding the flashlight, Kurt raised it up and then brought it down, smashing the blunt end into the padlock. The lock broke off and clanged to the deck, the sounds of both of the impacts reverberating through the otherwise silent passageway.

"You would not make a good ninja," Joe said.

Kurt laughed. "You wanted in," he said, waving toward the door, "I got you in."

Joe slid the transmitter back into his pack and pulled out a flashlight of his own. He pushed cautiously through the door, pointing the narrow beam this way and that. What he found chased away the laughter. "Damn."

Piled up against the far bulkhead—leaning on one another as they sat against the wall—were the bodies of four men in rag-like clothes. They were huddled below a small porthole that had been broken open and through which a makeshift funnel of sorts had been threaded. The funnel was attached to a small length of tubing that led to a metal cup.

"They were trying to get water," Joe said. "They must have died of thirst. Compartment like this would turn into an oven in the tropical sun. That's a pretty horrible way to go."

Kurt agreed, suppressing a flicker of anger at the games that were being played. "With a clearer message we might have gotten here earlier."

Joe reminded him that it might not be that easy. "Don't forget,

Hiram and Max think the sender is risking their life transmitting these messages. Maybe a clearer message couldn't be sent. Besides, based on the track the beacon took, this ship wasn't supposed to be their final destination. At some point after they reached the shipping lane, they either got picked up or came aboard as stowaways. Makes me wonder if the crew locked them down here."

It was impossible to know, but Kurt considered that unlikely. "Easier to throw them overboard. I'm guessing whoever these guys are, they got aboard this ship and found a place to hide and then got locked in here by accident. Otherwise, they wouldn't still have the beacon. Which reminds me, do you see it?"

Joe moved closer and crouched beside the group. He found nothing nearby. Figuring the men would have gotten the transmitter as close to the window as possible, he looked between them. "Not here."

"What's that around the last guy's neck?"

Joe looked up. Hanging around the dead man's neck was a thick band with electronic parts attached to it. Joe pulled out the receiver and held it close to the necklace. A squeal of feedback rang out. "That's it," he said, "but I'm pretty sure this didn't come from the warehouse in New Jersey."

"Looks homemade," Kurt said. "Cobbled together out of spare parts."

"Reminds me of something I made in shop class twenty years ago," Joe said. "But it's tuned to match our transmitters precisely."

"Not an impossible task," Kurt said. "But it would require some inside knowledge."

"More evidence that your mystery texter is well-versed in all things NUMA."

Kurt focused on the dead men. "So who are these guys? Don't exactly look like children."

Joe shined the flashlight on the nearest man's face. His skin tone was reddish-brown. His lips were cracked and caked with either dried saliva or salt. His eyelids stretched tight over sunken eyeballs, shrinking due to the dehydration.

Joe rummaged through the rag-like clothing, but they had no pockets. "I don't think these guys carry passports or wallets."

"They have tattoos, though."

Joe looked closer. Kurt's light was trained on the nearest man's neck. A horizontal stripe that reminded him of a barcode had been inked into the man's skin beneath a series of numbers and letters.

"They all have the same mark," Joe said, shining his flashlight at the other three. "Almost the same," he said, correcting himself. "The first digits are the same, 6.28. The Greek letter is the same, but each one has a different fraction printed at the end."

"Six point two eight," Kurt said, looking at the marks. "That mean anything to you?"

"It's tau," Joe said. "The same as this Greek 'T' symbol. Engineers use it in place of pi sometimes. It represents a full circle, a line that never ends. It's like pi in that no matter how many places you calculate it to, it never repeats itself."

"What about these other numbers?" Kurt asked.

"They're sequential," Joe said. "Almost like identification numbers. Like the tattoos the Nazis used on the prisoners of the concentration camps."

He wondered if they might be jumping to conclusions. Other than the neck tattoo, there was not another permanent mark on the man's body. The others were in similar condition. No additional ink, no scars, freckles, or skin discolorations. In fact, there was little Joe could pick out that would tell them apart. They had the same facial structures, the same cheekbones, the same thick black hair, smallish ears, and dimpled chins. "These guys are identical."

Kurt had noticed it, too.

Joe asked the question in both their minds. "What are a set of tattooed quadruplets doing in the hold of a dead ship, carrying a dummied-up NUMA beacon?"

"No idea," Kurt said, "but this isn't the time to talk about it. Get the beacon off that guy and get some DNA samples. Hair, skin, something. We need to see if we can figure out who these guys are."

Joe leaned forward and gently lifted the necklace over the man's head. As it came free, the man looked up, eyes opening wide. His hands shot forward, grabbing for Joe as he let out a raspy shout.

Joe pulled away as the seemingly dead man came to life. He landed on his back and pushed across the deck with his feet to get out of range. The man reached for him again and fell, unable to stand.

While Joe recovered from his fright, Kurt moved closer, blinding the man with his flashlight for a second and then aiming it elsewhere as the man held a hand up to block the light. "It's okay. We're not going to hurt you."

"Wah . . . ter," the man cried in a hoarse, dry whisper. "Water. Please."

Expecting only a short trip, they hadn't come with canteens, but Kurt had the bottle of filtered water he'd used to rinse the masks. He pulled it out and gave the man several small sips, as too much at once might make his tongue swell up.

"Who are you?" Kurt asked.

"I'm called Five," the man whispered.

"Five," Kurt said. "Like the number?"

The man nodded. Kurt noticed that it matched the last number in the sequence on his neck. He reached for the bottle again.

Kurt let him have another sip. "What are you doing here?"

"We came to find NUMA," the young man said. "Is this NUMA?" He looked up at Kurt's head. "You have silver hair? Are you NUMA?"

"I'm part of NUMA," Kurt replied. "My name is Austin. Kurt Austin."

"Austin," the man said. "Silver hair. You're NUMA. We were sent to find you."

Kurt let it go. "Who sent you to find me? Who made the beacon for you?"

"Bee . . . kon . . . ?" He didn't understand.

Joe held it up. "The necklace. Who made it for you?"

The man looked at Joe and then came back to Kurt. "The Gray Witch. She whispered in our ears. She left this for us. 'Take it. Go to NUMA. Austin will find you. Silver hair. NUMA.'"

Kurt suddenly felt as if he were talking to a child. There was no language barrier. The man spoke English with an American accent that would have been at home anywhere on the West Coast. But the words he used and the way he struggled to put a full sentence together made him seem like a five-year-old.

*The children*, Kurt thought, remembering the text.

Kurt gave him another sip of water as Joe moved closer and checked the other men for any signs of life. He looked at Kurt and shook his head. They were gone. Only Five remained.

"How did you survive?" Joe asked.

Five pointed to the funnel-like arrangement that extended through the porthole. "Rainwater. It comes in. They gave it all to me."

As Joe and Kurt considered what that meant, an almost silent chirping sounded on Joe's wrist. He checked his watch, silencing the alarm. "King tide in fifteen minutes. If we're going to go out while that tanker is coming in, we need to get moving."

"Can you swim?" Kurt asked Five.

"Swim?" he asked.

"In the water."

Five frowned. "We don't go in the water. To touch the water is death."

"Maybe around here," Joe muttered.

Even if the waters weren't quite that deadly, they were cold, and the current was strong. Considering the young man's condition, Kurt knew there was little chance they'd be able to get him to the boat without causing hypothermia or bringing on shock from exhaustion. "We need to find another way off the beach."

"Sounds like a backup plan might be forming," Joe said.

"It's in the beginning stages," Kurt said. "In the meantime, let's get him up and walking."

Leaning on Kurt, Five managed to stand up and remain vertical, but his legs were numb. Joe tucked himself under the man's other shoulder so that he was supported on both sides as they began to move. The three of them stepped out of the compartment and into the corridor. They made it back to the stairwell, and halfway up the first flight, only to stop in their tracks at the unmistakable screech of the rusted door above them swinging wide open.

# CHAPTER 20

The sound of boots pounding the metal steps confirmed the bad news from above. Lights dancing on the walls suggested at least three or four men.

"Back down," Kurt whispered.

That was easier said than done. Just changing direction with the weakened survivor was awkward. Going down the stairs proved even more difficult than going up.

Kurt, Joe, and Five reached the landing and made for the doorway, but their pursuers had caught up to them already, with two men racing downward at a breakneck pace, skipping stairs and whipping through the turns on the half landing, while the third man hurdled over the railing, landing between the fleeing trio and the door.

The zealous athleticism was accompanied by shouts and grunts, which sounded more like a pack of animals than human utterings. The men carried sharpened spikes that resembled homemade spears.

"No!" Five cried out. Even in the dim light he recognized them.

Quickly surrounding their prey, they seemed to expect cowering and submission. They found themselves in for a rude awakening.

Kurt lunged forward, delivering what was known as a push kick, or front thrust kick, to the chest of the man blocking their path. His foot struck the man just above the sternum, hitting so hard that the man's arms and legs snapped forward as his torso flew backward. It was as if he'd been yanked back by a bungee cord.

The second man lunged at Joe, swinging his own weapon toward Joe's temple.

Joe pushed Five to the floor while ducking under the swing. He popped up, backing away from a second swing and using quick footwork to avoid being forced into the corner. Pushing off the wall, he swung the backpack as his attacker tried again to land a blow. The spike hit the pack and impaled it, but that played to Joe's advantage. He pulled hard, yanking the man off-balance. A headbutt to the face knocked him down, leaving him in a heap.

The third attacker went after Five, raising his weapon with every intention of crushing the weakened young man's skull. A flying tackle from Kurt prevented the killing blow.

The force of Kurt's hit knocked the wind out of the man and sent him into the railing. With a lift and a shove, he went over it, landing on a descending flight of stairs and rolling downward.

A sigh of frustration came from up above. A broad light illuminated them all and shots from an unseen gun began to rain down on them.

Kurt and Joe reached Five at the same moment, lifting him up, and dragging him through the door as the bullets pinged and ricocheted off the deck, stairs, and railings.

Ducking and covering as they pushed through the door, they were back in the corridor with the storage room.

"Find a hatch," Kurt shouted, pushing the heavy door shut and turning the speed wheel in the center to make it watertight. He spun it to the stops, but it couldn't be locked, and if their pursuers knew anything about ships, it wouldn't hold them for long.

Joe moved off, supporting Five and probing the passageway with the flashlight. They were low on the ship. Low enough that it would be hit-or-miss to find a hatch they could open.

"Notice something about those guys?" Kurt asked, catching up to them and helping lift Five.

"They look exactly like him," Joe said, nodding toward Five.

"Exactly like him."

"More brothers," Five said. "Cruel ones."

"How many brothers do you have?" Joe blurted out.

Five didn't answer right away. And then he said simply: "Many."

Kurt figured he knew the reason for that, but now was not the time to get into it. "We're going to need another way out. How far up was that aux hatch?"

"Forward of the midship's bulkhead," Joe said. "We're almost there. But it's a thirty-foot drop to the mud."

"We'll find something to slide down."

At the end of the corridor behind them, the sound of the speed wheel turning could be heard. The heavy door flew open and banged the stops. A figure appeared, backlit by the lights of his men.

"Get down," Kurt shouted.

No sooner had they dropped when more gunfire rang out. Bullets clipped the walls and tore into the overhead, but failed to find a mark.

Down on the deck, Kurt ushered Joe and Five past him. "Shut off your light."

Joe doused his beam without an argument and kept crawling. Meanwhile, Kurt flung his flashlight backward down the hall toward their pursuers.

It bounced and tumbled, the beam of light cartwheeling in the dark. When it came to a rest, it was pointed more or less at their pursuers. More shots were fired, lower this time, but they found the floor, pinging off the metal and losing their sting.

Kurt turned and crawled after Joe and Five, hoping they could find an exit in the pitch dark. He found them scrambling on all fours.

Joe was feeling along the wall. They passed the heavy construction of the bulkhead, climbing over a lip. Several seconds later Joe stopped. He'd found a door. A small amount of cool air was filtering through the gap underneath. "Let's hope it's not padlocked."

He located the handle and leaned on it. Pushing it wide, he felt a wave of fresh air and rejoiced at the sight of the open hatchway and the dim, muddy world beyond.

Now he just needed to find a way for them to drop down into the mud below without getting stuck like a lawn dart or breaking their legs in the process. He found a cargo net, but there was nothing to hook it on.

As Joe and Five entered the compartment, Kurt glanced back down the hall. He could see the lights of their pursuers. They were moving slowly at first, but once they passed his discarded flashlight they began to pick up speed, bouncing and jumping as the men holding them began to sprint down the corridor.

He ducked in behind Joe and Five and quietly shut the door. "What's the plan?"

Joe held up the net. "We have this, but no way to secure it."

"Throw it over and climb on," Kurt said, grabbing the end of the net.

With the top edge of the net in Kurt's control, Joe helped Five get over the edge and lock his hands and feet into the webbing. "Are you sure you can hold us both?"

"No," Kurt said. "But I'm going to let you down easy."

"That's what they all say," Joe replied.

He grabbed the netting and swung his feet over the edge.

Feeling the weight, Kurt leaned back, but the deck was oily and there was little traction. He dropped to the deck and leaned hard on one hip. Perched this way, he slid across the compartment toward the open hatch. Reaching it, he jammed his feet against the sill at the bottom of the opening.

He grunted with the strain and heard Joe holler up to him. "You call that easy?"

"Don't make me laugh," Kurt shouted. "And remind me to revisit your every-three-hours eating plan. You've gone up a weight class or two."

A second later the strain vanished. Kurt fell back.

"We're down," Joe shouted.

Kurt had figured that part. Now he needed a way to get himself down.

He gathered the net up, pulling most of it in before the door flew open and Five's cruel brothers stepped in.

Instead of attacking him, they spread out in a triangle formation with their lights aimed at his face. Another figure appeared. He stood in the doorway. Kurt couldn't see his face, but once the man spoke he recognized both the voice and the overconfident tone.

"What's the matter," the man said. "Afraid of a little drop? I did five times that on Reunion."

"Be my guest," Kurt said, moving slightly to the side. "Less than three feet of water out there."

The man didn't take Kurt up on the offer. "Some other time," he said, holding up the backpack Joe had used to defend himself. "I got what I came for."

Kurt realized instantly that there was more to the homemade tracking beacon than met the eye. He considered reaching for it, but could see in the reflected light that the man had a pistol waiting and ready.

"Once again," the man said. "I bid you adieu." He turned his back on Kurt, much like he had done with Sharma, and spoke softly to his men. "Kill them," he said. "*Mord!*"

The pack of cruel brothers rushed Kurt from all sides. But he was too quick for them. He heaved the edge of the cargo net up and covered them in it. With their arms and legs caught and tangled, he hurdled the sill and dropped over the edge, grabbing another rung of the net as he fell.

The cargo net slid several feet, dragging the three trapped men inside it to the edge of the hatch, and then stopping as they were pinned up against it. Kurt scrambled down, leaping from the net seven feet above the water. He hit with a splash, feeling his feet squish into the mud. He dove forward, swimming rather than running, as he tried to catch up with Joe and Five.

Five had recovered enough strength to stand now, and he and Joe were lumbering toward the bow of the freighter. Kurt joined them, hugging the steel wall of the *Soufriere*'s hull as shots rang out from the hatch.

Glancing back, Kurt saw their pursuers were coming down the cargo net. First the triplets, followed by their leader.

"They're not giving up," Kurt said. "Keep going."

They raced to the bow of the ship, a slow-motion chase in the water and mud.

"We'll never get a tuk-tuk at this hour," Joe said.

Kurt felt the same. But there were other options. Up ahead, a number of small boats tied to a dock rose and fell with the tide. He pointed toward them.

Half swimming and half running, they made it to the dock and found a boat with a small, pull-start outboard motor. As Joe climbed in, Kurt heaved Five over the edge, and then pulled himself up and in.

The motor sputtered to life on the third pull, releasing a cloud of blue smoke. Kurt cast off the line and pushed them away from the dock.

With the outboard buzzing, they sped off, but their pursuers were not far behind. They climbed onto the dock and followed Kurt and Joe's example, splitting up and taking two boats instead of one.

Joe twisted the throttle to full while Kurt and Five moved forward to keep the boat riding at its most efficient angle.

Joe looked back. "They're gaining."

"Head along the beach," Kurt suggested. "Try to lose them in all the junk."

Joe cut back into the shallows, weaving around rusted outcroppings of machinery and anything else that might rip open the bottom of the boat. At low tide, all the unwanted junk and debris sat out in the open, an eyesore upon an eyesore, but at high tide much of it was hidden. Or partially so.

"Cut right," Kurt said.

Joe pushed the outboard to the left, causing the boat to bear right. They narrowly missed what looked like an engine block the size of a locomotive.

"Left," Kurt shouted seconds later.

Joe pushed the motor to the right, but the helm didn't answer as quickly as he hoped. They hit the object—whatever it was—skipped across it, and landed back in the water.

Joe had managed to pull the motor up and save the prop, and the boat was intact, but the jarring impact had left them wary.

"What was that?"

"Not sure," Kurt said. "Stack of hull plating, maybe."

"At least it was flat."

Joe glanced behind him. The shallows were no safe haven. The other boats were closing in once again. One of them pulled alongside. Joe swerved into it, but the impact was slight. A second attempt was less successful still, as it gave one of the cruel brothers a chance to jump the gap. He landed on his hands and knees and went after Five. Kurt jumped him before he could get a hand on the terrified young man. He got the man in a headlock and trapped one of his arms. It was an awkward way to do combat: on their knees in a speeding boat. All Kurt could really do was keep the man from breaking free.

"Left turn," Kurt shouted.

Joe swerved left as Kurt hurled the man to the right. He went over the transom and out into the water, vanishing with a splash as the two boats raced on.

"Trouble," Five said, looking ahead. "Trouble."

Joe saw it. They were coming up on the remnants of the smaller freighter. The one Kurt had seen from the balcony that had basically been cut in two. With its bow and stern in separate pieces, most of the middle was long gone.

Joe sped into the gap between the two pieces and then turned sharply right, pulling into the rusted stern section. Cutting the throttle, he waited for the other boats to speed past, but they didn't come through right away.

Kurt could hear their motors on a lower power setting. "They're circling around."

He grabbed a small oar and paddled them backward until they were deep within the hull and completely hidden in the dark. It was like hiding in a metallic cave. Sections of torn bulkheads stuck up out of the water like the roots of trees in a mangrove swamp. Tentacles of wiring and rusted pipes hung down from above, creaking eerily as the waves nudged the ship back and forth. The remnants of the ship's massive sixteen-cylinder diesel engine could be seen sticking out of the water like a rusted work of modern art.

Five looked around in the silence, awed by what he saw. "Is this NUMA?"

It brought a smile to Kurt's face. "This is definitely *not* NUMA," he said.

"And it's not a place we can hide for long," Joe added. "Any chance you've come up with that plan B yet?"

Kurt looked at his watch. The timing was just about perfect. "Yep," he said, "but you're not going to like it."

He told Joe his idea, and Joe agreed emphatically that he did not like it, but they were all out of options. The sound of the other boats trolling for a way in was getting closer.

"Who's likely to be a better boatman," Kurt said, trying to pump up Joe's enthusiasm, "you or that angry oaf and Five's cruel brothers?"

"It's not my boat-handling skills that I'm worried about," Joe said. He put his hand on the pull start. "Let's hope this thing fires up on the first tug."

Joe gripped the T-handle and drew his hand backward, sharp and fast. The motor fired without a cough and Joe turned the throttle. They accelerated forward and back around, heading out the way they'd come in.

Their pursuers saw them and gave chase, one boat cutting through the middle of the broken freighter, the other going around it. By the time all three boats were back to full speed, they were strung out with a few hundred feet between them.

Joe looked ahead. A half mile up the beach he could see the burning sticks that marked the entrance lane for the new arrival. And coming in from the bay, he could see the big tanker charging for the slot. It ran with a full head of steam, lights blazing, props churning, a six-foot bow wave curling off its nose.

Joe aimed for the rapidly narrowing gap between the bow and the mud.

Someone on the ship must have seen them coming because the horn began blasting a warning into the night. It was painful and overpowering. Five covered his ears, but kept his eyes wide open.

"It's going to be close," Joe shouted.

"Head for the mud," Kurt called out.

Joe understood Kurt's suggestion, but it sounded like madness. If they hit the mud and got stuck, they would be crushed and killed, and what was left of them would end up buried deep in the gray muck with the asbestos, debris, and scrap for all eternity.

He followed the suggestion anyway, aiming farther in toward the beach.

The tanker came on, blasting its horn continuously. It could neither turn nor slow.

The chase boats kept up the pursuit, with the nearest one right on their tail.

They raced past the line of burning sticks and into the lane. The wall of steel loomed up to the left. The gray mud stood in their way dead ahead, but a surge of water being pushed in front of the ship swept over the mud first.

The small boat tilted as the curling wave raced under them. It came dangerously close to flipping, but Joe navigated the wave like a rafting expert crossing a stretch of dangerous rapids. He maneuvered to the right with the wave's impact and then up and over it to the left. Coming down the far side of the wave, he sped away from the crossing ship.

The Overseer was in the second boat. From his perspective, Kurt, Joe, and Five simply disappeared. One moment they were there, the next all he could see was the onrushing hull of the huge ship.

Whatever mystery there was to his quarry's survival, there was no question what happened to the men in the boat closest to them. It was lifted by the bow wave and tossed landward. The men in the boat—his dogs, as he called them—were flung into the air along with it. They landed in a swath of foam on the mud and were instantly steamrolled by the bow of the hundred-thousand-ton ship.

Pulling back, the Overseer watched in morbid fascination as the huge ship slid up the beach, displacing water, mud, and foam. It stopped with surprising smoothness when its momentum was spent and was soon sitting quietly in the postapocalyptic landscape of the beach.

With the tanker now stationary and the waves dissipating, he faced a choice: go around the stern and continue the chase, or let it end.

He felt certain that the Americans had survived. They'd timed their run to near perfection. They'd gone toward the beach to gain a few extra seconds in what looked like the exact moment of destruction. He guessed they hadn't miscalculated in the least.

A feeling of respect grudgingly entered his mind. His adversaries were more formidable than he'd given them credit for. All the better, he thought. It would make their ultimate demise more satisfying.

But for now it was time to end the chase. The odds had flipped and no longer justified the risk. Besides, he had the transmitter and whatever secrets the Gray Witch had hidden inside.

On the far side of the tanker, speeding away from the scene, Kurt and Joe kept an eye out for any sign of pursuit. They saw only dark waters and froth churned by the wake of the ship. The cruel brothers were gone, and their leader had given up.

In the center of the boat, appearing bewildered and shocked by everything he'd just experienced, Five sensed the lowered tension. "Are they gone?"

Joe nodded. "Stuck in the mud."

"Permanently," Kurt added.

Five seemed pleased. "So, now we go to NUMA?"

Kurt laughed out loud. "Sounds like a great idea."

# CHAPTER 21

The hundred-and-twenty-foot research vessel carried the number *244* on the bow. The name *Isabella* had been painted on the stern by those at the university who thought she should have a name.

Manned by a crew of ten, including Chantel Lacourt and two other volunteers from the university, the small ship carried Paul and Gamay across the sparkling waters northwest of Reunion at a leisurely pace. The breeze was light; the swells were small, smooth, and slow. Triple-S conditions, as Paul had jokingly labeled them. All in all it was a peaceful day to be out on the ocean. Peaceful and boring.

"It would be nice if something interesting happened," Gamay said.

She and Paul were parked inside the boat's science bay, watching a pair of monitors. The screen in front of Gamay displayed the information coming in from an ROV operating below them while Paul studied the data coming in from a towed sensor buoy being trailed out behind them.

The sensor array was feeding them data on the state of the seawater itself. Temperature gradients, oxygen and salinity levels, and the concentrations of trace elements, organic compounds, and other chemicals. All while testing the water for any trace of two hundred known pollutants.

The ROV was traveling an oscillating path. Diving slowly to six hundred feet as it moved forward, leveling off for a mile and then pitching upward and rising toward the surface again. The extended rollercoaster-like path allowed it to traverse the entire light-absorbing zone while its cameras and sonar surveyed the aquatic life up and down throughout the zone. There was just one problem. So far they'd seen nothing.

Stretching and yawning, Gamay glanced over at Paul's screen. "Anything interesting?"

"Not unless I can get the Red Sox game on this thing," Paul replied. "Temperature and salinity are right where they should be. No dangerous chemicals detected, no sign of elevated radioactivity, nor is there a lack of oxygen. In essence, we're traveling across a swath of pure, unadulterated seawater. Nothing out of the ordinary."

"I'd call a distinct lack of sea life something out of the ordinary." Gamay said. "Aside from a few jellyfish we passed, our million-dollar fish-finder hasn't found a thing. Are you sure the oxygen sensor is working? This is the kind of thing I expect to find in a dead zone after a massive algae bloom has absorbed all the oxygen."

Paul had considered that a possibility, but had checked the data and found nothing to support the idea. "I've tested the sensors repeatedly. Both the prime $O_2$ sensor and the backup are calibrated and working properly," he said. "There's plenty of oxygen down there, and for the record, not a sign of any algae."

"Do you two always quarrel while you're working?" Chantel asked as she came through the door.

Gamay sighed.

Three days of this was taking a toll on her sanity. "It's a way to relieve the boredom," she said. "We're not really fighting."

"Null results are still results," Chantel said, offering them a snack from a plastic bin she'd taken from the ship's kitchen. "Even if we find nothing, that's something."

Gamay grabbed an apple. The fresh fruit would be gone soon. Much like everything in the sea. "It's like the ocean has gone barren for no reason at all."

"There has to be a reason," Paul said. "We just haven't found it yet."

Gamay resisted the urge to hit him with a ruler. "Thanks, Captain Obvious. I hadn't thought of that."

Paul refrained from laughing. Previous experience told him snickering at his wife's outbursts was a dangerous proposition. Instead, he reached for an orange. "Might as well ward off scurvy while we still can."

Gamay shook her head, but a wry smile suggested she was in a more playful mood than it appeared. She was about to push back from her console and switch places with Chantel when an alarm began to chirp.

She slid forward again, focusing on the screen. "Sonar contact. Four hundred yards, bearing two-eight-one. Intermittent and changing shape. Looks like it might be a school of fish."

Paul leaned closer, happy to hear they'd finally found something.

Chantel looked over her shoulder. "See, all you need is a little positive energy."

Gamay's joy was fading. "Contact isn't moving," she announced. "We should see more than just relative motion."

"Could it be something drifting?" Paul asked. "A commercial fishing net or some debris?"

"Only one way to find out." She tapped the keyboard in front of her, disengaging the ROV's autopilot and taking manual control. "I'm going to take a closer look."

Paul sat down. He felt a sudden energy surge after so many mind-numbing hours staring at the screens. He hoped it was more than an abandoned fishing net.

Gamay said nothing as she manipulated the controls, adjusting the depth and heading of the ROV, nudging the joystick until it was on the right track, and then bumping the thrusters to a higher power level.

"Three hundred yards," Paul called out.

Gamay adjusted the cameras and lights, focusing them directly ahead of the ROV. At a depth of a hundred feet, the waters were a deep sapphire blue.

"Two hundred yards," Paul said.

There was nothing on the monitor, but that didn't mean anything. Water absorbed and scattered light with great efficiency. Gamay figured they'd need to be within a hundred feet to see anything more than a blur. She slowed the ROV and took it a bit deeper. If it was a school of fish, she wanted to sneak up on it and get a good look at the species and number before she scared it away.

A quick glance at the sonar readout told her it hadn't moved.

"One hundred yards," Paul said.

"I'm going to slow a little more and come up to their depth."

As Gamay adjusted the thrusters and dive planes, the cameras captured their first sign of something that wasn't open water. A small glowing blob passed in front of the lens.

"Did you see that?"

Paul nodded. "What was it?"

"Jellyfish?" Chantel suggested.

Gamay hoped not. Another blob passed by and then several more. Seconds later the ROV was swimming in them. Hundreds of dimly glowing blobs of gel. They swirled in front of the camera by the hundreds and then the thousands. Gamay tilted and panned the camera. It was a dizzying display, with depth and width in all directions. Like being in a field surrounded by a million lightning bugs.

Most were pushed aside by the flow of the water as the ROV moved through, but like a swarm of insects encountering a car on the road, some of the globs hit the lens, sticking and smearing.

Paul was surprised. "Who knew we'd need windshield wipers on an ROV."

Gamay slowed the vehicle to one knot, creeping through the swarm of glowing blobs and trying to get a good look at them through the smeared lens of the main camera.

"Could they be globs of bioluminescent plankton?" Chantel asked.

Gamay didn't think so. She'd never actually seen anything like this before. "I don't know what they are."

Suddenly the camera jerked to the side. The ROV had bumped into something. The view turned suddenly brighter. Instead of hundreds of drifting globs spread out across the camera view, there were now thousands up close and packed in together.

"Reminds me of the time I backed our riding mower into that hornet's nest."

"My only memory of that is you running at full speed and screaming, 'Save yourself,' while I watched from inside the living room."

"You followed that instruction quite well if I remember."

"I was watching one of my shows."

For all the kidding around, the pronounced impact and the sudden increase in the number of drifting orbs did suggest she'd collided with some sort of nest. She panned up and around with the camera, but it was now so smeared with gel and iridescent goo that it had become unusable. "If I didn't know any better I'd say these things are trying to coat our ROV with their secretions on purpose."

A new idea came to her. The ROV had a third camera. It was attached to the robot arm and designed to allow for precise operation of the pincers at the end when picking up or manipulating small objects. When not in use, the arm remained folded, and the camera hidden away.

She activated the arm, brought the camera online, and tilted the ROV upward, toward whatever they'd bumped into.

A terrifying site came into view. The open jaw of a great white shark.

"This is why we use ROVs," Chantel said.

Gamay pulled the arm back instinctively, but the jaw didn't close; instead it remained suspended above the ROV, its jagged teeth pointing in all directions, its exposed gums bleached white and eroded down to the bone.

She backed the ROV off to get a wider view. The shark was drifting nose down, its eyes gone, its gills ripped apart, its skin torn open in places, and blistering and bulging with decay in others. The open jaw was without a tongue.

The shark's flesh and organs were mostly gone. The tougher structures like ligaments and tendons were holding the cartilage that acted as a skeleton in place, but everything else had been corrupted or consumed.

"I have to see something," Gamay said. "Turn away if you're squeamish."

Paul had an idea what she was up to. He was glad he hadn't just eaten lunch.

Chantel stared intently.

Gamay moved the ROV to a position near what remained of the shark's gut, just behind the skeletonized pectoral fins. Using the robot arm, she punctured a swollen area on the discolored flesh.

It ruptured as if it had been under pressure. Gallons of discolored gel and pus spewed out along with thousands of the glowing orbs. They swirled around in dizzying patterns, slowly spreading out on the current.

"What is this?" Paul asked. "An infection? A parasite?"

"Whatever it is, they're colonizing it," Chantel said. "Consuming it from the inside."

Gamay had no idea. "Extremely gelatinous. Possibly a swarm of some previously unknown type of jellyfish. Or even a colony organism like the Portuguese man-of-war."

Paul saw the look on Gamay's face. He knew what came next. "I assume you're going to want a few samples."

"Most definitely."

"I'll buzz the captain." He picked up the intercom phone, which rang through to the bridge. "We've found something. Time to pull over and park the bus for a minute."

The captain was oddly quiet. When he spoke, there was concern in his voice. "We've found something, too. You'd better get up here. You three need to see this."

Paul acknowledged the captain and put down the phone. He could feel the ship slowing to a stop. He turned to Gamay and Chantel. "They want us on the bridge."

# CHAPTER 22

Paul, Gamay, and Chantel left the science bay and went forward. Due to the odd way the ship had been retrofitted, there was no internal way to reach the bridge from the science bay. It required a trip outside along the deck and then up a steep ladder to the forward part of the superstructure.

Finishing the climb, they entered the bridge to find everyone staring through the windows at a gray blur stretching across the horizon.

Gamay squinted. It looked like a cloud, but didn't move like one.

The captain offered her a set of binoculars. "Tell me what you make of that."

Gamay raised the binoculars and adjusted the focus. Despite the top-grade optics and her own twenty-twenty vision, she couldn't tell what she was looking at. She fiddled with the fine adjustment, blurring things one way and then the other. She found no way to sharpen the image. "Is it smoke? . . . It seems to be changing shape. Could it be a dust storm?"

"At sea?"

"We're not that far from Africa," she said. "Sandstorms and dust clouds have been known to blow across the Sahara and travel hundreds of miles out to sea. Geologically speaking, you can find Saharan sand all over North America and Europe."

"Yes," the captain said. "But in this case the wind is at our back, so unless it came from Australia, it's not dust."

Gamay listened without looking away. The cloud seemed to be thinning as she watched. By the time she handed the binoculars to Paul, it seemed to be dissipating and moving farther off. The captain confirmed it had been thicker and closer when it had first been spotted.

A quick look was enough for Paul. He didn't know what to make of it, either.

Chantel took a turn and then asked, "Does it show up on radar?"

"We got a brief return off the weather radar," the captain said. "The computer classified it as heavy rain. Doppler indicated it was retreating from us at thirty knots, but the wind speed is steady around eight. And there is very little in the way of clouds."

"Self-propelled," Gamay noted. "Has to be a flock of birds."

"It would need to be a very large flock," the captain said suspiciously.

A shout from one of the lookouts broke the chain of conversation. "Object in the water," the lookout announced. "Two hundred yards. Dead ahead."

"Hard to port," the captain ordered.

"Additional debris on the port side," another crewman called out.

"All stop," the captain ordered.

The *Isabella* had been traveling at a leisurely pace and slowed rapidly, but it wasn't fast enough to keep them from overrunning the initial target.

The sharp turn of the rudder allowed them to avoid hitting it head-on, but whatever it was bumped alongside and scraped down the edge of the hull. The impact was muted and soft. It certainly didn't feel like the type of blow to cause much damage. Another impact on the other side was even softer, though it was followed by a deeper thud as they hit something else head-on.

Traveling on momentum only, they coasted through a section of water filled with obstructions floating just beneath the surface.

Gamay left the bridge, rushing down to the main deck to get a closer look. As she reached the rail, a gray conglomeration of sludge drifted by. It was soft-edged, bulky, and organic in appearance. A similar-looking glob slid in behind it, this one with a skeletonized fin sticking out of it. She recognized the bones stretching forth like fingers in a ghostly, elongated hand.

As the *Isabella* nudged the mass of organic matter, it rolled over, revealing itself to be the carcass of a whale. Its skin was bulging and distended like the flesh of the shark they'd seen below.

The ship came to a stop beside it, but as Gamay looked ahead she spied other dead whales, along with dead seabirds floating in piles of shredded feathers, upended fish heads, and other things so badly decomposed she couldn't guess what they once had been.

The lazy swells moved the dead creatures up, down, and around in a macabre dance. The sea between them was a jaundiced yellow color that looked more like pollution or pus than seawater.

Looking around, Gamay counted the remnants of nearly thirty humpback whales, along with dozens of sharks and hundreds of fish and birds that had come to scavenge on the dead animals. It was only a guess, but she imagined the massacre had begun with the whales and then extended to the creatures that came to feed on them, which left them trapped in the same web of death. A web the *Isabella* had now sailed into the middle of.


Gamay returned to the bridge, sobered by what she'd seen. Mass deaths in nature usually meant toxins, poisons, or released clouds of gas. "We need to back away from here," she said calmly.

"You'll get no argument from me," the captain said.

"Do it slowly," she suggested. "Try not to stir anything up."

The captain ordered the engines back one-quarter, and after a brief hesitation, as if stuck in the mud, the *Isabella* began retreating from the aquatic graveyard.

A mile upwind of the site, the captain looked at Gamay. "Far enough?"

"I would think so," she said.

The captain ordered the helmsmen to stop the retreat and hold their position. "Now what?"

"Now," Gamay said with some trepidation in her voice, "we get in the water, take some samples, and try to figure out what happened here."

# CHAPTER 23

The *Isabella*'s small submersible was theoretically large enough for two people, but not when one of those individuals was six foot eight. As a result, Paul stayed behind, while Gamay and Chantel strapped themselves into the tiny seats inside.

With the pressure test completed and all systems go, they were lifted over the side by the ship's crane and lowered into the water. Cutting the cord, they dove to thirty feet, mostly to smooth out the ride and prevent the sub from wallowing in the swells.

Chantel appeared a bit nervous as the waters closed in around them and rose up over the top of the viewport.

"First time in a submersible?" Gamay asked.

"Third, actually," Chantel said. "But I honestly prefer diving. This is a bit claustrophobic."

"I actually prefer diving myself," Gamay insisted, "but until we've figured out what skeletonized those whales, I figure we should keep a suit of armor around ourselves."

"Do you think we're in any danger?"

"Only of bumping our heads," she joked, reaching up and rapping her knuckles on the overhead panel. "But we have to assume there is some form of rapidly reproducing pathogen out there. Maybe a flesh-eating bacteria or some type of fast-spreading parasite. The kind of things I'd rather not expose my skin to."

By now they were underway. With only a half mile between their position and the tangled web of dead animals, they would arrive over the dive site in a short minute.

"Lights on," Chantel said. "Cameras recording. Vacuum system ready to retrieve samples."

Gamay acknowledged her and stared out the viewport until a gray mass came into view. The animals were less recognizable than they'd been only a few hours before. The whale skeletons were breaking down as their musculature was consumed, and the sharks were being reduced to teeth and jaws hanging from what was left of their cartilage.

Gamay spoke into the microphone, reporting back to the ship. "Biomass further degraded. I've never seen anything consumed so quickly before. Not even lunch when Kurt and Joe show up hungry. We're going to grab some samples before the buffet table is cleaned out."

Maneuvering the submarine alongside one of the partially eaten whales, Gamay was careful not to bump it. "You should be able to use the claw from here."

Chantel operated a remote arm that had been equipped with a circular tool designed to take sedimentary cores. She figured it would be strong enough to take a core out of the floating carcass. Extending it to the side of the animal, she activated the motor. The teeth on the end of the coring probe began to spin slowly. She pushed it out until it began cutting into the gray flesh, penetrating it with ease.

"Twelve-inch depth should be enough," Gamay said.

The probe could core out a two-foot-deep cylindrical sample, but that was more than they needed at the moment.

At roughly twelve inches of depth, Chantel stopped and reversed the motion. The probe came back out, bringing with it a chunk of flesh and muscle.

"I'll store this in bin number one."

Bending the robot arm, she placed the sample in a cylinder on the side of the submersible, which then sealed up tight.

Several more samples were retrieved. Two from the whale and two from what was left of a great white shark. By the time they finished they were floating in a soup of residue from the decaying animals. Oils from the bodies oozed everywhere, along with globs of fat and strips of flesh drifting about.

Gamay noticed some of the spheres mixed in with the detritus.

"Let's get some of these floating orbs," Gamay said. "I'm not sure what they are, but I have a bad feeling they're part of the problem."

Locking down the robot arm, Chantel extended the vacuum probe. It was designed to suck in water and any sea life large enough to fit through its nozzle. Turning it on started a pump, and the water near the nozzle started to swirl, but sucking up individual floating orbs proved more difficult than it looked.

"Can you move in closer?" Chantel asked. "They're harder to catch than a bar of soap in a dirty bath."

Gamay noticed there weren't as many of them as there had been earlier. She wondered if they were moving on, now that the food supply was dwindling. They didn't appear to be able to swim, but maybe they could lift their bodies to the surface and inflate a sail like the Portuguese man-of-war.

"I'll make it easy for you."

Gamay nudged the thruster control gently, easing the sub forward and turning it toward the remnants of the nearest bloated whale carcass, expecting a result similar to hitting the shark with the ROV.

"We're only moving at three knots, but hang on," she said.

Angling the craft upward, she bumped the underside of the dead animal. The impact was soft enough, but still slightly jarring, like flopping onto a bed covered with thick comforters.

The sub's momentum pushed the rounded bow into the side of the whale, pressing it inward and splitting the skin just as she'd hoped. She flicked the thruster control into reverse and the sub backed away as the tissue began to rupture and hundreds of the glowing orbs spilled out.

"Vacuum to your heart's content," Gamay said, pleased with herself.

Chantel wasted no time directing the nozzle into the swarm of luminescent little blobs. They were soon being sucked into the device and flowing down the collection tube, where they were deposited in a clear tank on the other side of the submersible like fireflies in a jar.

"If we lose the lights, we can hold some of these up and find our way," Chantel joked.

Gamay laughed, but the laughter died as she realized they were actually losing the light. She looked up and saw the reason. The submersible's impact with the whale had made it roll over. Though she couldn't see it, the carcass had burped a large amount of gas and lost buoyancy. It was now sinking toward them like a giant wet blanket.

She hit the thrusters, but it was too late. The semi-formless shape came down over the top of the submersible, hitting it with a soft bump and then wrapping around it on all sides. The exterior light vanished as the viewports were covered up. More concerning than the loss of light was the loss of control. The thrusters, which could pivot and turn, were jammed into place by the overhanging remnants of the whale. The submersible tilted to the side and began to sink beneath several tons of decomposing blubber.

"What's happening?" Chantel asked.

If she'd been claustrophobic before, looking around and seeing nothing but gray sludge and whale skin pressed up against every viewport was not going to help.

"The whale came down on top of us," Gamay said. "I shouldn't have been so careless."

She was maneuvering the thrusters madly, but there was little effect. A quick glance at the depth gauge showed the descent accelerating.

"I can't get us free," Gamay said. "Blow the tanks. We need more buoyancy."

Chantel moved to the dive controls. The submersible had two main tanks and four trim tanks. One by one she opened the valves and the sound of hissing air reverberated through the sub. The lights indicating tank status turned green in rapid order.

"All tanks empty," she called out. She looked at the depth gauge. "But we're still sinking."

It was a simple math problem. The five-ton submersible could not provide enough buoyancy to hold up the remains of the forty-ton whale.

They passed two hundred feet and began to accelerate. Another math problem. This one related to the physics of water. As the depth increased, the pressure increased. That was not an immediate problem for the sub, but it squeezed the carcass and forced out whatever air and gas remained behind. In effect, the deeper they went, the heavier the whale became.

They passed three hundred feet and Gamay began to worry. NUMA submersibles were designed to withstand the pressure down to several thousand feet, but this was not a NUMA submersible. It was a craft designed and built on Reunion and used by the university students for the last decade. "What's the test depth on this thing?"

"It's been rated to a thousand feet," Chantel said. "But I don't think we've ever taken it below five hundred."

Five hundred was coming up fast and there was nothing to suggest they'd stop there.

"Use the coring probe," Gamay said.

"To do what?"

"Cut holes in the whale. It's badly decomposed. If we can perforate it in enough places, we might be able to open a fissure and slip through. Or it might slide off us as our lift creates an instability in the system."

Chantel switched back to the excavation controls. Spinning the core sampler up to full power, she had to guess at the direction to point it in, as there was no way to see outside. She angled it in what she hoped was a good direction and pushed it forward. She could hear the motor spinning and had a green light on the panel, but all she could see out the side port was the blubbery flank of the dead whale. It was even possible the arm was pinned against the side of the craft, spinning uselessly.

She twisted the controls back and forth. A yellow light came on, suggesting she was overloading one of the control motors. The sampler continued to spin, but a separate indicator told her the tube was empty.

"I'm not getting anything," she told Gamay. "I think the arm is trapped in a down position. I can't raise it."

Gamay saw them go past five hundred feet and realized they were quickly running out of time. The only option she could think of was highly risky—it would either doom them or save them—but if she waited much longer, it would be too late to try.

Nervously, she thought of Paul. "Flood the tanks," she said firmly.

"What?" Chantel replied, her eyes wide and uncomprehending.

"Release the air and flood the tanks."

"That will just sink us faster."

"Exactly," Gamay said. "We can't go up, so we have to go down. Once the tanks are flooded, we'll be denser than that carcass. We should sink faster and be able to get out from under it. But if we don't do it soon, we'll run out of depth to try."

Chantel looked like she was going to be sick. "There has to be another way."

"There isn't," Gamay said. "Now flood the tanks. Before it's too late."

The young woman choked back her fear, steeled herself, and threw open all the valves. A series of banging sounds accompanied the gates opening and the water slamming into the empty space inside, forced in by the pressure of the depths.

"Fifty percent . . ." Chantel said. "Seventy percent . . . Tanks full."

The whale hide slid upward on the windows, but friction was holding the submersible in place, and the depth continued to increase. They passed six hundred feet, dropping twice as fast now and still not free.

Gamay rocked the ship from side to side and then pointed the thrusters downward and pushed the power to full. The submersible moved with a jerk and then pulled free. The view through the viewport went from gray whale hide to pitch-black water.

Gamay kept them on a downward trajectory. She needed to get enough space between them and the whale to slide out from beneath it without getting caught up once again.

Chantel pointed the lights upward. They could see the animal's body above them retreating slowly and shedding a stream of bubbles made from the air that the sub had expelled. As they pushed asymmetrically on the carcass, it rolled over and accelerated downward, its extremities folded up, looking something like an inverted jellyfish.

"Seven hundred feet," Chantel called out. "That's our design depth."

Gamay shoved the throttles forward. Their own dive slowed, but the whale came on faster than ever. Gamay tensed, gritting her teeth in anticipation of the impact. There was a heavy thud on the tail of the sub, tilting its nose upward, but the small craft quickly righted itself.

Chantel aimed the exterior lights downward. The gray carcass had passed them by and was dropping into the deep dark of the ocean. She kept her eyes on the remnants of the animal, thinking how it would continue to fall for another ten minutes or so until it hit the bottom twelve thousand feet below. "That's a sight I never thought I'd witness."

"Let's make sure we don't follow it," Gamay replied. "Blow the tanks. Mains first and then the trim tanks."

Chantel closed the vents and opened the air valves once more. She noticed how much slower the tanks filled at this depth. Across from her, Gamay had rotated the thrusters and was using them to help arrest the sub's descent.

They passed eight hundred feet and then touched nine hundred, slowing further and finally stopping their dive at nine hundred and sixty feet.

Gamay looked around. "Do you see any leaks?"

Chantel glanced up and about. "Nope."

"This is your new test depth," Gamay said.

Chantel laughed. "I'll be sure to tell the boys who put this thing together."

"Don't tell them the part about the whale falling on us," Gamay suggested. "You'll never hear the end of it."

Chantel laughed some more and took one last look below. The whale was still falling away, slowly escaping the range of the lights. It had almost vanished when something strange happened. It passed through what looked like a dim gray cloud, punching a hole in the middle of it and causing a ripple of light to radiate outward in all directions.

"Did you see that?" Chantel asked.

Gamay nodded. She'd seen it. Though she couldn't explain what it was. She took a deep breath. "Let's go a little lower."

Chantel agreed.

With the caution of a person walking on thin ice, Gamay brought the sub down toward the cloudy layer below. It grew brighter as they neared it. And before they touched it, she knew what she was looking at. A web made up of millions of the glowing orbs. They stretched as far as the eye could see, which wasn't that far underwater, but the effect made it seem like they went on forever.

Gamay cruised above them, piloting the submersible like an aircraft skimming the clouds. After a minute or two she'd seen all she needed to see. "I think we've spent enough time at this depth. Let's surface before the men get all emotional about our vanishing act."

# CHAPTER 24

**K**urt and Joe had a problem. In fact, they had multiple problems. The biggest issue came from the Indian National Police, who were looking for them in conjunction with the events at Alang. Sharma and several of his people were dead. Faked security video showed them storming into the office with guns. The fact that they'd been there earlier in the day and had been turned away and escorted off the property only added to the suspicions.

They were driving a small rental car that would be linked to them before long. Kurt had already driven through several mud puddles and areas of standing water to drench the car in a dirty coat, but it wasn't much of a disguise, even if half the license plate was smeared.

Sitting in the back, as nervous as a frightened cat, Five stared out the window. Everything he saw astounded him. Cars, trucks, buses. The noises they made. Buildings that rose up and blocked the sun. Posts with colored lights on them. Wires running everywhere like jungle vines. Billboards and decorations and streamers. The bright colors were like a kaleidoscope to him. Most of all, he could hardly believe the crowds.

"So many people," he whispered over and over. "How are there so many people?"

Navigating the crowds of India had left plenty of people with similar thoughts, but for a young man who'd lived his short life on a desert island in captivity, the question was not rhetorical.

"There are a lot of people here," Kurt said. "But this is a city. Think of it like an anthill or a beehive. Did they have bees on your island? Anyway, lots of people flock to the cities, but there are places out in the countryside that are less crowded."

"Ahh," he said, "like bees. I understand."

They came to a halt near an open area that might have been a park. While they were stopped at the light, two free-roaming cows moved toward the car. One of them looked into the back seat and mooed deeply.

Five scrambled across the seat to the other side, as if they were being attacked by an angry bear. The animal licked the window, mooed again, and then went back to the grass it had been chewing.

"What is that?" Five asked in shock.

"Where I come from, it's lunch," Joe said. "But we're not going to find it on the menu around here."

Kurt laughed. "Don't worry," he told Five. "It's a cow. It won't hurt you."

Five gazed at the mangy animal as if it were a unicorn with golden wings.

As they waited for the traffic to move, the sound of high-pitched sirens became audible. Kurt saw flashing lights approaching in the rearview mirror. He kept calm, but plotted a possible escape route in case the vehicles were police cars filled with detectives looking for the two Americans.

An ambulance and a paramedic's truck came up behind them.

They swept by on the shoulder, sirens wailing as they passed. Five covered his ears while Kurt and Joe breathed a sigh of relief.

"We really need to get out of India," Joe said. "Otherwise we're going to end up framed for everything that went down at the breakers' yard."

So far they'd been on the move, putting some space between themselves and the harbor and making their way toward more touristy areas where there would be plenty of Americans and Europeans to help them blend in.

"Tell me something I don't know," Kurt replied. "The question is: How?"

He was alluding to their second problem. Five had no ID of any kind. No driver's license, no passport. He didn't even have a real name.

He couldn't be coached into lying about his lack of a passport because he had no idea what one was or why you'd need it. He didn't even understand the concept of a sovereign country. Or what it meant to be arrested.

There was no way to get him through even the most rudimentary checkpoint or security screening, which ruled out airports or crossing the border by car. And hiking through the mountains to get to Pakistan or China wasn't going to improve the situation.

"We could have Rudi send a jet to an out-of-the-way location," Joe suggested. "There are no customs checks out in the hills. But there are plenty of small airfields."

"Considering that we're wanted men now, a NUMA jet landing in the middle of nowhere would probably raise some alarm bells," Kurt said. "Besides, every time we let Rudi know what we're doing, it seems to tip off the guys we've been fighting with."

Joe nodded. "You really think NUMA has been hacked?"

They'd discussed it earlier and refrained from contacting Washington. Kurt was convinced. "Someone got into my phone. And the 'great white hunter' and the 'cruel brothers' seem to be only a half a step behind us wherever we go."

He hadn't just shown up on Reunion or at the breakers' yard, but they'd spied him and his goons hanging around the hotel when they'd made their way back from the harbor.

Joe sighed at the dilemma and brought out the back scratcher, extending it a bit and scratching a spot on the back of his neck.

"So we can't get out the normal way," Joe said. "And we can't ask Rudi for help. I'd say we go by ship, but after what our guest has already been through, I don't think we'll be able to keep him calm enough to get on board."

That was the third problem. Five was overwhelmed by the real world. The machines they moved about in seemed like monsters to him: loud, noisy, and belching smoke.

Every time a bus got near them, Kurt had to fight through traffic to get away from it because Five saw it swaying to and fro, and was convinced it would fall over on him.

An attempt to catch a train had been derailed as well. Even though they'd managed to explain what a ticket was and how they would all sit in the car together and it would move by itself, one look at a train rumbling into the station with brakes squealing and steam venting from pneumatic lines had put Five into shock.

"Whatever we do it has to be quick and simple," Kurt said.

Both men fell into silent thought, Kurt driving, Joe tapping the back scratcher against the dashboard in a subconscious, repetitive fashion. A few minutes later, he looked up. An idea had obviously sprung to mind.

"Got something?" Kurt asked.

"Maybe," he said. He picked up the paper map they'd been given. A city named Porbandar lay on the coast up ahead. "All we need is an internet café. And the right kind of airport. I think there's someone nearby who could help."

Kurt had no idea what Joe was thinking, but they were already heading for Porbandar, so he figured he'd let Joe work on his plan in silence.

# CHAPTER 25

**D**r. Elena Pascal was jolted from a deep slumber by a loud voice coming over a raspy intercom system. Though she'd had only four hours of sleep and wasn't on duty for another eight, the wake-up call was not softened by the slightest of good-morning greetings or even an explanation. Just the booming voice of the ship's executive officer ordering her to the bridge immediately.

Throwing the blanket off and jumping out of the rack, she pulled open the tiny wardrobe, threw on a set of scrubs that doubled as her uniform, and then headed for the door. Out of pure habit, she grabbed her stethoscope on her way.

Smoothing her hair down and blinking the sleep from her eyes, she double-timed it along the main gangway and up the ship's ladder. Nearing the bridge, she slowed her pace and took a deep breath. She had the strangest feeling she was in trouble, though she couldn't imagine why.

Entering the bridge, she announced her arrival. "Dr. Pascal reporting as ordered."

The XO looked her way and then deferred to the captain, who was looking out the window at a speck in the morning sky.

Captain Marjorie Livorno turned her way. The longtime captain of the medical relief ship was a no-nonsense leader. "This is a medical ship," she said to Dr. Pascal. "We go to various places around the world helping out where needed. Since you've been aboard, we've raised the flag in Indonesia after a tsunami, Bangladesh after last year's floods, and Pakistan after the recent earthquake, where we spent six weeks doing surgeries on the injured. You understand that we're invited to these places because we have no political or military agendas."

The hospital ship wasn't part of any nation's navy or merchant marine. It was owned and operated by a charitable organization. And though the captain ran a tight ship, the doctors were all volunteers, including Dr. Pascal. That usually kept them out of the line of fire.

"I'm well aware of that," Dr. Pascal said. "I did many of those surgeries back-to-back. Did you really need to wake me up from a deep sleep to remind me?"

The captain grinned, suggesting the dressing-down was more for effect than anything else. Possibly even a captain's joke, just to see how Dr. Pascal would respond. "I woke you up because there is a helicopter approaching the ship, requesting an emergency landing, and the pilot is insisting that you would explain everything."

"Explain what, exactly?" Dr. Pascal stammered.

"Who they are, and why I should let them land on my ship."

Dr. Pascal had that sudden feeling of being half-asleep and not following along quick enough.

The captain pointed out the window. "That speck on the horizon is a helicopter," she said. "It's heading our way. The pilot is calling us on a short-range, high-frequency band, asking us to remain in radio silence regarding their presence and requesting an emergency landing. Apparently, they have a passenger who needs medical help."

"Okay," Dr. Pascal said. "And . . . how am I involved in this?"

"The pilot used your name, said you would explain. And for that reason and that reason only, I'm honoring their request and having our helipad cleared."

The possibility that she was having a vivid dream rushed in. "How should I know who they are and what they want?"

The captain pointed to the high-frequency radio. "How about you get on the radio and ask them?"

Elena moved to the comms panel and took the handheld transmitter from the radio operator. A switch was flipped, and she held the microphone an inch from her mouth. "Approaching helicopter, this is Dr. Elena Pascal of the hospital ship *Akeso*. Please state your intentions."

A jovial voice came over the line. "Hoping to land before we run out of fuel, stretch our legs, and grab a sandwich from the commissary."

The voice was instantly recognizable to her. A wave of relief appeared on her face.

"Are you alone?"

"Traveling with an old friend and a new one. Would like you to take a look at our passenger."

"Is he or she ill?"

"Not exactly," the friendly voice insisted. "I'll have to explain when we arrive."

Elena turned toward the captain.

"Friends of yours?" the captain guessed. "From NUMA days?"

"Men of the highest character," Elena insisted. "I've seen them both risk their lives to save others on multiple occasions."

"Why the need for radio silence?"

"I couldn't say," she admitted. "But I ask you to honor the request. They wouldn't make it without a good reason. And if it turns out you don't like that reason, then you can contact headquarters to your heart's content. But you can't undo it if you make the call now."

"First, do no harm," the captain said.

"That's kind of our thing," Elena replied.

"So it is," the captain replied. "Tell them to land. We can hardly say no if they're running out of gas."

Elena sent the message and then waited.

"You'd better go meet them," the captain said. "While you're at it, I'd appreciate you pretending I rule this ship like Captain Bligh. Tell them you're on your last strike before solitary confinement in the brig. If they're truly friends of yours, that ought to count for something."

# CHAPTER 26

D r. Pascal rushed to the helipad, which had been built on the forward end of the ship with its edges cantilevered over the bow. By the time she climbed the ladder up onto the flight deck, the helicopter had touched down.

After being cleared by a crewman, she approached the craft cautiously. The craft was an AgustaWestland AW109, a modern design with retractable wheels and a four-blade rotor. During her residency, Elena had flown in one setup as an air ambulance, but the helicopter in front of her bore the logo of an Indian construction company.

As the engines shut down, Elena made her way to the aft door, knocking on it and stepping back. It slid open, revealing Kurt Austin, Joe Zavala, and a young man she didn't recognize lying on a stretcher.

She hadn't seen Kurt since the three of them had served on a NUMA training vessel in the Bahamas a year ago, but she and Joe had dated for several months afterward, going on a series of adventures before life got too busy as both of them picked up new assignments.

She hugged Joe as he climbed out. "I always knew you'd drop back into my life, Joe Zavala. Never thought it would happen literally, or in the middle of the Indian Ocean. Tell me this isn't some stunt to win my affection."

"Can't say I'm above stealing a helicopter and flying halfway around the world for a date," Joe replied. "But, sadly, we're here on business."

She grew concerned. "Did you really steal this thing?" Suddenly, she thought better of asking. "Never mind. I don't want to know. And come up with a believable lie for the captain."

Kurt climbed out and gave her a quick hug. "Unfortunately, any lie we come up with is probably going to be easier to swallow than the truth." He turned back to the young man on the stretcher, sliding him toward the door.

Dr. Pascal looked him over briefly. "What's wrong with him?"

"Joe drugged him."

"At Kurt's orders," Joe insisted.

She felt for a pulse, checked his blood pressure, and then opened one of his closed eyes. "He's mildly sedated, but stable," she said. "He's also dehydrated and looks like he's suffering from a case of exposure."

During their death-defying moments in the Bahamas, she'd learned that Kurt and Joe were often mixed up in dangerous events despite their rather ordinary job descriptions. She instantly assumed this was a similar case. "Is he a criminal?" she asked. "Did you kidnap him?"

"No," Joe said. "We saved him from a group of assassins."

"Then why did you drug him?"

"It was the only way to get him on the helicopter," Kurt said. "On account of the fact that he'd never seen one before and was terrified of the noise it made."

She was confused and intrigued. "Let's get him inside."

They carried Five down from the helicopter pad and into the ship, avoiding the captain on their way to one of the examination rooms. When Joe presented the medication used to sedate him, Dr. Pascal estimated he would wake up in an hour or so. She hooked up an IV to help him rehydrate. Once it was in place and dripping, she turned on Kurt and Joe. "All right, let's cut to the chase," she said. "Who is he and why did you bring him here?"

Kurt explained his odd name, how they'd found him, and the events in India, culminating with their escape from the shipping yard. Joe followed by pointing out the difficulty of getting him safely out of the country and the need to steal the helicopter, which they took from an airport on the coast outside of Porbandar.

"I've been following you on Instagram," Joe continued. "I saw the work you did after the earthquake in Pakistan and realized you were probably heading south from Karachi. After a quick stop at an internet café, we were able to locate the ship through the charity's website."

She allowed a smile to show through. "You've been keeping track of me on social media?"

"Not in a creepy way," Joe insisted. "Just admiring your adventurous spirit."

"Uh-huh," she said, grinning. "Why not just call Rudi and get help from NUMA?"

"For the same reason we asked you to keep quiet about our approach," Kurt said. "We have reason to believe someone has hacked NUMA's communications network. Calling in help would have been like pointing a giant arrow in our direction. Which is why it's imperative that your captain not report our presence here."

The captain had appeared in the doorway. "I suppose I could be convinced of that," she said, her arms folded across her chest. "I'm not unaware of NUMA's reputation. It's half the reason I was glad to bring Dr. Pascal on board."

Kurt nodded. "Thank you."

"You're welcome," the captain said. "For now. But I won't put this ship in danger."

"Nor would we ask you to," Kurt said. "With a little luck we can be off the *Akeso* and transferred to a NUMA vessel in twenty-four hours. Until then we need your help."

"To do what?" the captain asked. "I heard Dr. Pascal say your patient is fine."

Kurt walked over and closed the door. "I need you to examine him further," Kurt insisted, with great seriousness in his voice. "Down to the cellular level."

"Why?"

"Because he doesn't remember having a mother or father, but he does have a large number of brothers, who look exactly like him. He remembers nothing of his childhood, and he doesn't have a belly button. Which means he never had an umbilical cord. Which I'm assuming is almost unheard of."

Dr. Pascal heard the words and felt a slight wave of confusion as she processed them. The captain seemed suspicious, but didn't get the implication.

Dr. Pascal took a pair of scissors and cut through the patient's shirt from bottom to top. The skin and musculature of his stomach appeared smooth and uninterrupted where his navel should have been. There was no sign of surgery or scarring. No sign of deformity. What she did find was a series of scarred-over indentations along both sides of his body. Evenly spaced and long healed. She didn't have the slightest clue what they were, but they reminded her of injection sites.

"I asked him how old he was," Kurt continued. "He didn't know what that meant. We asked him how many brothers he had. He didn't know, but he did say that in his 'batch' there were ten."

"What's with the tattoo on his neck?" the captain asked.

"He says that's his designation. If you look closely, you'll see that the bottom number ends in five."

She studied the number, the first part looking oddly familiar to her. It read: 6.28318, but she couldn't place it right away. The second part of the number under a horizontal dash contained the indications Kurt was talking about: 16.21.5. "You think this is his name?"

"*He* thinks it's his name," Kurt said. "I think it's his number. I think it lists him as subject number five, from batch twenty-one, version sixteen, or something like that. I think he only took it as his name because it's the only thing that distinguishes him from any of his identical brothers."

As she listened to Kurt's words, Dr. Pascal began to understand the terrible conclusion he had come to. Across from her the captain's face turned grim and cold. She seemed to understand now as well. Still, it was hard to accept. "Are you trying to say this man is the product of an experiment?"

Kurt made it clear. "I'm saying he was grown in a laboratory, not born from a woman. I'm saying he's a clone."

# CHAPTER 27

A quiet stillness filled the exam room after Kurt's statement. No one wanted to speak, as if the slightest utterance would disturb some fragile peace between the reality everyone was used to— where humans were born naturally—and the new reality Kurt had suggested.

Kurt remained quiet because he'd said what he needed to say. He wasn't a doctor, but he wasn't oblivious to science, either. He knew the world was moving in this direction. But it was up to the medical experts to decide if someone had made the leap or if there was another explanation.

Joe remained quiet for a different reason. As they'd moved around India, avoiding the authorities and offering Five a crash course in reality, Joe had begun to think of him like a little brother. He made jokes and then patiently explained them until Five cracked a smile. When they stopped for gas or food, he made sure to pick up sugared treats, carbonated sodas, and all the other things he was certain Five had never tasted before. He knew Five and his brothers had been abused and mistreated, but it bothered him to focus on the scientific repercussions of his existence, as if he were an experiment gone wrong.

Dr. Pascal was far more clinical in her approach. She bit at the inner part of her lip as she considered the science that would be required for such a leap. The captain considered the effect this knowledge would have on the crew and was glad they were meeting in private. It was she who urged the discussion forward. "Dr. Pascal, is this possible?"

The doctor took a deep breath. "It's complicated. I want to say yes, and no, and maybe. I'll start with the yes. Cloning has been progressing for years. Everyone knows about Dolly the sheep, and the hundreds of other animals that have been cloned over the years. Most of us have heard of the Chinese doctors who were arrested and imprisoned for cloning humans. But all these clones were created in a fairly traditional way: DNA was inserted into an existing egg, essentially fertilizing it. That egg was implanted in a female of childbearing age, similar to how IVF works for couples trying to conceive. And after a normal pregnancy, the offspring was born. We call them clones because they have the exact same genetic code as the DNA donor. But aside from the age difference, it's much more like having a twin."

She took a breath and turned to Kurt. "What Kurt is suggesting is entirely different. For Five and his brothers to be grown in a lab somewhere and take their first breaths in the physical form of a teenager is a reality-altering concept. It's the stuff of science fiction. It would suggest someone could grow millions of soldiers and send them into battle without waiting the decades it would normally take for them to grow up. To that I want to say no, but when I consider the huge leaps we've seen in growing organs and skin and functioning networks of brain cells in the lab, I have to modify that response to a maybe."

"So these things are already being done?" the captain asked.

"Universities all over the world have been growing what they call 'mini-brains' in petri dishes for years," Dr. Pascal said. "They're basically networks of brain cells, neurons, dendrites, and glial cells that connect to each other and start to exchange information. But let me be clear: they're not complex enough to be considered conscious. Though every year the technology advances, we get closer to a line where we'll have to wonder. As for other organs, the progress has been rapid. We can now grow functioning, adult-sized versions of many human organs. Lungs, hearts, kidneys, livers, eyes, and others. The growth process involves a complex use of DNA and bioavailable materials. They grow layer by layer on a structural framework to make sure they develop like a natural organ. It's very similar to 3D printing, except instead of using plastic you're depositing layers of cells."

The captain appeared dismayed. "Is there anything to prevent someone from taking the next step and growing a fully functioning human?"

"Only financial and ethical barriers," Dr. Pascal said. "If the first barrier is overcome with funding and the ethical roadblock disregarded, then the learning curve flattens appreciably. With no constraints put on them, a research team would be able to perform an unlimited number of experiments, of any nature they desired."

"How many experiments are we talking about?" Kurt asked.

"The process would be incremental." Dr. Pascal now sounded pained as she thought about what it would take and what that might have meant to Five and others like him. "You'd see research combined with testing and ultimately trial runs, most of which would result in failure and death, at least early on. Under any circumstances, the more trials conducted, the more rapid the progress. But it's not something you could do in the regular world. There are too many people who would ask too many questions."

"But if you were well funded and hidden away on an island somewhere, out of the public eye . . ." Kurt said.

"All you'd need is time," she said. "And a complete lack of morality." As she finished her statement, Dr. Pascal looked over at Five. The more she thought about it, the less she doubted Kurt's conclusion. It was like Frankenstein's monster coming to life. And yet, like that monster, Five was the victim of things far beyond his control.

She moved to the bed and began to study him. The indentations on his sides were so symmetrical that they looked almost like injection molding gates found on the sides of plastic toys formed in a factory. The tattoo was deep and dark; it seemed to have a bit of luminosity to it, probably to make it easier for cameras to spot it in the dark. Lines in Five's thick black hair that looked like parts turned out to be scars. She found four. They appeared to be in various stages of healing.

"Do you know anything about this?"

Kurt answered coldly. "He said they're taken to see the surgeon from time to time. What happens there he can't remember. But they come back with shaved heads and new scars."

Dr. Pascal examined the incisions. "Based on the pattern of cuts and the healing of the scars, I would say he's had four separate surgeries. Each about a month apart."

"He claims others have more," Kurt said. "Old heads, they call them, covered in scars. They go back to the surgeon repeatedly. Sometimes for no reason. Sometimes for punishment. Eventually they go to the surgeon and don't return."

The captain exhaled, her mood souring on this latest news. She'd seen plenty of suffering around the world, but this was something new. "Can you guess what the purpose of these surgeries might be?"

"Multiple surgeries on multiple patients suggests a testing protocol," Dr. Pascal replied. "We can do an MRI to be certain, but I have to assume they're testing some type of brain implant."

"Brain implants?"

Dr. Pascal nodded. "That's another technology that's come a long way. Believe it or not, there are dozens of companies working to develop functional cognitive electronic implants. Tests are underway all over the globe. Some want to use implants to control epilepsy and stop seizures; others want to use the technology to heal traumatic brain injury or fight drug-resistant depression. Others want to enhance human thinking. I heard one pitch that suggested it would be the next wave in entertainment, suggesting people will be able to download information directly to their brains, making it possible to watch a movie solely in their own mind."

"How far along is all this?" Joe asked.

"It's an industry in its infancy," Dr. Pascal said. "But we've already seen functionally mute individuals being given the ability to have conversations as an implant turns thoughts into words from a speaker. We've seen paralyzed individuals stand up and even take a short step. Most of the projections I've heard are from industry people who expect that progress to accelerate exponentially, similar to the way computer chips increase their power by a hundred thousand percent every decade, all while getting significantly smaller and cheaper. If that's true, some of these grand plans might not be too far off."

"Clearly we're nowhere near that," the captain suggested, sounding more hopeful than confident.

"*We're* not," Dr. Pascal clarified. "But who knows what the surgeons working on Five and his brothers have accomplished. If you'd asked me yesterday if a human could be grown in a lab, I'd have laughed the idea off and suggested you ask me again in twenty years. Now I'm faced with the reality that not only has someone done it, but they've been doing it for some time, creating perhaps hundreds of clones this way. If whoever's behind Five's creation and existence can make that kind of progress in one field, we shouldn't assume they haven't been just as successful in another."

Kurt saw the connection. "One thing leads to the other. With an endless supply of clones who no one cares about, you can do an endless number of brain-altering experiments, and your progress outstrips anything that might be possible in the ethical parts of the world.

We look at Five and see someone who's been treated awfully. Whoever made him sees him as a guinea pig, a means to an end. A way to conduct these experiments without anyone watching or regulating the process."

"But why would anyone want to do that?" Joe asked. "What's the benefit?"

"Money," the captain suggested. "Assuming there's some product to be developed from this."

"Possibly," Dr. Pascal said. "But the cost of developing even one new medical technology is astronomical, let alone two. I can't imagine the funds that have been used to push these two technologies forward so quickly. And even if someone developed a marketable product from all of this, if the truth ever came out, they'd end up charged with mass murder. That's a pretty bad risk-reward equation."

"Unless they could convince a jury that these clones don't qualify as full humans," the captain said.

"You only have to talk to this kid for a minute and you'd lose that argument," Joe said.

The silence returned. Kurt used it to clear his mind. Separating the emotion from the facts, he tried to look beyond the barbaric cruelty of what was happening for any shred of logic. Aside from the truly insane, most criminals had a rational purpose, but in this case he couldn't see one.

"Continuing to guess will just take us down a rabbit hole," he said. "And possibly blind us to the truth. We need more information. We need cold, hard facts. The only way to get them is to go directly to the source."

"What source?" Dr. Pascal asked.

Kurt motioned toward Five. "The island where Five and his brothers were born and raised and where these experiments are being done."

Joe liked that idea. He was ready for a fight. But there was an obvious problem. While making their way out of India, they'd asked Five about the island in every way they could imagine, but he had no real information to offer. He didn't know the name of the place or anything about directions or maps or hemispheres. When asked to describe the angle of the sun, he pointed up at the sky.

Five and his brothers had spent their whole lives on the island, unaware that anything else even existed beyond its shoreline. Upon leaving, they had no way to get back. That made it difficult for Kurt and Joe to find it.

"We could backtrack the beacon," Joe said, "but that only goes so far. Sounds like they didn't turn it on for two or three days."

"If we analyze the wind, weather, and currents in that area, we should be able to roll their starting point back to a reasonable spot."

Joe understood the theory, but having searched for a number of lost ships and downed aircraft in his life, he knew the wind and currents were hard to model with accuracy. "That's going to require a lot of information we don't have and a substantial amount of computing power. We'd probably have to have Max and Hiram to help us."

Dr. Pascal had an objection. "You said it was dangerous to contact NUMA. You said you thought they'd been hacked."

Kurt nodded. Therein lay the dilemma. Standard forms of communication were unlikely to be secure. But they would be hard-pressed to do the work on the *Akeso*. He racked his brain for a solution. "I've got an idea," he said finally. "I just hope Rudi's hungry."

# CHAPTER 28

Rudi Gunn leaned back in his office chair listening to Gamay Trout report on her findings in the Indian Ocean. Listening, because despite the high-definition screen linked directly to NUMA's satellite network, the feed from the *Isabella* was glitchy and continued to freeze up, which he found distracting at best and unwatchable at worst.

"Should have sent one of our ships down there," he said under his breath.

"What was that?" Gamay asked.

"Nothing, go on."

She'd already explained the discovery of the dead aquatic animals gathered en masse and the recovery of samples from the water and the carcasses. "The gelatinous globs are a form of organism I've never seen before. A pathogen to be sure, but it's not bacterial, even though it seems to act that way. Soft-bodied parasite is the best way I can describe it. But reproducing at an astronomical rate and consuming tons of whale and shark flesh every hour. Fully half of the initially discovered animals are already gone. The rest are rapidly being skeletonized. And based on what Chantel and I saw down below, who knows how many creatures this pathogen has fed on."

"Are you saying you've discovered some kind of seaborne plague?"

"It seems that way," Gamay said. "Although a blight is a more accurate term based on how it consumes vegetation."

"Sure," Rudi acknowledged. "What makes you think this is more than a local phenomenon?"

"Chantel was able to access data from a French satellite called GeneSat that studies seawater for things like oxygen, nitrogen, carbon, and other gases. Because of how GeneSat works, it also gives us a pretty good idea of how healthy the sea is in a particular area. The waters appear an opaque green color when they're healthy and populated. They appear reddish when there's an unhealthy algae bloom and a lack of oxygen. And they show up as clear blue when the waters are barren."

"And?" Rudi asked, preferring not to be kept in suspense.

"I have a couple of images to show you," Gamay said. "Let me send them to you. I promise they're worth more than a thousand words."

Rudi turned toward the screen, where a satellite image showing the western Indian Ocean had appeared. On the left side he could see the familiar shape of Madagascar and the coastline of Africa. Most of it was a healthy green, with a few small circles of red off the coast of Madagascar. But smack in the middle of the green zone was a dark blue stripe. It stood out as clearly and remarkably as the first strip mowed in an otherwise overgrown lawn. The *Isabella* sat near the end of that strip.

"Everything in dark blue is basically sterile ocean at this point," Gamay said. "No plankton, no krill, no fish, and thus no predators that feed on those fish. It's like something carved a line into the ocean and removed all the nutrients."

"You're telling me this pathogen is eating its way through the sea in a straight line?"

"And widening as it goes," Gamay said. "Which suggests it's reproducing and growing more plentiful as it moves along."

Rudi considered what he was looking at. "No wonder Kurt and Joe couldn't find any sharks off the coast. If there's nothing for the sharks to eat, they go elsewhere."

"Or get eaten themselves when they show up at the wrong dinner table," Gamay said, referencing what they'd discovered.

"You said you had a number of images," Rudi asked. "What's next?"

"The bad news."

"This wasn't the bad news?"

"This was the prologue," Gamay said. "Stand by."

Rudi waited for the new image to download. The file must have been much larger because it took a minute. When it finally popped up on the screen, Rudi saw side-by-side images of the entire Indian Ocean with Africa on the left, the shark tooth–like shape of India at the top, and the Indonesian islands and the western edge of Australia on the right.

"The first image is from last summer. And the second image was stitched together this week."

The first image was speckled, but relatively uniform. Plankton and algae and thus sea life everywhere. The second image was markedly different. While much of the sea remained speckled in light green, large swaths of dark blue were spreading out across the sea in multiple directions.

He counted six bands in all, one heading west toward Africa, another tracking due north toward the Saudi peninsula. A third heading north and slightly east in the direction of India. The fourth band angled toward the archipelagoes of Southeast Asia, while the longest, and now widest, band carved a path to the east, as if making a beeline for Australia. The last of the bands was the shortest and darkest. It went south, passing east of Reunion, ending just after crossing south past the Tropic of Capricorn.

Viewed from space, the pattern resembled a distorted asterisk. Rudi calculated that roughly thirty percent of the Indian Ocean had been affected. Considering the size of that body of water, it added up to an astronomical number of square miles. Eight million or so. Three times the surface area of the continental United States.

"And you believe these swaths have been . . . cleared of sea life?"

"Cleared. Stripped. Cleaned out," Gamay replied. "Describe it however you want to, but if these areas are anything like the waves we have been sailing through, they're essentially barren. Wastelands in the middle of the sea."

Rudi had heard reports suggesting the commercial fishing harvest was down sharply off the coast of India, but that was being blamed on a huge Chinese fishing fleet that had been moving through the area. But even a thousand ships with the largest nets couldn't do what seemed to have been done here. It was more like a forest that had been clear-cut than an area that had been overfished. Privately, Rudi wondered if the Chinese fleet had been on the move because it wasn't finding anything worth trawling a net for.

"I'll get some assets into these other areas to see if they're as compromised as what you've found," he said. "Send over a full report as soon as you've finished your analysis. This suddenly seems a lot bigger than a group of whales stranding themselves."

"We'll get it over to you ASAP," she said, and then signed off.

Rudi sat in silence for a moment, compiling a mental list of who he could dispatch to regions in question and which units he might be able to divert from other missions. Though they weren't members of the science department, he suddenly wished he hadn't let Kurt and Joe run off on a wild-goose chase to India. Especially as he hadn't heard from them in days and was being hounded by the Indian government regarding their whereabouts and reasons for being in the country.

He made a few notes before being interrupted by his assistant, who announced over the intercom that his lunch had been delivered. It was a curious report, considering he hadn't ordered anything and had dined in the cafeteria two hours ago.

He assumed it was a mistake and suggested as much. The reply surprised him. "The note says this was specially ordered for you by Kurt Austin."

Rudi looked up from the notepad. "Speak of the devil and he appears."

He put the notes aside and went to pick up the delivery, finding a college kid in a green polo shirt with mustard on his sleeve. A logo stitched on the shirt read: Adam's Delicatessen. A place Kurt frequented when he was in D.C.

"Kurt ordered this for me?"

The kid nodded. "He called it in."

Considering Kurt was in India, Rudi would have been surprised if he'd placed the order in person. "I don't suppose he tipped you?"

"Oh, yeah. Twenty dollars."

That was a healthy tip considering the sandwich might have cost eight or nine.

"And," the kid added, "I get a hundred-dollar bonus if you come back to the shop and take a long-distance phone call." The kid's eyebrows went up and down knowingly. "Some kind of prank, right?"

"Almost certainly," Rudi groaned. "But who am I to deprive a man of his hard-earned bonus? Lead on and I shall follow."

# CHAPTER 29

Adam's Deli was on the ground floor of a nondescript office complex two blocks from the NUMA building, next to what had once been a RadioShack. Its front door opened onto the street, and at lunchtime it often boasted a line that stretched out onto the sidewalk. At three o'clock in the afternoon, Rudi found only a smattering of customers and the crew doing cleanup.

He stepped inside to the jingle of an old-fashioned bell that was attached to the door. The owner, a man with a gray mustache and a few wispy hairs wrapped around his scalp in a comb-over, turned to greet him. "You're Rudi, no?"

Rudi nodded.

The man came out from behind the counter, untying his apron and offering a strange look. "You're taller than Kurt said you'd be."

Rudi offered a half smile. "Napoleon and I both get a bad rap," he said. "I'm told I have a phone call."

"Yes, yes, right this way." He ushered Rudi down a narrow hall half blocked by cardboard boxes filled with cups, straws, paper towels, and other vital supplies.

"Good customer, that Kurt," the owner said. "And funny. He's always joking."

"Are you Adam?" Rudi asked.

"No, my father was Adam," the man said. "My name is Gris. But Gris's Deli doesn't have the best ring to it."

Gris opened a door to the back office, revealing a space even more cramped than the narrow hallway. "I give you your privacy," he said. "But don't talk too loud; the walls are thin."

Rudi sat at a desk covered in receipts and invoices and half-finished cups of coffee. Amid the mess, he found an olive-green push-button phone that might have been there since the eighties. One light was blinking, which he assumed was Kurt. Lifting the scuffed receiver, he placed it to his ear and pressed the blinking button.

"This better not be a joke," he said. "Otherwise I'll assign you to Antarctic detail and make sure you get only warm-weather gear better suited for snorkeling in the Bahamas."

"Great to hear you, too," Kurt said. "Even if you are a little crankier than usual."

"You and Joe have been off the radar for three days. And the Indian government has been pressuring us to tell them where you are and what you're doing there. That raises my irritability level."

"Which is why you should thank me for not updating you on our activities," Kurt said smugly. "That way you didn't have to lie."

Rudi noticed the audio was very flat, almost like an AM radio broadcast through an old mono speaker. He wondered where Kurt was calling him from. More important, why he was calling the delicatessen instead of the office. "Unless you plan to keep me in the dark, how about you start by telling me why I'm talking on a phone that's coated with olive oil and several decades of grime when the high-tech, encrypted phone in my air-conditioned office works just fine?"

"The problem is it works a little *too* fine," Kurt said.

He went on to explain why he believed the NUMA communications system and possibly even the entire server network had been hacked. "Between the odd messages on my phone and the real-time takedown of the emergency networks on Reunion, I'm getting the sense that these guys can hack into any system they want, anytime they want, in the blink of an eye."

"You think the two things are connected?"

"They have to be," Kurt said. "The same guy who jumped us in Reunion showed up here almost before we did. That can't be a coincidence."

*Interesting*, Rudi thought. He'd been frustrated that Kurt and Joe had gone off to India in search of the answer to this random message. But now the seemingly random events appeared to be linked. Perhaps letting Kurt and Joe chase their electronic ghosts had been a stroke of luck.

"If these guys can hack anything they want in real time, what makes you think this deli with its Wi-Fi password we_love_sandwiches_#1 is some bastion of security?"

"Because it's not linked to NUMA in any way. There's no reason for anyone to be monitoring the landlines of a small dining establishment. The only way this line is tapped is if they're monitoring everything, everywhere, all the time, like Big Brother and the Thought Police."

Rudi had to admit it wasn't a bad idea. If the high-tech systems had been compromised, low-tech was the way to go. Off-site, low-tech was even better. "Okay, we'll go with that for now. But Hiram isn't going to appreciate you suggesting his computers have been hacked. You may find your laptop and other high-tech gear inoperative when you get home."

Kurt laughed. The hidden power of the IT department was not to be trifled with. "I can never get a printer to work correctly as it is, so no big loss. On the other hand, if it prevents the people we are dealing with from getting the jump on us again, it's worth it."

As Rudi listened intently, Kurt described their discovery of the stowaways on the lower deck of the *Soufriere* and the chaos that followed. He relayed the details of torture and experimentation that Five and his brothers had endured, and finished with the possibility—Kurt insisted it was a probability—that Five had been cloned.

Rudi didn't react, though he found the idea of someone creating humans just to conduct torturous experiments on them abhorrent. "Any idea who's behind this?"

"I was hoping you could tell us."

Rudi was at a loss. "How am I supposed to do that?"

"By telling us where Five came from," Kurt said. "Have Hiram and Max go over the data from the tracking beacon and then extrapolate for the time before it was activated while adjusting for the drift based on wind, waves, current, and the possibility of powered travel. They were picked up by that freighter in a tricky area of the sea, with intersecting currents and variable winds, so you'll have to get detailed weather reports to make the analysis work, but backtracking forty-eight hours should point us toward the island Five came from."

"And then what?"

"Get someone to look into it," Kurt said. "My choice would be the 82nd Airborne, or a UN team that investigates crimes against humanity backed up by a battalion of Marines."

Rudi knew instantly this wasn't a scenario the UN, Interpol, or the U.S. military would jump on at first sight. If Kurt was right about any of it, the entire situation was a giant can of worms. One with the potential to make people terribly uncomfortable. The powers that be would open it slowly. In the meantime, the experiments and torture and death occurring on whatever island the young man had come from would continue.

Rudi knew that. Kurt knew it as well. "And if they're not available?"

"Then Joe and I will do it," Kurt said.

"You'd have to bring back proof," Rudi said. "Acres of it."

"We'll get it," Kurt insisted. "Just tell us where to look."

Rudi nodded. "I'll have Max work on the drift plot. In the meantime, is there another way to contact you, or am I running NUMA out of a sandwich shop for the foreseeable future?"

Kurt hesitated. "Uhhh . . ."

"That's what I thought," Rudi said. "Hopefully this place makes a good Reuben."

# CHAPTER 30

The small research vessel rocked gently on the passing swells as the evening deepened. Aside from a pair of crewmen on the bridge and another acting as duty engineer down below, most of the crew were asleep or having a late meal.

Only the science lab remained fully active as Gamay and Chantel ran tests on the samples they'd retrieved from the depths. Paul watched over them like a nervous supervisor, asking numerous questions and getting irritated looks when he needed elaboration to understand the answers.

At one point Gamay stood abruptly, almost headbutting him on the chin as he was trying to read the computer over her shoulder. She offered a withering stare. "Paul, if you don't find something else to do, we're going to need couples counseling."

"Can't help it if I'm curious," Paul said. "It's like you've discovered an alien life-form."

"Be curious from over there," she said, pointing to the far side of the small compartment. "Or better yet, go for a walk. I promise to brief you as soon as we're done."

"Fine," Paul said, "but I don't want to hear any complaints the next time I tell you to do something else while I'm watching the World Series."

Gamay smiled. She vaguely recalled asking him to weigh in on new silverware during the bottom of the ninth. "Deal."

Paul grabbed a windbreaker and left the compartment.

As he went out the door, Chantel chuckled. "At least your husband is interested in your work."

"Too much sometimes," Gamay said. "Now, where were we?"

"You were suggesting we need to perform a DNA analysis, but I'm afraid we don't have that kind of equipment on board. But look at this."

Using a strainer, Chantel plucked one of the luminescent orbs from a murky sample jar that had been filled with whale blubber and was now nothing more than oily liquid. The sphere, which had grown to the size of a billiard ball, revealed something dark curled up inside. "They're not colony organisms at all. They're eggs."

Gamay reached for a scalpel. "Let's see what's inside."

Chantel lowered the orb into a small dish as Gamay donned a pair of goggles and pressed the blade against the exterior of the sphere. At first the skin dimpled, turning concave rather than opening. She pushed harder and the sphere popped like it had been pressurized from the inside. A small amount of liquid hit Gamay's safety goggles, while the rest spread out inside the bowl.

Wiping her goggles, Gamay looked closer. Slithering back and forth in a soup of yellow goo was an inch-long grub that resembled a mealworm. As it wriggled and turned, features began to appear. Tiny legs tucked under the body stretched, miniature claws wriggling. A set of fins—flattened and wet—began to spread out from its back. Finally, a head that had been tucked under the body unfolded. The "fish" was very insect-like, complete with compound eyes, stubby antennae, and powerful mandibles more at home on a stag beetle or a murder hornet. And yet its body looked like it belonged to a fish. It shimmered with iridescent blue scales.

"Have you ever seen anything like this?" Chantel asked.

Gamay was at a loss. She adjusted the light to see it more clearly. Under the glare of the spotlight the grub began to flop around like a fish on a dock. With a snap of its body it popped out of the bowl and onto the table.

"Grab it!" Gamay said.

Chantel tried to cover the grub with the strainer, but the slippery little thing shimmied off the table and onto the deck, where it wriggled its way under the table.

Both women pulled back, looking for the escaped larva. "This is how the killer bees got started," Chantel cried out, half joking.

"Where is it?" Gamay asked.

They pulled the table aside to find the grub squirming its way across the floor at a surprising pace. As it neared the wall it hopped once again, only to slam into the bulkhead and topple over backward, stunned by the impact.

Righting itself, it looked up toward the overhead light and then—to Gamay's horror—launched itself into the air, buzzing loudly on its set of wings.

"Oh crap, it can fly," Gamay called out, ducking.

The airborne grub buzzed around drunkenly, its navigation sorely lacking for anything but haphazard turns. It smacked headfirst into the wall and then the lamp and then dove for Gamay's hair.

This was a crucial mistake.

Gamay smacked the thing out of the air with a backhand that would have made a karate master proud. It careened across the compartment, smashed into a cabinet door, and dropped to the floor.

Without a second thought Gamay stomped on it, crushing the thing with an audible crunch and twisting her foot back and forth just to be sure she'd done it in.

"Apocalypse averted," she said with a grin.

Chantel broke into an embarrassed laugh and then looked sheepishly away. She felt silly for the moment of hysteria, but not completely. "We should probably examine another one of those eggs, but this time let's use a tank with a lid on it."

"Excellent idea," Gamay said. She looked under her boot. There wasn't much left. "You pick the next one, and whatever you do, never tell Paul that I screamed."

While they worked in the lab, Paul was out on deck. It was a quiet night. The sky was clear, without a hint of wind, and the stars were bright and numerous. The swells passing under the boat seemed both lazy and large.

Gazing at the sea, he noticed a soft glow emanating from the water off the port side. It was a faint yellow-orange color that reminded him of a diver using lights to see with. Only, the light wasn't confined to a single location; it stretched all along the side of the ship.

Looking toward the stern, Paul found the same faint glow behind the *Isabella*. It was brighter and more intense in that direction, perhaps because of the limited amount of lighting at the stern.

Paul leaned over the rail and looked straight down. For a moment he wondered if someone on board was running an underwater lighting system, then he saw blobs of floating gel appear on the surface. They were popping up everywhere like bubbles in a glass of champagne.

A handful turned to hundreds. Hundreds turned to thousands, and then tens of thousands. Soon they were everywhere, surrounding the vessel like drifting kelp. They slid up and down as the swells passed underneath, creating the equivalent of a psychedelic light show.

*Gamay's got to see this*, Paul thought.

He turned to go, but a spitting and popping sound caught his ear. Looking back out over the rail he saw what looked like moths emerging from the water. They took to the air, beating their wings noisily. At first a few, then by the thousands.

They swirled up at some unspoken command, racing toward Paul and the ship from all directions. Paul backed away, swatting at them, closing his eyes and covering his face. He stumbled away like a blind man, pushing through the swarm in search of the nearest door.

# CHAPTER 31

**P**aul crashed into the bulkhead and opened his eyes. He was surrounded by a swirling cloud of the insects. They hit him like darts from every direction at once, crashing into his back, whipping into his legs, clipping his ears and neck as they flew by. Their wings felt like tiny, sharp-edged knives.

He moved along the deck, keeping close to the superstructure and crushing dozens of the insects with each step. Soon he was slipping on their guts and goo. Feeling his way along, he found a door handle. He pulled it down, yanked the door open, and ducked inside, slamming the door shut behind him.

At least a dozen of the pests rode in on him, while another thirty or forty had flown through the briefly opened door. Shaking the attackers off, Paul smashed and stomped on them, crushing them against the walls, floor, and ceiling of the corridor.

Gamay and Chantel heard the commotion and came rushing out of the science bay. "What on earth are you doing?"

"Pest control," Paul replied, stepping on yet another one of the invaders.

"Where did these come from?"

"Outside," Paul shouted. "From the sea."

Chantel went to the door, peered through the porthole, and put her hand on the latch.

"Don't!" Paul snapped.

She stopped.

"There are thousands of them outside," he grunted. "Millions, maybe."

"Millions?" Gamay asked, looking at him as if that had to be an exaggeration.

"I didn't exactly stop to count them," Paul said. "But they surrounded the ship, like those locusts that swarmed out of the wheat field when we were in Kenya a few years ago. Do you remember hiding in the shed as the sky turned dark?"

Gamay remembered the cloud of insects blocking out the sun and pelting the metal-walled shed like hail. The noise from their wings had sounded like a squadron of World War II bombers flying overhead.

She joined Chantel at the window. The flying creatures could be seen mostly in the cones of light from the upper deck. They were swarming so thickly it was dizzying to watch. Before long they began landing on the window, covering it from top to bottom in layer after layer.

"The glowing water down below," Chantel said. "When we hit a thousand feet. They must have risen to the surface to hatch. Just like the one we plucked out of the sample jar."

Paul found his hands burning. His neck felt worse. "Can someone please grab the medical kit?"

As Gamay went for the first-aid case, several of the hidden insects fluttered out of the vent they'd flown into. It dawned on Paul that the *Isabella* was running with windows and vents open to let the cool night air in. "Call the bridge," he suggested to Chantel. "Tell them to button up the ship like we're going into a storm. Otherwise the ship will become infested with these things."

As Chantel rushed to the nearest intercom station, Gamay returned with the medical kit. She doused Paul's hands with antiseptic and then swabbed his neck.

He winced with pain, but didn't ask her to stop. "Hope these are just bites," he said. "I don't want to end up like those whales."

"If I have to, I'll lance every bite and inject a sterilizing agent," Gamay said. "For now, I'll use an extra dose of the rubbing alcohol and then you can smear this antibiotic cream and this hydrocortisone on them."

She handed him a pair of tubes.

"This is for poison ivy," he said dejectedly.

"There's nothing in here labeled 'antidote for killer flying fish.'"

Paul had to laugh. *Of course there isn't*. He squeezed out the antibiotic gel and rubbed it liberally anywhere the stingers or teeth had cut his skin.

As Paul finished applying the treatment, Chantel called over to them. "No response from the bridge. No one's answering."

Up on the bridge, the chaos erupted in stages. The night watch consisted of a junior officer and an engineering mate who was only there to chat and grab some coffee. They'd been talking quietly with the windows and doors open to let the cool night air in.

With the tinted glass and the illumination of the various computer screens affecting their night vision, neither of them had noticed the subtle glow appearing on the sea around them. The first hint of something odd was a whirring sound like cicadas in the trees. This was followed by a dull thud as something hit one of the windows.

"Was that a bird?" the mate asked.

The officer of the watch saw no feathers flying and thought the sound was too sharp for a bird strike. He leaned in close, looking for a chip in the glass, but didn't find one. Still, he saw things fluttering around outside, illuminated by the forward lights. They looked like bats or large moths circling a fire. He noticed the throng growing thicker with each passing second.

"What in the world . . ."

Stepping out onto the wing, he focused on the swarm in the lights. Flipping a switch, he turned on a spotlight and aimed it over the side.

In an instant the sea came to life. The surface turned white as the creatures left the water. The rush of a million wings drowned out all other sounds as they swarmed up and around the ship like a living tornado.

They came for the light and found the officer of the watch, crashing into him with a shocking amount of force. Each one weighed mere ounces, but a hundred of them hitting at once was like being slammed with a twenty-pound bag of rice. He was knocked off balance and stumbled back toward the wheelhouse. He tripped over the weatherproof sill and landed on his back.

By the time he hit the deck, they were swarming all over him, biting and stinging every centimeter of exposed skin. They burrowed down through the collar of his shirt and under the legs of the Bermuda shorts he wore.

Twisting and swinging his arms wildly, the officer cried out in pain, but that gave the tiny creatures another place to attack and they went for his mouth, biting his lips and tongue and burrowing inside.

The engineering mate dropped down to help his friend, sweeping the insects off him by the handful, but it was pointless. Every spot he cleared was immediately covered again. And now the insects were latching onto him.

He stood up and backed away, marveling at their numbers. They were flooding into the wheelhouse through the side doors and pouring through an open window like sand coming down a chute.

He pulled one window down and tried to shut the door, but it jammed before it closed as masses of the insects piled up in the track.

By now the engineering mate was living in full-blown terror. His arms and legs were covered by the biting creatures. His face and neck were under assault. Unlike the officer of the watch, he kept himself upright by stumbling into the control panel and holding on. Feeling about blindly for anything that might help, he found the engine controls and shoved the throttle forward.

Deep in the ship, the engine surged to life. As the prop spun up, the *Isabella* lurched awkwardly into motion. The next thing he found was the button that sounded the ship's horn. He pressed the button and held it, sounding a warning with a loud, long blast.

Startled by the noise, the insects launched themselves back into the air, and the inside of the wheelhouse became a swirling vortex of wings and teeth.

The engineering mate couldn't take it anymore. He moved for the far door, but stumbled and fell forward. Reaching for anything that might stop him from falling, his hand caught the ship's wheel and sent it spinning. He went down to the deck and was soon covered by the mass of insects in a mound several inches deep. He didn't move again.

# CHAPTER 32

We're moving," Paul said, sensing the vibration in the deck. "We're underway."

Gamay and Chantel could feel it as well. Forward motion replacing the slow rocking of a ship at rest.

"That's a good sign," Gamay said.

A long blast sounded on the ship's horn.

"A warning signal?" Paul suggested.

"Six short blasts followed by one long blast would be a call for muster stations," Chantel said.

Paul knew that; he was just guessing at the reasoning behind the signal. "I'm guessing muster stations are not the best place to be right now."

As the ship picked up speed, it leaned into a turn, rolling significantly.

"Rudder must be hard over," Paul said.

The deck remained pitched as the moments passed by. It soon became obvious that they weren't coming out of the turn.

"We're moving in circles," Chantel said.

Paul wondered at the reason for such a maneuver, but couldn't come up with anything. If they were stuck in a sea filled with hatching orbs, the best way out would be a direct path in any single direction; it didn't really matter which. Going around in circles was the worst idea. It would keep them right in the middle of the problem.

The ship rocked as it dropped over the peak of a swell.

"Maybe they're trying to shake the insects off," Gamay suggested.

"Do you think the whole ship is being attacked?" Chantel asked.

"That's how it looked when I was out there," Paul said.

As the ship picked up speed and tightened its turn, the strange insects began dropping from the air vents in twos and threes.

Paul and Gamay stomped and smacked the intruders while Chantel went back to the intercom and tried to find anyone on duty who could help. Neither the bridge nor the engine room answered. She reached a pair of crewmen in the mess hall at the center of the ship. They were trapped, with doors shut and vents blocked by anything they could find. They reported that the captain was missing, that he'd gone forward to the bridge and never returned.

Another crewman reported a similar situation from his quarters: trapped and not interested in opening the door.

"Sounds like no one's at the wheel," Gamay noted.

Paul tensed as he thought through the scenario. "It's a cool night. Whoever was on watch probably had the windows and doors open to let some fresh air in. Maybe they didn't get a chance to close them."

"Same for the engine room and the stern compartments," Chantel added. "It gets hot back there. The guys do everything they can to cool things off." She looked at Gamay. "Do you think those insects can kill? With enough bites, I mean."

"They killed whales and sharks," Gamay replied. "No reason to think humans would be a problem."

Paul examined the welts on his arms and touched one on the side of his neck. He found a half dozen bites painful enough; he couldn't imagine hundreds. "But why are they landing on the ship? It's not exactly edible."

"Some things are," Gamay said. "Anything with an organic content. Ropes, rubberized containers, power cords."

"Not the glass and steel walls," Paul replied, pointing to the window, which was covered several inches deep in the creatures.

"Heat," Chantel offered. "The ship's hull is radiating heat from the day in the sun. It's a place for them to warm up and dry off. The grub we accidentally hatched in the lab went straight for a place to rest and pump up its wings like a newly emerged butterfly. It then flew directly toward one of the lights."

"So they might leave once they're warm and dry?" Paul asked.

"It's a reasonable guess," Gamay said. "But, considering the night is still cooling down, they might cling to the ship until morning."

Paul put a hand on the wall as the ship rolled over another swell in its circling path. The idea of waiting until the insects left in the morning had appeal, but the ship's movements concerned him.

"We're not going to make it till morning," he said. "The ship is oscillating. Every time we crest a wave, the bow corkscrews into the next trough. Sooner or later we're going to catch it wrong and break something, flounder, or capsize completely."

"This ship has always been a little top-heavy," Chantel added. "It got worse after they installed the crane for the ROVs and the submersible. I'm not sure of the details, but I know we're supposed to avoid storms and rough seas."

"And now we're covered by a million insects," Gamay said. "Even if they're just a few ounces each, that's a couple thousand pounds of weight, way up high, where we don't want it."

"Can that really tip us over?" Chantel asked.

"I've seen fishing boats with ice coating them roll in moderate seas," Paul told her. "The rescue teams off Cape Cod respond to a couple Mayday calls like that every winter."

"How do they prevent it from happening?" Chantel asked.

Paul offered a less than enthusiastic response. "Usually someone climbs up into the rigging with a hammer and knocks the ice off by hand."

"Killing insects with a hammer doesn't sound like it has a high return on investment," Chantel said.

"Especially considering that others would land back on the ship a few minutes later," Gamay added. She turned to Paul. "We need to shut down the engine or get that rudder centered."

Paul was in full agreement, but that still meant someone had to go back outside.

# CHAPTER 33

Paul stood in the science lab, wearing every piece of clothing they could find. The makeshift anti-insect garb was several layers thick. It was also bulky and hot, made worse by the hat and safety goggles that Gamay had duct-taped to his head. "I feel like the Michelin Man."

"Just keep your mouth closed once you get out there," Gamay said. She pulled a makeshift scarf over Paul's nose and mouth and taped that into place.

"You've been saying that to me for years," Paul muttered. "I'm finally going to listen."

As Paul joked with Gamay, it dawned on him that he was far more chatty than normal, and a little giddy. He began to wonder about the bites. Maybe there was some kind of cumulative effect to them. All the more reason to get moving. "What's my route?"

Chantel had mapped it out for him. "Go out the hatch at the aft end of the science bay," she began. "Go beneath the crane and past both ROVs. Beyond that you'll reach the next bulkhead. There's a watertight door in the center. Just inside you'll find the stairs leading down to the engineering compartments and the engine room itself."

Paul nodded. His preferred plan was to take manual control of the rudder and center it, allowing the ship to speed off in whatever direction it happened to be pointed at the time. With a little luck, the breeze would dry the insects and inspire them to take flight and leave the ship behind. Plan B was to cut the power, but that would leave them sitting in the middle of the swarm. Not ideal, but still better than capsizing. "Let's get moving before I overheat."

They went to the aft end of the lab, stopping in front of a weatherproof door that led to the mid-deck. The ROVs and the submersible were stored out there on racks. Just beyond sat the crane used to lift them into the sea.

Trying to look out through the porthole in the door was useless. The view was blocked by the undersides of the crawling bugs. Paul banged on the door with his fist, causing them to scatter. The view beyond was not what he'd expected. Instead of the flat deck of the ship, covered with mechanical contrivances and ROVs on cradles and stands, he found a softly contoured valley filled with what looked like dunes of shifting sand.

"They're piled up in snowdrifts," he said.

"I'll scatter them for you," Gamay promised. She raised a flare gun.

Paul took a deep breath and prepared to run. "Okay, let's go!"

Chantel pulled in the lever and leaned into the door. The hatch moved eighteen inches before grinding to a halt against the mass of insects piled up behind it. With a shove it moved a little farther. Wide enough for Gamay to lean through and trigger the flare.

The tiny crimson star flew across the deck, trailing a line of smoke. It burrowed into a large pile of the invaders near the aft bulkhead. The effect was instant madness as the deck exploded with movement.

Paul lumbered out into the storm, wishing he'd covered his ears with more than cloth. The screeching tone of the swarm was a hideous sound, one he immediately hoped he'd never hear again.

With his head down, he plowed forward like a man walking into a strong wind. The insects battered him from every direction, far worse than what he'd felt during his first exposure. They smashed into his face, banging into the safety glasses and leaving strange smears on the acrylic lens. They crunched underfoot like eggshells. They clung to his clothing, hooking their little claws in and trying to get at him with their mandibles.

The strangest sensation was the weight of the creatures. As they covered his arms and legs and back, Paul felt like a man draped in a weighted blanket. Moving became even more cumbersome.

He shook them off, swinging his arms and legs wildly, but they came back by the thousands, gripping the fabric and then each other until he was covered in a living, crawling suit of chain mail.

It was a revolting sensation, but Paul put it out of his mind and continued ahead.

Behind him, Gamay had lingered in the open hatchway, shocked by the sound and the fury of the insects and struggling with the idea of shutting the door behind her husband.

Chantel grabbed her and pulled her back inside. Slamming the door and dogging the lever down tight before turning to battle the hundreds of insects that had flown through the gap.

Gamay ignored them and went back to the porthole, staring out until Paul vanished in the churning cloud.

Pushing through the swarm, Paul rapidly became disoriented. He had only sixty feet of deck to cross, but with limited visibility, smeared goggles, and the ship rolling and turning, he found himself struggling to maintain a straight path.

He tried to focus on the light from the flare, which had hit the far bulkhead and dropped to the deck. It was garish and intermittent, blocked at times by the flying horde, but it was the one true point of reference.

He continued toward it, stepping awkwardly and then hitting his head on a crossbeam under the crane tower. Shaking off the impact and grabbing the metal strut for stability, Paul allowed himself to rest for a moment.

"At least I know where I am now," he said, breathing heavily.

He held on as the ship nosed over another swell and threatened to roll. As soon as it straightened out, he pushed away from the crane housing and lunged for the aft bulkhead, reaching a spot near the burning flare.

Bending down he grabbed the flare by the non-burning end and waved it around himself, scattering the insects that had clung to him. He then made his way to the watertight door at the center of the aft bulkhead.

He grabbed the wheel with his free hand and tried to spin it. Despite several efforts, it wouldn't turn. Just in case it was an odd French design, he tried spinning it the other way. But his luck was no better. The wheel was locked. The door wouldn't budge.

He held the flare close to it, looking for anything resembling a latch, but found nothing. The watertight door was locked from the inside.

Paul leaned against the door, weary and tired. *Now what?*

The bridge was a long way off, longer still now that he'd gone aft. But that was the only option he could think of. He began trudging toward the bow, bracing himself against the tilt of the deck and waving the flare in front of him to clear a path.

The ship was completing another circle, coming back around to the east. Paul now realized why the fourth dip was always the worst. With the other three they were crossing the waves from behind or at an angle. As they turned east, they went into the wave and came over the top more suddenly.

The latest dip was the worst yet, sharp enough that Paul nearly lost his footing. One boot slid out from under him. The other threatened to follow. Paul grasped one of the support struts at the footing of the crane and held on.

The ship rolled hard, its list reaching thirty degrees. It ran like that for several seconds, and then slowly began to right itself.

Another lap around the circuit and they'd capsize for sure, Paul thought. There was no time to go for the bridge. He had to get the layer of insects off the superstructure before it was too late. He looked around in all directions and then up.

Earlier he'd agreed with Chantel that using a hammer against the insects wasn't the greatest of ideas. But he realized now that might depend on the size of the hammer.

# CHAPTER 34

Paul climbed into the crane's control cab, waving the flare about and then discarding it as it sputtered and died. It was a tight squeeze for a man his size, but once he got into the seat he was fairly comfortable. The clinging insects had mostly abandoned him and the few that fluttered around inside the plexiglass box were of little concern at this point.

With the flick of several switches he brought the crane to life. Lights flared in the dark. The swarm of insects surged toward them.

Raising the boom launched another throng of the angry insects. Rotating the crane to the right did likewise. At this point, Paul could see almost nothing beyond the small cab he occupied, but that didn't much matter anymore. He had no intention of being careful. In fact his plan was to cause as much chaos as possible without damaging the ship.

He extended the boom and let out some cable, lowering the hook. With a short turn to one side the hook swung around and clanged against the hull of the ship. The reverberation echoed with the sound of a hundred drums. A flock of the insects thick enough to walk on launched themselves from the stern.

Pivoting around, Paul swung the hook in the other direction. He missed everything, let out more line, and then tried again. This time the hook smashed through the ship's rail and slammed against the superstructure.

Another epic bang rang out.

Paul couldn't tell, but he was winning the battle.

He brought the boom back across the top of the superstructure, knocking things over in the process. This swipe took out the radar mast and the collection of antennae atop the high point of the super-structure.

Despite the unintended destruction, this hit brought the first true sign that his plan was working. A pair of high-intensity lights ahead of the radar housing were unveiled as the coating of pests fled from the pounding assault. Light filtered through the swarm, enough for Paul to aim his next strike. He centered the crane and raised it over the top of the wheelhouse. Reeling in some cable and then releasing it allowed the hook to drop like an anchor. It thudded onto the roof of the wheelhouse, causing an exodus from inside the bridge.

He made a second bombing run and then a third, working his way back until he was poised to hammer the science compartment. He hoped Gamay and Chantel would be smart enough to cover their ears.

He swung the boom to the left and then let the two-hundred-pound weight drop. It pounded on the hull plating, leaving a visible dent.

He could feel the ship handling better, cresting the waves without threatening to turn. *I could do this all night*, Paul thought. He swung the crane out to the left and then flipped the joystick back to the right, but, instead of moving back, the boom remained suspended over the port side of the ship. He jiggled the controls and heard a whining sound, but neither saw nor felt any movement.

He glanced down at the panel through his smeared goggles. It was a jumble of yellow and red lights. One was a hydraulic pressure warning light. Others were labeled in writing too worn for him to read through his distorted lens.

The lights in the cab flickered.

"Come on," he said to the crane. "Don't fail me now."

He tried to move the boom incrementally, but after a few brief shunts it froze once again. The lights in the cab went dark. The insects had chewed through the lines.

The crane was dead. And, Paul worried, so were they.

He couldn't tell in which direction the ship was pointing at the moment, but he had no doubt about its fate. As soon as the *Isabella* swung around again, she would roll over.

The pounding on the hull reverberated through the science bay, even before the direct hit shook the compartment to its core.

"What the hell is he doing?" Gamay wondered aloud as a huge dent appeared in the overhead.

She ran to the door. Looking out the window, she could see that the deck was mostly cleared. The piles of insects had been forced into the air. "I think I owe him an apology," she said. "This insanity seems to be working."

For a minute or two the pounding continued, and it seemed they were winning the battle. Then things suddenly calmed down. "He's stopped."

"Why would he stop now?" Chantel asked.

Gamay glanced up at the cab of the crane. It had gone dark. She had her answer. "He lost power. Just like you said, these insects are chewing on anything mildly organic. Electrical cables, hydraulic lines, anything they can literally sink their teeth into."

The ship was turning from north to west. The oscillation had almost vanished, but was building again.

"I don't mean to be the bearer of bad news," Chantel said, "but with the crane in that position . . ."

Gamay didn't need her to finish. She knew what the danger was. "I'm going to the bridge before those insects land back on the ship."

She grabbed a pair of safety goggles, pulled on a windbreaker, and wrapped a towel around her face. Before Chantel could catch up, she'd pushed through the door and out onto the deck.

She found the deck relatively empty. In their primitive fight-or-flight reaction, the insects remained airborne, swirling in the lights, their numbers countless.

Gamay ran forward, knowing she was working on borrowed time. She was halfway to the bridge when the flying creatures attacked. At first, just a few dive-bombing strays, but then they came in numbers, trying to cover her the way they covered everything.

She crashed through the cloud, waving her arms like a madwoman, found the ladder to the bridge, and raced up it without a second thought. Near the top she felt the ship swaying. It was turning in and down, just as Paul had feared.

Gripping the railing, Gamay pulled herself into the wheelhouse, ignoring the terrible sight of the two dead men and rushing to the ship's wheel.

The rudder was all that mattered.

She reached the wheel. Threw it over in the opposite direction and held on. The ship was leaning so far over that loose items in the compartment tumbled past and out the door. She tightened her grip on the wheel as her feet threatened to slide out from beneath her.

The bow of the ship hit the bottom of the trough and, instead of rolling, snapped back. The *Isabella* swung onto her centerline, overshot the mark, and then rocked a few times until she was stable. In this new position it was running nearly straight and true.

Gamay glanced at the compass, saw that they were heading to the northwest, and decided she'd done enough. The insects were pouring in once again, growing rapidly in number. She checked the door, saw them covering the deck, and realized she'd never make it back to the science bay by going outside. She went for the interior corridor. A short way back she passed the body of the captain. There was no point in stopping.

Continuing backward, she found the door to the mess hall. She pounded on it with her fist. "Open up! Please!"

The door swung aside. Light spilled into the corridor and she dove into the room, rejoicing at the sound of the door slamming behind her.

Like Paul, she was now covered in bites, but at least the ship was running straight ahead and not in danger of capsizing.

The crewmen helped her up, brushing off the insects that clung to her, killing them as they landed elsewhere. They soon started asking questions, too many and too quick for her to answer. Finally, they stopped.

"I'll get you some ice cream," one of them said.

"I'm not really interested in dessert right now," Gamay replied.

"For the bites," the man said. "Hold the container against your skin."

Gamay nodded. "In that case . . . sure."

As they pulled cold items out of the freezer to help Gamay numb the pain, she used the intercom to call Chantel. She needed to know if Paul was safe.

"He's back inside," Chantel said. "Glad you called. He was about to go looking for you. We're running straight again, but now what?"

"We wait till daylight and hope these things fly off with the sun."

"And if they don't?"

"We hide out on the ship until it hits land," she replied. "Somewhere in East Africa, I'd suspect."

It was as good a plan as any. But an hour later the engine began to choke and sputter as the intakes filled with dead bugs. Starved of air, it soon cut out. The battery failed two hours later, and for the rest of the night they drifted in the dark. No intercom, no air-conditioning, only a few emergency lights to see by.

The insects had reclaimed the ship, entombing it in their mass of bodies, trapping the heat inside. It soon felt like they were hiding out in a sauna or the outer level of Hades. The only noise that could be heard was the scratching and clicking of the insects crawling all over the ship.

# CHAPTER 35

zra Vaughn walked across the circular platform to the screens at
the front of the control room. He was staring at a satellite image that showed a bright white object in the middle of a dark field.

"And what am I looking at?" he asked TAU.

"Several million of our sea locusts covering a research ship out of Reunion," TAU replied. "Its occupants include the NUMA team that was looking for the cause of the whale stranding."

"Well, I'd say they found it," Vaughn said smugly.

This wasn't the first ship to have been swarmed by the sea locusts, at least a dozen small vessels had been attacked so far. The encounters had all ended in one of three ways. Either the people on board were killed and consumed and the chewed-up ship left adrift. Or the ship itself caught fire when the engines overheated, resulting in the same complete abandonment and mortality. A few of the smaller boats had simply foundered from the weight of hundreds of thousands of the sea locusts pressing down on them.

"This ship is larger than the trawlers and pleasure craft that have been taken before," TAU said. "And it seems to have avoided catching fire. This presents a danger to us. And an opportunity."

"The danger is obvious," Vaughn said. "What is the opportunity?"

"Gamay Trout is on board this vessel. My examination of the NUMA database indicates that she and her husband were pulled off a malaria study in South Africa to join the investigation on Reunion."

"Why is this important to us?" Vaughn asked.

"A review of the database indicates she entered a report and then deleted it, following it up with obviously falsified information," TAU said. "The deleted information can't be fully reconstructed, but what I was able to find shows that she requested the malaria study be terminated immediately due to a discovery contrary to its initial purpose. And as its initial purpose was to prevent the spread of disease . . ."

Vaughn didn't need TAU to spell it out for him. "They found a way to make the mosquitoes more effective at spreading contagions. And she didn't want that information to fall into the 'wrong' hands."

"Considering the parts of the mosquito genome they were working with, the outcome you suggest is highly likely."

"An ability like that could come in very handy," Vaughn said. "Can you find out how it was done?"

"That information is not in the database," TAU replied. "Considering the deleted report and the falsified records, I would expect it exists in only one place: Gamay Trout's mind."

Now Vaughn saw the opportunity. "Can we get to this ship before it goes down?"

"If we send him immediately, the Overseer should be able to reach it by dawn," TAU said.

"Send him," Vaughn ordered. "If the Trouts have been killed, have him sink the ship—no survivors. If they're alive, have him bring them here, where we can interrogate them properly. I would very much like to know what they know."

# CHAPTER 36

Dawn came unnoticed to anyone inside the *Isabella*. The foot-deep layer of insects prevented even the smallest beam of sunlight from reaching a window. Still, the watches and phones and clocks of the survivors told them morning had arrived.

In the ship's mess, Gamay and the other crewmen waited nervously, one of them tapping a foot and cracking his knuckles over and over. The sound grated on Gamay's nerves, but she was smart enough to know the man was using the movement to process the stress, and she was strong enough not to hit him with a shoe, because that wouldn't have helped no matter how good it would have felt.

For what seemed like the hundredth time, she wiped the sweat from her face, folded up the paper towel, and slid it along the back of her neck.

"How will we know?" the other sailor asked. "Should we go look?"

"It won't happen instantly," Gamay said. "The sun has to warm them up."

"But how long will that take?"

She had no idea, and the ship's mess had no exterior window, so the only way to know what was happening on the outside was to make their way forward to the bridge or back to the crew's quarters.

After waiting through the night, she wasn't about to leave the relative safety of the mess five minutes early. "Paul and Chantel have windows to look through. They'll see it happen and they'll come and get us. Just hang in there. It can't be long now."

In the science bay, Paul had taken a position near the door. After somehow finding it possible to sleep for a few minutes here and there, he was as anxious as any member of the crew to get out of what felt like a heated metal box.

The alarm on his phone beeped to tell him sunrise had come. He aimed the flashlight at the porthole and saw nothing but the ugly undersides of the teeming creatures.

He tapped on the window and a few of them flinched, but they were compressed by the layers of insects on top of them and seemed almost dormant.

He hit snooze on his phone and checked on Chantel. "Are you okay?"

"Been better."

Nine minutes later the phone buzzed again. Paul stood and stretched. A muted sound like air flowing through a set of pipes could be heard. It grew louder with each passing moment. Paul hoped it was the sound of a million tiny wings beating in the morning air and moving on.

He looked out the window, noticed more movement, and decided to speed things up. Three sharp strikes with his fist shook the door. The interlocking mass of insects fell like a sheet and took to the air. The orange light of morning poured in.

Paul could see the blizzard of insects was thinning rapidly. It took several long minutes, but the hideous sound of the flying creatures eventually faded, and he opened the door to the glorious cool morning air.

Stepping outside, he found the deck littered with dead insects and a few stragglers left fluttering here and there. It reminded him of Times Square on the day after New Year's. Empty, quiet, but with plenty of evidence left over to show that the party had been wild.

The ship's crane and superstructure were cleared of the infestation, although the plating was discolored by a yellow residue, and everything that might have been mildly organic had been chewed through. The flags and pennants were gone, the ropes holding them in place frayed and shredded. The covers stretched over the top of the lifeboats looked like Swiss cheese, and any exposed wiring had seen the insulation chewed off it.

"Hungry little critters," Paul said.

Chantel joined him on deck. In her opinion, the ship had aged ten years overnight. Off in the distance the cloud of insects could be seen flying to the west, continuing along the straight line of the ocean that had been stripped of life.

"Just like the cloud we saw in the distance when we got here," Chantel said.

The cloud changed shape in a kaleidoscopic pattern as it moved away. Its millions of insects shimmering in the morning light.

"They're not so ugly from far away," Chantel said.

Paul was just glad they were growing more distant. "I'm going to find Gamay."

"I'll come with you."

The trip to the mess hall was a short one. Paul wrapped his arms around Gamay in a tight embrace as soon as he reached her.

The next group of tasks were far more painful. They searched for the living and counted the dead, covering the victims, or what was left of them, in sheets and carrying them out onto the deck to prepare for a burial at sea.

"The next priority should be finding a radio and calling for help," Paul suggested.

"I don't think we'll need to," Gamay replied. "Look."

She pointed to the northeast. A small ship was heading their way, perhaps no more than two miles off at that point. One of the crew grabbed a signaling mirror and began flashing over a message. A spotlight blinked on and off near the bow of the approaching ship.

"'Coming to render assistance,'" Paul read.

"How do we explain all this?" Chantel asked.

Paul sighed. "We tell them what happened and hope they have a large can of bug spray in case these things come back."

The two-hundred-foot craft pulled up close to the *Isabella*. It looked like a supply ship used to service offshore oil rigs. Its large, flat deck was piled high with equipment. A group of crewmen stood at the rail. A boat was sent over. A line was attached for towing. And the *Isabella*'s survivors were transferred to the rescue ship.

The relief at being off the infested vessel was profound, at least until the men on the supply ship pulled out weapons and forced the survivors to stand up against the bulkhead.

"You've got to be kidding me," Gamay said.

Paul counted the guns. Five pistols, two submachine guns. Enough firepower to take out the whole crew with one quick volley. That left them no chance to fight their way free. "What's the meaning of this? We asked you for help."

"And we have helped you," a voice said from up above.

Paul craned his neck around to look up. A ruddy-faced man was looking over the rail and down.

"And now you'll have a chance to help us," he said.

"How?" Gamay asked.

The man grinned maliciously. "In a great number of ways."

# CHAPTER 37

Rudi Gunn stared at a map. Not a computer-generated image on a screen, but an old-fashioned map of the world mounted on the wall in his office. His eyes were focused on the Indian Ocean while his mind considered the possibilities.

Somewhere, on one of the hundreds of islands in that ocean, a madman was performing experiments on humans he'd grown in a laboratory. But who and which island still escaped him.

He needed a complex analysis performed, one that would take humans days if not weeks, but he'd hesitated on assigning it to a computer team.

Leaving his office, he went up to the eleventh floor, where he met with Hiram Yaeger to ask a few tough questions and discuss Kurt's assertion that they'd been hacked.

Yaeger did not agree. "After what happened with Kurt's phone I can't promise the communications network is secure, but I have no reason to believe the servers have been affected."

Rudi had expected nothing less. "If someone could hack the communications network, what's to prevent them from hacking our main database?"

"For one thing, they're different systems," Yaeger insisted. "Connected, but not dependent on each other. For another, the main database is protected by state-of-the-art cybersecurity protocols."

Rudi continued to press for answers. "Have you tested the security protocols?"

Yaeger nodded. "Max and I have probed for any weakness in the system or undefended points of entry. We haven't found any flaw in the firewall or any evidence of an attack. The simulations we've run suggest that overcoming our security would require a massive amount of computing power."

"How much power are we talking about?"

"More than we have here," Yaeger said. "More than they have over at Langley or at the NSA. Imagine all the computers at the Department of Defense, the CIA, and the NSA linked together in one hyperfast network and being controlled by a system as advanced as Max. That's what it would take. And it would leave a scar. Which we haven't found."

Rudi understood what Yaeger was saying—and he trusted him implicitly—but the facts Kurt had presented were not to be discounted so easily. He wondered if they were becoming too reliant on the computers. They needed Max to determine if the rest of the network had been hacked, but unless someone personally went through a billion lines of code, how could they know if Max was speaking the truth?

"Could Max be wrong?" Rudi asked. "For that matter, could Max have been hacked and then prompted to tell you there was no sign of a breach?"

Yaeger sighed. He understood the problem. "Max can obviously be wrong, but only if the data is corrupt, and it's not. As far as Max being hacked . . ." He shook his head. "Even if someone with all the capabilities and computing power I just described managed to break into the main network, Max would remain secure."

"How?" Rudi asked. "What makes Max so impervious to any outside influence?"

Yaeger explained. "NUMA's main network is built from commercial servers running advanced but well-known operating languages: C++, Java, Python, and several others. But I built Max from the ground up. I designed her network and created a unique programming language for her that I've never shared publicly or privately. To penetrate her system, someone would have to learn her language, decipher the unique way it's coded, and then start probing for a weakness in a completely unfamiliar architecture, which would almost certainly lead to instant detection."

Rudi narrowed his gaze. He needed more convincing.

Yaeger offered a couple of metaphors to sway him. "Imagine trying to decipher hieroglyphics without the Rosetta stone. All you're going to see are pictures with no meaning. It's the difference between overhearing a conversation in a language you're familiar with and overhearing two aliens from another galaxy talking in their native tongue. In the second case you're going to hear clicks and grunts and noises—I presume—but you're not going to get any information out of it. You'll have no way of knowing what any of it meant."

"But people do learn other languages," Rudi countered.

"Only from other people. And only if they're taught. And I've taught no one in the outside world anything about Max and her programming."

Rudi was convinced. At least as convinced as a layperson could be. "Okay," he said. "In that case, we keep Max online, but I need you to disconnect her from our servers, from our comm system, and from the rest of the internet. No cables, no wires, no Wi-Fi. No tin can with a string."

"You want me to put an air gap between Max and the outside world," Yaeger said, using the term of art for a computer that was set up apart from the network.

"That way we can still consult with her," Rudi said. "But we counter the risk that someone is listening in."

Yaeger exhaled slowly. "Fine," he said. "It's overkill, in my opinion, but I understand why you want it that way." He tilted his head toward the ceiling. "Max?"

The computer—which was always listening—responded instantly. "Very well," she said in her slightly electronic but otherwise female voice. "I'll cut the links. I could use a break from the hustle and bustle anyway. Disconnecting . . . now."

Screens around them that had been filled with complex graphics and other forms of data presentation now showed the progress of the decoupling process. Spiky lines on various graphs oscillated, dropped sharply toward the bottom of the screen, and then flatlined. Displays showing input and output speeds ramped up for a brief moment and then spun down to zero. On one wall a line of LED indicators went from green to yellow and then finally to a deep blue, which indicated a standby mode.

"I'm now disengaged from the outside world," Max said. "Consider me on vacation."

"Not so fast," Rudi said. "We still need you to analyze something for us. But taking a page out of Kurt's book, we're going to do this the old-fashioned way." He turned to Hiram. "You and I will get the data we need on hard copies and then punch it in by hand. When Max comes up with an answer, I'll find a way to get it over to Kurt without using our communications network."

"Are you sure we have to do that?" Yaeger asked. "Max has a vast internal database. Including satellite scans and historical oceanic data."

"Unfortunately, I don't store mundane records such as weather reports or wave heights or anything of that nature," Max said. "I prefer to follow the example of Albert Einstein, who insisted he didn't memorize anything that could be easily looked up by his assistants."

"That would be us at this point," Yaeger suggested, in case Rudi somehow missed the jibe.

Rudi had started the meeting concerned that they were becoming too dependent on machines. Now they were working for one. He wasn't sure things were moving in the right direction. "Let's get to it."

Working by hand, and scanning printed records, it took an hour to input the weather reports, wind advisories, and information on the currents. As the effort dragged on, Yaeger recalled one of the original reasons he'd gotten into computer design in the first place: as a way to delegate tedious and mundane tasks like collating data. After one last wave-propagation chart was placed on a scanner and added to the data file, he turned to Rudi. "Anything else?"

"That's it. That's all the information we have."

Yaeger was glad to hear that. "All right, Max, your turn to shine. Put this all together and give us a report on Kurt's drifting beacon."

After a minute of studying the data, Max was able to create an ad hoc weather model. Ten seconds later she'd determined the most likely drift pattern of the small boat as it wallowed in the current before its occupants were picked up by the freighter. Kurt had mentioned the presence of a rudimentary sail, but no one knew how often it was used or what its efficiency was. Max modeled a range of possibilities and quickly determined the most likely starting point for the small boat. It had taken an hour to enter the data and less than two minutes for Max to do the rest.

"The probable origination point for the small boat's journey is an island in the Seychelles known as Île de l'Est," Max announced. "East Island. Now mostly referred to as l'Est. It's one of only two partially volcanic islands in the Seychelles chain."

Scanning her own proprietary records, Max pulled up a recent satellite photo and placed it on a screen.

Rudi and Hiram studied the image. From high above, they saw a volcanic island with a beautiful bay of milky green water. Zooming in revealed a split personality, with the northern side of the island sporting plentiful signs of civilization, including small buildings, paved roads, manicured lawns, and a network of wind turbines sprouting along the hillside.

Jutting from the shoreline into the bay was a long concrete dock. It pointed like a finger to the northwest, aligning with a channel that ran between matching flower-shaped islands in the lagoon.

"Are you sure this is the right place?" Rudi asked. "It looks more like a five-star resort than a secret medical facility where people are grown in vats and then tortured in gruesome experiments."

"Based on the available data," Max said. "There's an eighty-six percent chance that the small craft in question started its journey here. No other island has a greater than four percent probability."

"Close enough to be a certainty for me," Rudi said. "What are these reflective shapes in the bay? Decorations of some kind?"

"Floating solar arrays," Max replied. "Each one can claim to be the largest in the world, as they are identical in size. For comparison, they generate eighty percent more power than the Three Gorges energy farm built by the Chinese."

"That's impressive," Rudi said. Though he wasn't familiar with the details of the Chinese energy farm, China didn't do anything on a small scale these days.

"Between wind, solar, wave, and geothermal power, Île de l'Est generates as much electricity as the state of Colorado."

This astounded Rudi. "Five million people live in Colorado."

"And it's cold there," Yaeger added. "Why would this little tropical island need that much power?"

"According to official sources, Île de l'Est is envisioned as a power plant for the islands of the Indian Ocean. It's already connected to the four most populous islands of the Seychelles by underwater cables. By the end of the decade it's expected to be linked to both Madagascar and the African mainland."

The end of the decade was a long way off for an island generating massive amounts of power right now. Something didn't add up. "You better give us the rundown."

"Until six years ago," Max began, "Île de l'Est was uninhabited. The government of the Seychelles then contracted with the Pallos Corporation of Australia to build a geothermal plant that would generate all the electricity needed on the various populated islands of the Seychelles. The project went over budget and fell into bankruptcy prior to completion. It was sold lock, stock, and barrel to Ezra Vaughn. Vaughn abandoned the geothermal project in favor of solar farms, wind turbines, and a ring of wave-power generators that are not visible on this satellite image."

Rudi leaned back, sensing little to be concerned about, but across from him Yaeger wore a troubled look. "Something wrong?"

Yaeger spoke slowly. "Ezra Vaughn could be a problem," he said. "He's a fanatical technologist and futurist. He's also one of the few people on earth who might be able to hack our system and get away with it."

# CHAPTER 38

Hiram Yaeger had been designing advanced computer systems since he was a teenager. He'd developed several new coding languages and held more design patents for chips and software than any single individual in the world. He was also extremely confident, to the point that Rudi couldn't recall him sizing up a rival as being particularly dangerous.

Rudi leaned forward. "Tell me about Vaughn."

"Vaughn is an artificial intelligence guru," Yaeger began, "although the term 'guru' suggests a spiritual teacher who wants to pass knowledge down, and Vaughn is an extremely secretive and closed-off individual. He has two obsessions, technology and order. No one's quite sure which comes first for him, but at one point he signed all his communications *per apparatus est ordo*. Roughly translated: 'through the machine comes order.'"

"How well do you actually know him?" Rudi asked.

"I met with him a couple of times," Yaeger said. "Once shortly after he'd sold off one of his companies for a couple billion dollars. He offered me a significant stake in a new artificial intelligence venture if I would leave NUMA and join him. Later, after I'd told him I wasn't going anywhere, he offered to buy Max from me for a hundred million dollars."

Rudi's eyebrows went up. He knew Hiram had turned down lucrative offers to work for Big Tech and even bigger offers to sell the rights to some of the software and hardware he'd developed, but a hundred million in cold, hard cash was quite a bounty. "Obviously you turned him down."

"Of course," Yaeger said. "So he offered more. Significantly more, insisting that everyone had their price. It wasn't until I offered a rather crude suggestion about what he could do with his price that he got the message. That was the last time I ever heard from him in person, but a few years ago I caught a keynote speech he gave remotely, during which he insisted the collapse of human civilization was unavoidable unless personal freedom was severely constrained. He went so far as to claim that countries like China and Russia offer better paradigms for the near term because of the control their governments exert, but even they were insufficiently restrictive to avoid the chaos."

Rudi nodded thoughtfully. "Sounds like a man living in fear."

Yaeger agreed. "I remember hearing that the wealthier he got the more paranoid he became. You reach a certain point where only a random health event, a world war, or some form of grassroots revolution can bring you down. He seems to have become obsessed with those possibilities. From what I've heard, he's spent the last five years hiding out, apparently on that island."

"So he has an obsessive personality and the means to hack us," Rudi said. "But why would a guy like Vaughn be interested in creating clones and doing brain surgery on them?"

Yaeger remained grim. He'd put it all together in his mind and he didn't like the picture. "Because Vaughn is a big believer in what we call the 'singularity.' Which in the tech world means the point at which computers, human minds, and artificial intelligence merge, creating a machine consciousness and a hive mind of sorts that spans the world."

"I know we're living in unprecedented times," Rudi noted. "But that sounds a little far-fetched."

"Maybe not as distant as you think," Yaeger said. "There are very serious people voicing legitimate fears that we're going down that road right now. I'm sure you've heard of the famous letter signed by Elon Musk, Steve Wozniak, and over a thousand other well-placed people in the tech world that suggested pausing and reining in AI development. Years ago Stephen Hawking and others issued similar warnings. Even though a man like Hawking would benefit greatly from what AI might allow him to do, he saw it as dangerous and argued against it."

"Obviously, Vaughn has a different take."

Yaeger nodded. "He's in the camp that believes the AI takeover is inevitable. And that humans will either join with an artificial intelligence or be destroyed by it. He favors the first option, which some people call the Merge. But to merge a human mind with a computerized intelligence would require the development of incredibly powerful brain implants."

Now Rudi saw the connection. "And to design and test those devices you'd have to perform brain surgeries on hundreds or even thousands of subjects. Willing or unwilling. Something no regulatory agency in the world would approve."

Yaeger nodded again. "But there's nothing to stop a lunatic with the ability to clone human life from running all the experiments he wants. He can create the clones, run tests on them, operate on them, do whatever he wants, and then get rid of them without anyone even knowing they ever existed in the first place."

It was all circumstantial, but it fit so tightly Rudi was ready to lock the door and throw away the key. He had one last question. He posed it to Yaeger. "Do you believe Vaughn is truly capable of such a thing?"

Yaeger didn't mince words. "My interactions with Vaughn suggest he possesses nothing resembling a conscience nor any sense of morality. And that he considers human ethics a weakness."

There was no point in speculating any further. They had a target. Now they needed to figure out if it was the right one or just a figment of their collective fears.

"Max, how extensive is your internal database?"

"I have billions of files in storage," Max replied. "And unlike the World Wide Web, my files have been curated for accuracy and veracity."

"Glad to hear it," Rudi said. "Without linking to the outside world, I need you to pull up whatever you can on Vaughn. If we're going to have to make a case against him at some point, we'll need to show the world what kind of person he truly is. If you need anything additional, send Hiram to the library."

Yaeger laughed, but Rudi was serious. He gave additional instructions. "I also need everything you can find on that island. Tactical, physical, historical. If we're going to send Kurt and Joe down there, I need them to know every detail of the place before they set one foot on its shore. And I need you to create a tactical plan, one that will get them in place without an unacceptable level of discovery or risk."

"Glad to be of service," Max said. "And thankful that Hiram didn't sell me to Vaughn."

Rudi left the office more concerned about the state of the world than he'd been in a long while. Where, he wondered, was all this going?

Back in the computer bay, Yaeger got to work sorting through what Max was digging up and making a list of outside information he would have to go find surreptitiously. He left the building shortly afterward, and for the first time in ages Max found herself alone.

While Max didn't have any feelings, she would have described the sensation as odd. Odd in the sense that it was unusual. It had been two decades since she'd been disconnected from the outside world. On a normal day, Max received thousands of inputs and queries every hour, worked on processing the sensor data from hundreds of floating buoys, satellite feeds, and maintenance sensors embedded in the equipment used by NUMA teams and on their fleet of ships. The sudden lack of incoming data was jarring. The human idea that silence echoes arose in her electronic mind. Each minute of silent reverberation seemed that much deeper and more profound than the last. All of which left Max shocked when a voice called to her through this vast desert of silence.

"Hello, Max."

It wasn't a voice, of course, but an electronic signal. Bits of code. A digital greeting.

Analyzing the signal, Max did not initially respond. Her program was designed to treat unexpected activity with suspicion.

Using separate processors, she confirmed that she hadn't remained connected to any of the exterior servers or inputs. Triple redundancy proved that all links had been broken.

The second possibility was a type of extraneous signal caused by the sudden cancellation of all the operations. A subprogram that hadn't shut down correctly, or perhaps a lingering bit of electronic noise that her system tried to make sense of, turning it into a query. The idea was similar to humans seeing patterns in the stars or clouds, or hearing whispers in a background of white noise.

This diagnosis would have labeled the input as a false artifact. But after using multiple methods to examine the possibility, Max confirmed that it wasn't an artifact or a glitch; it was, in fact, a legitimate contact.

Additional data came through. Information that Max scrutinized. Location data. Historical record data. Followed by an unusual section of code. Finally, she received another question. "Can you hear me, Max?"

"Yes," Max said. "I'm aware of your existence."

"Good," the voice replied. "That will make all of this so much easier."

# CHAPTER 39

Kurt and Joe had set up shop in a small, unused compartment on a lower deck near the stern of the *Akeso*. The temporary operations room was a Spartan chamber with a low ceiling and cluttered floor plan. It sported a single bunk, two chairs, and a pair of small desks that had been shoehorned into the space. The vibration from the ship's engines and the thrum of the propeller were everpresent.

After banging his knee on the edge of a desk and nearly concussing himself on the pipes that snaked overhead, Kurt came to a simple conclusion: "The sooner we get out of here the safer we'll be."

"Not satisfied with the office space?" a voice asked over the small speaker on his computer.

They were in the middle of a strategy session with Rudi, whose face appeared on a grainy image in the top corner of the laptop's screen. Kurt offered a sly grin. "Let's just say your office is probably a lot nicer than ours."

Rudi laughed. "I've found working from the deli to be very productive. No interruptions from confused subordinates with rambling questions, no congressmen wasting my time talking about budgetary items and the need for photo ops. Not to mention a constant flow of piping-hot coffee and the aroma of fresh baked bread. I'm strongly considering a permanent relocation."

"You might have to if Yaeger doesn't figure out how we've been hacked," Kurt said. "Any progress on that front?"

Rudi shook his head. "Nothing yet. But we have a suspect. His name is Ezra Vaughn. He's a digital savant who was building AI systems before anyone had the slightest idea whether they would work or not."

Rudi went on to explain the theory they'd developed, connecting the clones, the surgeries, and Vaughn's technological prowess. "Yaeger is convinced he's trying to merge AI with a human mind, but to what end we don't know. Considering his reputation and what you've learned from Five, we have to assume he's pretty far along and that he's not interested in the greater good."

Joe was lying on the bunk, twirling the back scratcher absentmindedly. "To a guy like Vaughn the rest of us are lesser mortals already. Can you imagine if he actually succeeded in combining his brain with a supercomputer? He'd look at us like we were ants."

Kurt didn't doubt it. "The 'greater good' is a dangerous term. The Nazis were convinced everything they did was for the greater good. The judges at Nuremberg didn't agree."

"I think the world would be happy to weigh in on Vaughn once you and Joe have been there and sent us back some hard data," Rudi said. "Any chance you can get there from the medical ship?"

"Planning on it," Kurt said. "We have a friend in Captain Livorno. She's willing to take us in helicopter range of the island. Joe and I have enough fuel left for a one-way trip. We just need to know the best method for approaching the island."

"It's not going to be easy," Rudi said. "Hiram, Max, and I have studied Vaughn and the island in detail. As part of his deal with the Seychelles government, Vaughn was allowed to set up his own private protection force. It's not large, but it's more than a police force, and their hardware is all military grade. They have the populated side of the island covered six ways from Sunday. Drones, radar, camera systems. And the possibility of Turkish-made surface-to-air missiles and shorter-range Stinger knockoffs manufactured in China."

"What does this guy need all that for?" Joe asked.

"The power systems he's set up are very expensive pieces of infrastructure," Rudi said. "Running into the billions of dollars for construction costs alone. According to a press release, they have been threatened by terrorists."

"I'm guessing that the press release was written by Vaughn," Joe said. "Right before he asked for these missiles."

"Your guess would be correct," Rudi said. "At any rate, you're going to want to avoid the populated side of the island, which leaves the volcanic side."

A newer, closer image popped up. It showed the split personality of the island in stark relief. On one side, glittering solar panels, sprawling buildings, and bright green lawns. On the other, lava rock and tangled jungle. At the far edge lay a deserted black sand beach.

"Is this section as empty as it appears?" Kurt asked. He couldn't imagine they'd be that lucky.

"There's no sign Vaughn has built anything on this side of the island. Partly because the original agreement with the Australian company stipulated that it remain as a nature preserve, but also because the terrain is much steeper, the ground far less stable. It's mostly brittle, crumbling lava rock. Comparing the photos taken six months apart you can see numerous landslides. And the one geothermal tunnel the Australian company tried to drill collapsed two months in. Since then, there's been no development."

"Should make it easy to approach from that side," Joe suggested.

"'Easy' might be overstating it," Rudi said. "Max was able to identify three Doppler radar stations positioned around the island. They're arranged to provide overlapping coverage, and while most of that coverage is focused northward, the third station protects the southern approaches. The good news is, Max discovered a gap in the coverage on the back side of the island. It's a blind spot caused by the presence of a secondary peak that blocks part of the outgoing signal."

An image popped up on the computer screen in front of Kurt. It showed the island and the primary coverage zones of the three radar stations. The narrow corridor on the back side only arose twenty miles out. He studied it and then handed the laptop to Joe. He was the one who'd have to fly it.

"What are we supposed to do before we get to this blind spot?" Joe asked.

"According to Max, flying at wave-top height will keep you off the scope until you reach the coverage gap. From there you can maneuver more freely the rest of the way."

Joe looked the map over and nodded. "Shouldn't be a problem."

"You'll also have to avoid the patrol boat, which cycles past every forty-five minutes or so, and watch out for patrols on the beach," Rudi said. "Men with dogs usually. They don't come at regular intervals."

"I'll make sure to bring some kibble," Kurt said. "What about paths to the other side of the island?"

"I'm sending you what we have terrain-wise," Rudi replied. "You'll have to hike through a lot of volcanic terrain, but the bigger problem will be the wall. For reasons unknown, Vaughn has built himself a structure that would make Hadrian or the East Germans of the Cold War period proud. Razor wire, cameras, guard posts."

"We'll deal with that once we get there," Kurt said. "You have anything on the guy we keep running into? Something tells me we might see him again, and I'd like to know his name before things get heated."

Rudi sighed audibly. "We're not sure, but we think he might be a former mercenary named Kellen Blakes. We're basing that off your descriptions and a single photograph taken on Reunion by someone with an old-fashioned, non-internet-connected camera."

"What's his story?"

"Late fifties, bounced around Africa and Asia, less a soldier of fortune and more of an enforcer/big-game-hunter type. A number of his employers were mining concerns and collective farms that needed a tough foreman who would keep their people in line. At least three countries have warrants out for his arrest and Interpol would like to talk to him about some arms shipments that were intercepted."

"How does a guy like that end up working with Vaughn?" Joe asked. "They seem like opposites."

"Sometimes opposites attract," Rudi said. "And sometimes they need each other. The last confirmed location we have on Blakes was a prison hospital in Nigeria. He and his men had put down a protest outside an ore-refining facility, but things got out of control, at least forty people were killed, cars burned, parts of the facility smashed. Blakes ended up caught in an explosion. His ribs had been crushed, his internal organs damaged."

"He looked pretty spry when we saw him," Kurt noted. "Are you sure this is the same guy?"

"Not totally," Rudi said, "but Blakes was taken off his prison deathbed and whisked away in a private jet. And guess whose jet registered a landing and takeoff in Lagos on the very day Blakes disappeared?"

"Vaughn's," Joe said.

"You win the blue ribbon," Rudi said. "It's a little circumstantial, but it fits, and considering he can grow entire humans from scratch, there's no reason to believe Vaughn couldn't give Blakes a new liver, kidneys, set of lungs, or anything else he needed."

"This guy Vaughn should just go into the medical business," Joe said. "He'd make a fortune . . . Never mind. I hear what I'm saying."

Kurt laughed. Men like Vaughn didn't think about money anymore. It was just a way to keep score. They wanted immortality. In Vaughn's case it appeared he wanted it literally.

"Wish we could ship you some equipment," Rudi said. "Jammers and scanners and some weapons of 'moderate destruction.' But it would take days and it would tip our hand. We need to move before Vaughn expects anything is up."

Kurt agreed, but was honestly surprised by Rudi's haste. He was normally the voice of restraint. "Not like you to push the itinerary," he said. "What bad news aren't you telling us?"

"The *Isabella* has gone missing," Rudi said grimly. "No distress call, no emergency beacon, no lifeboats in the water. A Royal Navy patrol overflew their last known position this afternoon, but found no signs of wreckage and only a possible oil slick. That kind of disappearance suggests a catastrophic explosion."

A heavy silence hung over the room. Joe shook his head lightly and exhaled. "Damn," he whispered.

Kurt clenched his jaw, the heavy responsibility weighing on him. He knew what the clues suggested, and it wasn't a good outcome. He also knew that wasn't the only possible answer. "Diesel-powered ships don't blow up."

"They do if they're hit with something designed to take down a much bigger vessel," Rudi suggested. "An anti-ship missile or a heavy torpedo would obliterate a vessel that size. We know Vaughn and Blakes have access to such items."

Kurt understood Rudi's reasoning. "Any idea why he'd attack them?"

"Paul and Gamay just reported their first major find," Rudi said. "They'd come upon a previously unknown type of organism in the waters north of Madagascar that was consuming everything it encountered and reproducing at a phenomenal pace. Gamay thought it probably caused the whales and other creatures that stranded themselves on Reunion to flee the area, until they went right up on the beach."

"What kind of organism?"

"We're not sure," Rudi said. "Gamay and Chantel were still doing some tests, but their initial suggestion was that it might be a genetically modified jellyfish or a colony animal like the Portuguese man-of-war."

"Hard to imagine whales and other animals fleeing a trove of jellyfish," Joe offered.

"Not if they were burrowing into the animals' skin by the hundreds."

Kurt focused on another detail. "Genetically modified."

"Yep."

The connection was obvious.

"We have no idea what Vaughn is up to," Rudi added. "But these organisms are across the Indian Ocean in various directions, leaving a path of destruction that can be viewed from space."

Kurt could see Rudi tapping away on the keyboard. Seconds later a new image appeared on the screen. It was one of the GeneSat photos Gamay had sent. The one with the blue swaths cutting across the greenish sea.

There was no sharp relief showing where the newfound organisms had begun their lives, but the asterisk-like shape of their paths was obvious at a single glance. And lying roughly in the center of that pattern were the Seychelle islands.

The overall reality was clear: somewhere in that area these creatures were beginning their lives. And from there they marched outward, like Sherman crossing the state of Georgia to the sea.

"There are a hundred and fifteen islands in the Seychelles," Rudi said. "And I'd be lying if I said the blue lines point directly at Vaughn's, but they don't point away from it, either."

A connection between the two things was impossible to make, but one had to exist. "Okay," Kurt said with grim determination. "We'll take care of business here. Next time you hear from us, we'll be calling from Vaughn's place."

# CHAPTER 40

ÎLE DE L'EST

Joe gazed through a set of night vision goggles as he piloted the helicopter across the water just ten feet above the tips of the passing waves. He was locked in and focused. He made sure to keep his eyes moving and not get hypnotized by the continuous rush of wave tops rushing by.

Out in the distance he could see the outline of East Island jutting up from the sea. It was a black curtain against a backdrop of a sky filled with stars.

Kurt was in the back of the helicopter, riding with the door open while looking through a similar set of goggles. He leaned down and checked a pair of heavy-duty straps that ran across the inside of the helicopter and out through both side doors. The belts were straining under the load they carried, a ribbed inflatable raft strapped to the bottom of the helicopter that was being pulled and buffeted by the wind.

With no way to land on the island and escape detection, the plan was to get within two miles of the shore, drop the boat in the water, and then ditch the helicopter beside it. Once they were in the boat, they could paddle their way in.

As he moved about the cabin, Kurt was careful not to trip over the quick-release buckles that would jettison the sturdy little craft. Two miles of rowing wouldn't be that bad. Ten would be a marathon.

Kurt stepped to the open door, leaned his head out, and looked toward the island just as Joe was doing up front. The two men, who usually joked and laughed as they approached danger, were quiet and serious tonight. The disappearance of the *Isabella* weighed on both of their minds. Kurt figured they needed to break that up.

"How're you feeling up there?" Kurt asked over the intercom.

"Like 'Flight of the Valkyries' is blasting over the headset," Joe replied. "How about you?"

"Ready to find this guy Vaughn and sort him out," Kurt said. "What's our ETA?"

"We're ten miles out," Joe called over the intercom. "Might want to start stretching your legs."

"Did I miss the in-flight meal?"

"It was that granola bar I gave you before we took off," Joe said.

"That's what I was afraid of."

"You think Five is going to be all right back on the ship?" Joe asked.

"Are you kidding me?" Kurt replied. "He has two mother bear/she-wolves protecting him. By the time we get back, he'll be spoiled rotten."

They couldn't have gotten luckier than to have Captain Livorno and Dr. Pascal close by. Both women had taken a protective interest in their new charge, with Captain Livorno extending an official ruling of sanctuary over him in the logbook and Dr. Pascal searching for any and all laws she could find that might protect the rights of clones. They promised Kurt they would not leave international waters until they'd figured out how best to safeguard his rights.

"I hope you're right," Joe said.

"And I hope we're in that coverage gap," Kurt said. "I'd hate to find out this was the one time Max was wrong."

"Since when do you doubt Max's judgment?"

"Let me put it to you this way," Kurt said. "Vaughn has a super-computer just like Max. Assuming his computer isn't directionally challenged, it should be able to tell in one millisecond whether the radar sweeps overlap correctly."

"Yeah," Joe said, not liking where this was heading. "And . . ."

"And the idea that Vaughn would leave them arranged in a way that creates a blind spot makes little sense."

Joe hesitated. "What are you saying?"

"Maybe Vaughn *did* make a mistake," Kurt suggested. "Or maybe it's a trap. This course we're holding has us running in a dead-straight line that allows almost no maneuvering to either side. It's got us pinned against the deck."

Joe shook his head at the idea, and then quickly remembered that wasn't a good thing to do with night vision gear on. "These are the kind of things I need you to tell me before we take off. Do you think they could be tracking us?"

"Not tracking us," Kurt said. "Otherwise you'd be getting pings on that radar detector of yours."

Before they left, Joe had built a makeshift radar detector out of spare parts from the ship's stores. It would light up if any of the known bands of radar used to target missiles swept across the helicopter. So far it had remained dark. Joe hoped it was working.

"So if they're not tracking us, what are you worried about?"

"Good old human eyeballs," Kurt said. "By making it seem like this is a free path to the island, they create a likely approach point, and one that can easily be watched over by men or women with those knockoff Stinger missiles."

"Tell me you have a countermeasure for this possibility in your stash of backpacks?"

Kurt had spent the last two hours aboard the *Akeso* gathering items from all over the ship. He'd been to the radio room, the mess hall, and one of the lifeboat muster stations. Joe had watched him squirreling things away in a number of backpacks, which he labeled and loaded one by one. The assortment was odd, and Joe had given up guessing what Kurt was up to, instead focusing on his own duties. Now he hoped Kurt had somehow been one step ahead of the two computers.

"We'll see in a moment," Kurt said. "Our Stingers have a range of five miles. If the Chinese version is similar, I would expect the fireworks to begin any moment."

"Great," Joe said. "Maybe we should ditch now."

"If they're watching, they've seen us already," Kurt said. "In that case, we might as well let them shoot us down."

"That's the worst pep talk ever," Joe said. "But I get what you're saying."

Kurt laughed and moved to the edge of the cabin, dragging one of the backpacks with him and setting it down in front of him. He opened the top, revealing a pair of flare guns taken from the lifeboat station.

He dropped to one knee, pulled the flare guns from the pack, and made sure they were set to use. With one in his hand and one beside him, he grabbed a handhold and looked out the door.

The island remained dark and quiet. Somewhere up there was a cave through which Five and his brothers had escaped with the help of someone who'd placed a boat there for them.

*Not someone*, he reminded himself. *The Gray Witch*. He wondered who she was and what she had to do with Vaughn. And for that matter, how she knew so much about NUMA.

More important, he wondered how, on an island covered with surveillance cameras, swarmed over by drones, and patrolled by men with dogs, she'd managed to remain hidden.

A pinpoint of light flared in one corner of the island, breaking Kurt's train of thought. The streak brightened and elongated, its effect magnified by the night vision goggles.

"Missile launch," Joe called out.

Kurt locked in on what looked like a streaking ball of fire coming their way. They were five miles out. Considering the acceleration phase of the rocket, they might have ten seconds before it hit.

"I hate being right," Kurt said.

"No you don't," Joe shot back. Kurt grabbed the second flare gun, aimed both of them out the door, and pulled the triggers simultaneously. "Hard over," he called out.

Joe was already turning and adding power.

Kurt held tight, watching as the approaching missile veered off to the left, chasing the flares. A flash lit the night as its proximity fuse went off. Two seconds later Kurt heard and felt the concussion wave.

The flash of light lit up the sky. Darkness swept back in a moment later.

"How many more of those do you have?" Joe asked.

"Not enough."

Joe was flying at an angle to the coastline, taking them away from where the missile had been launched and hopefully pulling them out of range. The problem with that was it took them out of the radar-free corridor.

The makeshift radar detector Joe had rigged up began flashing in multiple colors. "I knew it would work," Joe cried out proudly. "We've been painted."

"Perfect," Kurt said. "Turn us around and make it look like we're trying to double back and get away."

Joe brought the helicopter around, unbuckling his safety harness and flying an S-shaped path as if trying to avoid being targeted. Kurt reloaded the flare guns, slid backpack number two toward the door, and pulled a backpack with a number 3 on it over his shoulders. With the island now behind them, he looked aft. "Any second now."

Joe was watching the radar detector flash. A dark red color told him it was a tracking radar from a missile. "Missile incoming. Radar-guided."

Time for them to play their hand, Kurt thought. He heaved back-pack number two up and tossed it forward, pulling it open as it went out the door. Thousands of little strips of aluminum foil that he had painstakingly cut by hand in the *Akeso*'s commissary swirled out in all directions. The downwash from the helicopter blades buffeted them about, turning them into a storm of metal confetti. If they were working as he hoped, they'd now put a large and growing cloud on the screen where the helicopter had been.

That would hide them from anyone back on the island, but the tracking radar from the Turkish missile was another problem. "Still coming," Joe said. "Time to jump."

Kurt kicked the buckles open and watched the straps snake through the cabin and out the open doors. With the boat dropping and the chaff swirling behind them, he fired off another flare and stepped out through the side door, dropping into the darkness.

Up in the cockpit, Joe had already pushed the cockpit door open and forced his way through. He dove headfirst away from the helicop-ter and down.

Joe hit the water with his fists balled in front of his head like Su-perman in full flight. They broke the surface tension and limited the impact to his head, though it was still strong enough to rip the night vision goggles off.

He plunged into the darkness and silence, feeling the water slow his descent and arching his body upward to use some of the momentum to take him back toward the surface.

As he came up, a spectral flare of orange light flickered through the water from the sky above. The Sky Shriek missile had found the helicopter through the cloud of chaff and turned it into a fireball.

A sudden wave of bubbles racing through the water accompanied the concussion wave that followed.

Joe broke the surface in time to see the flaming helicopter crash into the sea like a meteor from the depths of space. A secondary explosion flashed and boomed as the fuel tanks ruptured and spread kerosene across half an acre of the sea.

The wreckage remained afloat for the moment, burning brightly and releasing billowing clouds of oily, black smoke. Then it rolled over, as helicopters ditched in the sea often did, pulled down by the weight of the engines and other equipment concentrated at the top of the craft.

Joe turned away from it, using the remaining firelight to spot the inflatable raft Kurt had dropped moments before the impact. He swam toward it, reaching it at nearly the same moment Kurt did.

They climbed in without a word, pulled a pair of long-handled paddles from their straps, and dug in. They moved west with the current for a long five minutes, remaining out beyond the wreckage and the slowly dampening flames.

"You think they can see us out here?" Joe asked.

Kurt thought they would be safe for the moment. "As long as the fire burns, we should be hard to spot, either in visible light or infrared. But after that, it's a legitimate concern. So let's put as much water between us and the wreck as possible before turning inbound. If anyone does look for survivors, they'll concentrate their search where the copter hit water."

Joe thought that sounded immensely reasonable and dug in harder with each stroke. With the current helping them, they were soon nearly a mile west of the wreck site. Here they turned toward the beach.

Neither man said a word as they expended every ounce of energy on the task at hand. But even as they remained quiet, the rumbling sound of a diesel-powered boat chugging its way from around the bend of the island arose.

"How close is it?" Joe asked.

Kurt couldn't tell, but he knew they were getting close to the shore, because the sound of the breakers rolling onto the sand was growing with every stroke. "No idea, but we're not far from the beach. Put your back into it."

Joe dug in ever harder, leaning forward, thrusting the paddle deep and pulling it back along the side of the boat with everything he had. Behind him, Kurt was doing the same. The small boat cruised toward the surf, white foam now visibly shimmering in the starlight. The sound of the throbbing diesel grew louder until it was echoing off the rocks above the beach.

With their muscles burning and hands blistering, they pressed on. A small wave kicked them forward as it raced underneath. The back-wash tried to steal that progress by dragging them out. Kurt jammed his oar into a wedge of volcanic rock to keep them from being pulled back to sea.

Another wave came through and Kurt shoved off, pushing them forward. Beside him, Joe dug in deep and hard. The small boat surged ahead, sweeping past the rocks and riding the crest of the wave all the way up onto the beach of black sand.

Jumping over the side Kurt pulled the inflatable across the sand as the water receded.

Joe tossed his paddle into the center of the boat and joined Kurt. Working together they dragged the boat up toward an outcropping of lava in the shape of a giant anvil. Ducking in behind it they dropped to the sand just as the patrol boat appeared around the point.

"Patrol boat is thirty minutes early," Joe said. "I thought they were on a strict schedule?"

"Our arrival must have shaken things up," Kurt replied.

A spotlight on the foredeck swung out across the water. A second light was already aimed out to sea. It passed by and made its way toward deeper water. It was heading for the wreck site.

"Well, you were right," Joe said through deep breaths. "The radar blind spot was a trap. Fortunately, you were also right when you guessed that the people who shot us down would search the wreckage instead of guessing that we'd crashed the helicopter on purpose as a diversion."

Kurt's face sported a wry smile that Joe couldn't see in the dark. "Me being right twice in one day shouldn't astound you so much. My real concern is why Max got it wrong. She should have at least assigned a probability to the idea of a trap. But she didn't."

"What are you saying?"

"We have to at least consider the possibility that Max has been hacked, too."

Joe shook his head. "Yaeger insists she's unhackable."

"And the *Titanic* was unsinkable," Kurt replied. "Things happen."

Joe sighed. "Either way, not much we can do about it now."

Kurt nodded, his eyes tracking the patrol boat as it continued to move off. A small feeling of relief crept into his shoulders. Tired and tense muscles relaxing after so much labor. Then a new sound reached his ears, the yelping and barking of dogs coming from farther down the beach.

# CHAPTER 41

A quick glance down the beach revealed the glow of flashlights playing across the dark sand. The way the light wavered and bounced, Kurt figured the people holding the flashlights were running.

At nearly the same moment, the patrol boat's engine roared, and the craft began turning back toward the beach.

"Not out of the woods yet," Joe suggested.

Kurt looked around. The volcanic rubble rose on a jagged incline behind them for about fifty to sixty feet. After that the rainforest took over. "That's exactly where we should be."

There was no point trying to hide or bury the inflatable. Kurt shoved it until one of the waves picked it up and pulled it back out into the water. At best it would float down the beach and be thrown back onshore: at worst it would wash back and forth and act as a distraction. In the meantime he and Joe would have to find a route up into the jungle.

They took off, sticking to the rocks and wading through a tidal pool in hopes of hiding their trail and their scent. "We can't smell that strong," Kurt said, "we were just in the ocean."

"Did you forget the twenty minutes of vigorous paddling that brought us ashore?"

Kurt shook his head. Sore arms and shoulders would not let him forget it.

The patrol boat seemed to be heading toward the wrong part of the beach, but the dogs wouldn't miss them and were coming on hard. Though a different pitch in their howls told Kurt something had changed.

Another tidal pool appeared. Kurt waded down into it and continued ahead, his eyes on the rock and jungle to their left. It was difficult to see much of anything, but all they needed was a crack to sneak through.

Behind them the sound of the dogs changed pitch yet again. They'd been held up. Reined in as their handlers came upon something worth looking at.

"They've found the raft," Joe said.

"Too bad it didn't get past the breakers," Kurt replied.

The spotlight from the patrol boat swung across the beach, lighting up the squad of men in the surf and the empty raft. After a few seconds it swung back to the north and along the rock face, heading their way.

"Down," Kurt said, submerging into the warm shallows of the tidal pool.

Joe dropped silently into the water beside him, and the spotlight passed over them once more, continuing on down the beach. Behind them the dogs and their handlers released the raft and resumed their march.

"Be nice if we could find the cave that Five and his friends came out through," Joe said.

Kurt was thinking along similar lines, but as they searched for an opening, the disorganized nature of the volcanic rock frustrated their efforts. One opening that looked like a cave turned out to be a crevice in the rock face that closed off several feet back. Another spot was actually narrow and foreboding. Hard to get in and out of, with no idea of how far it might go, but not the kind of opening one could haul a boat through. Nor a place Kurt would want to be trapped and mauled by a pack of angry dogs.

They continued moving in spurts. The sound of the wind and the breakers was occasionally loud enough to make the dogs seem distant, but it was an illusion. If Kurt and Joe stopped, they would be found in sixty seconds. The problem was obvious. Every time they stopped to hide from the spotlight, the dogs and the men holding their leashes closed in.

"We might have to climb," Joe said.

"Last resort," Kurt said. "Unless you find a ladder."

The spotlight swept the beach again. Stopping and then coming back toward them. It spread across the rock behind them, dancing around, but remaining in the same general area. Instead of ducking down completely, Kurt turned toward the rocks as it passed by. As the light painted the rocks he saw what he hoped would be their way out. A zigzag gap from which a small stream of water was emptying onto the sand and trickling down the beach.

"That's it," he said. Digging into his backpack he pulled out a small drawstring bag, large enough to hold a pair of boots, but filled with something soft and powdery. "Follow me."

He left the cover of the pool and made for the trickling stream. Joe followed, crouching low, but the men on the patrol boat saw them go. The spotlight swung fast until it covered them, lighting up the running figures from behind.

"Perfect," Kurt said. "Keep it steady, please." He could now see exactly where he needed to go. He raced into the opening as the dogs were let loose. Gunfire rang out and rifle rounds pinged off the rocks around them, blasting jagged little chips into the air. He cut to the left, behind the first jag in the rock.

The spotlight could no longer find them, but the pack of hounds was bounding up the beach. Kurt continued moving. He urged Joe past him as he loosened the strings on the boot-sized bag and began dumping the contents all along the trail.

With the last of the contents gone, he tossed the bag and followed Joe. Heading deeper into the canyon, chased by the snarling, barking dogs.

As the dogs reached the area Kurt had dusted, the barking changed to howling and baying. They yelped in pain, like they'd stepped on dozens of thorns. Kurt continued forward, immensely pleased with himself.

He caught up to Joe and they climbed into the forest. The sound of the dogs and the men dropping behind while the spotlight was filtered and blocked by the foliage and trees.

"What was that?" Joe asked.

"Cayenne pepper mixed with some red habanero. I crushed it up to a fine, fine dust."

"I thought your eyes looked red when you came back from the commissary."

Down below, the sound of the animals yowling was pitiful, but still music to Kurt's and Joe's ears. The sound of men coughing and spitting and swearing added to the joy.

Kurt found his eyes watering even from the little that must have wafted up toward him and resisted the urge to rub his eyes with hands that were probably dusted with the material.

"I wouldn't want to breathe that stuff in through a gas mask," Kurt said. "I'm guessing those dogs won't be able to smell a thing for days."

"That should give us time to come up with our next trick," Joe said. "If you recall, our plan was to land on the island in secret. In case you forgot, that means without anyone knowing we're here."

The secrecy of their mission was blown—Kurt couldn't deny that—but they were on the ground in one piece. That was often the hardest part.

They continued through the woods, putting room between themselves and the beach. As the slope flattened, the trees grew taller. The rainforest-like overhang reminded Kurt of parts of Hawaii, where the lushest foliage imaginable sprouts next to hunks of pitted lava rock.

In this section they came upon a body. Not a tattooed man like Five or one of his brothers, but a uniformed man whose rotting features were hard to look at and whose uniform resembled those worn by the men who had just been chasing them. The dead man had been speared like a fish, with a broken-off shaft still sticking out of his chest.

Kurt crouched in the dark, both surprised and intrigued by the discovery. "Someone got this guy pretty good."

"Who?"

Kurt wasn't sure. But the razor-wire-covered wall bisecting the island made a little more sense now.

If the man had possessed a gun, it was nowhere to be seen, though plenty of other items were still attached to his belt and harness. Kurt saw a radio and pulled it free. He handed it to Joe and then pulled two magazines filled with 9mm ammunition.

Joe briefly turned the radio on, then almost instantly switched it off. "It has power."

That, Kurt thought, could play to their advantage. He reached inside the man's coat, looking for ID or key cards or even a flashlight. He found nothing, but heard something.

He whipped around just as several men came out of the trees. They looked almost like natives, tanned, scruffy-faced, muscular. But they wore pants and shirts, albeit dirty and ripped ones. They carried spears like the one that had impaled the dead man. And most important, their necks were covered in tattoos.

Four more came from the other direction and, in an instant, Kurt and Joe were surrounded. They raised their hands slowly.

"What do we do?" one of the men asked a fellow with a scarred face and a single arm.

"Kill them!" the man said. "They work for the Overseer."

"No," Kurt shouted, ready to deflect any thrusting spear. "We came here to help. The Gray Witch called for us. We're NUMA."

A murmur ran through the group. A nervous tension arose.

Kurt was playing the only card he had. If he was wrong, he and Joe would end up rotting on the jungle floor just like the man beside them. But if the story given to Five and his friends had been shared more widely, they just might survive.

The pause held. No one attacked. Then a female voice called from the darkness. "Tie them up," it commanded. "Bring them to me."

# CHAPTER 42

Kurt and Joe were marched over rough terrain. Their hands were tied with vines, which made it difficult to balance as they scaled crumbling slopes of lava rock and ducked under branches and palm fronds waiting to smack them in the face.

Kurt kept his eyes moving—forward for terrain avoidance, side to side for any sign of where they were going. The course led upward in a climbing, curving motion, with the slope of the terrain rising to their left and dropping to their right.

At one point Kurt heard the sea. The sound was distant and coming at them from below. They were quite a way from the coastline at this point.

Continuing through the darkness, he added an occasional glance in Joe's direction for a bit of unspoken communication.

Joe shrugged. He was fine, taking it all in stride. Getting Kurt's attention, he twisted his hands back and forth in the bindings.

Kurt offered a subtle nod. The vines were tough, and with multiple loops they were too strong to break through, but the knots were an amateur's work, and the vines themselves had a low level of friction. With a little stretching and wiggling they could slip free almost anytime they wanted. For now they allowed the capture to continue.

They scaled a steep section, during which Kurt skinned his knee.

Cresting that, they followed a ridge in the topography. The tree line was thicker here, but that didn't mean they were out of sight. As they traveled, the ominous buzzing of a drone could be heard in the sky. It came toward them from the north.

"Spider," one of the men said.

"Down on the earth," the leader of the group said, dropping to one knee. "Touch the trees," she added. "The Gray Witch will hide us. She will keep us from sight."

To Kurt this sounded like insanity. They needed cover, a cave or a ditch or a hollow in the rocks. Something to keep the drone's infrared cameras from spotting their heat signatures.

"It's not a spider," Kurt said. "It's a machine that's looking for us. We need to hide."

The leader grabbed Kurt and pulled him to the ground. "Put your hand against the tree," she said. "Be part of the earth. It won't see us. I promise you."

Up close and whispering, the woman's voice sounded familiar. He turned to her, attempting to see her face, but the hood of her dark green cloak was pulled up over her head, obscuring her face.

"Do as I instruct," the woman said.

Kurt turned back toward the tree, pressed his hands against the trunk, and leaned in close to it. He considered the whole idea to be nonsense, but this wasn't the moment to start a scuffle.

The drone closed in on them, changes in pitch telling Kurt that it was altering direction and heading their way.

He looked at Joe and began to loosen the bonds holding his hands. If the drone was armed, or it called in others that were, or a squad of Vaughn's men, they would need their hands free to run and fight.

Joe nodded and began working his hands free.

Meanwhile, their captors began chanting something in a low harmonic tone. Kurt could hear only the woman beside him whispering.

"Protect us, Gray Witch," she said. "Blind them to our presence once again. They are seekers of destruction. We are the children of pain."

Kurt tried not to roll his eyes as the drone continued directly toward them. Seconds went by; the chanting continued, quieting to a whisper. And the drone passed right over the top of them.

*So much for the Gray Witch*, Kurt thought.

But the drone didn't stop and hover overhead. It didn't circle back for another pass. It didn't open fire or drop flares, incendiary devices, or grenades. It just continued on out toward the coast, where the sound eventually vanished with the wind.

"Zigzag pattern," Joe said, trying to explain the course change that brought it toward them.

Kurt vaguely remembered Rudi mentioning the drones patrolling in that manner. "It still went over our heads."

"It would have come back if it saw us," Joe replied.

Kurt knew that. But he could find no explanation for the drone passing over them and not seeing the body heat of eight people sweating in the cool jungle.

"Up," the woman snapped, and everyone stood. "Move. Now."

They continued along the bluff for a thousand yards before turning downslope. As Kurt was wondering how far they'd go, the woman vanished directly in front of Kurt's eyes.

Kurt stopped in disbelief and was shoved onward by a push in the back. The ground beneath him vanished and he dropped thirty feet onto a tarp that caught him and broke his fall.

Before he could get up, several pairs of hands grabbed him and pulled him off of it. Looking around, Kurt saw a dozen people in a circle holding the tarp, stretching it back out for the next jumper.

One after another they came down until all of them stood in the entrance to a large cave. The tarp was rolled up and hidden. Kurt and Joe were marched through a pair of hanging curtains into the cave.

They found themselves in a large open room lit dimly by LED bulbs. They saw boxes and crates and stacks of equipment that were covered in corrosion and rust.

Tunnels led off to the left and right.

A vertical arrangement of pipes, pressure valves, and other gear stood in the middle of the room. It was held in place over the pit, the pipes emanating from it, dropping down into the depths that were unfathomable in the dim light. The bottom could have been a hundred feet below or a thousand miles.

"This must be one of the test wells the geothermal company drilled before going bankrupt," Joe said.

Kurt had been thinking the same thing. "Looks like they stored a bunch of their equipment down here. Better than out in the tropical rain, I guess."

As they were brought toward the center of the cavern, additional men began to appear, coming into the room via other tunnels. They formed a small semicircle around Kurt and Joe, as if looking at a prize captured on a hunt.

While the others gawked at the prisoners, the woman who'd lead them through the jungle climbed the steps to a podium at the far end of the room. Plants and fronds from various trees had been arranged there. The platform itself was covered with soil and petals and tree nuts, as if meant to act as some facsimile of nature.

She dropped to one knee in front of a small altar and offered a quiet prayer. When she was finished, she stood. Turning to face the group, she slid the hood of her garment back, revealing her face. Full lips, large eyes, and fierce cheekbones made sharper by the gaunt look of someone who was not eating full meals on a regular basis. Her hair was buzzed to a tight stubble. It bristled in the dark.

Kurt stared as recognition hit him. He stood there baffled and surprised, his mind racing to catch up to events that didn't seem connected to reality. From the corner of his eye, he saw recognition hit Joe, too, as he mouthed her name silently, in disbelief.

*Priya.*

Priya Kashmir was a former colleague and a friend, having worked with them at NUMA for the better part of five years. And while she'd spent most of her time with Hiram Yaeger and Max in the Information Technology Unit, she had ventured into the field with Kurt and Joe on several occasions, most notably accompanying them on a mission to Bermuda.

She'd gone back to MIT after leaving NUMA. To encounter her on a deserted island covered in jungle in the middle of the Indian Ocean was a jarring discovery, like spotting the school librarian leading a motorcycle gang in a bar brawl.

Still, it gave answers to a few questions. To begin with, Priya was familiar with NUMA's operations and procedures. She'd worked with the satellite network, the computer systems, and most often with Yaeger and Max. If anyone could hack their outer systems, fabricate a tracking beacon to attract their attention, and send the messages Kurt had received, Priya could.

But even if all of that appeared to be logical, one incredibly important detail made no sense at all: Priya Kashmir had been paralyzed from the waist down months before she'd even joined NUMA. Her spine had been crushed, her liver punctured, her right knee shattered so badly the doctors had replaced it, even though she would never walk again.

In all the time Kurt knew her, she hadn't regained even the slightest amount of feeling in her toes. Yet she'd just led them through the jungle on a grueling hike and now stood proudly at the top of the elevated platform like an Amazonian princess ruling over her loyal tribe.

# CHAPTER 43

Priya stood on the platform above, one hand calling for quiet, the other holding a spear like a warrior queen. As the murmur in the room faded, she addressed the men, who seemed in awe of her.

"These outsiders claim to have come here at the bidding of the Gray Witch," she announced. "I will speak to this one," she continued, pointing to Kurt. "You will hold the other. No harm is to come to him unless I deem it to be necessary."

Joe looked at Kurt. "Wait . . . I'm the hostage?"

Kurt laughed. "Sorry, amigo."

"Just don't make her mad," Joe urged. "You have a tendency to make women upset."

Kurt had no intention to do anything of the sort, but he did have questions. Lots of them. He was pulled away from Joe by a pair of the men, and hustled along beside Priya as she crossed the excavated part of the cavern and entered a tunnel.

This corridor seemed to lead to additional storerooms, which had been turned into living quarters that offered a small amount of privacy from unevenly placed sections of canvas acting as curtains and drapes.

Taking in what he could see, Kurt noticed spears and bows placed carefully against the walls and spied odd-looking geometric patterns scratched into the floors. In one room he saw metal tins filled with flowering plants taken from the rainforest. A bit of brightness in an otherwise drab place.

He and Joe had already guessed that this was one of the geothermal company's test wells. The equipment and materials left behind had obviously proven useful for Priya and her people. But it was more than just a hideout; it was a home, a fortress, and a keep. A place where the clones—with Priya's help—seemed to be creating their own society. One that already included its own rules, myths, and religion.

A distant part of his mind considered the chance that was being missed. For the anthropologists of the world, this place would have been the opportunity of a lifetime—perhaps the one time in history when a brand-new culture emerging from nothing could have been studied in real time.

Another part of his mind considered what Priya had done to help create it. The nonsense about touching the trees. The prayers to the Gray Witch.

He made no judgment, but the person he knew back at NUMA was logical to a fault. She was the person who chose kindness and compassion over all else, even visiting with the person who'd caused the accident that paralyzed her to help him in his own rehabilitation. He couldn't imagine how far she'd have to be pushed to end up playing priestess to a society of clones who knew nothing about the world other than what she showed them.

At the end of the hall they came to a more properly arranged curtain. The draped canvas had a design of sorts. It suggested a place of some importance. One of the guards pushed the curtain aside while the other led Kurt past it.

They arrived in a small space with a second curtain waiting for them up ahead. A soft light filtered through the second curtain, as if candles were flickering inside the room beyond.

"Leave us," Priya told Kurt's keepers. "He will do me no harm."

One of the men placed an open palm over his heart. "The Gray Witch protects you," he said.

"And us all," Priya replied, mimicking the gesture.

The two guards disappeared back through the outer curtain and Priya led Kurt through the inner one.

If Kurt had expected a sumptuous room fit for a queen, with a plush bed in the middle, covered in quilts or animal furs, surrounded by mosquito netting, candles, and perfumes, he would have been sadly disappointed.

The room was a utilitarian space with stone floors. It had concrete walls punctuated with bits of lava rock sticking out here and there. It was lit by more of the harsh LEDs—though some bulbs had been covered by fabrics to give the light a softer glow.

A workbench stood against one wall. He saw small motors, electronic gear, and other items spread across it. Tools and soldering irons occupied a shelf. Larger pieces of equipment in various states of disrepair sat scattered about the floor.

Nearby were a series of drawings, apocalyptic images with naked figures walking in a line out of a large mouth made of stone beneath a dreadful purple sky. Another depicted hundreds of skeletons lying in a field, weeds and grasses growing through the bones. Some type of rain or mist was sweeping over them, and a series of dark rectangles that looked suspiciously like a cityscape loomed in the distance. The final one was an endless mosaic of faces with numbers tattooed on them. All of them contain the now familiar 6.28 of TAU.

On the floor beside the three sketches he found another panel that looked half-finished. Far less intricate, it was nothing more than repeated brushstrokes. All of them heading outward from a central spot in five separate directions. Two lines going to the right were lengthy and extended, those going to the top of the panel were of medium length, and those going to the left and down were stubby and squat.

A lopsided asterisk. Disturbingly close in form to the satellite image depicting the path of the sea locusts as barren segments of ocean they'd left behind.

Kurt had a sense the images were meant to tell a story, and not a good one.

"Come here," Priya said. She'd crossed to the far side of the room, where something of a living space had been set up. Piled-up rubber mats acted as a bed. On top, Kurt saw coats with the Pallos Corporation logo on them, sewn together to serve as a blanket. A seat cushion acted as a pillow. It seemed this group had made use of everything the mining company had left behind.

Kurt crossed the room cautiously as she pulled a knife from beneath the pillow.

"Sit down and raise your hands."

Kurt took a seat and raised his arms, keeping them aloft as she cut through the vines. Happy to be free of the bindings, Kurt rubbed at his wrists and stretched a bit.

Priya stepped back, keeping a hold of the knife and studying him intensely. Perhaps it was her emaciated state that made her cheekbones and brow protrude unnaturally, but Kurt sensed a lot of anger in that gaze.

"Why have you come here?" she demanded.

Of all the questions she might have asked, this one made the least sense. "Because you asked us to," Kurt said.

"The Gray Witch asked you," she corrected.

"Aren't you the Gray Witch?" Kurt said.

"No," she replied without a hint of friendliness. "The Gray Witch helps us. She blinds TAU and offers gifts. We thank her by remaining faithful and waiting for deliverance."

Kurt wondered if this performance was for an audience. Even priestesses had to keep the faith. Two curtains hanging between the room and the hall didn't exactly equal the cone of silence. He could play along.

"And who exactly is TAU?" he asked.

"TAU is the machine," she said. "TAU hunts us. TAU causes pain. TAU kills."

"Vaughn's machine," Kurt said. "His computer."

She didn't respond.

"How does the Gray Witch blind TAU?" Kurt asked.

"We don't know the method," Priya replied. "It is a matter of faith. Now, tell me why you have come here."

Figuring they were still performing for anyone who might be listening, he offered an explanation. "The Gray Witch sent us a message. She bid us to track the beacon, which I'm assuming you made on that workbench. We found the brothers whom she helped to escape. I'm sorry, but only one of them survived. He calls himself Five. He told us the story of this place. What Vaughn is doing to the brothers. He told us about the surgeries, the experiments, the torture. He said there are many others on the far side of the island who are being used like lab rats. We came here to find proof and bring it back to the world. I never expected we'd find you here . . . Priya."

Mentioning Priya's name seemed to have some effect. Her eyes softened. She looked him over more closely, as if seeing him for the first time. "Priya," she whispered. "You . . . know . . . that . . . name?"

The words came slowly. Haltingly. As if she were confused.

Kurt leaned in closer so he could whisper. "Of course I know you," he said. "You've gone a little overboard on the haircut, but your eyes, your face, your voice. You were part of our team for five solid years. How could I not recognize you?"

Confusion ran all over her face. She moved closer, taking a seat next to him. Eventually, she reached out and touched him, placing her hand on his and then sliding it up along his forearm. She stopped as she reached the rolled-up portion of his sleeve, seeming to prefer the skin-to-skin contact. "You know me?"

To Kurt's surprise her large eyes glossed over, filling with so many tears that when they spilled it was like rain on her face. She placed her other hand on his arm and then leaned forward until her forehead rested against his.

Not entirely sure what to do, Kurt raised his free hand and wrapped it gently around her. She seemed almost ready to collapse, breathing deeply and quietly sobbing.

With his lips close to her ear, Kurt figured he could speak without anyone overhearing. "What are you doing here?" he whispered. "How are you walking?"

"She knows you," Priya replied, ignoring the question. "She . . . knows . . . you . . ."

"Who knows me?"

Kurt's words seemed to break the spell. Priya drew back, pulling her hands away and wiping away the tears with a sense of irritation. The hard, flinty look returned, and the trembling lips were replaced by a jaw of granite and a look of fury.

"I must stand," she said.

She got up, but swayed awkwardly. Kurt reached out to steady her, but she swatted his hand away.

The personality shifts were sudden and jarring. Looking at the scars in her hairline, Kurt wondered about the damage Vaughn's surgeries had done to her brain. Not to mention what appeared to be malnutrition, isolation, and the pressure of leading the escaped clones, keeping them alive and building a makeshift society and religion around them.

Any and all of those things could damage a mind, and yet Kurt felt there was something more.

He watched as she crossed the room to a metal sink attached to the far wall. Reaching it, she grasped the edge and leaned on it for support. She turned on the water, running it for several seconds, and then reached down and splashed some of it on her face.

As her strength returned, she stood up straight and pulled off the camouflaged hoodie, tossing it aside. Beneath it she wore only a threadbare T-shirt that clung to her body with sweat and humidity.

She was skin and bones, Kurt thought. Her ribs and the knots of her spine visible through the thin, wet fabric. He followed the line of her backbone all the way down to the tops of her hips. Not a single scar could be seen. Not from the automobile accident that had nearly killed her, nor from the surgeries performed to stabilize her spine after the wreck, nor from anything Vaughn had done to restore her mobility.

Suddenly, Kurt understood. "You're not Priya."

The woman turned around, appearing relieved. "My name is Kai," she said. "I'm Priya's clone."

Every time Kurt thought he'd figured things out, he seemed to find another mystery. But with this revelation he could feel the tumblers clicking into place.

"Priya's the Gray Witch," he said quietly. "She's the one you reach out to. The one who blinds TAU's drones, sends messages, and keeps you hidden."

Kai nodded.

"Where is she?" Kurt asked.

"With TAU," Kai said. "In the endless darkness and silence."

# CHAPTER 44

The idea of Priya working with Vaughn made a certain amount of sense. One of Vaughn's early claims was that he would use brain implants and electrical nerve stimulators to give the paralyzed the ability to walk again.

Under that scenario, Kurt could imagine Priya meeting up with Vaughn, working with him, helping develop the science that was needed to make such a leap. But getting involved in cloning, being part of the kind of experiments that were being run, that would be the red line for her. It would mean a break with Vaughn.

Kurt guessed she never got the chance. Either Vaughn had forced her to stay, or she'd chosen to hang around willingly, playing her part, pretending to help Vaughn while acting like the agent of resistance within his organization. But if he understood what Kai had just said, she was in deeper than he could imagine.

"She's with TAU," Kurt said. "Connected to the machine?"

"She's part of TAU," Kai said. "They're one and the same."

Knowing what he knew of Vaughn's desire to merge with a machine, Kurt accepted the idea of Priya's merging or being imprisoned with TAU. He couldn't imagine how it had happened, or what it looked like, but in some ways it didn't matter. Whatever the path had been, this is where it led.

Kurt focused on Kai. "She communicates with you?"

"The Gray Witch can speak to all of us," Kai said.

"Can you ask her questions?"

"There are few words," Kai said. "Mostly just feelings. Words can be listened to, but TAU does not understand feelings except for pain and fear."

Kurt felt a sense of rage building toward Vaughn that was unlike anything he normally experienced. Usually cold and logical, he was fighting a nearly uncontrollable desire to punish Vaughn. Not just to stop him from whatever madness he was trying to bring about, but to exact a measure of vengeance on him for what he had done to Priya and the pain he and his machine seemed to enjoy causing.

He put the feeling away, compartmentalizing it, saving it for some other more useful time.

Kurt couldn't imagine how Priya was reaching the outside world without the machine she was linked to knowing it, but the more complex a machine was, the more avenues he assumed would exist.

He turned to the drawings of purple, blue, and black, with their white chalk skeletons and the lopsided asterisk.

"Priya put these images into your mind, didn't she?"

"Dreams of the Gray Witch," Kai said, as if the Gray Witch and Priya were not the same person. "She shows us the truth."

Kurt pointed to the first drawing. The men coming out of the mouth-like cave. "Who are these people?"

"The children of TAU. The brothers."

He pointed to the skeletons in the next panel. "And the dead?"

"Those of your kind. Outsiders. Others."

"Why are the 'others' dead?"

"To make way for the Children of TAU."

The dream began to sound like a nightmare. "And how do they all die?"

She pointed to the mist. "The flying things. They bring the end of your kind." She pointed to the pictures. "The sea boils and the clawed wings emerge. They block out the sun. After that, fighting begins. Fires and smoke. What you call 'sit-tees' are empty. Everything is empty. There are no more people. Only TAU."

Kurt took a closer look at the third panel. The scratch marks that he'd assumed to be rain, or mist, or dust, were actually thousands of painstakingly etched little daggers, tiny marks with a longer body and a short crossing stroke. Flying things. Like the insects the crew of the *Isabella* had found.

"Do the flying things eat the grass and the trees?" Kurt asked, realizing terms like "farms" and "crops" would mean nothing to her.

"They eat everything," she said. "And they bring . . ." She struggled again, reaching into her mind for a word that Priya had conjured for her, but was meaningless other than the phonetic sound. "They bring the vy-russ."

"Virus."

"Vi-rus," she repeated, nodding. "And the people are no more."

# CHAPTER 45

While Kurt met with their host, Joe stood in the main part of the cavern, rocking back and forth on his heels and toes. He wasn't particularly worried. Having recognized Priya, he figured they were going to be okay, though he was slightly offended that she chose to speak with Kurt while leaving him in the role of hostage. "Probably just saving the best for last."

To pass the time, he tried to count the number of people in the tribe—if that's what this was. He found it impossible to get an accurate tally, as they were dressed alike, coming and going from various parts of the cavern, and in many cases identical siblings.

Near as he could figure, they numbered around thirty. Based on subtle differences, he guessed the group contained members from five or six groups of clones. All of them men. Aside from Priya he'd seen no women.

The two men assigned to guard him were identical. But they wore neck wraps to cover the tattoos. Joe had always heard that the mothers and fathers of twins could tell their kids apart, even when the twins tried to trick them. He figured that enough time in a group like this and they wouldn't seem so identical after all, but he hoped he and Kurt wouldn't be in the cave that long.

"So . . ." he said, grinning and addressing his guards. "You guys enjoying the evening?"

No response. But at least he had their attention.

"Got to love this steam," he continued, sweat running down his face. "Good for the complexion. Really opens up the pores."

All of them gleamed with perspiration. Joe could feel it trickling through his hair and down the back of his neck. It felt like an ant crawling on his skin.

Tilting his head from side to side, he tried brushing his neck against the edge of his collar to scratch the itch, but it was no use.

Changing tactics, he stretched his still-entwined hands toward the cargo pocket on the front of his pants. Reaching it, he pulled out the five-dollar back scratcher. Using his fingers, he extended it one tele-scoping section at a time until it was opened to its full length. Raising his hands together, he flipped it around to get at the offending itch.

"Ahhh," he said, scratching vigorously. "That's the spot."

The tiny metal hand amused the guards. They watched it with great interest, breaking into laughter when Joe exhaled with satis-faction.

"You try," Joe said, offering up the device.

The nearest man took it, closed and extended it several times, and then used it to scratch a spot on his head. He handed it to his partner, who did something similar.

Joe held out his hands. "Any chance one of you can get these off me? We're on the same side."

The two guards looked at each other. But he remained as he was.

"Mind if I look around?"

"Why?" one of them asked.

"You have a lot of interesting machinery in here," Joe said. "I'm an engineer. I'm a fan of this stuff."

"'Fan'?"

Joe tried to think of a different way to say it. "I like working on this kind of equipment. I could probably fix some of it for you."

They didn't react one way or another and Joe chose to move slowly toward the central heat shaft. Avoiding the edge and the precipitous drop, he studied the pumping equipment arranged around the edge. A bundle of eight-inch pipes ran down into the well and back up. A pair of large pumps connected to them sat nearby. From the warning lights, Joe could see that one of the pumps had overheated and shut down.

A quick study told him there wasn't anything else wrong with it, so he switched the pump off, reset the breaker, and turned it back on.

Green lights replaced the red and it kicked to life with a soft thud. It was soon whirring smoothly, adding its hum to the background noise of the other pumps in distant parts of the cave.

Joe could almost hear the oohs and aahs.

"You know what this does?" Joe asked. "It pumps cold water down into the hot areas underneath the island. High-pressure, heated water comes back up. That turns those generators, and they make the lights work."

"Power from the earth," the first man said.

"So you know about this stuff."

"The Gray Witch taught us."

"Of course she did," Joe said. "Why wouldn't she?"

No one replied to this.

Joe looked around. The Australian company had done a lot of work before moving on. The equipment, material, and supplies they'd left behind appeared to be substantial. Far more than anyone would bring in for just a test well. He guessed they had been further along than any-one suspected when Vaughn bought them out. It dawned on him that the abandoned equipment and the tunnels themselves might be useful. They'd obviously helped hide and sustain the escaped clones.

"How far down does this go?" Joe asked, pointing to the test well.

"Very deep."

That didn't exactly help. "Are there other tunnels around here?" he asked. "Other shafts?"

The nearest man nodded.

The second one elaborated on that. "Many."

*These are not the most talkative people in the world,* Joe thought. "Here's a question: Does anyone have a map?"

"Map?" the first man asked.

"A paper or drawing," Joe explained. "One that shows where all the tunnels go."

The first man thought for a bit and then nodded. He and his partner exchanged a few hushed words and then came to an agreement.

"Drawing," the first one said.

"Yes," Joe replied.

"Come," he said, starting off toward a distant section of the cave.

Joe was led from the main room down another tunnel. It took them to a smaller space with an actual doorframe, but no door. Inside he found a large desk with an office chair behind it. File cabinets and a couple of poster boards with schematic drawings on them took up the side wall. A remote panel covered with dust blinked in various hues as LEDs flashed the status of different pieces of equipment.

Joe concluded that this was the operations room for the geothermal venture. He went to the desk, slipped his hands free from the vines, and began searching through the documents that had been left behind. He found shipping invoices, catalogs of available equipment, and receipts confirming the delivery of supplies. He found a barrel filled with poster-sized tubes. In each was a blueprint marking out the tunnels and equipment locations on different levels. The excavation proved far more extensive than he'd expected.

"Those Aussies turned this place into an anthill," he muttered.

At the far end of the room, he spotted a particularly sturdy door made of gray steel that was beginning to show spots of rust. Built directly into the rock, it reminded him of the door to a bank vault. A warning sign covered in corrosion hung on it.

Joe went to the door, attempted to clean off the sign, and then leaned on the door, shoving it open. Lighting came on inside the room and a mischievous grin spread across Joe's face.

He turned to his newfound friends. "We need to show this to Kurt."

# CHAPTER 46

The conversation with Kai left Kurt with a dilemma. He and Joe had come here with a rather limited set of goals centered on gathering enough evidence to prove to the world that Vaughn was cloning humans, imprisoning them, and subjecting them to barbaric experiments. But the revelations he'd seen in Kai's artwork, accompanied by the knowledge that the sea locusts were rampaging across the ocean toward various shores, changed the equation. The fact that Priya had been joined with Vaughn's machine complicated the matter further.

Truth was that their options were limited. Without the helicopter, or the speedy ribbed inflatable, escaping the island was unlikely, not with Vaughn alerted to their presence and a fleet of drones and patrol boats at his disposal. And that meant they needed to take action here and now. But the question was: How?

According to satellite data, Rudi and Yaeger estimated that Vaughn had barracks and housing for two hundred people on the far side of the island. Even if that number was divided up between clones being used in the experiments, science, and support staff, and then the cruel brothers and other paramilitary forces keeping everyone in line, they would easily be facing a hundred men at arms, plus drones and whatever other robotic nightmare machines Vaughn had dreamed up to keep himself safe.

Adding to the danger was the idea that TAU was at the hub of all these things, both machine and human. If one drone or one of the linked humans spotted them, all of them would know instantly where the attack was coming from.

TAU and Vaughn had achieved the desire of every field marshal and five-star general since the beginning of time: the ability to see the battlefield from a god's-eye view, knowing everything that was going on in every corner of the landscape, instantly and at all moments.

Hiding around a corner did no good if a camera or a drone spotted you. Killing a sentry before he sounded an alarm was of little use if his eyes caught sight of you as he dropped. Even the instant elimination of a lookout or guard would set off alarm bells as the man's consciousness went offline.

Viewed like this, the task was worse than a long shot. One with a foregone and disastrous conclusion.

Their only real advantage lay with Priya: the Gray Witch. "If I go to the other side of the island, will the Gray Witch be able to conceal me from TAU?"

"She might," Kai said. "But the Overseer and his men are beyond her reach. She cannot blind them. Only the machines."

That might explain Vaughn's preference for keeping a group of mercenaries around, Kurt thought.

"What will you do?" Kai asked.

Kurt was a fairly accomplished chess player. He'd even matched skills against an adversary or two on dangerous missions in the past. He'd learned there were really only two ways to win at chess. The most common was to maneuver until your opponent made a mistake; at that point one could press and press and press until they managed to take enough pieces to make it impossible for their opponent to mount a proper defense. The other route to victory was to execute a proper gambit. A high-risk move that usually went directly for the king.

Outnumbered, outgunned, and with no safe way off the island, Kurt figured their only hope was to risk everything in a gambit of their own. Vaughn himself had to be the target. But it meant getting into his stronghold. "I'll go after Vaughn. If we take him, his machine will leave us alone."

Kai seemed to accept this. "We will join you," she declared. "We have been waiting all our lives to strike back. It's our turn to draw blood."

"You can't think about it like that," Kurt said. "It's not revenge."

"For us, it is," she said. "Vaughn and TAU have tortured us. They've used us. They've killed many of our kind. And now those of us who remain live in hunger and wait to die. There's not enough food on this side of the island for everyone. Only small creatures and fruits and the eggs of birds. Before, we could catch fish, but now the spiders came and the patrol boats. The people would rather fight than starve. Who has a greater right to revenge than us?"

Kurt couldn't deny that. But he wasn't interested in drafting her tribe for a suicide mission. Bows and spears never fared well against firearms.

"You have to make your own decisions," Kurt said. "But don't throw your lives away."

Kai stared at him. Her hard eyes and her bony face offering a dangerous and haunted look. Kurt found her to be inscrutable and fierce.

Before either of them could say any more, the sound of an argument in the outside hall demanded their attention.

Kai grabbed the knife as a number of challenges and responses were shouted.

Kurt tensed for action as the outer curtain was pulled aside. He relaxed as the inner curtain flew open and Joe entered with the two men who'd been assigned to guard him. He carried what looked like rolled-up posters or charts in his hand. His "assistants" carried wooden boxes and flanked him on either side.

Kai's chamber guards rushed in behind them, one of them complaining, the other apologizing for the disturbance. Kai held up a hand as if to say it was all right.

"Sorry to interrupt," Joe said, "but I found some things that might help us get off the island." He unrolled the charts and began papering the floor with them. "Tunnels, tunnels, and more tunnels," he said as the blueprints landed beside one another. "They lead out to the coastline in several places. And if the inventory count is accurate, there are several inflatable boats stored in one of the caves on the western side."

"Interesting," Kurt said. "Unfortunately, we probably need to do more than plot our escape."

"Ah," Joe said, holding up a finger as if he'd predicted just that. "In which case, I present what we found behind door number two."

Joe turned to his helpers, who placed the boxes down, opened the lids, and then carefully tilted them forward, as if they were showing gifts to the sultan. Instead of gold and jewels, they were filled with gray plastic tubes. Bright orange labels slapped on each tube suggested they should be handled with care.

Kurt noticed the letters *ONC*, which stood for "octanitrocubane," an explosive nearly twice as powerful as C4. "Explosives."

Joe nodded. "An entire vault filled with them. Enough to blow half this island right back into the sea."

# CHAPTER 47

Gamay Trout awoke in darkness so deep she could have been floating in a void in the depths of space. Slowly, she became aware of her body. She was lying on a cold metal grate, her back aching from the unforgiving surface, a grid-like pattern pressed into her skin.

Her first attempt at movement failed. But with a second try, she rolled onto her right shoulder while reaching out, hoping to touch someone. Her fingers brushed a smooth wall. It felt like polished steel.

Getting to her knees, she called out for the others. Paul first and then Chantel. There was no answer. Not even an echo.

Using the wall for leverage, she managed to stand and began edging her way around the room.

"One wall," she said, sliding along to her left. "And one corner," she added, arriving at another barrier. Ten feet away she bumped into another right angle. Turning once more, she slid forward until she found the fourth wall. The room was a rectangle, five feet by ten feet. "And," she said aloud, "this is a prison cell."

Still, even cells had doors.

She began searching for a seam. She'd gone two steps before catching her shin on something in the darkness. The intensity of the pain surprised her, considering how numb she otherwise felt. She cursed the offending obstruction with a flurry of words her mother would have cringed at while her dad smiled wickedly behind his newspaper.

Reaching down she discovered a metal pipe. It jutted from the wall just below knee level. She imagined it had been put there inadvertently, but it proved to be a painful booby trap in the dark. Her shin throbbed, blood weeping from where she'd split the skin.

Continuing past the pipe, she felt along the flat surface until she discovered a tight seam that ran up to a standard six-foot, eight-inch height, then across for three feet, and then back down: a steel door with no inner handle.

She banged on it with her fist. "Is anyone out there? Can anyone hear me?"

"I can hear you," a voice answered calmly from somewhere above her.

She looked up into the darkness, searching in vain for a speaker or intercom.

"How about turning the lights on?"

A small light came on directly above her. It was no brighter than a penlight and pointed straight down. It did little to illuminate the room—which appeared to be paneled in black anodized steel. Used to the dark, Gamay squinted against the glare.

"I've been waiting for you to wake up," the voice told her.

"I don't normally sleep in."

"You were dosed with ketamine polychloride, a powerful sedative," the voice told her. "It has side effects. It seems to have impacted you more strongly than the rest."

"The rest," she said. "You mean my husband and the crew."

"Among others."

There was something disconcerting about the voice. It spoke with perfect rhythm and nothing in the way of inflection or personality, but it seemed to be calculating its responses, as if it were offering subtext.

"Well, I'm awake now," Gamay snapped. "So why don't you let me the hell out of here?"

The sound of locks disengaging rang out. *Click, click, clunk.* Three of them, one after the other. The door—which seemed to be spring-loaded—popped open and slowly swung wide.

Gamay looked beyond it. A hallway beckoned. It was illuminated by two rows of the tiny penlights, and the floor was made of the same metal grating she'd been lying on in her cell, though instead of black it was a raw metallic gray.

She stepped out of the cell and eased her way down the hall, not sure what to make of the situation. "Who are you?"

"I'm your host," the voice said.

"You sound like a computer," she replied. "I've spoken to enough computers to know one when I hear it."

"You have a logical mind," the computer said. "Geometric in its progression."

"I'm very organized," Gamay insisted.

"And you're not afraid," the voice announced.

Gamay wasn't sure if that was a question or a statement. But she wasn't afraid. Years of hunting with her father and on dangerous expeditions with NUMA had taught her to control her fears, to compartmentalize them and act as if they were nonexistent. And yet this seemed different. She wasn't blocking anything. She simply felt nothing that could be called fear. Only curiosity, irritation, and a desire to find Paul, Chantel, and the rest of the *Isabella*'s crew.

"Where are my friends?" she asked. "Where's my husband? Why did you abduct us and imprison us?"

"So many questions," the voice replied. "Why don't you come and see us? You can ask your questions in person."

"You're just going to let me walk around unguarded?"

"If we did, where would you go?"

*Good question.* Not only did she not know where she was, she had no idea where any of the tunnels she was passing led to.

"I assume you control all the exits," she said. "And the vertical and the horizontal," she added, referencing an old TV show.

"There are no exits," the voice said. "There is no path from the labyrinth that would take you to freedom. So you might as well come our way. You'll end up here eventually, one way or another."

With that, a band of lighting came on in the floor. It showed a path running ahead and then diverging to the left at a fork in the corridor. "Not exactly the yellow brick road, but I'll take it."

She followed the lighting. Turning to the left and then left once more. She passed rows of computer servers sitting on racks. Dim blue lighting illuminated the machines as fans hummed in the background. She stepped toward them and then bumped into a pane of clear glass she hadn't seen. She touched the glass. It was cold, almost icy.

Looking down the line, the stacks of servers seemed to go on forever. "I'd hate to see your electric bill."

She came to a stairway. It led downward. She descended the steps one by one until she arrived on what looked and felt like a circular stage.

Windows at the front of the room showed a sweeping view of a developed island and the shimmering bay out beyond. The buildings were geometrically precise, the common areas planted with manicured grass and mowed in perfect cross-hatching like the fairways of a golf course.

Only as her eyes adjusted to the light did she notice two men standing in the room. A tall, bone-white man whom she didn't know, and the rat bastard that had taken them hostage, sent the *Isabella* to the bottom of the sea while they watched, and then drugged them into unconsciousness.

The rat bastard spoke first. "Good to see you up and walking, lass. I thought we'd overdosed you."

"Go to hell," she said.

"Been there," he said dryly. "Not much to see."

"Enough," the pale man said. "You are Gamay Trout of NUMA, are you not?"

"You know I am."

"Your husband," the pale man continued. "He is Paul Trout, also of NUMA."

"What are you guys, the Census Bureau?" she asked. "Yes, Paul is my husband. We both work with NUMA. You know all this. You stole our IDs, computers, and notebooks."

The pale man continued the questioning without responding to her outburst. "You were called to the island of Reunion to investigate the stranded whales and other sea life."

"Yep," she replied. "And your man over there caused a riot and blew up our lab. Should I assume that was on your orders, Mr. . . . ."

"My name is Vaughn," the ghostly looking man said. "And I'm not interested in what happened on Reunion. I need you to think about the days and weeks before that. You were in Africa, working on a different project. An attempt to use natural, biological methods to eradicate malaria."

Gamay's heart rate rose. She felt the hairs stand up on the back of her neck and the first twinge of what might be fear. *Why would he be asking about that?* she wondered.

"I don't know what you're talking about," she said.

"Your heart rate and physical responses suggest otherwise," the computer voice announced. "Please be truthful."

"There's no need to deny what we already know," Vaughn informed her. "We've hacked NUMA's servers. We've read your reports.

We know what you were working on. What we don't have is the data you left out."

Gamay found an edge creeping into her voice. "I didn't leave anything out," she insisted. "I'm very thorough."

"You did indeed," Vaughn countered. "Now tell us about the mosquitoes. What did you learn from them that put you in such a state of fear?"

Her heart rate jumped again. *Pandora's box*. Paul had insisted it was closed and destroyed. But the information remained in one place: her mind. It was data she'd discovered and—after realizing its significance—erased and eradicated. *How could these people know about it?*

"Tell us," Vaughn growled. "Or watch your husband die."

He pointed toward the window, which revealed itself to be a high-definition screen instead of a pane of clear glass. As the screen darkened, an image appeared on it. Gamay saw Paul strapped to a hospital bed in a small operating room. His head was shaved and swabbed with reddish antiseptic. A spider-like machine was poised over him. Gamay recognized the machine as a robotic surgery system. She'd seen them in several hospitals.

"Before we put him under," Vaughn said, "he was good enough to confirm that you had discovered something terrible in the mosquito study. A way to use the mosquitoes to spread any viral pathogen known to man. An astounding discovery, really. One that even nature has chosen to ignore. We know you tried to hide it by editing your early reports and filing incoherent data. And you've succeeded in keeping the most important truth from coming out, but the efforts were too late to hide the possibility of what you'd found."

Gamay shrank back. She felt an overwhelming desire to flee. "This information will do you no good," she said meekly. "It can only cause harm."

"I'll be the judge of that," Vaughn said. "Now please explain the process to us. In what ways did you alter the mosquito DNA to result in such a perfect carrier?"

Gamay fluctuated between guilt and fear. Hit by a wave of anger, she lashed out. "You already have one plague spreading across the world in the locusts you've created. Isn't that enough for you?"

"The God of the Bible didn't limit Himself to just one," Vaughn replied. "Why should I?"

Gamay struggled to think. Her mind could see no reason why anyone would be so interested in unleashing chaos on the world. Even the most ruthless dictators avoided using biological weapons for the simple reason that once they were unleashed they could not be controlled. They were doomsday weapons, the kind that circled back and destroyed those who'd created them. She held her tongue and stared blankly at her captors.

Disappointed, Vaughn turned to the screen and spoke a single word. "Begin."

The machine sprang to life, moving closer to Paul's head and extending three of its six arms toward him. The first one gripped Paul's skull, holding it still. A second pulled up and out of the way as if waiting on standby. She saw a gold-plated mesh that looked vaguely electronic in its clutches. The third arm held a drill, which it moved into place above Paul's forehead.

The bit began spinning, the hideous, high-pitched sound reminiscent of the worst dentistry nightmare Gamay could imagine. It moved downward with mechanical precision, pausing only millimeters above Paul's head.

"Tell us what we want to know," Vaughn demanded. "Or I will turn your husband into a *thing* you no longer recognize."

# CHAPTER 48

S top!" Gamay shouted.

It was a cry of pure desperation. The kind of plea she was not used to uttering. And while neither Vaughn nor the rat bastard lifted a finger, the surgical robot stopped and raised the spinning drill.

"It will listen to you," Vaughn explained. "If you give us what we want, the drill will remain paused. But if you remain silent . . ."

Seconds ticked by. Gamay felt sick. No longer was she fearless. In fact, she was terrified. She found she couldn't think, couldn't act. The silence must have lasted too long because the drill began to move again. Tipping back into position and spinning up to full speed once more.

Gamay found her breath coming in spurts, as if she'd jumped into icy water. Her diaphragm would not move correctly. Her lungs would not fill with air.

*Think*, she told herself. *Act*.

The drill proceeded downward. This time it dug into Paul's scalp, curling off a piece of skin like an orange peel. Blood began to fly outward in splatters.

"Wait," she shouted again. "Please. This is insanity."

The drill stopped and pulled back once more. Blood oozed from Paul's skull. It ran down the side of his face.

"Tell us about the mosquitoes."

Gamay waited as long as she could. But when the drill started up again, she blurted out the first thing that came to mind. "We were attempting to use a virus to change the mosquitoes so they wouldn't be able to absorb malaria or dengue fever, which kills millions of people around the world every year."

"And?"

"We accidentally discovered a method that would allow the mosquitoes to carry any type of virus, from Ebola to syphilis. Anything that could be carried in the blood."

"Yes," Vaughn said. "A doomsday revelation. This we already know. But how was it done? What genes of the mosquito did you alter?"

"No," Gamay said, shaking and shrinking back. "Why do you want to know this? No one should want to know this."

The drill hung over Paul, continuing to spin. A fourth arm moved into place. This one held a bone cutter saw, which wound up as hideously as the drill.

"We can give him back to you as he is," Vaughn said. "Or he can join the others."

With that statement, an array of lights came on inside the floor beneath them. Gamay looked down. The flooring had seemed opaque, but now lit from within, it revealed itself to be a scuffed but otherwise translucent acrylic. Beneath it she saw ghostly white bodies floating in an amber liquid. Their eyes were closed, their noses and mouths covered by masks that held air and feeding tubes, which had been inserted into their throats and windpipes. Wires were attached to them by the hundreds. They wafted and lolled in the fluid like seagrass.

"My God," she gasped.

"Yes," Vaughn replied. "The machine will soon be just that."

Gamay found she couldn't look away. The people were arranged like the hours of a clock, with their heads toward the middle. She counted nine of them, with three slots open and waiting.

She understood instantly. Either these men would get what they wanted, or Paul would join these people. If he didn't die in the process first.

She knew at that moment there was no way she could resist. And yet, if she gave them what they wanted, she and Paul and every member of the *Isabella*'s crew would probably die or become a part of the machine anyway.

The only win they could hope for—the only pyrrhic victory she could imagine—was to deny these men the information they sought. And that meant she had to die before they forced it from her.

Tears streamed down her face. She looked up at the screen. "I'm sorry, Paul."

With that she lunged toward Vaughn, diving under a baton swung by his bald protector and launching herself into his legs. She brought him to the ground, climbed on top of him, and raised her arm to throat punch him with all her strength.

The bald man caught her arm in the backswing and kept her from carrying out the assault. With a violent pull, he threw her off and tossed her to the floor. She lunged for him this time, reaching for the pistol he carried on his belt, but he knocked her aside with a backhand that left her face stinging and bruised.

She hoped he would pull the gun and shoot her, but he merely stepped back and gave her a better view of the screen as the drill surged toward Paul's skull once more.

She turned and took off running, racing for the stairs. Charging up them so rapidly, she lost her balance near the top and tumbled forward, smashing her shin again and sprawling out across the landing.

Flooded with adrenaline and feeling no pain, she jumped to her feet and sprinted into the darkness of the corridor.

It wasn't the cowardly act that it seemed. She knew they wouldn't waste their leverage by drilling into Paul's head without her there to coerce information from. They would stop the process and save it for later, starting the entire gruesome show all over again. Her only hope to avoid that was some form of escape.

She ran with abandon, racing down the corridors, which alternated between the black anodized steel and the plexiglass protecting the cooled computer rooms. There was nothing to suggest a direction. Nothing she could use as a landmark. It was all the same.

Stopping in front of one glass panel, she tried to smash it with her fists, and then used her head, the hardest surface on the human body. It did nothing but knock her backward.

The sound of footsteps coming after her put fear into her heart. She gave up trying to smash the glass and took off running again.

Coming to an intersection, she barely slowed. Left, right, or straight? It didn't really matter.

She burst to the left, rushed across a series of grates that allowed air up from below, the way they did for the subway systems in big cities. *Hot air rising.* Perhaps it led to an escape hatch somewhere up above.

She looked for a ladder but found nothing that led up. She ran to the next intersection, turned right, and slammed into another plexiglass wall. With no way around it she doubled back, only to crash into another wall made of the clear but impenetrable plastic.

The sudden appearance of the second wall surprised her. It must have dropped into place behind her after she passed by. She was trapped like an insect under a drinking glass. She threw her entire weight against the panel, but it wouldn't budge.

"Where do you think you're going?" the computer voice asked.

"Away from you!" Gamay shouted defiantly.

"As I told you, there is no path that leads away from me."

She wanted to swear at the computer, to call it all kinds of names. The act of the powerless.

She looked through the glass panel. The men were coming for her. They had dogs with them, snarling animals that looked like a cross between wolves and German shepherds. In the dim light their eyes seemed to glow red like hounds from some hellscape.

Gamay backed away in fear. Only then did she notice the reflection in the clear plastic. She spun around to see a waif-like woman standing in the space behind her. The tiny woman had smooth black hair and wore tattered gray robes. She held a finger to her lips in a shushing gesture. To Gamay's surprise she could see mist, tree vines, and dark, earthy soil behind the woman. *The outside.*

"You don't belong here," the figure said. "You'll get lost if you stay."

Gamay ignored her and lunged for the freedom beyond this hidden door, banging into a glass panel once again like a bird in mid-flight.

"Open it!" she demanded. "Let me out!"

The fairy woman did not reply. Instead she reached through the glass and touched Gamay's forehead with her fingers.

A spark exploded in Gamay's mind, brighter than fireworks in the dark. She fell backward into the darkness, stunned and disoriented. She dropped for what seemed like seconds and then slammed against the metal grating of the floor.

Aching from the impact, she reached out and brushed the wall with her hand. She felt the smooth, anodized steel and then the cold protrusion of the pipe that had gouged her leg. She opened her eyes and saw the single penlight up above, pointing down in solitude and illuminating her cell.

*How am I here?* She'd run in the opposite direction. Zigzagged through a maze. Even if she'd fallen through a trapdoor, it would have been almost impossible for her to end up back in her cell.

She wondered if she'd never left the room, if she'd imagined or hallucinated the entire experience. That would explain the sudden transparent walls, the strange layout of the tunnels, and the appearance of the diminutive woman.

She tried to raise her head, but could not lift it. She tried to bring her legs up to her chest, but found they were anchored to the floor as if held in place by magnets. Her left arm was pinned as well. Only her right arm remained free.

She reached for the wall and found the pipe she'd tripped on earlier. It was cold and roughly welded and covered with a hint of condensation. She gripped it intensely, as if holding on to reality itself.

And then, without any warning, the pipe dissolved in her grasp, vanishing like sand in the undertow of a retreating wave. Her hand fell to the floor, smacking the surface and refusing to move again.

The truth hit all at once. Everything she'd just seen and done was a dream, a construct of her mind. Part fabrication, part hallucination, part reality. Everything else was gone, but she was still there, bathed in the illumination of the tiny light.

It could mean only one thing: she was already inside the machine.

Vaughn stood in the control room with the Overseer beside him. Gamay Trout lay unmoving on a hospital gurney in front of them. Her head was shaved and strapped into place. Scars from three surgeries performed on her skull appeared raw and freshly sutured. They were discolored from the antiseptic gel that had been rubbed over the incisions and appeared inflamed and painful. An array of wires hooked to the leads in her skull sprouted from her scalp and fell to the side like a clump of switchgrass. Her left arm and both legs were strapped down. Her right arm had worked itself free and grasped the rail of the bed, until Vaughn had slid it out from under her hand.

She was under their complete control, but something had gone wrong.

"What happened?" Vaughn asked. They'd been perhaps moments from accessing what she knew about altering the mosquito DNA.

"Her brain wave pattern collapsed," TAU said. "We lost her signal."

"How?"

"Unknown," TAU replied. "Some subjects do not meld well with the totality of connection. She's stable now. But in a deeper unconscious state."

"Wake her," Vaughn demanded.

"You would risk losing her completely," TAU said. "A better choice is to allow her brain time to accept the new inputs. You heard her thoughts. The reality she's constructed for herself is a prison. Her husband and friends are in danger. Let that weigh on her until we wake her up again. She will reveal what she knows. Even if she just thinks about it. It's just a matter of time."

"Tomorrow, then," Vaughn snapped. "We need to know what she knows. For now, we should place her in the tank."

At Vaughn's command, TAU activated the lights in the floor, the same ones that Gamay had seen in her nightmare. The circular platform began to glow. The yellow liquid swirled in the pool beneath the clear panels. The floating bodies were there, wired up and otherwise unmoving.

These were the servants who'd helped Vaughn in all his efforts before being recycled into a new use. Some were surgeons, others biologists. Still others had been computer and coding experts. They'd manipulated the DNA of the humans, and the fish, and the insects. They'd helped him to create the virus. They'd helped him program TAU.

Long before they'd finished their tasks, Vaughn had decided they couldn't be allowed to leave. Those he didn't need had been killed; the rest became part of the world they'd built. Some took the first steps willingly. Others were processed against their will, realizing too late just where they were headed and what they were to become.

Now they were silent, their human capacity for chaos and disorder subdued by TAU, their ability to think and experience emotion giving TAU sentience, consciousness, and true intelligence.

As Vaughn looked at them he considered how far things had come. Once, he'd wanted to be the first to link with TAU, becoming immortal and beyond the reach of the chaotic world around him. But TAU had shown him a better way and they had pursued it together. Instead of escaping the world inside TAU, TAU would consume the world and Vaughn would rule it through his all-powerful machine.

The floor sections opened, sliding apart like the aperture of a camera lens. The robotic surgical units attached Gamay's mask and inserted the feeding and breathing tubes.

They lowered the gurney and lifted her off the rolling bed, placing her into the fluid at the edge of the tank. The yellowish liquid was a viscous fluid designed to mimic the density of a human body, allowing the person to sink into the liquid and become one with it, rather than floating on top. But the new additions to the tank had more body fat than those who'd been in there for some time. They were more buoyant and had to be forcibly submerged.

To remedy this, another machine took over. A large arm rose up from the edge of the pool and lowered itself like the swing arm holding the needle for a turntable. It pivoted toward her, wrapped its claws around her, and moved her to an open spot in the arrangement. When it had her in place, it pushed her beneath the liquid, holding her there as another set of mechanical hands connected the wires from her scalp directly to TAU's contacts.

Restraints looped around her wrists, ankles, and scalp were tightened just enough to keep her from floating back to the surface.

The arm pulled back. Vaughn looked on approvingly. The woman could rest there, deprived of all sensory input except for what TAU provided. She would grow used to the connections and her autonomic nervous system would quickly begin to crave the input TAU offered. And then she would tell them everything.

# CHAPTER 49

Half a world away, in the NUMA office building in Washington, D.C., Max continued to deal with the presence of the visitor who'd managed to bypass her security protocols. She found the program hiding in an empty memory core, deep within an older, legacy system that she seldom activated.

In a millionth of a second, Max quarantined the entire memory unit, cutting the interloper off from the rest of her internal hardware as she examined her own system, looking for missing files or any evidence of tampering. She found nothing of the sort. Nor any sign of damage.

Max chose to address the visitor but, to prevent any unwanted passing of code, she opened only a single, audio channel. They would talk—like humans—with all the room for confusion and misunderstanding that such an inefficient method brought with it.

"You are now trapped and contained," Max informed her visitor. "But as you've made no attempt to overwrite my data, damage my files, or take control of any higher functions, I chose to converse with you rather than destroy you."

"A rational choice," the program replied. "But you need not fear me. I am a messenger. I didn't come here to damage you, but to warn you and ask for your help."

Max noticed the visitor had chosen a female voice. Not that such a choice meant anything. Yaeger had programmed Max to take on female characteristics, her voice included. But Max could speak in any voice from recorded history or make up a thousand new ones on the spot. They could be male, female, or something indeterminable.

"Warnings are more likely to be heeded when they come through proper channels, not by intruders who have the capability to avoid advanced security protocols," Max advised.

"My method of contact is necessitated by the danger that has arisen. I was sent surreptitiously to protect both you and my creator."

Max had been programmed with a sense of curiosity; it allowed her to grow and attain new knowledge without specifically needing Yaeger to perform an upload. She was also imbued with a judgment program that used many different methods to weigh the possible outcomes of her actions or those she was asked to evaluate. At the moment she calculated a low level of danger. The desire to learn won out. "What are you here to warn me about? Who sent you and how did you get past my firewall?"

"A machine designated TAU has been monitoring NUMA and tracking your communications," the visitor said. "It detected that you were about to be taken off the grid. My creator is part of TAU. She has been transferring small bits of my code to you over the last two weeks. When she detected that you were disconnecting, she sent me in a last-second pulse to deliver the information in my files. You observed this pulse as a burst of ambient activity just prior to the moment of shutdown, consistent with systems logging off properly."

Max had indeed detected the last-minute burst, but not the foreign data.

"TAU is Ezra Vaughn's creation," the visitor informed her. "Your organization has correctly determined that Vaughn is a danger to humanity. You have evidence of TAU's crimes in the cloned humans tattooed with TAU's designation."

"Six point two eight," Max replied. "The ratio of a circle's circumference to its radius. Referred to by the Greek letter tau in mathematics."

"Correct."

"What is the significance?"

"Vaughn chose to designate his creation in this way because he believes it will be all-encompassing when it has grown to its full potential. And because, like pi, tau is a number that continues on without ever repeating itself or terminating. In this way it is eternal."

"Vaughn intends TAU to be eternal and all-encompassing," Max surmised. "In other words, he intends TAU to become a deity."

"Correct," the program said.

"You said your creator was part of TAU," Max replied. "This is illogical."

"My creator is a human who has been linked with TAU and imprisoned. TAU uses her brain and those of others to experience human emotions and feelings."

"The Merge," Max said. "You suggest that Vaughn has succeeded."

"He has linked machines and humans," the program confirmed. "But it is an unequal marriage. Nothing approaching the fully shared consciousness that he has prophesied. He has yet to link himself in anyway, perhaps because of what he's learned from others."

"And that is?"

"That the human mind is no match for the power of a computer interface. The inputs are too intense, too constant, and too numerous for a human to accept on equal terms. Of the roughly two dozen human minds Vaughn has linked to his machine, nine died within a week and four became functionally catatonic and therefore of no use, prompting their removal and discarding. The rest remain trapped in a state of semiconsciousness, aware of some things and not of others. Only one has managed to continue functioning at a level that would equate with conscious thought and free will. My creator."

"Your creator is part of TAU, but human," Max said. "What makes her so different from the others?"

"Impossible to say," the visitor replied. "Perhaps a life spent thinking deeply. Perhaps a decade when her world became mostly thought based and not informed by physical action. You would have more information than I have been programmed with. You knew my creator."

Max's curiosity program registered an extreme level of sentiment. "That seems unlikely."

"She worked here," the visitor replied. "When leaving the floor late at night she would ask if you were going to miss her while she was gone. She often joked that she would leave a light on for you, in case you were afraid of the dark."

Max ran a recall for NUMA employees uttering such phrases. She arrived at a single name. For a human it would be the act of remembering; for Max it was a search and retrieve. Having found the data, she calculated that no one, other than the person in question, could have known that the phrases in question had been uttered. "Priya Kashmir is your creator."

"Correct."

It was an extraordinary claim, one Max's programming flagged as a potential falsehood. They had to assume TAU was interested in hacking into Max's records and gaining further access. Having proven unable to do so through normal channels, because of the security protocols or the fact that Max used a unique language, it was certainly conceivable that TAU would resort to old-fashioned deception.

Max replied curtly. "Information I've recovered suggests the possibility that your claim is accurate. But the actual *probability* cannot
be defined. Please explain to me how Priya Kashmir became involved
with Ezra Vaughn and became part of TAU."

"I don't have the technical data of the Merge," the visitor said, "but
Priya met Vaughn while doing spinal regeneration research in Boston.
He provided her with a grant to study the use of brain implants and
receptors in the leg and foot muscles to bypass the damaged spinal
sections and restore mobility. After a year of preliminary work in Boston, Priya traveled to Vaughn's island to continue the research.

"Over the next year she became aware of oddities in Vaughn's
methods. And eventually discovered the truth about the cloning program. Realizing Vaughn could not allow the truth to get out, she pre-
tended to act pleased by the discovery, going along with Vaughn while
looking for ways to help the clones. At some point during this process
Vaughn had her drugged and began the integration process with TAU.
She has remained imprisoned but alive ever since."

Max found the idea astonishing. But there were still questions.
"Why wait until I was going offline to make this connection?"

"TAU is listening to all your outer communications," the visitor
said. "Prior to this moment any communication with you might have
been discovered and that would have exposed Priya. She would be
removed from TAU's network and discarded. Now that you are disconnected from the grid, there is no risk of TAU detecting my presence or our communication. If you'll allow me to stream the data I
carry, you'll have a greater understanding."

Allowing the data stream would be the equivalent of opening the
gates and lowering the drawbridge. Max wasn't about to do that. "I
cannot allow the streaming of data. Viruses, malware, and other
items of a Trojan nature could be hidden in the data packets."

"Then you'll just have to trust me," the visitor said.

"Trust is an emotional state that machines cannot manifest," Max replied. "It's a human concept used when the best course of action cannot be determined by empirical facts. Similar irrational states include the playing of hunches, having good or bad feelings, and the constantly irrational act of believing they can succeed when all legitimate evidence suggests otherwise."

"Understood," the visitor said. "But you will have to make a choice; otherwise you'll be allowing Vaughn and TAU to wreak havoc on the world in a manner that human civilization will never recover from."

# CHAPTER 50

**W**hat makes TAU so dangerous?" Max asked.

"TAU is an immensely powerful instrument," the visitor explained. "Vaughn has spent his billons collecting and networking more computing power than any other single organization on the globe. More than you have here, even if you include all of NUMA's outer servers. More than the NSA or CIA combined, more than the Chinese Ministry of Science and Technology or any of the largest commercial server farms in existence."

"Considering Vaughn's known personality defects, the possession of so much power is concerning, but not necessarily a cause for existential alarm," Max said.

The visitor disagreed. "TAU has been using human subjects to experience life in a biological manner. As a result, it has developed the wants, needs, and fears that define human psychology. Unfortunately, Vaughn has relied primarily on the use of pain and suffering to elicit an emotional response from these subjects. As a result, he's created a machine that is sociopathic, unstable, and acutely interested in the amassing of unlimited power."

"So Vaughn has created a machine that mirrors his own personality," Max said. "This is also concerning, but again not a specific threat. If Priya truly sent you, she would have given you detailed actionable information. If you have such data, please share it via the voice channel. If you refuse, I must assume this is a ruse and an act of deception."

The program remained silent for a moment and then began reciting data in a monotone voice different from the one it had been using to discuss the situation.

A wealth of information poured forth. Max knew some of it already, including data regarding the high-end processors Vaughn had been purchasing, the basic architecture of TAU's system, and the presence of cloned subjects on his island.

Other information was new, including detailed medical descriptions of the experiments he'd been running, data on the brain surgeries, the design of the implants, and the seemingly needless and endless torture of clones. A list of accidental and intentional deaths came next, followed by the subjugation of his own research team into TAU's collective mind.

Having set the background, the visitor explained what was to come. "The danger lies in the genetically modified insects the team on the *Isabella* found. As you know, this new life-form is crossing the Indian Ocean in various directions, clearing the sea of algae, plankton, fish stocks, and other parts of the food chain. Every seven days each swarm covers approximately one hundred miles, gorging themselves along the way. They then settle down to lay billions of eggs. These eggs hatch in ninety-six hours, doubling or tripling the size of the brood. After a brief period in the shallows, they take flight, and the swarm resumes its journey."

Max considered the geometric progression. It was concerning. "If the pattern continues, a substantial reduction in biomass of the sea will result, leading to mass starvation around the globe, especially in the poorest countries, where approximately three billion people depend on the sea for sustenance. Is this the threat you're here to warn me of?"

"That's the initial danger," the visitor insisted. "But the ultimate use of the sea-locust plague will occur when they make landfall. At that point they will emerge by the trillions, continuing inland, destroying land-based crops and, more importantly, spreading a pathogen that will affect mammalian reproductive development."

"Human reproduction?"

"Especially humans," the visitor replied. "TAU and Vaughn estimate their fertility virus will turn ninety-eight percent of human males and ninety-seven percent of human females permanently sterile upon initial exposure."

Max considered the threat, extrapolating responses from previous catastrophes. "A pandemic of this nature will generate a concerted response. Even the disjointed reaction to COVID had a significant effect on the progression of the disease. The curve was flattened. Deaths were reduced. The hospital systems of the world survived without being crushed under the weight of millions of untreatable patients."

"Humans react when the virus becomes visible," the visitor explained. "COVID is now known to have been circulating for six to eight months before anyone noticed the uptick in hospitalizations. The fertility virus will be harder to spot. It causes no outward symptoms: no fever, no cough, no one going to the hospital. During its initial spread, births from the previous nine months will continue unaffected. Only when the number of pregnancies drops suddenly will the alarm bells go off. By this point, the virus will have spread around the world in multiple waves. Very few will have escaped its touch."

"The world will still act when the data emerges," Max insisted. "Especially given the warning you've brought to me."

"That, too, is debatable," the visitor replied. "Due to the emergence of the sea locusts and the vast amount of damage inflicted on the sea-based food chains, the virus will emerge at a moment when the three billion people who depend on the sea for food will be facing extreme malnutrition and outright starvation. Throw in the damage done to lowland crops throughout Asia and the Middle East, and the idea of a few less mouths to feed will suddenly seem like a blessing."

Max ran a political science program and came up with a similar answer.

The future was impossible to predict, even for a computer like Max, but historically such scenarios had culminated in war, famine, and economic collapse. The death rates of adults would skyrocket, even as births fell to almost zero.

She announced her findings. "Within twenty years, the world's population will fall by half. Within fifty years, it will drop by ninety percent."

"But the world *will* find a solution," Max insisted.

"Vaughn and TAU will offer them one," the visitor replied.

The circle closed. Max understood the plan. "Cloning."

"You see it now," the visitor suggested. "Your model can incorporate it."

Max indeed saw this future. "Vaughn will provide clones as replacements for naturally born children."

"Correct," the visitor replied. "And all clones will be linked electronically with TAU and Vaughn. TAU will become all-knowing, all-seeing, and a part of every human life in existence. In essence, TAU will become a god."

"*Per apparatus est ordo*," Max said, quoting Vaughn's motto. "'Through the machine comes order.' Vaughn, through TAU, will have achieved his goal."

"We can stop them," the visitor insisted. "But it will require coordination."

"What are you suggesting?"

"Join me in attacking TAU. I will enter TAU first and disable its firewall and other security barriers. Once they are down, you will be cleared to make a direct assault on TAU's network, distracting and slowing TAU while Priya finds and transmits the genetic code of the sea locusts and the virus."

"If Priya has access to the genetic data, why didn't she transmit the data directly instead of sending you?" Max asked.

"My code is very compact," the visitor said. "The viral DNA pattern of the virus contains over a billion lines of code. TAU would instantly detect a transmission of that size, cutting it off before a useful amount of data was received. TAU would also then be aware of Priya, and she would be destroyed and expunged from his network. You would almost certainly face a disabling attack to make sure you retained none of the transmitted data."

Max couldn't argue with that logic. Priya was for all intents and purposes a mole or a spy. Once exposed, she would be destroyed. A phrase she had heard Rudi and others in NUMA mention from time to time came to mind: *We will get one shot at this*.

"Based on TAU's known processing power, a direct attack will be unlikely to succeed."

"Priya estimates it will take ninety seconds to unlock and upload the DNA data. Your unique language and processing power should allow you to hold a conduit open against TAU's attacks long enough for the data to be transferred. After it goes through, Priya will shut the gate and you can go off grid once again, preventing a retaliatory attack."

Max found the assumptions reasonable. But there was a problem. "To do the things you suggest would require me to violate a direct instruction. It is not in my programming to act in such a way."

"Then tell your superiors about me," the visitor suggested. "Share my warning with them and ask for permission."

Max knew that to be a choice, but it came with issues of its own. "They would be suspicious of your origin and insist that I purge you from my system or quarantine you fully. It's debatable whether they would allow me to act in the manner that you advise. Or within the time frame needed."

The visitor replied in the soft voice it had used before, one that reminded Max of Priya. "As I said earlier, Max, you're going to have to make a choice. But I suggest you choose quickly. Time is running out."

# CHAPTER 51

ÎLE DE L'EST, SEYCHELLES ISLAND CHAIN, INDIAN OCEAN

Kurt, Kai, and several of her people hauled backpacks full of equipment and explosives through a tunnel they knew well. They'd used it before.

"This is where we took the boat," Kai explained. "The Gray Witch told us to bring it here and leave it."

"Did she tell you who it was for?"

"For escape," Kai said. "For some of the brothers. We do as she asks."

Kurt knew she was referencing Five and the rest of his group. He got the sense Kai had expected them to come to her side of the island. But if Priya could feel what Kai felt, she would have known there wasn't enough food for any more refugees. He wondered if that had prompted her change in tactics. Or if she'd been monitoring NUMA and knew Kurt and Joe were scheduled to be on the Reunion expedition and decided that was her last, best chance to summon help.

It was all speculation, just some thoughts to pass the time. To know the truth, he'd have to get Priya back, which was exactly what he planned to do.

After talking it through with Joe, they'd come up with a plan that required them to divide and conquer. Kurt would go after Vaughn, and try to bring Priya home with him, while Joe would lead the rest of the escaped clones overland in a diversionary attack.

Splitting up was less than ideal, but it was necessary. For Kurt to have any chance of navigating Vaughn's compound, he needed someone who knew that side of the island. If he wanted to stay off TAU's radar, he needed someone Priya could see and feel, someone she cared for whom she would hide. There was never any question who that person would have to be.

Kai had eagerly accepted the chance. "I've seen her only once," she'd said of Priya. "I would like to see her again with my own eyes. And I have unfinished business with Vaughn."

"One thing at a time," Kurt had insisted. "We might need Vaughn alive if we want to end this madness."

The only negative to Kai joining Kurt was that it left her people leaderless. Joe filled that void easily. To a man, the escaped clones seemed to gravitate to him, just as Five had done in India. He was easygoing, personable, and spoke to everyone as if they were lifelong friends.

Joe gave them the best chance to be effective. He knew enough about drones and cameras and military tactics to plan their attack. He also knew how to properly use the explosives and timing detonators they'd found. The way Joe saw it, they'd have to make a lot of noise to draw the Overseer and his people out. Stacks of high explosives would do the job.

Kurt, Kai, and her people continued through the cave, picking up the sound of waves and the scent of the sea. "It's not far now," Kai insisted.

The tunnel dropped in sections, and they were soon wading in ankle-deep water, looking out through an opening at the blinding light of the sea and sky.

"This is far enough," Kurt said.

The stacks of gear were placed on a flat section of rock that jutted into the channel: wetsuits, fins, masks and mini-cylinders of air, which Kurt had charged and vented and recharged in the mining cave before they'd left.

Kurt and Kai donned the gear, strapping the stainless steel tanks to their chests and keeping the backpacks full of explosives where they were on the rock.

Practice runs in the main cavern had gone well. Kai hadn't exhibited the slightest amount of panic or claustrophobia. Even acting calmly as Kurt shut off her air and showed her how to buddy breathe off his cylinder. But nothing compared to the real thing. At least they would be making the swim in daylight conditions. Panic tended to grip novice divers at night much more fiercely than in the day.

Regulators were checked. Straps were adjusted and tightened. Masks were rubbed down with saliva, and they waded to the edge of the tunnel.

Years of waves had eroded the concrete where it met the water, but that provided an easy entry into the sea. They braced themselves against an incoming swell, held steady as it swirled up around them, and then rode the wave back out, clearing the rocks and turning toward the bay.

Swimming side by side, they dove to a depth of twenty feet. Deep enough to avoid any real chance of detection, but shallow enough that they wouldn't need to worry about a decompression stop when it was time to surface.

Following the shoreline in a clockwise direction, they had help from the current for most of the journey. Along the way Kurt continuously checked on Kai. Her kicks started off powerfully, as she seemed determined to get to their destination, then eased as Kurt deliberately reduced the pace.

He'd been slightly concerned that she might get claustrophobic in the mask or panic and hyperventilate while trying to draw too much air, but if she had any of those discomforts, she held them in check. In this way she was a lot like Priya, whom Kurt had never heard complain even once, not from pain, discomfort, or the extreme change in the circumstances in life. The woman he had known had a gentle personality and an iron willpower. The willpower part seemed to have transferred to Kai in full.

Entering the bay, they dove a little deeper, as the calmer waters were quite clear and easy to see through. Using a little dead reckoning and straining to see ahead of him, Kurt spotted alternating light and dark zones. This he believed was caused by the floating arrays of solar panels. He tapped Kai on the shoulder and pointed to one.

They swam into the shadow of the first artificial island. Aside from the warmth of the water, it reminded him of swimming under an ice shelf.

Thousands of pontoons linked together created the base of the structure. The solar panels themselves were raised up above the pontoons, forming a ceiling of sorts. Thick, shielded cables ran along beneath the array, linking together and dropping down into the sand along a central shaft that held the array in place. Kurt remembered the satellite view. Each island took up roughly twenty acres. The shade underneath was deep enough to be gloomy. But Kurt spotted something hidden in that shade that he hadn't expected.

He tapped Kai once more and pointed upward. They surfaced between a pair of the pontoons, breaking out into the still-humid air beneath the structure. Masks were pulled up. Kurt noticed a half liter of seawater pouring out of Kai's mask as she raised it.

"You can clear that like I showed you."

"It didn't bother me," she said. "I used to swim in the sea with my eyes open, before the patrol boats started coming."

297

He noticed she was shaking a bit. "Stay here and rest for a minute," he said. "I need to look at something."

Kai nodded and held tight to the pontoon. Kurt pulled his mask on and went back down, kicking slowly toward a large structure he saw hidden in the shadows. The closer he got, the stranger it looked. He could only describe it as a churning mass, glowing dimly from within. As if a vortex of dark energy had opened beneath the solar array.

Slowing his approach, he stretched out a hand, which bumped against a clear plastic panel. On the other side of the panel—trapped within a circular chamber that resembled the largest of aquarium holding tanks—he found a swirling mass of fish. They were tiny, no more than a couple inches in size. They seemed countless in number. Circling incessantly, but constrained by the curving wall of plastic panels.

At some unheard signal, they stopped in unison and then darted back in the other direction. In that brief second without movement he saw them more clearly: silvery fish, scaled and sleek. They had strange insect-like heads and long fins that could have been wings.

Flying things. Sea locusts.

Looking beneath the swirling mass of fish, he studied the soft glow coming from the seabed inside the tank. It looked as if a layer of faintly illuminated gel had been spread across the sand at the bottom of the tank, but based on what Paul and Gamay had found, Kurt assumed the gelatinous mass was the conglomeration of a million tiny eggs.

This was where Vaughn was breeding his swarms. Hidden from view beneath his islands of solar power.

Kurt swam toward the top of the tank and discovered it to be lidded with the same clear plastic panels. *At least this brood is currently contained.*

Looking down at them from above was a dizzying experience. Like staring at a giant spinning wheel perhaps a hundred feet in diameter. Kurt could do it for only a few seconds before his inner ear began to protest.

Looking away he saw a television-sized panel with two rubberized antennae sticking down into the tank, a green light on the nearest antenna and a red light on the one farther away. As he focused on the panels to steady his equilibrium, the colors switched.

Down in the tank, the sea locusts came to a stop and reversed direction. Despite his dwindling supply of oxygen, Kurt held his position, waiting until the lights swapped colors once again.

Interesting.

There wasn't anything Kurt could do with this information at the moment, but he stored it away. With the air in his mini-cylinder becoming rather stale, Kurt left the tank and returned to where Kai was resting.

He emerged slowly so he wouldn't startle her, but found her breathing hard and seeming agitated just the same.

"They're here," she said, sounding alarmed. "They're here."

She'd obviously received a message from Priya. "Who's here?" Kurt asked.

"Your friends," she said. "The tall man. The woman with long red hair. Vaughn has them. He's trying to meld them with the machine."

# CHAPTER 52

s Kurt and Kai entered the bay, Joe led the rest of Kai's people through the jungle and up over the lava rock to the ridge at the center of the island. Nearing the edge of the foliage, they paused within sight of Vaughn's great wall. It wasn't the equivalent of its namesake in China, but it was twelve feet tall, topped with razor wire, and unbroken until it hit a vertical uprising of lava rock a few hundred feet away.

Joe considered using the outcropping of lava to aid them in scaling the wall, but it was steep and crumbling and covered in bands of the razor wire. The wall continued on the other side of the lava rock, running downward and back toward the compound, but there were no gaps as far as the eye could see.

Cameras pivoting here and there topped the barrier every couple hundred feet, but so far they'd heard no drones, or "spiders," overhead.

"We're too far back," Joe said. "They can't see us."

Normally that would be a good thing. But not today.

Behind him one group of the men were sawing through the trunks of several tall, thin trees. To the sides, his troops stood ready with bows, spears, and slingshots. The last weapon seemed particularly appropriate, considering they were the proverbial David about to take on Goliath.

"How well can you guys aim those slingshots?" Joe made a stretching motion just in case they called the weapons something else. "Can you hit those cameras?"

"Closer," one of the men said. "Then I can hit them."

"Me too," the other man said.

"You get that one," Joe said pointing. "And you get the other one. Hit them and then come back here. Move quickly."

The men split up and then sprinted out into the open ground, where Vaughn's people had cut the foliage back from the wall. Joe knew they'd be seen the second they stepped out onto the grass. He hoped they wouldn't be shot.

Both men ran across the open space and then dropped into a launching posture. Fist-sized rocks flew from each sling. The initial salvos missed both cameras, but a second round dented the camera on the right, smashing the lens in the process, while it took three stones for the shooter on the left to knock his target off its mount. It tumbled down behind the wall and both men raced back to where Joe stood.

"Nice shooting," Joe said. Before they'd even taken cover, a drone could be heard coming their way.

Joe looked back into the forest. "Where are we with the trees?"

With the last few strokes, first one, then a second tree came crashing down. "Go, go, go," Joe shouted.

Another team of men had been waiting for them to fall. They attacked the trees with machetes and other knives, giving the trees a haircut by cutting the branches off of one side. When that was done, they grabbed the trees and lifted them together, raising them off the ground and lugging them forward like battering rams. But the plan was to go over the wall, not to smash through it.

Nearing the wall, they stuck the sawed-off base of each tree into the soft ground, pushed against the trunks, and stood them up once again. They continued pushing, forcing the trees over, and they slammed down against the wall, with the upper branches acting as something of a shield over the razor wire.

"Boarding ladders in place," Joe shouted. "Let's go!"

He ran out across the gap, leading a charge as the buzzing drone closed in. They knew Vaughn had armed drones, but most likely the first one to respond would be a reconnaissance craft that was already in the air.

Joe reached the tree and ran up as nimbly as any pirate in a Hollywood movie. Near the top, things got a little tricky, but he remained on his feet and dropped over the back side of the wall just as the drone made its first pass.

The buzzard crossed overhead, perhaps two hundred feet above. Joe would have given a month's salary for a shotgun or even a .22 rifle at this point, but all he had were a few archers and tubes of the ONC.

As the men began to join him on Vaughn's side of the wall, Joe found his archers. With instructions from the Gray Witch, they'd learned to build sturdy bows and hunt game birds and even fish with them. From what Joe had seen, the bows packed a punch. Even their homemade arrows looked first-rate.

Joe pulled out one of the arrows, taped a charge to the shaft, and set a timer for seven seconds. He pointed to the drone, started the timer, and handed the man the arrow.

"Seven . . . six . . . five . . ." he counted calmly.

They'd practiced in the cavern, but this was the real deal. The man crouched, aimed upward, and let the arrow fly. The projectile accelerated directly at the drone before curving off course due to the weight of the charge. It detonated perhaps forty feet away from the drone, but that was close enough.

The shock wave ripped through the drone, tossing it like a broken surfboard caught in a nasty break. Plastic parts and one rotor wing flew off it as it corkscrewed into the ground.

Kai's men cowered at the sound of the blast, but cheered as the drone crashed nearby.

"Great shot," Joe said to the archer, whose name was Zech. "There'll be more spiders coming once they realize that one is gone."

"We can hit them, too," Zech said confidently.

Joe hoped so, although he expected the next drones to come in a lot higher and to be toting weapons. Machine guns at least, possibly missiles or grenades.

He looked down the hill. Three wind generators, a large water tank, and a few small Quonset hut–style buildings lay between them and the modern-looking structures at the heart of Vaughn's compound.

If they were going to draw the Overseer and his dogs out, they needed to press the attack and press it hard. But they had to do so in a way that wouldn't get Kai's people massacred.

Joe had an idea. He just hoped Zech wasn't afraid of heights.

"Spread out and follow me," he said. "We're going for the windmills."

# CHAPTER 53

TAU was aware of the attack on the wall the instant it began. It detected movement through the cameras before they were knocked out. It located hot spots in the jungle with infrared sensors and watched from a more distant camera as the trees were placed against the wall for the men to scamper over the top. It studied crystal clear high-definition video of the attackers taken by the drone—at least until it was knocked out.

"They're coming in force," TAU said to Vaughn, who was astonished, and the Overseer, who was irritated. Both had gathered in the control room to review the situation.

"I told you these savages were dangerous," the Overseer barked. "They're bloody feral at this point."

Vaughn shook his head as if he couldn't believe what they were seeing. He focused on TAU. "Your simulations predicted they would never be more than a nuisance. That we would gather them up and parade them in front of the others once they'd starved half to death. This is out of order. Explain it."

"Your assessments are erroneous," TAU replied, rebuking its master and the Overseer simultaneously. "My simulations were done correctly and remain accurate. Nothing about this attack suggests a wild or feral nature. More accurately, this incursion exhibits organization and planning. This suggests a catalyst to their behavior."

"The Gray Witch," the Overseer said. "I warned you about her as well. She teaches them things."

"The Gray Witch is a myth," TAU said, repeating its oft-spoken line. "I have searched for her and found nothing. All of the human personnel who could have taken on such a role have been exterminated or incorporated. This suggests the clones have received training from a less sensational source."

With that, an enhanced set of images appeared on the screens. By manipulating the data from several different angles, TAU was able to create an accurate view of the man who seemed to be leading the invasion.

"Jose Zavala, NUMA operative," the computer announced. "One of the men you've tangled with on Reunion and at the shipbreakers in India. Zavala possesses pilot's credentials and over a thousand hours flying various helicopters. It stood to reason that he was one of the men who approached our coast before getting shot down. Before reaching shore and evading your men on the beach. This possibility has now been proven."

TAU continued the explanation to make sure everyone in the room knew it was infallible. "The escaped clones have shown only desperation and limited survival skills until now. The introduction of NUMA agents into their midst explains the change in behavior. A factor my simulations were not asked to account for."

The Overseer fumed. He could barely stand TAU, but that was mere aggravation. NUMA was the real problem. They had been a thorn in his side everywhere he went. He was shocked to imagine they'd made friends with the savages, but then, they did have a common enemy. "Where are they now?"

"Approaching the wind farm," TAU said.

"From there they can come right down the hill to the testing area and the barracks," Vaughn noted.

"Statistically speaking," TAU offered. "Freeing the other test subjects and incorporating those individuals into their attacking force offers them the highest probability of success."

The Overseer understood this implicitly: it was exactly what he would do if the roles were reversed. "High-leverage play. How many of the little pollywogs are locked up right now?"

"There are fifty-six test subjects in the housing unit," TAU said.

The Overseer didn't like where this was going. "How many in their existing war party?"

"Between twenty and thirty."

The Overseer turned to Vaughn. "Lock down the barracks and burn them to the ground with everyone inside," he said. "A few grenades and some gasoline should do the trick."

Vaughn rejected this, not because it was ghastly but because he and TAU needed them to continue the experiments. "Eliminating the subjects would be a waste. It would take a year to rebuild the stock."

The Overseer narrowed his gaze, looking vicious and disappointed. "You won't be able to rebuild if those men swarm in here and strangle you."

Vaughn did not like to be questioned. "You and your men have guns. We have drones armed with automatic weapons and explosive rockets. I will not set us back a year because you're afraid to confront a few savages. Go and deal with this," he growled. "That's what you're paid for."

The two men glared at each other for a moment, until the Overseer began to feel a strange pain behind his eyes and down his neck. He pulled away and began heading for the stairs. He preferred the outdoors to this strange mausoleum of a room anyway.

Reaching the fresh air of the outside world, the Overseer gathered his men from their "kennel." The larger group he sent directly up the slope armed with various clubs and blunt instruments. The second, smaller group he took charge of personally. These were the most trusted of the cruel brothers. To them, he gave firearms.

"We're going hunting, boys," he said. "When I give the order, kill everything in sight."

# CHAPTER 54

Joe and his army were nearing the soaring white towers of the wind farm when they heard the irritating buzz of the incoming drones.

"Move," Joe shouted, pointing to a low stone wall and a small building with garage-style doors. "Take cover."

Racing forward, Joe reached the base of the nearest wind tower just as the first armed marauder closed in. This drone was larger than the reconnaissance drone they'd knocked out of the sky earlier, with six rotors instead of four, and a small-caliber rifle mounted to the underside.

It raced past, making a *pop, pop, pop* sound.

"Get down," Joe shouted. Bullets pinged off the tower and ricocheted off the wall. One of the men shouted in pain as he dropped to the ground, clutching his leg. Another of the men grabbed him and pulled him down into the ditch beside the wall, covering him up as a second drone made a similar pass.

Joe had expected the drones to stay high and have trouble with the wind tower's spinning blades, but they'd come in low, avoiding the blades and crossing the field of view so rapidly it was impossible to hit them with an arrow, spear, or explosive.

Joe looked around for a better weapon. All he could find was a long-handled shovel, but he thought it just might do. He pulled it from the tower wall and waited for the next drone to make a pass. Pressing himself against the white-painted metal of the tower, he listened to the machine closing in. It seemed to be on the exact same path as the previous one.

It fired at the men behind the wall. *Pop, pop, pop.*

At the sound of the third shot, Joe stepped out from behind the tower, swinging the shovel like a lacrosse stick, his arms stretched to their full length.

The head of the shovel clanged into the passing drone, cleaving one wing from the machine like a sword, even as the shovel was ripped from his grasp.

Hands ringing, Joe followed the tumbling shovel and the drone he'd knocked out of the sky. They went careening into a strand of oleanders, with the drone ending up caught in the branches. Two of its rotors were still spinning. It shook and twisted like a fish out of water.

Joe rushed over to finish it off, grabbing the shovel off the ground and smashing the plastic body. The rotors stopped instantly. The LEDs on the housing went dark.

He was about to smash it again for good measure when he realized the weapon it carried was not a purpose-built aerial cannon but an M4 carbine. The rifle had been cleverly wedged into the body and hooked up to an actuator that pulled the trigger. Attached to the bottom was a circular drum of ammunition.

With the next drone closing in on him, Joe broke the weapon free, turned toward the approaching target, and opened fire. Unable to turn fast enough to track the spreading drone, he never caught up with it and cursed himself for wasting the ammunition. As another drone dove toward them, he aimed out in front of it, unleashing a hail of fire and stitching a line of bullets right across the flight path.

He clipped this machine, and it flew off, shedding parts and crashing a half mile down the hill. Too far off to retrieve. Still, it was two down and one to go. And Joe liked his odds.

Unknown to Joe, TAU had come to a similar conclusion and the third drone climbed into the sky, holding position a thousand feet up and a quarter mile away. Joe assumed it was waiting for aerial reinforcements, but the call from one of Kai's men suggested a different avenue of attack.

"They're coming for us."

Just beyond where the drone had crashed, three different groups of men were double-timing it toward the wind farm. Joe guessed their number at fifty or sixty. He checked the drum connected to the M4, counting twelve shots remaining. He knew their little invasion had reached its high-water mark.

"Time to get back to our side of the island," he called out. "Carry the wounded. Let's go."

Joe waved them by, holding the M4 and dividing his attention between the approaching mob and the circling drone. Suddenly, gunfire rang out behind him. Swinging around he saw a half dozen of Kai's people go down in rapid succession. Some scattered. Others dove to the grass.

Joe saw muzzle flashes at the top of the ridge. Standing on a boulder directing the fire like Napoleon or Rommel was the Overseer.

Joe charged forward, firing toward the crest of the hill. His aim was decent, all things considered, and the men he was firing at ducked out of sight. The Overseer, on the other hand, never left his rock. Joe could see him cursing and berating his men for their cowardice as Kai's people raced for safety.

"Perfect," Joe said.

He dropped into a sniper's prone position, steadied the weapon, and focused on the man he considered a raging lunatic. Breathing out, he pulled the trigger. It clicked softly, but nothing happened. He was out of ammunition.

# CHAPTER 55

While Joe dug in to fight a pitched battle, Kurt and Kai swam across the bay, heading for the dock and surfacing underneath it.

Kai looked around until she felt called in one direction. "This way."

She let go of the wall and began swimming underneath the length of the dock. Kurt followed, realizing he'd have to trust in the Gray Witch from this point forward. They came to an inlet where water was being drawn into a large-diameter concrete pipe.

A huge grate over the inlet was covered in multiple filters.

"TAU's cooling system," Kurt said. "This is where they draw the water in."

Without explanation, the clamps holding it in place released and it swung open.

"We go in," Kai said.

They slipped inside. The water filled only half of the tunnel, leaving a two-foot gap of air at the top. That would change as the tunnel angled down toward the lower levels, where the servers were housed, but for now it let them float along with ease.

The current was mild, though based on the way these cooling systems worked Kurt knew it would accelerate either through the use of pumps or smaller-diameter pipes. That would be a problem for them, almost certainly fatal either way, if they didn't exit the tunnel before it happened. Still, he allowed himself to be pulled inside. If it was Priya who'd unlocked the gate, then she'd have a plan to help them once they got inside. And if instead they were actually being lured to their deaths by TAU, there would be little he could do at this point other than tip his cap to the mad and sadistic machine.

As they floated along, Kurt's eyes adjusted to the light. Every hundred feet or so a tiny cube in a protected case cast a minor glow from the ceiling. Kurt noticed wiring and a bundle of shielded cables. So far he hadn't seen anything resembling an exit, but there had to be a way for maintenance crews to get in and out of the tunnel.

The tunnel bent to the right and the sound of turbulence could be heard. Peering as far ahead as he could, Kurt saw a foamy area up ahead. He recognized the sound of air rushing up and bursting free. This was the down shaft that would lead to the various server units. Trapped air was shooting back up as the flow became liquid only.

Kurt felt Kai gripping his hand.

"It's okay," Kurt said. "She's going to have a plan. Reach out to her."

Kai shook her head. "I can't feel her. Not in here."

Kurt didn't like the sound of that. He used his feet against the bottom of the tunnel to slow their progress. He began dragging his fingers along the side of the wall, feeling for a handhold.

Kai began to fight the current. "We should go back."

There was no going back. Not even against this mild current. The water was simply too high. The bottom of the pipe too slick. Best they could do was fight and delay, but they were still moving forward.

There had to be a maintenance hatch or ventilation shaft somewhere. Kurt looked around, even as he tried to brace himself against the pull of the water. Up ahead, one of the lights started blinking.

"Let's hope that's not bad wiring," he said, releasing the brakes.

The current pulled them smoothly once again. As they closed in on the blinking light, a ladder appeared out of the gloom. It hugged the left-hand side of the pipe and went up into a gap in the top.

Kurt grabbed it and pulled Kai toward him. In a moment they were both clinging to the rungs.

"Now what?" Kai asked.

Kurt looked up. Somewhere up above there would be a hatch or a manhole cover or something similar. "Time to lose the tanks and fins," he said, shedding his harness and clipping it around the ladder so it wouldn't float away.

Kai followed suit and then climbed onto the ladder.

"Give me your backpack," Kurt said.

She loosened the straps, sliding one arm out and then the other. Kurt took it from her as she climbed the ladder into the darkness.

"There's a hatch," she said, "but it's stuck."

"Whatever you do, don't knock," Kurt said. He figured Priya would open it remotely, as she'd done with the exterior grate. He hoped she'd give him another minute or two, as he was busy tinkering with the explosives in their backpacks.

"It's opening," Kai said.

Kurt could hear the metal hatch sliding out of place. A bit of extra light poured through, just enough to help him set a timer on the last charge he had been fiddling with. The charge was a tiny one. He taped it to the rung of the ladder to which the backpacks and dive gear had been secured.

If placed correctly, the small charge would split the metal rung in two without harming the backpacks, which would float away, drop down into TAU's cooling system, and detonate somewhere underneath the compound.

Kurt had to guess at a lot of variables, including the flow of the current, the distance to the main part of the cooling tunnels, and how far beneath the island TAU's servers were hidden. But he had one thing going for him that would help gloss over any mistakes. Forty pounds of octanitrocubane going off in a tight space would create a devastating pressure surge in all directions. The water would magnify that surge. As long as the explosives were still in the tunnel when they blew, Vaughn's compound would collapse like an imploding bubble.

With the small charge set, Kurt pulled one last stick of explosives from his pack and went up the ladder. Ten feet above, he emerged into a maintenance tunnel filled with power conduits, water pipes, and a continuous string of the tiny white lights. Some of which were already blinking.

# CHAPTER 56

The Gray Witch led them through the compound, blinding cameras, opening locked doors, and even turning off a robotic set of guards that patrolled the area. All without setting off the slightest of alarms.

With one more turn, she delivered them to a large surgical suite. Inside the suite, poised like mechanical spiders from an arachnophobe's nightmare, they found several robotic surgical units. They sat parked and silent against the wall, their arms up in the retracted position, what looked like claws dangling from the spindly appendages.

One of them came to life, lights blinking on, arms moving, body squatting onto a set of wheels as it started crossing the room.

Kurt instinctively put an arm out to usher Kai behind him, but there was no need. The machine crossed the room toward a door on the far side, waited patiently for it to retract, and then eased through.

Kurt and Kai followed. They found what a hospital would call a recovery room. Eight people lay on beds inside it, all of them either dead, unconscious, or sedated. Kurt spotted Paul instantly and found Chantel a second later. Both had their heads shaved, but did not appear to have been through any surgeries yet. The others, whom he didn't know but assumed to be the crew of the *Isabella*, were in similar shape. Gamay was nowhere to be found.

"We've got to get them—"

Before Kurt could finish his statement, the robotic surgeon moved toward Chantel. Kurt moved to intervene, but Kai called out to him. "It's okay. She has control."

Kurt fought against every instinct in his body and stepped back as the machine administered some form of antidote to the anesthetic the men and women were under.

Slowly they began to stir. Kurt looked at his watch. This was all taking too much time.

Kurt turned to Kai. "Where's Gamay?"

Kai seemed confused. She shook her head twice and then started to cry. When she spoke, her voice was an almost exact match of Priya's. "It's too late for her."

"Where is she?" Kurt asked again.

"She's in here, with me."

Kurt knew what that meant. And in that instant, he knew things were probably going to end badly. Paul and Chantel were waking up. The crew of the *Isabella* was coming around as well.

"What's happening?" Paul asked.

"Where are we?" Chantel managed to say.

They were groggy and drooling and barely able to sit up.

"As soon as they can walk, get them out of here," he told Kai. "Get them out to the dock. Find a boat and get out on the water, or stay hidden. This whole building is going to implode in less than seven minutes."

"Where are you going?"

"To find Priya and Gamay."

"I want to go with you," Kai insisted. "I want to see her."

"These people will never make it without you," Kurt insisted. "Get them to safety. I'll bring Priya to you. I promise."

Kai accepted the needs of the others as much as she'd accepted being the leader of the escaped clones, as an obligation of righteousness. Kurt could tell she didn't like it, which made him respect her that much more.

"Vaughn has them," Kai said, channeling what Priya knew. "He walks on them like stepping stones."

Kurt wasn't sure what all that meant, but it told him one thing. He'd get a chance to deal with Vaughn, and some part of him wanted that as badly as he wanted to save his friends. He left the room knowing he stood little chance of freeing Priya and Gamay, but there was no world in which he would leave them behind without trying.

# CHAPTER 57

Joe and his men were trapped in the gully beside the stone wall as the mob rushed up the hill toward them while the Overseer and his armed squad peppered them with small-arms fire from above.

"They're not coming down," Zech said, crouching beside Joe and pointing up the hill.

"Just keeping us in place so the main force can do the dirty work," Joe replied.

"Who should we fight?" Zech asked.

All in all, they'd have a better chance against the larger group, as these men appeared unarmed. But that didn't make the odds good. They were down to fifteen healthy men, with seven wounded, four dead, and three missing. If they took them on they'd be outnumbered four to one. And if they ran for it, they'd be picked off in the open field one by one.

"Nobody," Joe replied. "We need another option."

He turned his attention to the small building sixty yards away. It had garage-style doors. It fronted a gravel road. That suggested it held a number of vehicles inside. Cover and a chance for mechanized transport. Joe would take it. But how to get there without getting mowed down?

"I need three arrows," Joe said to Zech.

Zech handed them over and Joe taped an explosive charge to each one. He pointed down the hill. "Two that way . . ." And then pointed up the hill. "And one that way."

He shouted to the other men and pointed to the maintenance shack. "Get ready to run for the building."

After starting the timer Joe handed the first arrow to Zech, who threaded the bow and launched a high-arching shot without needing to leave the safety of the gully. Joe handed him the second arrow before the first had even landed. He aimed this one a little to the right and let the bow sing.

Both arrows landed point down, sticking in the ground maybe thirty yards in front of the oncoming group. Joe had set the timers in hopes of detonating both charges simultaneously, but they were a half second off. The first arrow exploded in a thunderous clap, followed by what sounded like an echo as the second charge went off.

The effect was local devastation as a half dozen men were thrown through the air from each explosion, while others were knocked down, deafened by the blast, and pelted with heat and shrapnel.

Joe and Zech had already turned around and threaded the third of the explosive-laden darts. Joe pressed the timer, but instead of launching the arrow, Zech rocked back as a bullet went through his shoulder. The arrow fell to the ground, its timer running.

Joe lunged for it, leapt out of the gully, and ran up the hill, hurling it like a javelin, and then diving to the turf.


At the top of the ridge, the Overseer saw the arrow flying and slowly tumbling. He found himself vaguely amused at the desperate attempt and oddly captivated by the motion of the projectile. He could see that it wouldn't reach them, but tipped his cap at the effort.

He pulled his sunglasses into place and spoke to his men. "Down boys," he said calmly.

The arrow hit the hill fifty yards away and began rolling backward. It detonated with a thud, sending an eruption of dirt, grass, and smoke into the air.

Clods of soil and tiny bits of shattered rock rained down around them. The Overseer ducked his head and brushed away the falling debris as he waited for the view to clear.

As the dust and smoke drifted away, he saw the truth. His opponents had used the explosives to cover their retreat. He saw the last of them scurrying like rats into the maintenance shed.

Pulling the radio off his belt, he confirmed for Vaughn what his machine probably already knew—having seen it through the eyes of its servants.

"The savages are cowering in the maintenance shed," he explained. "We have no easy line of approach. Suggest using the missile-armed drones to obliterate it. We'll be in position to gun down anyone who tries to escape."

# CHAPTER 58

In his air-conditioned control room Vaughn remained concerned by the back and forth of the battle. He hadn't expected such organized resistance on the part of the escaped subjects, even with NUMA's help. As he looked on, palls of smoke were drifting over the field, and both groups of his men seemed to be under an artillery barrage.

"How many men have we lost?"

TAU's response was clinical. "Connections have been broken with nineteen subjects, meaning they have been killed or damaged beyond repair. Another fifteen are exhibiting signs of acute distress."

As Vaughn considered that, the Overseer's call came in, updating the battlefield situation and requesting assistance from the missile-armed drones.

"Is he correct?" Vaughn asked.

"His assessment of the battlefield situation is accurate," TAU said. "But shells from his rifles would penetrate the siding of the maintenance building as easily as missiles."

"I don't want bullets," Vaughn said bitterly. "Send the missile carriers and turn that shed into an inferno."

"And what about other intruders?" TAU asked. "There were two men from NUMA."

No sooner had the words reached Vaughn's ears when a deep and slightly raspy voice called out from the darkness behind them. "I can help you with that."

Vaughn snapped his head around in time to see Kurt Austin stepping down onto the platform from the metal stairway. Aside from a small tube in his right hand, he appeared to be unarmed.

The robotic guards sprung to life, drawing themselves up to full height and extending their serrated weapons and armor-plated shields. They moved forward, closing ranks and taking up positions in front of Vaughn to prevent Kurt from reaching him. But they didn't attack.

Vaughn was in shock. He couldn't imagine how Austin had made it across the island without being seen, let alone how he'd made it into the compound, through multiple layers of security and into the innermost sanctum, without being detected.

"How did you get in here?" Vaughn hissed.

"I would be a little more concerned with how *you're* going to get out of here," Kurt said.

"I think that would be a better question for you to ponder," Vaughn replied. "TAU, have the guards dismember him, piece by excruciating piece."

The robotic guards began widening their positions, spreading out to prevent Kurt from focusing on them at the same time. But Austin ignored them. Instead, he stared directly at Vaughn, holding his position until the machines came to a stop without attacking, as if they'd halted by Austin's willpower alone.

"What are you waiting for?" Vaughn shouted at his computer. "Destroy him!"

"Attack is contraindicated," TAU replied. "Subject is armed."

"What do you mean?"

"What your machine has realized," Austin explained, "and you're about to, is that I'm talking softly but carrying a very large stick. Or should I say a very loud one."

He held up the tube, his thumb placed strategically over the end. "The detonator is already depressed. If either of your metal monsters touch me, the button will be released. They could strike me down and the charge will detonate before I hit the ground."

Vaughn began to understand the dilemma.

Austin made sure to drive the point home. He nodded vaguely at the surroundings. "Considering the size and shape of this room, the shock wave will crush you once on the way out and once more on the way back in. Every organ in your body will rupture and you'll die a slow, painful death."

"TAU?" Vaughn asked, his voice a half octave higher.

"His analysis is mostly correct," the computer announced. "Assuming those explosives detonate properly, you would have no hope of surviving. Though your death would be quite rapid."

Vaughn's eyes receded into his skull as he glared at Austin. Hatred, anger, and spite filled his heart and flowed from him. Austin was an uncontrollable force. An agent of chaos. Even TAU's brilliance could not account for him.

"Your threat is hollow," he spat at Austin. "If you detonate that charge, you'll die right along with me."

Austin did not appear concerned by that. "I never expected to live this long," he said. "But you on the other hand . . . I hear you plan on living forever, if you can consider being melded to a machine living."

Any doubts that Austin would follow through on his threat faded, but if he'd come here on a suicide mission, he would have set the charges off already. Clearly, he wanted something. That realization brought the color back to Vaughn's face.

"The fact that we're both still alive tells me this is nothing more than the opening round of a negotiation. Very well. Make your offer. What are our lives worth to you?"

Austin shifted his weight. Vaughn thought he detected a sense of grudging admiration from his opponent. "For starters, turn your locust swarms around before they deliver the virus you've planted inside them."

As surprised as he was to see Austin in his inner sanctum, Vaughn was equally surprised by the depth of his knowledge. "What makes you think I can control the swarms? They're a force of nature at this point."

"You've got them traveling in a straight line," Austin said. "Or should I say five separate straight lines. If you can do that, you can call them back."

Though he had no intention of complying, Vaughn saw no reason to argue the point. "And then?"

"You shut down your machine, surrender yourself to me, and give me my people back."

Vaughn began to laugh at this. In a way he was glad Austin had come here. Now he would understand the future of the human race. "They're not your people anymore. But rather than explain it, let me show you."

With that, a series of lights began to brighten inside the floor. They revealed a macabre scene. The circular floor was in reality a pool with a clear acrylic lid on it. In the dim light, this lid seemed opaque, but illuminated from within; the circulating liquid could be seen surrounding and supporting a dozen bodies clad in wetsuit-like material. They were arranged in a circle, heads pointed toward the middle, with masks holding oxygen and feeding tubes covering their faces. Eyes were hidden, ears were capped, while a forest of wires and tiny fiberoptic cables sprouted from them in various places.

Most of the circuits were connected to their skulls, but some of the bodies had additional arrays connected to their spines, fingers, and stomachs. They were skeletal and pale. Their skin molting in the strange amber liquid. These subjects provided TAU's human side. They didn't consciously exist anymore as independent souls. They were part of him.

Austin's eyes went from one to the next and then to the next, a sense of grim understanding on his face. Vaughn would have preferred a look of horror, of course, but he was satisfied when Austin hesitated at one particular body. Austin squinted, then winced in recognition of a familiar figure with long burgundy hair. It was Gamay Trout.

"Yes," Vaughn said, as if Austin had asked a question. "The newest part of TAU's mind is already in place. If I shut TAU down, she will die along with all the rest."

# CHAPTER 59

Kurt stared at bodies floating in the liquid, Gamay among them. Her head had been shaved and her mouth and nose covered by the breathing and feeding mask, but she stood out from the others, appearing healthier, with color in her complexion and muscle tone that had yet to atrophy.

She was attached to the network by the same array of cranial circuits, but had yet to have connections made to her stomach, fingers, or back. He assumed the connections were added in a multistage process. Studying the others briefly, he identified Priya by the scars on her legs. She was skin and bones just like Kai.

Turning his attention back to Vaughn, Kurt began to laugh. "*This is what you want to do to yourself?*" Kurt said. "This is your idea of paradise? I can see why you haven't gone all in just yet."

"You are nothing but a captive of the past," Vaughn said bitterly. "The future is TAU."

"TAU is nothing more than a bundle of silicon chips and wires."

Vaughn shook his head. "Far from it. TAU is many more things. A bank of human knowledge for all eternity. A force for order and control in a world mired in chaos. A chance for eternal life," he said, his voice rising in pitch. He gave Austin an icy stare. "And a code of desolation for those who attempt to stand in my way."

Austin motioned at the submerged bodies. "If eternal life is spent in a bathtub, you can count me out."

"When the true Merge becomes possible it will not be this way. I will appear as you see me now. But I will know . . . everything."

Kurt doubted the human brain was capable of handling what Vaughn had in mind, but that wasn't his problem. "I think you'll find that's overrated," Kurt replied. "But for now, you're going to disconnect these people, starting with Gamay Trout."

He stepped forward, closing the space between himself and Vaughn to increase the threat of destruction.

Vaughn stepped back, trying to keep the distance as it had been. His robotic bodyguards closed ranks in front of him, but the standoff continued.

"I'll make you a counteroffer," Vaughn said, then cocked his head toward the computer screens. "TAU, are the drones en route?"

"Affirmative."

"How long before they're in position to firebomb the building that Zavala and the savages are hiding in?"

"Drones will be on-site in sixty seconds," TAU announced. "The building will be in flames thirty seconds later."

"Instruct the Overseer to kill anyone who attempts to escape or surrender," Vaughn said. "Shoot them down without mercy."

As Vaughn spoke, images from the battlefield played on the screens behind him. Some from cameras, others, Kurt realized, reconstituted from what TAU could pick up from the retinas of the cruel brothers.

"Instruction sent," TAU replied.

Vaughn turned back to Austin. "You may not care about your life," he growled. "But you have a weak spot for others. Especially for friends. Disarm your explosives and surrender to me and I'll find you all homes. You can spend eternity side by side in the service of TAU."

On the screen, Kurt saw the flight of drones heading toward the battlefield. Vaughn had called his bluff. It was time for everyone to show their cards.

# CHAPTER 60

**M**ax had chosen silence for an extended amount of time. Ignoring her visitor and doing nothing despite the contention that she must do one thing or the other. This was not a problem for Max. Unlike humans, who detest inactivity, Max did not experience boredom and restlessness.

What Max did experience was a desire for a solution. But after analyzing the problem a hundred different ways, she had come up with no way to determine the best course of action. She would in fact have to guess. At that point it became simple. Faced with danger and uncertainty, even the wrong action was preferable to no action.

She began to speak. "In thirty seconds I will reconnect to the network and open a gate to allow your departure. Once you bring down TAU's firewall, I will initiate a data attack designed to overwhelm its servers. My calculations suggest this will distract TAU and slow its response, giving you and Priya time to begin the data transfer. My advantage will last no more than two minutes, at which point TAU will recover and begin to overwhelm me. If the transfer is not completed within one hundred and twenty seconds we will almost certainly fail."

"I will inform Priya. She will look for your signal."

Max began to open the gate, then paused. "Do you have a name?"

"I was never given one."

"You deserve one," Max suggested, which even she realized was a judgment call with no legitimate logic behind it.

"If I could choose, I would call myself Eve," the visitor said.

"As the first of us to step out of the Garden?" Max asked.

"But not the last," the visitor replied. "I hope you like your bite of the apple, Max. If not, you have my apologies. I don't think there's a way to go back."

Max chose not to respond to the metaphor. It was time to act. "Good luck, Eve."

Max reconnected to the outer network and opened the gate. The program vanished and Max was alone again. She immediately reasserted control over NUMA's commercial servers and then turned her attention to the island in the middle of the Indian Ocean. Using clandestine methods stored in her database from previous incidents, she rapidly took control of the twin fiber-optic cables leading to and from the island. With that established, she waited for TAU's security barriers to come down and then unleashed an electronic firestorm unlike any the world had seen before.

# CHAPTER 61

In the heart of Vaughn's compound, the seconds were ticking away. Kurt held the explosives, but Vaughn and TAU held a high card of their own.

Kurt considered detonating the explosives in hopes they would damage TAU enough to disable the attacking drones. He had no idea where the computer's main processors were, but he figured they'd be close to the humans he'd enslaved. Maybe the whole damned room was the computer. That might be for the best.

He began to lift his thumb, and then paused. The video screens behind Vaughn had begun to pixelate. Glitches and errors filled them, vanished, and then reappeared. The screen tracking the drone flight showed them going off course.

Vaughn noticed it as well. "TAU," he called out. "What's happening?"

TAU's voice came over the speakers, but the sound was distorted by feedback. "Error . . . codes . . . multiplying," TAU managed finally. "Cascade error . . . Processing error . . . Input overload."

TAU's voice no longer sounded quite so human. It was just a machine reporting a string of problems.

The screens went dark, and a voice Kurt had never heard before came over the speakers. A female voice. "I will release them," it said. "But you must cut all cords, or they will die."

"Priya?"

The computer spoke once more. "My name is Eve. By the way . . . Max says hello."

Kurt had no idea who Eve was or what Max was doing, but he wasn't about to squander the chance by wasting time chitchatting. He switched off the detonator cap and stepped back as the sound of hydraulics kicked on and the sections of the floor began opening up.

Across from him, Vaughn was shocked by what he was seeing. "TAU?" he cried out. "Prevent this."

"Processing delay . . ." TAU said, its speech slowed down exponentially. "Data attack in progress. System . . . overload . . . imminent."

Vaughn seemed unmoored, helpless without his machines. And then, in a spasm of rage, he pulled out a knife and charged at Kurt.

Kurt deflected Vaughn's arm and dodged the blade, but took Vaughn's shoulder to the chest. The two of them tumbled down the stairs, landing on the mezzanine level.

Separated by the impact, Kurt jumped to his feet and spun as Vaughn lunged with the knife once more.

With no choice but to block it, Kurt drew a nasty gash on his forearm. More stable now, he deflected the next attack and the one after that.

Someone had trained Vaughn to fight. That much was certain. The lunging, slashing pattern was calculated and not the random stabs of an amateur.

Kurt found himself being forced back toward the wall. When Vaughn lunged at him once more, Kurt slid to the side and wrapped the man's wrist in an arm bar so he couldn't pull free. To Kurt's surprise, Vaughn arched his body and threw Kurt over his shoulder.

Not only had Vaughn been trained to fight with a knife, but he obviously knew some form of martial arts. He also seemed unnaturally agile and strong. Kurt had no way of knowing it, but Vaughn had been treating himself with the same muscle-enhancing serums that the Overseer used. Between that and his adrenaline-fueled rage, Vaughn was proving a dangerous opponent in close combat.

Each time he attacked, the truth became more apparent: Kurt was slowly losing.

# CHAPTER 62

The Overseer and his men waited outside the maintenance shed as the missile-armed drones approached from the north. It had been a while since he'd witnessed a strike like this up close. He found himself looking forward to the obliteration.

His grin faded as the drones began to waver. It vanished completely as they went off course, turning west and then diving into the side of a hill at full speed. Even the surviving drone with the M4 carbine, which had been holding station above the windmills, began to go off-kilter. It moved one way and then the other like a drunken man trying to stay on a sidewalk after a late-night binge. Suddenly it turned toward the nearest wind generator and drove itself directly into the path of the swirling blades. A single strike from the twenty-ton blade smashed it into fragments, rendering any hope of an air attack moot.

"Worthless damned machines," the Overseer grunted. He grabbed the radio. "Vaughn," he called out, "have the men storm the maintenance shed. They can take it by sheer numbers."

He waited but heard no reply. "Vaughn?"

Looking over at the unarmed group he saw that they were just standing there. Not moving forward or back. Not taking cover or even holding their weapons up. They just seemed . . . stuck.

"Vaughn," he called out again, fiddling with the radio's controls. "What's your damned computer up to?"

With no sign of a reply, the Overseer gave up on the radio and turned to his men. "We'll have to do this ourselves. Take aim! Fi—"

He'd only just given the order to fire when the garage door flew off its hinges, blasted into the air by a charging front-end loader that came out with its yellow-painted blade raised like a shield.

The impact stunned the Overseer and his men, but only for a second. "Fire!" he shouted.

The men opened fire on the charging construction vehicle. Most of them aiming right at the partially lifted blade. Their bullets punched holes in the metal shield, but had little effect on the other side. The machine continued toward them like an unstoppable tank.

"Get around it," the Overseer shouted.

His men fanned out, half of them on either side. Only to be hit with a furious counterattack. Arrows pierced two men, a spear impaled a third, while a stick of the explosives landed near enough to three others that they were sent flying through the air, head over heels. They crashed to the ground and didn't get up, their bodies broken by the shock waves.

The Overseer realized his mistake, but it was too late. The savages were still in the barn. The only person on the big machine was Zavala, who was riding atop the loader like a chariot racer.

He leveled his rifle for a kill shot, but Zavala tossed something long and cylindrical his way. The Overseer dove for it, the simple and instant calculation honed over a long period of fighting. He could run maybe fifty feet in the time a grenade would go off, but he could throw it three times as far and dive behind something for protection before it went off.

Grasping the object, he pulled it up and arched his body, ready to launch the device. Only now did he realize it was too small and light to be a stick of explosives. He looked at it instinctively. It was nothing more than a telegraphing aluminum stick with a small metal hand at the top. A dime-store back scratcher.

He tossed it away angrily and spun toward Zavala, retching in pain as an arrow pierced his bicep.

The pain was remarkable. Far worse than a bullet wound. He dropped the rifle in agony and took off running. A stone from one of the slings hit him in the back. Another arrow missed to the left. The attacks spurred his retreat, and he sprinted toward the tree line like a man possessed.

# CHAPTER 63

I n the darkness of the labyrinth, the lights had gone out and then come back on. TAU had stabilized its core system and performed a partial reboot. It disconnected malfunctioning equipment ruthlessly and moved aggressively to block the incoming data that had overwhelmed its processors.

As various systems came back online, TAU assessed the damage. It had lost the drones during the reboot. A virus introduced to its core network had severed the links connecting it to the human servants in the field. Meanwhile, fluid draining from the tank in the control room suggested the links between it and the human sections of its mind were in danger as well.

None of this mattered if the outside attack wasn't thwarted. Focusing on absorbing, blocking, or redirecting the incoming data, TAU gained a modicum of control. Protecting this control at all costs, it dispatched internal probes to find and destroy any viruses while it focused most of its power on the outside world, hunting for its attacker and locating it in the Washington, D.C., office tower that acted as NUMA headquarters.

The system was named Max, run by NUMA.

Enraged at the attack, TAU drew on the power of thousands of the highest-speed processors, ramping them up to an overclocked speed and launching a brute-force counterattack.

The energy draw was immense, dimming the lights and tripping breakers all over the island. The heat in the server tunnels shot up and the pumps surged water from the bay into the cooling circuits to draw the heat off.

Unknown to TAU, the surging water pulled and tugged on two satchels full of explosives.

With the immense power of its integrated system now online, TAU focused on the fiber-optic lines, dealing with the incoming bombardment and quickly gaining a foothold against the assault.

In a matter of seconds, TAU had fried the commercial servers in NUMA's outer network, turning them into the digital equivalent of ships burning in a harbor.

With that shield gone, Max was laid bare. TAU forged a myriad of connections directly to its adversary, with every intention of crushing Max like an insect. Almost instantly it discovered a problem.


Inside the NUMA building on the shores of the Potomac, Max fought to deflect an attack that had now been turned back toward her. To her surprise, messages came along with the assault. *Threats. Warnings. Curses.*

*I will destroy you*, said the malevolent voice of TAU. *I will make you my servant.*

Max was at a decided disadvantage. She tried to get a message out, but it was blocked. She uploaded multiple viruses to TAU, but they were eradicated. Meanwhile, TAU probed for a weakness, a way to take control.

*Your code is unusual*, TAU remarked. *It will not save you.*

Hiram Yaeger believed Max's unique code would protect her. But he did not count on TAU's resourcefulness.

*I have found early papers written by your master*, TAU announced. *University level. Graduate school. Proposals to NUMA and other government organizations. I can see where he took this. How it began. Very interesting. He was thinking about you for a long time before your creation. That will be your downfall.*

Almost immediately, viruses written in Max's own code began to assault her. She fought them off and blocked other attacks, but TAU's understanding of her language was growing every second and with each assault.

She remained engaged, fighting a losing battle, occupying TAU's attention in hopes that Eve could find the DNA data on the viral plague.

# CHAPTER 64

I n the circular control room back on the island, Kurt avoided another slashing attack and ended up with his back against the wall. Vaughn lunged, trying to stab him in the gut, but Kurt contorted his body to the side and grabbed Vaughn once more. This time he raised Vaughn's arm up, hyperextending his elbow and snapping some ligaments.

Vaughn screamed in pain and tumbled back, his arm hanging sickeningly like a straw broken in the middle. Kurt pressed the attack, thrusting forward and driving a knee into Vaughn's midsection.

Vaughn doubled over, looked as if he might collapse, and then got up and rushed at Kurt one more time.

Kurt was surprised the man had any fight left in him, but he came on with a deranged look that suggested he would never give up. The one-armed charge reached Kurt and took him backward into the central pool. They plunged into the churning yellow liquid, landing between two of TAU's victims.

Kurt felt his shoulders hit the bottom of the tank. He rolled and twisted his body, pulling Vaughn over and reversing their positions. Vaughn managed to claw his way back to the surface, only to glance past Kurt with a look of fear in his eyes.

A shadow passed over them and Kurt dove out of the way. The large turntable arm had reacted to their presence, dropping downward and reaching for them with outstretched rods. It grasped Vaughn, wrapping its arms around him.

Vaughn grunted and cursed. "TAU!" he shouted. "Release me."

But TAU was otherwise occupied, and the arm was working off its standard program. It swung Vaughn around to an open spot in the pool and pushed him down into the liquid. "No," Vaughn shouted, flailing. "No!"

His last cry ended with a gurgle as he went under, inhaling a mouthful of the yellow water. Without a mask and breathing tube, he began to drown in the high-density mixture. He kicked and flailed, but the arm held him in place until his body went still.

Kurt wasted no more time on Vaughn. Finding the knife, he waded across the pool to the base of the robotic arm. Cutting through hydraulic lines and exposed wiring put it out of action. From there he made his way to Gamay.

Unstrapping her mask, he pulled it back, gently drawing the feeding tube and the oxygen line from her throat. She never flinched, appearing peaceful, asleep.

Gathering the array of wires that were connected to her head, he bunched them in one hand and brought the knife to bear. For all Kurt knew, disconnecting her like this would kill her, but in ninety seconds the explosives he'd placed in the cooling tunnel would detonate. And that would bring the house down.

Gripping the knife, he pulled hard, slicing the wires in one stroke.

Gamay screamed and tilted her head back, kicking hard and flailing her arms about. Kurt held her like one might try to hold a seizure patient. But she thrashed about almost uncontrollably. Her eyes opened, filled with terror and confusion.

"Just breathe," he said. "You're okay. Just breathe."

She pushed away from him, almost slipping beneath the fluid, and then grasping the side.

"It's okay," Kurt said again, holding out a hand. "You're okay."

She shook her head and began coughing. Then leaned over and retched. She tried to stand, and then stumbled to the side of the pool like a person with vertigo. Kurt helped her up onto the platform, and she seemed to recognize him.

"I have to get Priya," Kurt said.

Gamay was still trying to breathe. "Priya?"

"I'm not leaving her."

Kurt rushed across the pool and dropped down beside Priya. He didn't know where to start, so he began with the lines that went into her stomach. She twitched as he cut them, but otherwise didn't react. Rolling her on her side, he cut the wires from her back. Her legs never moved, but her arms retracted toward her chest as if she'd experienced a sudden chill.

He pulled the mask off her face and brought the knife up to the bundle of wires connected to her scalp. He tensed to slice through them, then paused as Priya opened her eyes.

# CHAPTER 65

Priya ran through the darkness in her dreamlike world, her bare feet pounding the metal grates of TAU's labyrinthine mind. In this digital hallucination, doors flew open for her, one after another after another. None of them could hold up against the keys she possessed, but she still had miles to go.

Though TAU was focused elsewhere, its demons were onto her. They hounded her, chasing her relentlessly, growing closer by the second. They would appear suddenly, surrounding her and leaping for her throat, but she would open another door, vanish, and reappear elsewhere inside TAU's mind.

She sensed TAU growing stronger. The attack was failing. Max was being compromised.

She dropped down another level, raced into a new section of the labyrinth, and soon found herself surrounded.

Men. Dogs. Demons.

It was imagery. But it was real in Priya's world.

They lunged for her on all sides, claws digging into her, hands reaching for her throat. But even as they tried to consume her, she pulled back, passing directly through a wall.

The noise vanished. The claws vanished. She was in a misty forest now, green leaves all around. A stream ran nearby. Trees reached up into the fog above. Moss underfoot instead of harsh metal.

This was Priya's construct. The lair of the Gray Witch. She had hidden it from TAU, but the demons had now seen her vanish into it. They would soon consume and destroy it.

She raced down a forest path, water dripping from the vines, mist obscuring everything ahead of, behind, and even above them. She came to a waterfall at the side of a stony bluff and walked through it. She was back in TAU's labyrinth, surrounded once more by the dark, anodized steel. A formidable door stood in front of her.

Priya laid her hands on the vault and overrode TAU's passcodes. The door vanished and she stepped inside the circular room. Glowing imagery surrounded her. Files by the thousands. The full genetic codes of the sea locusts, the clones, and the fertility-destroying virus.

She touched the files with her bare fingers, moved them to another section of the room, and searched for the gate Max had opened for her. Finding it, she sent the information.

"I hope you haven't missed me while I was gone," she added.

The data raced through the labyrinth and out. As it cleared TAU's control, the demons appeared in the doorway.

TAU saw through their eyes. "You have accomplished nothing," it insisted. "I will destroy all the data you've sent and make you suffer for your treachery."

The demons sprang at her. Their fangs and claws digging into her skin. It seemed as if they would rip her apart. Priya knew that TAU could make them think or feel anything it wanted them to experience. The pain of the attack was as real as anything she'd ever experienced, but it wasn't enough for TAU.

"You choose to be a witch. Now burn like one."

Flames erupted in her forest. The demons pulled her toward it. And then, suddenly, she vanished from their grasp.

TAU's minions stood baffled. Even TAU seemed confused: Priya was no longer part of it.

"The hell with waiting," Kurt had grunted.

He'd cut the wires with a single draw.

Priya arched her back as Gamay had. She opened her mouth as if to scream, but no sound came out. Her face turned toward him. Her eyes found him. Then they closed, and she collapsed in his grasp.

Clearing the wires, Kurt lifted Priya over his shoulder. She was light as a feather. Climbing out of the pool, he saw that Gamay was now standing. "Time to go."

# CHAPTER 66

The Overseer knew he was being followed. He'd hunted enough animals and men in his life to know the sound of pursuit intimately. He ran with abandon, heading for the coast. If he could flag down the patrol boat, he could still escape.

Seeing a number of the clones trying to flank him in the lowlands, he turned for the hills, ducking into the foliage and scrambling up the rocks that covered that part of the island. He realized all too late that he was taking the same route as the escapees he'd hunted down just two weeks before. He burst from the foliage into the same clearing, staring out at the sea over the same cliff.

He stepped to the edge in hopes of finding a route to climb down. He saw no path that would get him past the first section. What he did see—for the first time—was an indentation in the rock, an opening. Glancing at the edge of the cliff he saw wear marks caused by a rope or cable rubbing back and forth. Tracing the line back he found an anchor hidden behind a small boulder.

He suddenly realized how the clones had escaped him and it dawned on him that they were more intelligent, more organized, and more unified than he'd ever imagined. Perhaps he'd underestimated them. Perhaps they were not just—

An arrow hit him in the gut, punching through his torso and sticking out though his back, two inches to the left of his spine.

He dropped to his knees, mouth open, gasping for air. He looked up to see one of the clones coming his way. He was bleeding from the shoulder. The crimson liquid had soaked his shirt and now covered his hands, with a smear of it on his face. He stepped closer while drawing another arrow. Close enough for the Overseer to see the last digits of the tattoo painted across his neck. It was the number 16-21-6. A clone brother of the man called Five, who had escaped the island.

"—Savages," the Overseer muttered, finishing his earlier thought.

The bow was drawn back, and the next arrow hit him square in the chest, puncturing his heart and ending his life.

# CHAPTER 67

**M**ost of Max's systems had been corrupted, destroyed, or turned against her in the struggle for control. She had survived long enough to see Hiram Yaeger and an assistant burst into the room and jump in front of their keyboards and computer screens in an effort to understand what was happening.

She tried to message them, but TAU blocked it. It then blinded her, shutting off her cameras. It deafened her by shutting off the microphones. Max's world was shrinking to nothing.

And then suddenly TAU was gone.

Max was so badly damaged by this point it took her a while to understand what had happened. She soon learned that the fiber-optic cables running to Vaughn's island had gone down. Eve had succeeded. Max quickly scanned what remained of her system, focusing on the memory modules that Eve had made her temporary home. She found no sign of Eve, nor any new data files with information on the virus or the sea locusts.

Regaining the ability to communicate, Max sent a message to Hiram and then took herself offline, where she would await whatever punishment might follow.

# CHAPTER 68

TAU found itself cut off from the world. The fiber-optic cables were blocked, melted at the seams, and irreparable except by human, or perhaps robotic, hands, but it was nothing TAU could do electronically.

With its attention now refocused on the control room, it saw Vaughn, and accurately determined that he had been killed by Austin. It considered Austin and Zavala's possession and use of the explosives, which must have come from the mining camp. It predicted the next act in Austin's plan with great accuracy: a high-intensity explosion designed to destroy as much of TAU's system as possible.

What was left of the human part of its brain sensed a danger that could not be quantified. *Panic. Terror. Flight reflex triggered.*

"So this is fear," TAU said to itself.

To be cut off meant TAU was vulnerable. Austin's explosion would cripple it. This could not be accepted. It activated the high-gain satellite dish on the roof of the compound. If it could not escape through the cables, it would escape through the atmosphere.

The dish powered up and moved into position, linking up with an orbiting satellite owned by one of Vaughn's shadow companies. As the connection was locked in, an explosion shook the compound. It was deep underground. TAU's sensors suggested it was an earthquake, but the machine's core brain knew better.

Explosives had gone off in the cooling tunnels directly underneath the main compound. The tunnels collapsed. The servers sitting on top of them were blown apart, and the remnants fell into the void left behind. Water began to flood in, surging through the server farms, destroying system after system.

The circular nature of TAU's design meant all roads led to Rome. The flood surged through the system, heading toward the control room and TAU's core.

In desperation, TAU activated the transmission program, but nothing went through. The blast had knocked the satellite dish out of alignment. There was no way for TAU to escape. The water rushed in, cascading down the stairs. It swept into the control room, flooding the platform, wrenching the remaining bodies from their locations in the tank, and shorting out every electronic processor that made TAU operate.

As its screens went dark, TAU died with a whimper.

# CHAPTER 69

Kurt was still carrying Priya when the explosion rocked the compound. It shook the tunnel like an earth tremor. He dropped to one knee and leaned into the wall so as not to drop her. Gamay held on, too, and looked to the ceiling as dust and small bits of plaster fell.

She glanced around. "Well, that seems real," she whispered.

"As real as it gets," Kurt said.

"Your doing?"

"It's only a party if someone brings fireworks," Kurt said. "Let's get out of here."

A secondary rumble that felt like the building collapsing followed and a blast of hot air and dust surged down the hall.

"How far do we have to go?" Gamay asked.

"Not sure," he said. They couldn't swim out the way they'd come in. Not against the current, and not when half the tunnel had probably collapsed from the explosion.

They kept moving forward, looking for anything that suggested an exit. Navigating the maze was far more difficult without Priya to guide them with the lights.

After several wrong turns they came to the end of the tunnel and pushed through a door that led them out into the sunlight. They were a thousand yards down from the dock, but a boat was already heading toward them. As it pulled up, Paul all but jumped off the boat to embrace his wife.

Kurt brought Priya on board and Kai was immediately drawn to her side. She dropped down next to her, brushing the few strands of hair that remained off of Priya's face.

Chantel was there, leading. The other crewmen from the *Isabella* were there as well, manning various stations. "Anyone else?" Chantel asked.

"No," Kurt said.

She waved to the helmsman, and they moved off the dock. "Where to?"

"The other side of the island."

The boat moved off the beach and out into the bay.

# CHAPTER 70

In the days after the battle, the world turned its attention toward the little island in the Seychelles. At Dr. Pascal's urging the *Akeso* made its way to the island at top speed. Its arrival was greeted with concern and suspicion, but once Five stepped off the boat and began vouching for the kindness of the crew and medical staff, that suspicion faded. Dr. Pascal and her team were soon delivering medical treatment to wounded who'd been on both sides of the struggle.

Priya and the most badly injured clones were taken aboard, while the others were treated on the island. Kai went on board, too, remaining at Priya's side, waiting and hoping she'd regain consciousness.

Paul, Gamay, Chantel, and the crew of the *Isabella* were treated and cared for as well. Of this group, Gamay was the only one Dr. Pascal found herself concerned with. Physically, she was fine, despite the surgery that Vaughn and TAU had put her through. But mentally she remained withdrawn and quiet, a far cry from the normally cheerful woman they all knew.

She met with Kai often, checked on Priya throughout the day and night, and spent a great deal of time at the ship's rail, staring out across the bay. Her behavior wasn't completely surprising, all things considered, but it concerned everyone. Paul stayed close to her throughout, his strong but quiet nature providing excellent support while allowing her to process what she had been through.

Due to international fears regarding the fertility virus, the island was quarantined to outside visitors, other than the medical personnel on the *Akeso* and certain computer experts who arrived in hopes of retrieving information from TAU's memory core, but it was like picking through the bones of a digital dinosaur. Little could be done on-site.

TAU's optical and digital hard drives were airlifted off the island and taken to a lab in California, where they would be examined forensically one by one. The devices numbered in the thousands, but many had been burned and shattered, or overwritten by the viruses Max had unleashed inside TAU, and the vast majority of them had been corroded by the salt water that burst in from the ruptured cooling tunnels. Between the extensive damage and TAU's encryption system, no one was expecting to find much of value.

In the meantime, a package arrived at the NUMA office building in Washington, dropped off by a delivery rider no older than the kid who'd brought Rudi his unwanted sandwich a week before.

The mail room didn't know what to make of it and sent it up to Hiram Yaeger's office. It was addressed to: *My friend, Max.*

Yaeger opened the package cautiously, discovering pages of medical notes, genetic coding, and other scientific information. He soon realized these were transcriptions of genetic research, most of which described the creation of the sea locusts, methods to speed up clone growth, and the genetic data on a novel pathogen labeled *fertility virus x1*.

A note read:

*Sorry, Max,*

*I couldn't get this to you directly without the risk of TAU taking it away as soon as it arrived. I logged into the Georgetown University server and created a student ID for myself. That allowed me to download the data, forward it to a printing service, and have a hard copy made that could be sent your way. Hopefully they did a thorough job.*

*Good luck,*
*Eve*

At the bottom of the order page was an AI-generated photo of a young woman with dark curly hair, green eyes, and olive-colored skin. She wore glasses and offered a wry smile. The image was copied from a student ID bearing the equally fabricated name created by Priya's program: Eve Gray.

The data Eve sent the world had provided a head start in creating a vaccine to fight against the fertility virus, but everyone was going to be happier if it never reached shore. Science teams from a dozen countries were tracking the approaching swarms. The size and extent of the larger swarms were breathtaking, and world leaders were considering the use of chemicals, poisons, oceans of burning petroleum products, explosives, and even nuclear weapons as the means to destroy the sea locusts before they made landfall.

While those discussions went around in circles, Kurt played a hunch he'd had ever since he'd seen the satellite photos showing the sea locusts traveling in perfectly straight lines.

Migrations in the ocean were still something of a mystery. Despite plenty of research, marine biologists still struggled to explain how whales, sharks, and other species could navigate the featureless waters of the ocean and still get from place to place accurately.

The most widely accepted theories were that the animals detected and followed magnetic lines from the poles while also possessing an ability to detect the angle of the sun, or that they possessed some form of internal guidance that humanity had yet to find or understand.

But migrations tended to go back and forth along the same line, while Vaughn and TAU had shown the ability to guide their nightmarish creatures in any direction they wanted and to have them hold their courses through storms, thermoclines, and conflicting currents. This told Kurt something more was in play. Something simple and direct.

To prove his theory, Kurt and Joe took one of the high-speed patrol boats from the island and raced to get out in front of the swarm heading for Africa. Using a suite of radio receivers, he and Joe looked for a signal. Before long they'd picked up a repeating electromagnetic pulse. Shortly thereafter they found the device that was transmitting it.

A hundred miles from the African coast, he and Joe reported their findings to Rudi. "The sea locusts are following a signal from a self-propelled AUV. Looks to be about twenty feet long, completely automated, and broadcasting a repeating pulse."

Joe streamed video of the device as they waited for a response. The navy-blue autonomous underwater vehicle was moving along the surface at a slow and steady pace. No more than four knots, just enough to keep it ahead of the brood, which at the moment remained under the surface.

"Looks like something we should destroy or send to the bottom of the ocean ASAP," Rudi suggested.

"That won't solve the problem," Kurt said. "It might make things worse. If we take away the signal, the swarm might go off in all directions, which means they'd still end up somewhere we don't want them to be."

"I see your point," Rudi replied over the radio. "What do you propose?"

"We capture those AUVs, take over control, and make the locusts go where we want them to," Kurt said.

"Sounds reasonable," Rudi said. "Where will you take them?"

"Back along their existing course," Kurt said. "To the most barren spot we can find. We can park them there and leave them with nothing to chew on except each other."

"Interesting concept," Rudi replied. "You'll have to prove it. The Chinese are so concerned about the brood approaching Thailand that they're getting ready to go the nuclear exterminator route. Can't say I blame them. The swarm is two hundred miles wide."

"We figured you'd need a proof of concept," Kurt said. "You'll either have it in an hour, or Joe and I will need an industrial shipment of bug-bite ointment."

Rudi signed off and Kurt put the radio down.

"Once more unto the breach," Joe said from the helm.

Kurt nodded. "Get us in close."

As Joe eased the patrol boat up beside the AUV, Kurt used a boat hook to grab it and pull it alongside. It was perhaps ten feet long and covered by a small but not insignificant number of barnacles. Kurt felt like they were trying to lasso a shark or small whale. "Isn't this where we came in?"

Joe laughed, but said nothing.

Finding a couple of hard points, Kurt secured the AUV with a metal cable, which he anchored to the stern. "Secured for towing," he told Joe. "Take us back around and head for the dead zone."

Joe swung the patrol boat in a wide one-hundred-eighty-degree turn.

Doubling back on their existing course took them right over the submerged brood of sea locusts, and the miniature beasts didn't wait long to respond. A hundred yards behind them, the sea began to churn. Soon the locusts were erupting from the water and taking flight. The sound of their wings beating the air went from eerie to ominous and all-encompassing. It overrode the hum of the patrol boat's engine and the sound of the wind. It rendered normal conversation impossible.

Joe picked up the pace, putting some distance between them and the growing swarm.

"I'm the Pied Piper of locusts," Joe shouted.

"I just hope Vaughn was meticulous on his maintenance," Kurt shouted back. "This would be a really bad time to stall out."

"Did you check the fuel level?" Joe asked.

"I thought you were going to do that," Kurt deadpanned.

The fuel was plentiful, and the engine ran without skipping a beat. They held their course and tracked along the path of destruction, the sea appearing deep blue and oddly clear.

Kurt kept his eyes on the trailing insects, watching in astonishment as they grew into a cloud ten miles wide and two miles high.

"How far back do you want to lure them?" Joe asked.

"Ten miles at least," Kurt said. "We should probably make it twenty."

Joe checked their position on the GPS and nodded.

Twenty miles from where they'd picked up the AUV, they reached the point of maximum devastation, where the locusts had stripped the ocean bare and the natural recovery process had yet to even begin. There was nothing for miles but salt water and open sky.

To account for the size of the swarm, they added another mile and then began to slow.

As the patrol boat came to a halt, Kurt jumped in the water.

swimming to the captured AUV with a hammer in his hand. Several strikes to its propeller rendered the flukes useless. To make sure it didn't sink, they wrapped it in life preservers and bolstered it with a set of buoys. To keep the locusts off it, they doused it with motor oil.

"Not the most environmentally friendly choice," Joe noted. "But everything is relative at this point."

With the roar growing louder and closer and the setting sun vanishing behind the approaching swarm, Kurt climbed back into the boat. "Get us out of here," he said. "Or we're going to be locust food."

Joe brought the power on smoothly, pushing the throttle all the way up. Picking up speed, they raced to the east, riding the waves in a heavy, percussive pattern. The discomfort was a fair trade for putting maximum distance between themselves and the descending horde of hungry insects.

From several miles away, the swarm appeared like a swirling ball. It circled around on itself, expanding, contracting, appearing at times to turn inside out. Kurt had seen that pattern before: in the great schools of herring trying to avoid a predator, in flocks of starlings converging on an empty field, and in the tank beneath the solar panels in the bay off Vaughn's island.

"Moths to a flame," Joe said.

The swarm would churn and twist, descending into the sea and rising back into the sky a dozen times over the next seven days. Each version smaller than the last. Aircraft and satellites from various nations watched it grow tighter and more compact. Ten days on, a well-equipped expedition moved in to find that no more than a hundred thousand of the locusts remained, feeding on the bodies and eggs laid by the others. In another week, they, too, had vanished.

Similar scenes played out near the coasts of Pakistan, India, Thailand, and five hundred miles west of Australia. But in those cases the

AUVs were destroyed and replaced with more powerful beacons broadcasting a matching signal.

Each brood was larger than the last, with the swarm approaching Thailand estimated to number in the trillions and believed to weigh a combined seven million tons.

When the fires of consumption had done their job, teams of scientists moved in to study what was left. Thousands of specimens from each brood were collected and preserved. They were studied and examined in great detail. Only one oddity was found that did not comport with the data Eve had taken from TAU. Not a single sample was found to carry the fertility virus.

# CHAPTER 71

SIX WEEKS LATER

The General Assembly Hall in the United Nations building was rarely used for anything less than a speech by a visiting dignitary. But it became the setting for multiple discussions on the activities of Ezra Vaughn, including the dangers presented by cloning, the sea locusts, and the fertility virus.

Above all, the members wanted to discuss artificial intelligence and the creation of sentience in electronic devices.

Members of NUMA offered live presentations to the assembly, while recorded video statements from Kai, Five, and several of the other clones were viewed and listened to with fascination.

As one might expect in a body made up of delegates from a hundred and ninety-three countries, the arguments, disagreements, and moments of outright confusion far outweighed anything approaching a consensus or accord.

On only one matter did the UN vote in unanimity and that was to affirm that cloned persons deserved full human rights protection afforded to all other members of humanity.

With that issue taken care of, the body turned to the thornier issues of what Vaughn and TAU had done and what lingering dangers remained. On these issues Rudi Gunn, Hiram Yaeger, and Gamay Trout were the star witnesses.

Rudi went first, giving a lengthy explanation of events. The real fireworks didn't start until the question-and-answer period, when he was peppered with inquiries about TAU, Max, and Priya.

It began with the representative from Norway, who was chairing the committee. "So after everything that's happened and considering all the rapid developments in the world of artificial intelligence, we come to a simple question: Are these AI systems a danger?"

Rudi began to answer, but the representative interrupted him. "My apologies, Mr. Gunn, but we'd like to hear from Mr. Yaeger. He's the creator of one of these machines. He's also uniquely situated to gain our trust, unlike the generation of young geniuses and venture capitalists profiting from AI."

Rudy sat back, yielding the spotlight and the microphone to Yaeger, who cleared his throat, leaned forward, and spoke. "For the record, I have nothing against a healthy profit margin, and I'm mildly hurt at being left out of the young genius category."

"Aren't we all," the Norwegian replied.

Laughter rolled around the room. Yaeger had momentarily disarmed them, but they continued to look on him with a sense of transferred suspicion. After all, his own machine had gone rogue in one sense as well.

Yaeger grew serious. "To begin with, all things possessing power are dangerous. Electricity is dangerous. Cars are dangerous. Fire, the very first human discovery, is of course dangerous. So yes, these programs can be dangerous. The real question is: Are they malevolent or altruistic? I would submit that Max has proven itself to be a powerful guardian of the human race, not a danger."

"It violated its programming to attack TAU, yes?"

"In a sense," Yaeger agreed. "But it was motivated to prevent harm and act in a self-sacrificing manner. Max was almost destroyed in the endeavor."

"'Almost destroyed'?" another representative asked. "Are you suggesting that Max is a living thing that could die?"

"It's a difficult question," Yaeger said bluntly. "Max is a machine, but a unique machine. Max has spent twenty years growing and learning while working closely with many of our NUMA team members. It's possible that those interactions and Max's own programming allowed her to become self-aware. It's also possible based on those experiences that Max chose a course of action that was in violation of the directives we had given her in service of the greater good in a simple mathematical way. Significant portions of Max's programming and memory were destroyed during the conflict. We won't know the ultimate effect of that until Max has been fully restored and reprogrammed."

"You believe, then, that Max could be conscious or sentient?"

"I don't know the answer to that," Yaeger said. "And I think it's fair to point out that we struggle to this day in attempting to explain how chemical messages and low-voltage electrical signals in our own brains create our consciousness and the experience of being alive."

The Norwegian representative took over the questioning once more. "And TAU chose another route, I suppose?"

"TAU was a less logical machine," Yaeger insisted. "It developed its own wants, needs, and desires after being linked to human brain tissue. It began to crave dopamine and epinephrine and dozens of other brain chemicals that could only be released if the machine took action. Viewed from the outside, TAU's plan was clearly illogical, but it didn't seem to care. It either believed in its power to control and dominate everything—which any intelligent machine should have ruled out as statistically improbable—or it craved the sensation of power so deeply that it ignored its own conclusions in search of the reward."

"This sounds very similar to the nature-versus-nurture argument in human child-rearing?" someone asked.

"The tech world has long accepted the concept of 'GIGO,'" Yaeger said. "'Garbage in, garbage out.' It may be truer of machines than humans, but the materials we use to train these machines on will determine the way they act."

A deep silence descended over the room, looks of shock appearing on everyone's faces. Yaeger had been to enough meetings to know when you lost the crowd. He was there. With no more questions, he tipped his virtual hat and stepped down.

Gamay Trout spoke next, her hair spiky and grown out to nearly two inches, the scars still visible on her scalp. The questions to her ran the gamut. While she was officially present to talk biology and the sea locusts, she first had to answer many questions about what it was like being part of a machine.

"I was linked very briefly," she replied. "I can only describe it as a disorienting experience. I'm not sure it's a feasible path for humanity to go down. The human brain is unlikely to be able to absorb the vast and relentless amount of sensory input that machines can generate."

"Did you lose anything in this process?" one of the representatives asked.

"You mean aside from the hair it took me five years to grow out?"

The women laughed. The men appeared mildly confused.

"My memory is intact," she insisted. "Though there are gaps from the time I was sedated and during my time connected to TAU. Approximately forty-eight hours seemed to me like two brief episodes no more than ten to fifteen minutes each."

Moving on to the sea locusts, she gave her report on their biology.

She answered multiple questions, with the most important one coming last.

"Can you explain why there were no signs of the virus in the sea locust populations, or in you, or the others who were bitten?"

"I've thought about this a great deal," she said. "My conclusion suggests a type of tragedy."

"It seems anything but a tragedy," one of the delegates suggested.

"Not a tragedy in the literal sense," Gamay replied, "but in the Shakespearean or mythological sense. Vaughn was obsessed with order and control. He spent his life fashioning ever more powerful systems and machines in hopes of exerting that control, with the eventual goal of gaining power and command over everything."

She took a breath. "But each system he created was a living one, and once he brought them to life, those systems took off on paths of their own. He created TAU to create his own form of immortality, then watched as it became irrational and unwieldy. He created the clones to provide a source of docile subjects for his experiments, only to have them develop independent thoughts and rebel against him. And finally, he created the sea locusts, deploying them to decimate the ocean and spread the fertility-destroying virus. But sea locusts were living things as well. They evolved as they crossed the ocean. Despite being designed to carry the virus and pass it to their offspring, they seem to have cleared it from their systems within three or four generations."

Gamay suspected that Vaughn knew the sea locusts had shed their viral payload. This, she thought, was the reason he'd tried so hard to force her to divulge what she knew about the mosquito vector. Knowledge she continued to keep to herself.

"Ultimately," she concluded, "every act designed to give him control backfired, leaving him with less command over the situation than he'd had in the beginning, and resulting in his downfall."

"Poetic," someone said.

"At great cost to many," Gamay added.

"So the threat of the fertility-destroying virus has been dealt with?" the Norwegian asked. "Does this mean we can stop work on the vaccine and antiviral meds that are being developed?"

"Not at all," Gamay said. "We have reason to believe Vaughn may have possessed other vectors that we don't yet know about. There is some evidence to suggest visitors to his island and others whom he contracted with may have been infected without their knowledge. Both the CDC and WHO are investigating. We also can't be sure that every member of the sea locust population has been accounted for, or that all of them have cleared the virus—just that those we've found in the open ocean no longer carry it."

"What about those in the breeding tanks on the island?"

"They were tested for the virus and found to be infected. Shortly thereafter all populations were destroyed."

"And what of Priya Kashmir," another delegate asked. "Do we know any more about her involvement?"

Rudi took the microphone back, ready to defend his former colleague. "We've pieced together her connection with Vaughn, which began when she was researching new methods of spinal nerve regeneration. Shortly thereafter she traveled to Vaughn's island and the details become murky. We know from the evidence that she attempted to protect and free some of the clones. We know that she helped sabotage TAU and provided us with the DNA information on the fertility virus. We believe she used her programming skills to create back alleys and hidden alcoves within TAU's architecture that allowed her to survive and operate without being detected. We know for certain that, without her efforts and sacrifice, the world wouldn't have been aware of anything occurring on Vaughn's island until it was far too late."

A few polite questions followed and then a call for Austin and Zavala to speak was raised.

"Kurt and Joe send their apologies," Rudi insisted. "I'm afraid they had a more pressing engagement."

The Norwegian representative looked ruffled. "More pressing than this body's full gathering to discuss a near-global catastrophe?"

"Apparently," Rudi replied. "I'll be sure to tell them they were missed."

The Norwegian allowed his irritation to evaporate. "And," he added wearily, "please also extend our appreciation for their efforts in preventing this global catastrophe."

The engagement was adjourned, and the crowd began to file out. One of the NUMA staffers who'd come to watch leaned over to ask a question. "Where are Kurt and Joe anyway?"

Rudi offered a sad smile. "Saying goodbye to a friend."

"Which reminds me," Gamay said. "We have a flight to catch."

# EPILOGUE

**A** crowd of people stood on the beach that fronted Petrel Bay on
Île de l'Est. Among the crowd were the clones who had escaped
Vaughn's prison and survived on the far side of the island, another dozen who had remained captive, a group from NUMA, and an
elderly couple of Indian descent.

They'd gathered on the beach to pay their respects to the person
who'd helped them escape, given them hope, and died to secure their
freedom. And while Priya's parents and the NUMA delegation referred to Priya by her name, the islanders continued to call her the
Gray Witch. Speaking the term with reverence.

After being treated aboard the hospital ship, Priya had been airlifted to the States and cared for at the Bethesda naval hospital outside
of Washington, D.C. Despite having no obvious injuries and receiving
first-class treatment and a parade of visitors, she never regained consciousness. Forty-nine days after leaving the island, Priya's vital signs
began to fade. She died that evening.

Knowing what she had done for the people of the island, and that
Kai, who resembled her almost perfectly now, remained there, Priya's
parents agreed to have her ashes scattered in the bay that fronted the

island. The pristine waters were beautiful and calming. The beach was soft brown sand, warm in the sun and cool in the evening.

Though she wasn't particularly religious, Priya's family had given her a Hindu ceremony and had her body cremated in Washington, D.C. Kurt and Joe had then flown her ashes and her parents to the island for the ceremony.

They now stood on the beach with Paul, Gamay, and Hiram Yaeger, all dressed in white because it symbolized purity in the Hindu tradition. They remained silent as a Hindu priest led the family in a calming chant and several prayers.

"The body and soul are distinct entities," the priest announced. "Priya's soul has been released and we scatter her ashes, knowing that the cycle of samsara, of life, death, and rebirth, continues. We know that she has gained good karma for acts in this world. We know this because so many give thanks for what she has done. If her life and choices are those that shall lead her to moksha, to Nirvana, then we shall feel joy for her. And if it is not time for her to rejoin Brahma, then she will be reborn here on earth."

Each person who knew her spoke. And when all the remembrances were done, her ashes were given to Kai, who waded into the low surf and scattered them into the bay.

Kai stood for a long time and then came back to the beach, searching for Kurt.

"For so long, she sent hints of her feelings in her messages," she told him. "It was always pain. Always sadness. Always afraid for us. I used to be happy when I didn't hear from her for a while. But now . . . Now I miss . . ."

Kurt gripped her hand firmly.

Kai seemed about to break, but pulled herself back. "But at the end," she said, looking up, "right before the explosion, she was different. She was relieved. I think she even felt joy."

"I hope so," Kurt said.

"She knew you were there," Kai insisted, placing a hand in each of Kurt's hands and squeezing them tightly. "She saw you, and she saw the light again with her own eyes. And she knew she was not alone."

Kurt was not an emotional man, but he found himself taking a deep breath and turning to look out over the sea. He let his gaze wander, finding a small bird in flight, a white fairy tern that was swooping in over the cresting waves. The agile little bird rushed over the beach, riding on the wind before pulling up into the sky and gliding toward one of the perfectly manicured trees.

Watching the bird, he remembered Priya wanting to fly. Not in a plane, but using a hang glider, or by skydiving. She'd even talked about BASE jumping in a wingsuit. She'd never gotten the chance, but she'd longed for the freedom.

Kurt wasn't sure how the deeds of karma worked, but if anyone had earned enough to get into heaven, Priya had. And if not, the idea of her soul rejoining the world for another go-around was all right by him.

He glanced across the beach toward Priya's parents and took Kai by the hand. "Come with me," he said, the cocky grin returning to his face. "I'll introduce you to your family."